WINDWARD WEST

MATT BRAUN

St. Martin's Paperbacks

WINDWARD WEST

Copyright © 1987 by Matt Braun.

ISBN: 0-312-99788-4
EAN: 80312-99788-5

Printed in the United States of America

Signet Paperbacks edition / February 1987
St. Martin's Paperbacks edition / March 2005

St. Martin's Paperbacks are published by St. Martin's Press, 175 Fifth Avenue, New York, NY 10010.

10 9 8 7 6 5 4 3 2 1

After tossing down a drink, Tate happened to glance along the bar. He hadn't spotted Clint before, but now his eyes assumed an ugly look. His mouth curled in a brutish smile.

"Lookit here, boys," he said, motioning to the other men. "It's the Injun-killer hisself."

As though deaf, Clint stared straight ahead. He casually swigged rye and returned the glass to the bar. The buffalo-hunters, sensing trouble, stared at him with interest.

"Only one thing wrong," Tate went on loudly. "He loses the redsticks quick as he finds 'em! Gawddamn, it's just plumb pitiful."

Clint turned, one elbow hooked over the bar. "Let it go, Tate. I've got no quarrel with you."

"Let it go, hell!" Tate blustered. "I heard how you led the 2nd around in circles. We oughta start callin' you Injun-lover."

"You heard wrong," Clint said tightly.

Tate glared at him. "You callin' me a liar?"

"Not exactly." Clint fixed him with a hard look. "You're just a sorry son-of-a-bitch."

Tate muttered an unintelligible oath. His eyes hooded and he pushed off the bar. What he lacked in height he made up in girth, bullnecked and broad through the shoulders. He lumbered forward, arms swinging loosely, and suddenly uncorked a looping haymaker. The blow snapped Clint's head back and set his ears buzzing. Shuffling closer, Tate let go a murderous roundhouse right.

Clint collected himself in the nick of time. He bobbed underneath the blow and exploded two splintering punches on Tate's jaw. The sergeant sagged at the knees, clutching the bar to hold himself upright. Clint shifted, measuring him, and hit him a clubbing blow upside the head. Tate dropped to the floor, supporting himself on his hands and knees. He was unable to rise.

Stepping back, Clint stared at the three troopers. His voice was quietly menacing. "Anybody else?"

To Harry, Eleanor and Bill
and all the Adairs everywhere!

1

SUNSET CAST a fiery glow across the parade ground. The last note of a bugle faded as the flag was lowered from a wind-whipped flagpole. A moment later the color guard marched off toward regimental headquarters.

Clint Brannock watched from the porch of the sutler's store. As chief scout for the 6th Cavalry, he was a familiar figure around Fort Dodge. His buckskin jacket and wide-brimmed hat set him apart from the spit-and-polish of a military post. At day's end, though he wasn't required to stand formation, he always observed the flag-lowering ceremony. It reminded him of a time past, when he'd served under another flag. He saw nothing ironic in the fact that he now served the Union army.

The troops were dismissed in a flurry of commands. A chill February wind whistled across the parade ground as the men broke formation and hurried toward the warmth of their barracks. Shortly, the bugler would sound chow call and there would be a rush on the battalion mess halls. Until then, no one cared to stand around in the bitter cold.

Dusk settled quickly over the post. Situated in the southwestern quadrant of Kansas, Fort Dodge was some fifty miles from Indian Territory. Nearby was the Santa Fe Trail, which snaked westward along the Arkansas River. Spring and summer, wagon caravans loaded with trade goods rumbled past, bound for New Mexico. Detachments

of the 6th Cavalry patrolled constantly to protect the traders from hostile war parties.

Winter brought a different mission. Only yesterday, the
2nd Battalion had returned from a sweep along the headwaters of the Canadian. Their objective had been to locate
a band of Southern Cheyenne who had jumped the reservation. A brief engagement, fought in a blinding snow squall,
had proved inconclusive. By the time the weather cleared,
the Cheyenne village had vanished.

Clint stepped off the sutler's porch. He walked to the
hitch rack and mounted his roan gelding. As he reined
about, his thoughts drifted once more to the aborted patrol.
While he'd done his job, locating the village meant nothing in itself. A combination of harsh weather and half-
frozen troopers had allowed the Cheyenne to escape. It
grated on him that the army seldom displayed the grit and
endurance of the hostiles. At least half the time he spent in
the field seemed to him little more than wasted motion. He
suddenly felt the need of a drink.

Dodge City was five miles west of the garrison. A
sprawling hodgepodge of buildings, it was inhabited principally by traders, teamsters, and buffalo-hunters. Last
year, during the fall of '72, the arrival of the railroad had
transformed buffalo-killing into big business. These days,
the western plains swarmed with hunters, all busily engaged
in the slaughter. Alongside the tracks, thousands upon
thousands of flint hides awaited shipment to eastern markets.

The permanent population of the town was something
less than five hundred people. At one end of Front Street
was the Dodge House, Zimmerman's Hardware, and the
Long Branch, flanked by a mercantile outfit and a couple
of greasy spoons. Up the other way was a scattering of
saloons, two trading companies, another mercantile, and a
whorehouse. Apart from buffalo hides, the town's econ-
omy was fueled by troopers of the 6th Cavalry and free-
spending hunters. Whiskey and whores were a profitable
enterprise on the edge of nowhere.

Outside the Long Branch, Clint dismounted and loosened the gelding's cinch. The hitch racks were crowded, and upstreet he saw a group of soldiers emerge from the whorehouse. Their noisy laughter echoed in the night as he moved across the boardwalk. A blast of warm, fetid air struck him as he pushed through the saloon door. The smell was a mixture of sweat, stale tobacco smoke, and cheap whiskey. The rainbow of odors was further enhanced by several buffalo hunters. They stank of blood and dried offal.

At the bar, Clint ordered a shot of rye. He downed it neat and waited while the barkeep refilled his glass. Then he hauled out the makings, creased a rolling paper and sprinkled tobacco into it. He licked, sealed the paper, and twisted the ends. After popping a match on his thumbnail, he lit the cigarette and took a deep drag. Exhaling smoke, he leaned into the bar and sipped at his rye. He ignored the buffalo hunters as well as a scattering of men seated at the tables. His gaze seemed inward, somehow faraway.

Other men seldom intruded on Clint. He was tall and solidly built, with wind-seamed features and a wide brow. His manner was deliberate, which combined with a square jaw and smoky blue eyes gave him a standoffish appearance. Nor was the impression dispelled by a thatch of sandy hair and a brushy mustache. He generally drank alone, and while he was pleasant enough, most men kept their distance. He allowed them the same courtesy.

Then, too, there were the rumors. Some years ago, in Denver, Clint and his two older brothers were reported to have killed five or six men. Later, while operating as special agent for the Overland Stage Line, he was thought to have killed at least four road agents in gunfights. However true the rumors, no one questioned his reputation against the hostiles. He was known to the warrior bands, and feared.

The door burst open while Clint was still on his second drink. Glancing up, he watched in the back bar mirror as

Sergeant Frank Tate and three troopers barged into the saloon. Apparently none of them had pulled duty today, for they were already flush with liquor. Tate slapped the bar with a loud whack and demanded a bottle. The barkeep brought a quart of snake-eye whiskey and four glasses.

Clint avoided looking at them. He'd had trouble with Tate in the past, and on one occasion they had almost exchanged blows. A veteran campaigner, Tate fancied himself an Indian fighter and a barroom scrapper. He was assigned to the 3rd Battalion, and by all accounts he was daredevil brave in battle. Yet he was a loudmouth and a braggart, and he made no secret of his contempt for civilian scouts. As a sergeant, he earned $18 a month, while a scout was paid more than five times that amount. He took it as a personal insult.

After tossing down a drink, Tate happened to glance along the bar. He hadn't spotted Clint before, but now his eyes assumed an ugly look. His mouth curled in a brutish smile.

"Lookit here, boys," he said, motioning to the other men. "It's the Injun-killer hisself."

As though deaf, Clint stared straight ahead. He casually swigged rye and returned the glass to the bar. The buffalo-hunters, sensing trouble, stared at him with interest.

"Only one thing wrong," Tate went on loudly. "He loses the redsticks quick as he finds 'em! Gawddamn, it's just plumb pitiful."

Clint turned, one elbow hooked over the bar. "Let it go, Tate. I've got no quarrel with you."

"Let it go, hell!" Tate blustered. "I heard how you led the 2nd around in circles. We oughta start callin' you Injun-lover."

"You heard wrong," Clint said tightly.

Tate glared at him. "You callin' me a liar?"

"Not exactly." Clint fixed him with a hard look. "You're just a sorry son-of-a-bitch."

Tate muttered an unintelligible oath. His eyes hooded

and he pushed off the bar. What he lacked in height he made up in girth, bullnecked and broad through the shoulders. He lumbered forward, arms swinging loosely, and suddenly uncorked a looping haymaker. The blow snapped Clint's head back and set his ears buzzing. Shuffling closer, Tate let go a murderous roundhouse right.

Clint collected himself just in the nick of time. He bobbed underneath the blow and exploded two splintering punches on Tate's jaw. The sergeant sagged at the knees, clutching the bar to hold himself upright. Clint shifted, measuring him, and hit him a clubbing blow upside the head. Tate dropped to the floor, supporting himself on his hands and knees. He was unable to rise.

Stepping back, Clint stared at the three troopers. His voice was quietly menacing. "Anybody else?"

The troopers seemed rooted in place. Clint watched them a moment, then turned and walked toward the door. Outside, he crossed the boardwalk and stepped down, circling the hitch rack. As he reached for the reins, the saloon door banged open behind him. A gunshot split the night and a bullet whistled past his head.

All thought suspended, Clint reverted to instinct. He flung himself to the ground, pulling the Colt .44 holstered at his side. Framed in the light from the doorway, he saw Tate with a pistol extended at arm's length. Thumbing the hammer, he touched off two quick shots, hardly a heartbeat apart.

The first slug caught Tate in the chest and the second drilled through his forehead. As though warding off evil spirits, he raised both arms, dropping the pistol, and pitched forward on his face. He lay perfectly still, blood and gore puddling around his head.

Clint slowly climbed to his feet. He started forward, then abruptly stopped and holstered the Colt. There was no need to look. Frank Tate was dead.

Something over an hour later two uniformed guards

marched Clint into post headquarters. Following the shooting, he'd been placed under military arrest and disarmed. His status as a scout made him subject to army law.

In the orderly room, Sergeant Major Jack Baxter gave him a dirty look. Clint had no illusions about the gravity of his situation. The army protected its own, and killing a noncommissioned officer was a capital offense. His only out was to prove self-defense.

Baxter ushered him into the office of Colonel Richard Dodge. Something of a martinet, Dodge was post commander and took pride in the fact that Fort Dodge had been named after him. Seated in a chair beside his desk was General Phil Sheridan. Clint had heard that the general was visiting the post on a routine inspection tour. He took Sheridan's presence at the hearing as a bad sign.

Sheridan was universally acknowledged as a hard man. A West Pointer, he had served seven years in western outposts prior to 1861. His advancement during the Civil War was attributable to impressive victories throughout the South. Following the Confederate surrender, he commanded occupation forces in Texas and Louisiana. There, because of his harsh rule, he'd become known as a tyrant. In 1869, he'd been promoted to lieutenant general and assigned the Division of the Missouri. His command embraced the western plains and virtually all of the warlike tribes.

Sheridan's immediate superior, General of the Army William Tecumseh Sherman, was equally pragmatic in his methods. Speaking of the Plains tribes, Sherman had once observed: "We must act with vindictive earnestness, even to their extermination . . . men, women, and children." As the instrument of that policy, Sheridan had devised a strategy to destroy the warrior bands. His solution was to avoid full-scale engagements with the hostiles. Instead, he struck at their base camp, their villages, and their families.

The Plains Indians were essentially nomadic. Spring and summer, they were constantly on the move, following the migration of the buffalo herds. Their raids against white settlements and isolated homesteads were also conducted during good weather. In the fall, the raids stopped and the tribes concentrated on buffalo hunts, stockpiling meat for the hard months ahead. During the winter they made permanent camps along wooded streams. For all practical purposes, the horseback warriors were immobilized while snow blanketed the plains.

General Sheridan spurned such limitations. Brooking no argument, he ordered his cavalry commanders onto the frozen plains. Their instructions were to seek out and destroy the villages. All food and shelter was to be burned, and any survivors were to be driven into the bleak wasteland. No quarter was asked and none was given, for it was war to the death. Hostiles were granted but one option: annihilation or surrender.

By his every act, Sheridan had demonstrated an implacable and unrelenting attitude. Clint had little doubt that the same attitude would extend to killing noncoms. He braced himself for a rough time.

Colonel Dodge motioned him forward. He halted before the desk, aware of Sheridan's penetrating stare. There was a tense moment of silence.

"Well, Brannock," Dodge demanded. "What have you got to say for yourself?"

"It's simple enough," Clint said evenly. "Tate tried to back-shoot me and I killed him."

"On the contrary," Dodge said with a querulous squint. "You beat Sergeant Tate senseless and left him on a barroom floor. I'd say he was provoked."

"Won't hold water, Colonel. Tate's the one that picked the fight."

"Indeed!" Dodge snorted. "According to several eyewitnesses, you called him a son-of-a-bitch. Isn't that true?"

Clint's expression was wooden. "Tate started it by callin' me an Indian-lover. Any son-of-a-bitch that says that deserves to be whipped."

Phil Sheridan smothered a laugh. Dodge glanced at him, momentarily flustered. Then he looked back at Clint.

"Don't confuse the issue, Mr. Brannock. The fact remains that you beat and then killed a man in my command."

"No, sir," Clint corrected him. "You've got your facts wrong. Tate threw the first blow and he fired the first shot. Any court in the land would say I acted in self-defense."

Dodge stared across the desk with a bulldog scowl. "I daresay a military court-martial would see it differently."

"Maybe so," Clint conceded. "But every scout you've got on the payroll would quit you cold. You'd play hell hiring new ones, too."

Dodge took a deep breath, blew it out heavily. "I want you off the post tonight. No one will serve with you now, Brannock. Not after this."

"Suit yourself, Colonel. I think you're shortchanging your men, though. They're generally a pretty fair lot."

Clint turned to leave. Sheridan halted him with a gruff command. "Hold on a minute."

When he stopped, Sheridan studied him with a judicial gaze. "Your name sounds familiar. Weren't you with Custer on the Washita?"

"Yessir," Clint replied. "Big Foot Wallace was chief of scouts then."

"That was our first winter campaign. I remember it well."

Clint managed a lopsided smile. "Scared the holy livin' hell out of the hostiles. They never expected pony soldiers in the middle of a snowstorm."

"I take it you approve of the tactic?"

"Yessir, I do, General. Figure it's the only way we'll force 'em to stand and fight. Otherwise they scatter like a covey of quail."

Sheridan gave him a searching stare. "How did you get into scouting, Mr. Brannock?"

"Long story, General."

"Give me the short version, then."

Clint tried to keep it brief. In 1865, after serving as marshal of Denver, he'd been appointed special agent for the Overland Stage Line. Shortly afterward, a stage coach on the Bozeman Trail was attacked by Cheyenne warriors. A woman passenger was taken captive and Clint was assigned to bring her back. With members of the Colorado militia, he located the Cheyenne village and attempted a dawn attack. In the ensuing fight, the woman was rescued, but he'd been wounded and taken prisoner. Always unpredictable, the Cheyennes made him a slave rather than torturing him to death. For six months he lived as an Indian, learning their ways, surviving the ordeal. Then, on a dark winter night, he stole a horse and escaped.

A week later he rode into Fort Laramie, Wyoming Territory. The post commander, impressed that he'd lived to tell the tale, promptly recruited him as a scout. For the next two years, he took part in campaigns against the Northern Cheyenne and the Sioux. After the treaty of 1868, he signed on with the 7th Cavalry, operating out of Fort Riley, Kansas. There, under George Armstrong Custer, he participated in the Battle of the Washita and several lesser engagements. In 1871, when Custer was transferred to the Department of the South, he decided to stay on at Fort Riley. Over the next year he served as a scout in actions against the Southern Cheyenne and the Kiowa. Late in 1872, he'd been hired as chief of scouts for the 6th Cavalry.

"Guess that's it," Clint concluded. "I've been at Fort Dodge ever since."

"An impressive record, Mr. Brannock. What is that, seven years active service?"

"Nearabouts, General."

Phil Sheridan rose from his chair. He was a stocky man, with a close-cropped beard and ascetic eyes that belied his profession. Striding back and forth, he paced the room, punctuating his speech with vigorous gestures.

"You're too experienced to lose, Mr. Brannock. But

Colonel Dodge is entirely correct. You've burned your bridges with the men of the 6th.''

"I'll take your word for it, General."

"Tell me . . ." Sheridan paused, staring at him. "Would you consider a transfer to Texas?"

"Whereabouts in Texas?"

"What's the difference?"

"Nothing special," Clint said. "Just that I've got a brother who lives in Dallas."

Sheridan wagged his head. "I had another assignment in mind. Colonel Mackenzie and the 4th Cavalry."

"Fort Clark?" Clint frowned. "Hell, General, that's damn near on the Rio Grande."

"After tonight," Sheridan pointed out, "you're hardly in a position to pick and choose. Wouldn't you agree?"

Clint hesitated, considering. "Yessir, I expect you're right."

"By jingo!" Sheridan laughed out loud. "It's a marriage made in Hades. You and Ranald Mackenzie."

"I don't follow you, General."

"Why, it's elemental, Mr. Brannock. Until you've met Mackenzie, you've never met a true son-of-a-bitch."

Chuckling to himself, Sheridan took pen and paper off the desk. He sat down, dipping the pen into the inkwell, and began scribbling. He shot Clint an amused look.

"Orders won't be enough. I'll give you a personal letter to Mackenzie."

"Sounds like a tough man."

"None tougher, Mr. Brannock. He's just your speed."

Sheridan went on writing, chortling under his breath. Clint watched him with a growing sense of unease and considerable second thought. He had a feeling he'd just been euchred by a two-star general.

2

"MR. GOULD?"

"You must be Virgil Brannock."

Jay Gould swung the door wider. Virgil moved past him into the parlor of a large suite. The accommodations were the finest of any hotel in Dallas, and befitting the man. Gould was a legend in financial circles back East.

"Won't you have a seat, Mr. Brannock."

Gould gestured amiably to an easy chair. Virgil seated himself and Gould took a chair across from him. They stared at each other a moment.

"No doubt," Gould finally said, "you're wondering why I asked you here."

Virgil nodded. "Your note indicated a matter of mutual interest."

"Far more than that, Mr. Brannock. I've come all this way from New York just to see you."

Virgil was at once flattered and wary. Jay Gould was known as the Mephistopheles of Wall Street. Financial correspondents had variously described him as dishonest, amoral, and rapacious. In his time, he had plundered a dozen railroads and several lesser business concerns. He was perhaps the wealthiest man in America, and certainly one of the most powerful.

In appearance, Gould was both disarming and deceptive. He was painfully frail, sallow-skinned and mild-mannered, and stood scarcely five and a half feet tall. An impeccable dresser, he wore a frock coat and striped trousers, with a vest and somber black cravat. Yet nothing about him was to be taken at face value. By all accounts, he had an absolute gift for subterfuge and guile.

"Correct me if I'm wrong," Gould said pleasantly. "I understand you're equal partners in the Texas & Pacific Railroad."

Virgil eyed him in silence a moment. "No reason to deny it. Tom Scott and I own it fifty-fifty."

"A nice turn of phrase, Mr. Brannock. Translated, I believe that means you own fifty thousand shares of common stock."

Virgil was instantly alert. Among other eastern Robber Barons, Gould had personally outwitted the likes of Jim Fiske and Henry Villard. His reputation preceded him, and he wasn't to be trusted. All the more so where it concerned railroad stock.

"Suppose we get down to cases, Mr. Gould. What is it you have in mind?"

"Quite simply," Gould said with perfect civility, "I propose to buy you out."

"Do you?" Virgil returned his gaze steadily. "What makes you think I want to sell?"

Gould laughed without humor. "A matter of avarice, Mr. Brannock. Not to mention good business sense. I'm prepared to offer you ten dollars a share."

"Why?" Virgil asked bluntly. "It's worth no more than eight on the open market."

Gould spread his hands in a bland gesture. "Allow me my secrets. Your only concern should be that I'm prepared to hand you a bank draft for a half-million dollars."

The figure represented a fivefold return on Virgil's original investment. Still, however attractive the offer, his mind was on the "secret" just mentioned. He knew that Gould had recently acquired control of the Kansas Pacific Railway. There were rumors of negotiations to bring about a merger of the Kansas Pacific and the Union Pacific. Should that happen, the next logical step was a takeover of the Texas & Pacific. Gould would then have what amounted to a monopoly of the western railroad system. Despite himself, Virgil had to admire the financier's audacity.

"Why me?" he inquired, one eyebrow lifted in question. "Why don't you buy out Tom Scott?"

"Because he wouldn't sell," Gould remarked. "I believe you will."

"What makes you think that?"

"Scott is a romantic fool. He sees himself as a visionary, a man of destiny. Now you, Mr. Brannock, you're a realist. You know when to take a profit and call it a day."

Virgil thought the assessment of Tom Scott was entirely accurate. He wasn't so sure about himself. "You make me sound a touch greedy, Mr. Gould."

"Not at all," Gould protested. "It's largely a matter of self-preservation. You won't stand in my way because you know I'll win. I always do."

"And if I refuse to sell?"

"Why, that should be patently obvious, Mr. Brannock. I'll ruin you."

Virgil gave him an appraising glance. "How do you propose to do that?"

Gould strummed the tip of his nose. "I have influential friends both in Washington and on Wall Street. I could make it impossible for you to obtain construction funds." He paused, smiling. "Or have you forgotten we're in the midst of a financial panic?"

Virgil hadn't forgotten. The Panic of '73 began when Cooke & Company, the most prestigious financial institution in the country, closed its doors. That same afternoon thirty-seven banks and brokerage houses went under. An hour later, the board of governors suspended trade on the New York Stock Exchange. Before the debacle ran its course, thousands of businesses would be forced into bankruptcy.

The West, for all its natural wealth, was still dependent on the East. Western railroads, in particular, were susceptible to the slightest quiver in the economic structure of a distant money market. As Virgil saw it, a gathering storm loomed just over the horizon. When it broke, a tidal wave of economic ruin would be set in motion, gaining momentum as it swept westward across the plains. He had no doubt whatever that Jay Gould could impose a freeze on construction funds. Which would leave him holding 50,000 shares in a bankrupt railroad.

"Come now," Gould prompted him. "I'm trying to make you a rich man, Mr. Brannock. Why fight it?"

"Why not?" Virgil said easily. "Maybe somebody will make me a better offer."

Gould chuckled, sardonic amusement in his eyes. "I do admire a man with moxie. You think I'll go higher, is that it?"

"Anything is possible."

"You're a clever one, Mr. Brannock. You intend to pit me against Tom Scott, start a bidding war. Am I correct?"

"Wouldn't you, Mr. Gould?"

"Tell you what." Gould steepled his hands, tapped his forefingers together. "I'll top Scott's best offer by five percent. How does that strike you?"

Virgil shrugged noncommittally. "I'll have to let you know."

Gould inclined his head. "I leave on the evening train. The offer's open until then, Mr. Brannock."

"Not much time."

"Enough for a man who knows his own best interests."

Gould rose from his chair. He walked Virgil to the door and there they shook hands. Neither of them believed the other's smile was genuine.

Outside the hotel, Virgil turned downstreet. His mind was racing with possibilities, none of them pleasant to contemplate. He walked toward the train depot.

Not three months past, the Texas & Pacific had laid tracks into Dallas. At the time, the town was little more than a settlement on the banks of the Trinity River. Since then, Virgil had watched it explode with growth, witnessing a boom brought about by the railroad he'd help found. Until today, he thought he had at last put down roots.

Late in 1865 Virgil and his wife, Elizabeth, had departed Denver. There too he'd been involved in a railroad venture that had turned sour. But he'd walked away with a hundred thousand dollars, and an undiminished belief in the future of western railroading. Early in 1866 he found a man who shared that belief and needed a partner. His name was Thomas A. Scott.

Tom Scott was a true visionary. Like many Southerners, he had long dreamed of a railroad that would extend from the Atlantic Coast through the southeastern states into Texas, and then on to the Pacific Coast. He visualized on a grand scale, and work progressed smoothly as track stretched westward from New Orleans. Yet he was a builder rather than a businessman, and no politician. Upon reaching the Texas border, he ran out of funds, and worse, he'd failed to obtain a state charter. His railroad stopped cold.

At that point, Virgil entered the picture. He had money to invest, and more important, he was an old hand at railroad politics. Texas was then controlled by the carpetbaggers, and corruption was rampant. For a price, the legislators in Austin would accommodate any need. While new to the Lone Star State, Virgil was only too aware of how the game was played. His lobbying efforts were already well under way when he met Tom Scott. He had several influential lawmakers in his hip pocket, and the promise of a railroad charter. His deal with Scott was predicated on his ability to deliver.

In quick order, Virgil produced the charter. The legislature generously awarded the Texas & Pacific twenty sections of land for each mile of track laid. Further, the railroad was granted tax exemption for twenty-five years

and authorized to float municipal bonds totaling $1,000,000.
On the basis of the land windfall, Virgil was able to
arrange an additional $5,000,000 in loans from northern
banks. Scott resumed laying track, his gaze now fixed on
the Pacific Coast. The first leg of his dream was realized
when end-of-track arrived in Dallas.

For all his success, Virgil found small gratification in
what he'd accomplished. He was prosperous, a man of
position and prestige, well on his way to making a fortune.
Dallas was growing apace, and as one of the town's
leading citizens, his future seemed assured. Yet he felt
personally sullied by his involvement with corrupt politicians and shady bankers. However many baths he took, he
still felt grubby, somehow tarnished. He reconciled all the
skulduggery by telling himself that it served a worthy
purpose. He was bringing the railroad to the frontier and
opening wilderness lands to settlement. Until today, that
had seemed enough.

He walked on with his hands stuffed deep in his pockets.

"Jesus Christ!"
Scott stared at him in baffled fury. They were in the
Texas & Pacific office, located on the upper floor of the
depot. Virgil had just finished recounting the salient points
of his meeting with Jay Gould. He evidenced no surprise
at Scott's reaction.

"It's a sorry mess," he said quietly. "The bastard's got
us between a rock and a hard place."

"Amen," Scott said in an aggrieved tone. "We've got
to figure a way around him—and damned fast!"

Virgil forced himself to stay calm. "That's a dead end,
Tom. Unless we deal with him, he'll put us into bankruptcy. He's got the connections to do it."

Scott looked surprised, then suddenly irritated. "Are
you suggesting we go along with the sonovabitch? Sell
out?"

"What's the alternative?"

There was an awkward pause. The partners stared at each other, and never was the contrast between them more apparent. Scott was short and thickset, a man of mercurial moods and volatile temper. Virgil, on the other hand, was tall and wide through the shoulders. His chestnut hair and full mustache gave him a rugged look, an air of assurance and enormous vitality. Unlike Scott, he brought to bear a force of character that commanded the respect of thoughtful men. He seldom had to raise his voice to be heard.

"Tell me straight out," Scott said indignantly. "Are you planning to sell me out?"

"No," Virgil assured him earnestly. "I figure Gould wants it so bad he'll buy us both out. At top dollar, too."

Anger mottled Scott's features. "Goddammit, I won't sell. I'll go under before I let that shifty bastard take over my line."

"Our line," Virgil reminded him. "We're equal partners, remember?"

"So we are," Scott grumbled. "But that doesn't change it an iota. I still won't sell."

"Then you put me in a tough spot, Tom. I won't go under with you."

"What the hell's that supposed to mean?"

Virgil's stare was direct. "Our agreement requires that I offer you my stock first. If you refuse, then I'm free to go elsewhere."

Scott's eyes narrowed. "He's got you convinced, doesn't he? You really believe he'll cut off construction funds."

"You'll recall that one of my brothers is a gambler. He once told me that the secret is knowing when to fold a bad hand. I think Gould holds all the cards."

"Not by a damn sight! I've been put to the wall before and I've always shook loose. I'll do it again."

"Well, I wish you luck," Virgil said softly. "I'll let you have my stock at eight dollars a share."

"I thought Gould offered you ten?"

"I just want out, Tom. I don't aim to break your back."

"Done!" Scott said with a terse nod. "I'll have a bank draft for you this afternoon."

"Sorry it had to end this way, Tom."

"No hard feelings, Virge. You got me as far as Dallas and I'll make it the rest of the way myself. You wait and see."

Virgil departed on that note. He doubted that the Texas & Pacific would make it as far as Fort Worth. California was strictly pie in the sky.

On the way uptown, Virgil found himself in a reflective mood. He was now a wealthy man, and there was something to be said for that. Yet his thoughts, oddly enough, centered on family.

Elizabeth was all things to him. They shared an easy intimacy, and even after eight years of marriage, he still felt starstruck in her presence. She was more than his wife, the mother of his children. Her quick insights and unwavering support made her a partner in whatever he achieved. She'd given him a daughter and a son, and they were the pride of his life. Jennifer, though only seven, was a cameo of her mother, fiercely independent and strikingly beautiful. Morgan, who was a year younger, already showed the Brannock stubborn streak and a determination that never quit. Virgil thought himself fortunate beyond measure. No man could want more.

Still, he was not altogether sanguine about family matters. He missed his brothers and often brooded on their welfare. Upon leaving Denver, the three of them had gone their separate ways. Earl, along with his wife, had settled in San Francisco. That was eight years ago, and apart from an occasional letter, he'd had no contact with Earl. The last letter, written in a shaky hand, had informed them that Earl's wife, Monte, had died of consumption. There had been no mention of Earl's son, now going on seven, or their plans. All the more ominous, there had been no response to the letters Virgil had written in the intervening months. He took that as the worst possible sign.

Clint, the younger brother, was no less worrisome. Head-strong and too rash for his own good, he seemed gripped by wanderlust. As an army scout, he'd drifted from one fort to another, always where the action was the thickest. Like metal to a magnet, he was somehow attracted to trouble, and obviously thrived on it. Virgil still carried the Remington pistol that Clint had given him back in Denver. Every morning, when he strapped it on, he was reminded that Clint, to a large extent, lived by the gun. Yet, on Clint's infrequent visits, he seemed no worse for the life he led. None of which relieved Virgil's concern to any great extent. As the eldest, he'd always felt a certain responsibility toward his brothers. Time and distance had done nothing to break the habit.

He found Elizabeth in the kitchen. She was kneading dough on a floured board and humming softly to herself. She turned, somewhat startled, as Virgil appeared in the doorway. Her expression was one of bemused surprise.

"What are you doing home so early?"

Virgil bussed her on the cheek. "You don't sound all that happy to see me."

"Of course I am," she said quickly. "It's just that I didn't expect you."

"Where're the kids?"

"Where they are every morning—in school." She gave him an odd look. Dusting flour off her hands, she cocked her head and stared at him. "You're acting very strange, Virgil Brannock. What's happened?"

A sudden grin cracked Virgil's face. "I'm out of the railroad business. Sold the whole kit and caboodle. To the tune of four hundred thousand dollars."

"Nooo," she breathed. "Really?"

"Yeah, really."

Virgil explained the morning's events. Her eyes got round and her mouth formed a perfect oval. Then, as he related the deal with Tom Scott, she laughed and clapped her hands like an exuberant child. She threw her arms around his neck.

"We're rich!" She laughed happily. "I can't believe it. We're actually rich."

"Go ahead and believe it. It's true."

Virgil leaned forward and kissed her on the forehead. Her eyes danced merrily and he thought she'd never looked so beautiful. Even after two children, she had kept her sumptuous figure and lost none of her vivacious manner. She was tall, with enormous hazel eyes and exquisite features, and wore her dark hair in the upswept fashion. He still found her irresistible.

She shook her head in mock wonder. "All that money, Virgil. It's just incredible." Her eyes shone. "We can do anything, go anywhere."

"Not so fast. I've got plans for that money."

"Oh?"

"I aim to double it. Hell, we might even wind up millionaires."

"Honestly?" she marveled. "You really mean it?"

Virgil nodded, then smiled a little. "I've had my eye on another situation for quite a spell. Figured I might take a trip to Colorado."

"Colorado? What on earth for?"

"To see a man named William Palmer. He owns the Denver & Rio Grande."

"Another railroad!"

Virgil laughed and lifted her high in the air. Then he brought her down and kissed her so hard it took her breath. Her questions were smothered within the iron band of his arms.

3

A BRISK WIND swept across the bay. Buffeted by choppy waters, the noon ferry from Oakland plowed toward San Francisco. Ahead lay the waterfront, a sprawling collection of wharves and warehouses below the hill-studded city.

Telegraph Hill, towering prominently above the waterfront, was cloaked in fog. Around the curving shore of the bay, the terrain formed a bold amphitheater, with inland hills surrounding the center of the city. The bay itself, perhaps the finest landlocked harbor in the world, was crowded with ships.

At anchor were vessels of all nations, tall-masted clippers and oceangoing steamers, their flags fluttering in the breeze. Westward, hidden by the fog-bound peninsula, was the Golden Gate. Through its channel and into the harbor sailed the ships of the China trade. Their cargo holds were filled with copra and raw silk, coconut oil and sugar, and myriad imports from the exotic Orient. The trade had transformed Frisco into one of the richest ports on earth.

Standing on the wharf, a youngster in tattered clothes watched as the ferry reduced speed. He pulled his worn coat tighter against the damp chill and the spray that peppered him as waves slapped into the pilings. When the ferry docked, he idly looked on as passengers disembarked

and hurried toward Market Street. The main thoroughfare
of the city, Market began at the waterfront and bisected the
business district. Farther upstreet a profusion of carriages
and hansom cabs stretched as far as the eye could see.

The boy's attention shifted from the ferry. Out in the
bay, anchored away from the wharves, were hundreds of
ships. Their silhouettes were fuzzy through the mist and
fog, a ghostly assemblage hovering beneath the overcast.
Small boats, their running lanterns lit, bobbed like fireflies
on the rolling water. Known locally as Whitehall boats,
the craft ferried sailors ashore for a fee. From there, once
their feet touched dry land, the seamen ventured forth at
their own peril.

All along the wharves were a seedy collection of gaming
dives, whorehouses, and busthead saloons. Vice was their
stock-in-trade, and after months at sea, the sailors were
victims of their own shipboard fantasies. On reaching port,
they set off in search of women, alcohol, and gambling.
The wilder the women, the better, and even popskull
whiskey was none too potent for a sailor with a thirst.
Waiting to accommodate him was an assortment of vultures in human form.

Those who operated the waterfront dives were special-
ists who dealt in live bodies. Their ostensible aim was to
provide the seafarer with diverse forms of entertainment.
Their principal business, however, was the traffic in shanghaied sailors. The seaman's origin, whether Scandinavian
or German, French or British, was of no consequence. The
first step was to fleece the sailor of his wages, either at the
gaming tables or at the hands of blowzy whores.

Once the seaman was penniless, the bartender slipped
him a drink drugged with sulfate of morphine. Afterward,
the warm body was delivered to a ship captain who paid
cash on the spot. The sailor awoke to find himself on a
voyage that lasted two to four years. Though the practice
was widespread, few seamen made any effort to avoid the

waterfront. The danger of being shanghaied was considered one of the hazards of shore leave in Frisco.

The Whale, a sleazy dive operated by Mother Bronson, was located at Battery Point. Crude even by Frisco standards, it was a saloon with girls for rent by the trick or by the hour. The ramshackle building squatted directly on the wharf, with water lapping at the pilings below. By rowboat, the trip from the Whale to a waiting clipper ship was only a matter of minutes. For the shanghaied seaman, it was also a one-way trip. His next port of call was generally halfway around the world.

Turning from the wharf, the boy walked directly to the Whale. A casual observer would have thought him one of the many street urchins who infested the waterfront. To the sporting crowd, however, he was one of their own. His name was Lon and he was the son of a gambler who had fallen on hard times. Scarcely seven years old, he had been born on the Barbary Coast and lived there all his life. His mother, who was now dead, had been a gambler as well. Her professional name was Monte Verde and she'd been known as the slickest twenty-one dealer in Frisco. With her death, the sporting crowd had unofficially adopted the boy.

While a step above the street urchins, the youngster was nonetheless a streetwise survivor. He'd been raised in an atmosphere of violence and crime, and life held few mysteries for him. Whores and gamblers, rather than a child's usual playmates, were his closest friends. He was a towhead, with snappy blue eyes and pleasant features. Yet he was old beyond his years, and jaded to the brutal world of the waterfront. He'd seen men killed in knife fights, and he already knew how saloon girls relieved sailors of their money. Nothing surprised him anymore.

The patrons of the Whale were rough-garbed seamen. They were rank with the smell of sweat and cheap whiskey, and all of them appeared stamped from the same mold. Several house girls were working the crowd, and a

woman with the stern look of a grenadier was posted near
the end of the bar. Her hair was pulled back in a severe
bun, and her drab dress somehow emphasized the massive
bulk of her figure. A lead-loaded blackjack was wedged
into the belt cinched around her waist. She looked entirely
capable of felling man or beast with one blow.

Her expression changed as the boy entered the door. She
waved him over with a matronly smile. "Well, now, look
who's here."

Lon bobbed his head. " 'Mornin', Mother Bronson."

" 'Mornin' yourself." She ruffled his hair with rough
good humor. "What can we do for you, dearie?"

"Thought maybe you'd let me have a pint."

She eyed him critically. "A wake-up for your pa?"

The boy dropped his gaze. "Yes, ma'am."

"How's he doing?"

"Oh, same as usual, I guess."

"Still not working the games?"

"No, ma'am," Lon said, studying the floor. "Not just
yet."

Mother Bronson seldom felt anything akin to emotion.
But the sight of the youngster always aroused some long
dormant maternal instinct. Like most of the sporting crowd,
she was moved to pity for both the boy and his father.
Their hard luck convinced her that God was indeed wrathful.

Earl Brannock had arrived on the Barbary Coast late in
1865. With him was his wife, Monte Verde, already famed
as a vingt-et-un dealer in the Colorado gold fields. Earl,
who was a noted poker player, had operated a gaming dive
in Denver. In short order, they established themselves
among the sporting crowd in Frisco. Monte began dealing
at the Bella Union, and Earl became a regular in table
stakes games. They seemed an unbeatable combination.

Then, in the spring of 1866, Monte gave birth to a boy.
She resumed dealing a month or so later, but there was a
general decline in her health. Gradually, her condition
worsened, and by late 1872 she was diagnosed as having

consumption. For the last few months of her life, she was bedridden, wasting away day by day. Earl brought in relays of doctors, and had around-the-clock nursing care, but all to no avail. She died New Year's Day of 1873.

After the funeral, Earl Brannock seemed a broken man. He began drinking heavily and lost all interest in playing poker. To his friends, it appeared he had lost interest in life as well. He was consumed with grief and deeply embittered by his loss. For the past several months he'd rarely drawn a sober breath, and rumor had it that he was now dead-broke. Some weeks ago, he and the boy had been evicted from their house on Russian Hill. They were now living in a seedy hotel.

Mother Bronson held a view shared by most of the sporting crowd. She agreed Earl Brannock had been dealt a cruel blow, but she also thought he was wallowing in self-pity. Her sympathies went, instead, to young Lon. As she saw it, the boy had lost both mother and father. Caring for a drunk was no sort of life for a seven-year-old. All the more so when the father seemed hell-bent on drinking himself to death. She admired the boy's spunk.

"Harry," she boomed to the barkeep, "give our young friend a pint of the good stuff."

Lon shuffled his feet. "All I got's four bits. Would you wait for the rest, Mother Bronson?"

"Forget it, dearie," she said gruffly. "Save your money for a rainy day."

"Well . . . Gosh!"

"Off with you now!"

She suddenly seemed embarrassed by her own generosity. She took a stoppered bottle from the barkeep and whacked the cork for good measure. Handing it to the boy, she brusquely waved him toward the door. Her attention turned once more to the crowd of sailors, and her hand went to the blackjack at her belt. She decided on a big Swede.

He looked ripe to be shanghaied.

*   *   *

Outside, the boy stuffed the bottle in his coat pocket. He felt no shame at having cadged the liquor. For the past week he'd hit a different saloon every day, and he still had the four bits. He turned uptown at a brisk clip.

A short distance away was the heart of the Barbary Coast. Infamous throughout the world, it was no place for greenhorns or the god-fearing. On the bayside, it was bounded by the waterfront and Telegraph Hill, and extended several blocks inland along Pacific and Broadway streets. A wild carnival of depravity, the area was devoted to dance halls and brothels, gambling dens and groggeries, and sinister crimp joints. Vice and debauchery were the district's sole source of commerce.

Legend attributed the hellhole's name to the African coastline of earlier notoriety. By whatever ancestry, the Barbary Coast transformed the lust of sailors and landlubbers alike into coarse and sometimes deadly reality. On average, there were five murders a night, with seamen the most common victims. Grifters openly worked the streets and robbery was so common that passersby hardly took notice.

Nor was the lighter side any less seamy. A dive billing carnal entertainment presented live shows involving feats of copulation that ranged from acrobatic couples to onstage orgies. Not to be outdone, a rival joint staged a showstopper in which the buxom star was mated on alternate nights to a Shetland pony and a bull mastiff. No man, however low his tastes, failed to get his money's worth on the Barbary Coast. By comparison, the western cowtowns and mining camps were downright tame. Frisco, as the natives proudly boasted, was in a class by itself.

On Pacific Street, Lon turned into the doorway of a hotel. One step above a flophouse, the establishment reeked of unwashed bodies and encrusted filth. His father hadn't paid the rent in a week and he hesitated in the dimly lit entranceway. When the desk clerk stepped into a cubby-

hole office, Lon darted down the hall. A moment later he
slipped into the room.

The furnishings were spartan. Apart from a rickety bed,
there was one straight-back chair and a washstand. His
father was snoring softly, covered with a blanket, head
buried in a ratty pillow. Lon moved to the side of the bed
and gently shook his father's shoulder. There was no
response and he shook harder.

"Dad," he coaxed. "C'mon, Dad. Time to get up."

"Lemme alone."

"For cripe's sake, Dad! It's already past noon."

Earl muttered a gruff oath. After a moment, he pushed
the blanket aside and sat up on the edge of the bed. He
was barefoot, dressed in dirty long johns, his face covered
with stubble. His features were ravaged, bruised-looking
rings under his eyes and ugly lines straining his mouth.
Head bowed, breathing raggedly, he seemed to age before
the boy's eyes. He was thirty-four and looked ten years
older.

Lon handed him the bottle. Without a word, he unstop-
pered the cork and tilted the bottle to his mouth. A tremor
passed through his hand as he took three long gulps. When
he paused, he shuddered slightly as though suddenly chilled.
He took another nip, noting that the bottle was half empty,
and replaced the cork. He looked up at the boy through
bloodshot eyes.

"You saved my life, kiddo."

It was their ritual morning joke. Yet they both knew that
the humor was nine parts truth. Without a shot of whiskey,
Earl might never have gotten out of bed. His system was
now dependent on alcohol.

"How about breakfast?" Lon asked. "Feel like you
could eat something?"

Earl pulled a face. He shook himself and glanced around
the room. His clothes were neatly draped over the straight-
back chair. He looked back at the boy.

"I take it you put me to bed last night?"

Lon avoided his gaze. "Yeah."

"How bad was I?"

"Not so bad."

"Where'd you find me?"

"Doyle's saloon," Lon said quietly. "Mr. Doyle figured you'd had enough."

Earl laughed sourly. "Guess he did, at that. Especially since he was setting them up free."

Lon fidgeted a minute, staring down at the floor. The memory of his mother was still sharp and painful, and he wished she were here now. When she was alive, his father had been a man of wit and great vitality. Since then, the man he'd looked up to with such reverence had become what the sporting crowd called a "rummy." His throat went tight when he thought about it, and he desperately wanted things to be as they were before. At length, he gave his father a sideways glance.

"You hungry?"

Earl motioned vaguely. "See how we're fixed for money."

The boy moved around the bed. He took Earl's trousers off the chair and extracted a wad of crumpled bills from the pocket. He looked back with a gee-whiz grin.

"Goddurn! You got nine dollars, Dad. We're flush!"

"Watch your mouth," Earl said in a parched voice. "You're starting to talk like some streetcorner grifter."

"Awright," the boy said half-aloud. "I didn't mean nothin' by it."

Earl hawked, coughing up phlegm. He took a swallow of whiskey and wiped the back of his hand across his mouth. "Where'd you get the bottle?"

"Cadged it off Mother Bronson."

"That witch," Earl mumbled. "Wonder you're not on your way to China."

Lon's gaze was suddenly direct, unblinking. "You got no call to say that, Dad. She likes you. Lots of people

do.'' His voice dropped to a whisper. ''They're just tryin'
to help.''

The innocence of the words somehow jolted Earl. Dull
despair struck him and his eyes appeared to turn inward.
His head felt queer, almost as though his eardrums were
blocked. A vein pulsed at his temple and he dropped the
bottle on the bed. He looked at the boy with a hollow
stare.

The youngster's eyes were guileless, brimming with
tears. Earl marked the tousled hair and the vulnerable look
around the mouth. He saw himself mirrored in the boy's
features, and something more. Lon possessed the resil-
ience and inner strength of his mother, that indomitable
steadfastness of spirit. Otherwise he would never have
sustained himself on the streets of the Barbary Coast.
When all the while his father was soaked in booze.

Earl scrubbed his face with his palms. He was abruptly
overcome with a sense of self-loathing and repugnance.
For months now, he realized he'd immersed himself in his
own pitiful torment. He'd been something less than a man,
and no father at all. Before he lost what remained of
himself—and the boy—he resolved to make amends. One
way or another . . .

Standing, Earl moved toward the chair and his clothes.
He nodded to the boy with a lame smile. ''Help me get
dressed, sport. We've got some business that needs
tending.''

''Business?'' Lon blurted. ''What d'ya mean, Dad?''

''I'm feeling lucky. We're gonna buck the tiger.''

A short while later Earl emerged from a pawnshop.
He'd hocked his last remaining possession, his gold watch.
With the ten spot the pawnbroker had loaned him, he now
had a grand total of nineteen dollars. Four of that went for
a breakfast of steak and eggs, with extra biscuits for Lon
and strong black coffee for himself. Their vigor restored,
they crossed Pacific Street not long after two o'clock.

With the boy at his side, Earl marched into the Bella Union. The batwing doors opened onto a large barroom and gaming parlor. Beyond the bar was a spacious theater, with an orchestra pit and curtained stage. The floor was jammed with tables and several men stood at the bar. None of them gave the youngster and his disheveled companion a second look.

Earl halted at the roulette table. At midafternoon, the only players were a bowlegged sailor and a whiskery miner. They appeared intent on the numbered layout and hardly glanced around. He nodded to the croupier.

" 'Afternoon, Cecil."

"How's tricks, Earl?"

"Never better, my friend. Never better."

Earl traded his fifteen dollars for three red chips. He studied the layout a moment and placed them on the black 20. Then, moved by a sudden hunch, he shifted the chips to a split bet, between the black 20 and the red 23. The odds on a winner paid seventeen-to-one.

"Spin the ball, Cecil."

"Hell, Earl. Why play a sucker bet?"

"Have faith," Earl assured him. "I can't be beat."

The croupier waited for the other players to place their bets. Then he spun the wheel and dropped the ball. Whirling round and round, the wheel gradually slowed. As they watched, it spun one final revolution and the ball clicked into a slot. Earl laughed aloud.

"A winner!" Cecil announced. "Red twenty-three!"

Earl collected two hundred fifty-five dollars in winnings. Turning from the cashier's window, he winked at Lon and stuffed the bills in his pocket. On their way out the door, he flipped Cecil a good-bye salute. They paused on Pacific Street.

"What'll you do with all that money, Dad?"

"Well, first," Earl said, "we'll get my watch out of hock."

"And then what?"

"Then we'll get the hell outta Frisco."

Lon's eyes went round. "Where'll we go?"

"How would you like to visit your Uncle Virgil?"

"I'd like it a lot."

"So would I, sport. Let's go."

There was no reason to return to their hotel. After reclaiming the watch, they caught the ferry to Oakland. Late that afternoon, they boarded an eastbound train.

Lon fell asleep in his father's arms.

4

THE SKY LIGHTENED to a muslin blue. There was a chill in the air and mist rose off the river. To the east, the vermilion of oncoming sunrise smudged the horizon.

Clint broke camp with practiced ease. He'd made no fire, and breakfast had been a strip of jerky washed down with river water. After saddling the roan gelding, he lashed his bedroll into place. What few supplies he carried were in the saddlebags, and a Winchester carbine rode beneath his leg. He mounted as the first rays of sunlight streaked the sky.

For the past week, he had drifted southward through Indian Territory. His only stop had been a night spent at Fort Sill, a post deep in reservation country. There, over drinks with a first sergeant of his acquaintance, he'd heard the latest reports on the hostiles. The talk centered on the Comanche, who were expected to take the war trail by late spring. No one doubted that the other tribes would follow.

Today, the Comanche were much on his mind. As he forded the Red River, he recalled that it marked the boundary separating Texas and Indian Territory. He reflected as well that it was a meaningless boundary where the warlike tribes were concerned. The Comanche and Kiowa, in particular, raided across the Red with what amounted to impunity. By treaty, everything north of the river was closed to cavalry units in pursuit. He thought it a hell of a note that the government provided hostiles with a sanctuary.

At bottom, the Comanche were the source of the trouble. Theirs was a history of bloody and unremitting warfare, extending backward in time through Mexican and Spanish rule. They called themselves the Nermernuh—the People—and considered themselves lords of the Southern Plains. Among white men, they hated *tejanos* with vindictive, unwavering ferocity. For it was the Texans who had first encroached on their ancestral lands.

Oddly enough, it was disease that drove the Comanche from Texas soil. Prior to the Civil War, the military had contained Comanche raids on *tejano* settlements. But the advance of white men brought with it the twin plagues of cholera and smallpox. An epidemic followed, infecting whole encampments, and thousands died. The Pehnahterkuh, southernmost of the tribe's bands, was decimated, losing fully half its members. The other bands retreated to *Comanchería*, that vast expanse of plains north and west of the Red River.

On the eve of the Civil War, however, all Union regiments were withdrawn from Texas. The hostiles watched the pony soldiers depart, and terror once again descended on the frontier. The Comanche and their allies, the Kiowa, savaged *tejano* outposts throughout the war. By 1864, the line of settlement had been pushed back a hundred miles or more, roughly where it had rested in the 1840s. Western Texas, by the close of the Civil War, was desolate and deserted.

To halt these depredations, the Treaty of Medicine Lodge was negotiated in 1867. The Comanche and the Kiowa, along with the Southern Cheyenne, were located on lands in western Indian Territory. The Texas Panhandle, as part of the ancient *Comanchería*, was reserved for their hunting grounds. Yet not all of the five Comanche bands signed the Medicine Lodge treaty. The Quahadi band, led by the war chief Quanah, refused to register at the Fort Sill agency. They retreated instead to *Comanchería*, far out on the Staked Plains, and from there resumed their raids on the *tejanos*. Other bands, joined by the Kiowa, were quick to follow their example. War parties jumped the reservation and made lightning forays into Texas. Afterward, by outdistancing all pursuit, they took sanctuary north of the Red River.

Under President Grant's peace policy, the Quaker religious order was appointed to administer the tribal reservations. But the Quakers, as well as the Indian Bureau in Washington, failed utterly in holding the Comanche and Kiowa to the white man's road. Texans, meanwhile, were up in arms because federal commissioners at Medicine Lodge had appropriated the Panhandle as tribal hunting grounds. Buffalo-hunters further aggravated the situation by commencing the slaughter of the great southern herd. Hostility and distrust spread to all quarters, more than ever pitting red man against white. The peace policy shortly collapsed in a shambles.

In 1869, Sheridan at last convinced President Grant that extending the olive branch to hostiles was a travesty. Thereafter, the cavalry regiments followed a policy of "pursue and punish." While unpopular with religious groups, and therefore unofficial, the policy nonetheless became standard operating procedure in the field. Cavalry patrols harassed the warlike bands for the next three years, restricting their bloody assaults on the *tejanos*. Still, these punitive campaigns were more a holding action than a war of attrition. Every spring raiding parties left the reservations and took the trail to Texas. Farther west, the Quahadi Comanche continued to follow the old ways. As yet, no army patrol dared venture onto *Llano Estacado*, the Staked Plains.

For all that, there was one cavalry commander who instilled fear and respect in the Comanche. Colonel Ranald Mackenzie, operating out of Fort Sill, had twice undertaken campaigns into the Texas Panhandle. In 1871, at

Blanco Canyon, he'd tangled with Quanah and forced the Quahadi chief to retreat higher into *Llano Estacado*. A year later, in the fall of 1872, Mackenzie's troopers stormed an encampment of the Kuhtsoo-ehkuh band and drove them back on the reservation.

The Comanche, always impressed by bravery, dubbed the pony soldier chief Mangaheute, Three Fingers. Mackenzie, as the result of a wound during the Civil War, had lost the index finger of his left hand. After honoring him with an Indian name, the Comanche were allowed a respite from Mackenzie's search-and-destroy brand of warfare. For the past six months, the 4th Cavalry had remained in garrison at Fort Clark. So far as the Comanche were concerned, it was good riddance. Quanah and the other chiefs wanted no part of Three Fingers.

Fording the Red River, Clint thought he'd played into luck. The shooting at Dodge City, far from damaging his prospects, had put him on the trail to Fort Clark. Like the Comanche, he too respected a commander who asked no quarter and gave none. The frontier, he told himself, was no place for the squeamish.

Three Fingers Mackenzie sounded like his kind of a man.

Four days later Clint rode into Dallas. The orders posting him to Fort Clark weren't effective for another two weeks, and that left time for family business. He hadn't seen Virgil and Beth in almost a year.

When she opened the door, Elizabeth at first appeared shocked. Clint was covered with trail dust and grime and he hadn't shaved in a week. Then she recovered, emitting a little shriek of delight. She threw her arms around his neck and kissed him soundly on the cheek.

"Well, now," Clint said when she let him go, "that's the kind of welcome I like."

Elizabeth laughed. "We haven't seen you in ages. What are you doing here?"

"Stopped by on my way to Fort Clark. I've been assigned to the Fourth Cavalry."

Surprise echoed in her voice. "Fort Clark! Goodness, that's somewhere on the border, isn't it?"

"Nearabouts," Clint admitted. "Only a hoot and a holler from the Rio Grande."

"How long can you stay?"

"Just the night. I've still got a long ride ahead of me."

"Oh, my," she said, clearly disappointed. "You won't get to see Virgil. He's not due back till the end of the week."

Clint frowned. "That's a helluva note. Where's he at, anyway?"

"Colorado."

"What for?" Clint interrupted. "He's got no business up there."

"Don't be upset," she said. "I wouldn't allow him to go anywhere near Denver. He's in Colorado Springs."

The remark needed no elaboration. Virgil had political as well as business enemies in Denver. That, combined with Earl's feud with the city's underworld boss, had resulted in violence. Fighting for their lives, the Brannocks had survived three shootouts in the course of one week. In the aftermath, a shaky truce had been negotiated that allowed the Brannocks to leave Denver in peace. To return would only invite further bloodshed.

"Colorado Springs," Clint repeated quizzically. "What the devil's he doing there?"

"Would you believe it?" Elizabeth said ruefully. "Another railroad . . ."

Before Clint could respond, the children appeared in the parlor doorway. Jennifer, who had a gamine quality about her, hung back shyly. Morgan, with a mop of curly hair and the look of a prankster, advanced a step further. In his buckskins, with a pistol at one side and a foot-long bowie knife at the other, Clint seemed to them some colossus off the plains. They stared at him with open curiosity.

"Mercy sakes," Elizabeth admonished. "Don't stand there with your mouths open. Say hello to your Uncle Clint."

Jennifer edged forward and bashfully nodded her head. Somewhat bolder, Morgan stuck out a tiny paw and manfully shook hands. Clint, looking a bit nonplussed, wondered what an uncle was supposed to say.

"You've grown some," he noted, glancing from one to the other. "How do you like Dallas?"

"Fine," Jennifer said softly.

Morgan studied him with an impish expression. "Pa says you're an Injun-fighter. How many have you killed, Uncle Clint?"

"Honestly, Morgan!" Elizabeth shook a chiding finger. "You two scoot out of here, right now. I'll call you when it's time for supper."

Jennifer took the boy's hand and led him somewhat reluctantly back through the parlor.

Embarrassed, Elizabeth watched them out of sight. At length, she turned to Clint.

"You'll have to excuse him. Virgil fills his head with tales of your adventures."

"No harm done," Clint told her. "Wonder if I could wash up before supper. I expect I'm a touch rank."

Elizabeth showed him to the spare bedroom. She brought him a washbasin and a teakettle of hot water, along with soap and towel. While he was bathing, she had Morg walk his horse down to the livery stable. The boy returned, proud as punch, carrying Clint's saddle carbine. She gave him a smart slap on the rump.

By the time Clint reappeared, she was working madly over the wood cookstove. An hour or so later she called the children and they sat down at the table. She had outdone herself, preparing a small feast in Clint's honor. He stuffed himself full on pork roast, mashed potatoes, brandied apples, and corn bread. For dessert she served

cherry pie topped with fresh cream. Upon finishing, he
had to let his belt out a notch.

After supper, Clint retired to the parlor for a smoke.
Elizabeth dragooned the children into helping her clear the
table and wash dishes. The three of them soon joined him
in the parlor, where a warm blaze crackled in the fireplace.
Elizabeth took a chair opposite him and the children seated
themselves on the sofa. Jennifer and Morg eyeballed him
as though he were a magician about to perform some
staggering sleight-of-hand.

Clint tended to treat children with amiable sufferance.
As a confirmed bachelor, he looked upon kids as one of
life's great mysteries. They were generally noisy and full
of questions, and seldom respectful of a man's privacy.
Then too, having lived among soldiers so long, he had no
idea how to talk to them. Their minds leapfrogged hither
and yon with baffling illogic.

Jennifer quickly proved his point. Having recovered
from her bashful spell, she inquired innocently, "Have
you ever met a squaw, Uncle Clint?"

"Well, yeah." Clint looked uncomfortable. "Here and
there, I've known a few."

"Are they pretty?" she asked ingenuously. "I've never
in my life even seen one."

"I reckon they're like anybody else. Some are pretty
and some aren't."

"Someday," she said dreamily, "I hope I get to meet
one. So I could see for myself."

Clint chuckled. "Just hope you don't meet the wrong
one. Lots of squaws would give their right arm for a
blue-eyed little girl like you."

"No kiddin'?" Morg said, his voice excited. "You
mean they'd steal Jen and take her off somewheres?"

"For a fact," Clint observed with exaggerated gravity.
"Happens all the time."

"Wow!" Morg crowed. "Wouldn't that be the berries?
Serve her right, too."

Jennifer made a face and poked him in the ribs. The boy doubled over with laughter, amused by his sister's beet-red blush. When they fell to squabbling, Elizabeth shooed them off to bed. Over their protests, she declared tomorrow was a school day, and that was that. She promised they would see their uncle at breakfast.

Clint was rolling a cigarette when Elizabeth returned to the parlor. He popped a match and lit up in a cloud of smoke. Seating herself, she shook her head with an apologetic look. He grinned, tossing the match into the fireplace.

"Guess they must keep you hoppin'."

"Never a dull moment," she said lightly. "They're a handful."

Clint was silent a moment. "What's this about Virge and another railroad? I thought he was partners in the Texas & Pacific."

"No more," she confided. "Last week he sold out."

"Knowin' Virge, he must've had a good reason."

"The reason was a scoundrel named Jay Gould."

Elizabeth started at the beginning and told the story through to the end. Though she mentioned no specific amount, she hinted at the fortune Virgil had reaped from his Texas & Pacific stock. She concluded by stating that he was now considering an investment in the Denver & Rio Grande. The line was a fledgling railroad, with plans to expand into New Mexico Territory. Clint sat as if lost in thought, taking in every word. He wagged his head when she finished.

"Virge always had a sixth sense for business. I'd bet my boots he's onto something good."

A note of pride entered her voice. "Sometimes he takes my breath. He's so certain of himself—so confident."

Clint scratched his jaw with a thumb. "Virge was always an ambitious man, bound to get ahead. Guess he's still got his eye on the brass ring."

"Isn't it the truth," she said wonderingly. "I really believe there's no limit to what he could accomplish."

Clint was taken by her spirited manner. There was an effervescent quality about her, at once sprightly and vivacious. Yet, at the same time, she was very much the lady. A woman of exquisite elegance and grace and undeniable beauty. His personal tastes ran to zestful, romping women of laughter and animal appetites. He nonetheless thought his brother a lucky man.

"Funny thing," he said after a time. "I reckon Virge and Earl aren't all that different. In their own way, they're both gamblers."

A troubled look came over her face. "When was the last time you heard from Earl?"

"When Monte died," Clint said in a low voice. "Letter caught up with me a month or so later. How about you?"

"The same," she murmured uneasily. "Just the one letter and then nothing. It bothers me."

Clint nodded thoughtfully. "Earl's deeper than he appears. Thing like that, he wouldn't shake it off too quick."

"I'm afraid you're right," she said in a faraway voice. "You don't think he'd do anything foolish, do you?"

"Like what?"

"Oh, I don't know. Perhaps hurt himself somehow."

"Huh-uh," Clint muttered. "One way or another, Earl always lands on his feet."

"Virgil says the same thing. But we've written letter after letter, and all of them have gone unanswered. I've begun to worry about the boy—Lon."

"No sense borrowing trouble. We'd likely hear if anything was wrong."

"I wonder," she said anxiously. "San Francisco's so far away, almost like another world. If anything happened to Earl, we might never hear about the boy. Don't you see?"

A flicker of humor showed in Clint's features. "You know what? You're starting to sound the least bit like a mother."

"What do you mean?"

"I'm sayin' there's no need to fret about the boy. No matter what, Earl wouldn't leave him high and dry."

Elizabeth studied him a moment. She'd always known that he was the strongest of the three brothers, harder and mentally tougher. There was something impenetrable about him, a sort of personal insensitivity. As though, somehow, his soul was like his hands, gnarled and calloused. She often thought he was a victim of the life he'd led, brutalized by all the killing and bloodshed. Yet, for all that, she felt a powerful tug of emotion toward him. No man was more loyal or true to those he loved.

At length, she fixed him with a disarming smile. "Well, on to more pleasant subjects. How's your social life these days?"

"How's my what?" Clint said, surprised.

Her lips curved in a teasing smile. "Don't be evasive, now. Surely there must be a lady in your life?"

Clint met her gaze, found something merry lurking there. "I get the feeling you're asking me why I haven't settled down with some good woman."

"Well . . ." she said speculatively, watching him. "Why haven't you?"

"God a'mighty," Clint mugged, hands outstretched. "You women just can't abide an unmarried man, can you?"

"Oh fiddlesticks! You won't get off that easy, Clint Brannock. Isn't there someone you're interested in?"

Clint smiled lazily. "Why, as to that, I reckon you couldn't pin it down to one. I'm interested in all the ladies."

Her eyes sparkled with suppressed mirth. "To hear you talk, anyone would think you've left behind a trail of broken hearts. Have you?"

Clint's smile broadened. "Ask me no questions and I'll tell you no lies."

"Well, Mr. Footloose and Fancy Free, there's always a day of reckoning. You'll regret it in your old age."

5

COLORADO SPRINGS was situated on a rough and barren plateau. The town lay in the shadow of Pikes Peak, a towering summit still capped with snow. In the distance, the Rockies marched northward like an unbroken column of sentinels.

Virgil arrived on a sunny morning in late March. By stage, he'd traveled to New Mexico and on through Raton Pass into Colorado. The trip had consumed the better part of a week, with a one-night layover in Santa Fe. He was bone-tired and yet strangely exhilarated, for he carried a confirming telegram in his pocket. At three that afternoon, he had an appointment with General William J. Palmer.

Stepping down from the stage, Virgil waited while his bag was unloaded from the luggage boot. His gaze was drawn to the majestic spire of Pikes Peak. The grandeur of the Rocky Mountains always infused him with a sense of greatness, as though standing testament to the limitless potential of the land. He realized he'd missed that feeling on the parched flatland prairies of Texas. Something told him he'd made the right decision, and he absently nodded to himself. He was glad to be back in Colorado.

Farther downtown, he saw the railyards and a chuff of smoke from a locomotive. He already knew that the narrow-gauge tracks ended several miles south of town. There, on the broken terrain, the Denver & Rio Grande abruptly

came to a halt. In the opposite direction, the line extended
northward to Denver, connecting with the Kansas Pacific
and the Denver Pacific railways. He found a certain irony
in the thought, for he'd been one of the founders of the
Denver Pacific. The memory, despite the lapse of years,
still stung.

After collecting his bags, he walked across to the Mani-
tou House Hotel. The main thoroughfare was clogged with
wagons and buggies, and the boardwalks were crowded
with shoppers. The arrival of the railroad, scarcely six
months past, had transformed barren land into a bustling
little metropolis. The street was jammed with shops and
stores, and a block away the new courthouse was under
construction. Colorado Springs, created virtually out of
nothing, had assumed a look of permanence. There was a
smell of boom times in the air.

A bellman carried Virgil's bag to his room. He ordered
a kettle of hot water and overtipped to ensure it was
speeded along. When the water arrived, he stripped and
took a birdbath in the washbasin. After emptying the dirty
water into the johnny pot, he refilled the basin from the
kettle. With a mug and brush, he soaped his face and tested
the edge of his bone-handled straight razor. Watching
himself in the mirror, he began shaving with dulled concentration. His mind was on William J. Palmer.

Unlike many railroad builders, Palmer was a man of
fairly decent reputation. Prior to the Civil War he had
spent four years with the Pennsylvania Railway line. When
hostilities broke out, he'd organized the 15th Pennsylvania
Cavalry, serving with the regiment from Antietam to the
burning of Atlanta. A shrewd tactician and a gifted leader,
he had retired with the rank of brigadier general. He had
been twenty-nine at the time.

In 1865, Palmer joined the Kansas Pacific Railroad. As
superintendent of construction, he had surveyed the western approach to Denver and later completed the line to
Colorado's capital city. At that point, he'd gone on his

own, establishing headquarters in Denver. After forming a company and obtaining a railroad charter, he had organized the Denver & Rio Grande. His immediate objective was to build to El Paso, Texas, with a long-range goal of extending the line into the interior of Old Mexico. He began construction late in 1871.

So far as Palmer was concerned, the route by which he ultimately arrived at El Paso was of no particular significance. Experience had taught him that there was more money to be made from organizing townsites and peddling real estate than from operating a railroad. Whether the towns withered and died for want of an economic base was a worry he left to others. While he was no Robber Baron, he knew the essential secret of lining his own pockets. Federal land grants and private land companies were what made railroad builders rich.

Some sixty miles south of Denver was a small town called Colorado City. Before starting construction on his railroad, Palmer checked around and found the land prices in Colorado City to be rather steep. With no one the wiser, he went farther out and acquired a large block of land for less than a dollar an acre. A year later the Denver & Rio Grande bypassed Colorado City, establishing a terminus in the new townsite he'd named Colorado Springs. Shortly, Colorado City vanished and Colorado Springs was designated the county seat. Palmer made a killing selling town lots.

Some people called him a buccaneer and others lauded him as a trailblazer. By whatever name, he was like all railroad builders in one important respect: without construction funds from banks or outside investors, he was out of business. While he'd reached Colorado Springs, the Denver & Rio Grande was still 130 miles from the New Mexico border and a world away from his primary goal, El Paso. The operation was stalled for the most fundamental of reasons. He'd been caught short by the Panic of '73.

Virgil saw it as an opportunity. He had no intention of capitalizing on another man's misfortune. Instead, he perceived himself in the role of a financial savior. Apart from a direct infusion of cash, he had something Palmer needed even more. When it came to raising funds, there were few men Virgil's equal. And he had a trick up his sleeve that could spell deliverance for the Denver & Rio Grande. He was confident the general would listen with a receptive ear.

As he finished shaving, Virgil was reminded of a long-past event. In 1865, when Lee surrendered at Appomattox, he'd been a captain in the Confederate army. A month later the President of the Confederacy, Jefferson Davis, was captured while trying to elude Union pursuit. The cavalry unit that ran him to ground was the 15th Pennsylvania. Their leader was Brigadier General William Palmer.

Virgil thought it an amusing sidelight to today's meeting. All the more so since he intended to take Palmer captive. Along with a large chunk of the Denver & Rio Grande.

The offices of the Denver & Rio Grande were located north of the railyards. The building was constructed of planed lumber and painted forest green. On the roof was a large sign identifying it as the general headquarters of the railroad. The first impression was that of a substantial operation.

At three o'clock sharp, Virgil walked through the door. He was attired in a black broadcloth coat, with gray-striped trousers and a elegant diamond stickpin thrust into his tie. The outfit, along with a touch of gray at his temples, gave him a distinguished look. He thought it appropriate to the occasion.

A clerk took his hat and ushered him into the inner office. Seated behind a polished walnut desk was a large, round-shouldered man. He was rangy in build, with angular features and wire-rimmed spectacles perched on the bridge of his nose. His eyes were deep-set and dark, curiously flat. He rose, extending his hand.

"Good to see you, Mr. Brannock."

Virgil accepted his handshake. "My pleasure, General. I appreciate your making time for me."

"Not at all."

Palmer motioned him to a wing-back chair. Virgil seated himself, extracting a leather cigarcase from an inside pocket. He lit up in a haze of blue smoke, dropping the match into an ashtray. From behind the desk, Palmer eyed him like a pugilist waiting for the bell. Virgil purposely forced him to open the discussion.

"Your wire indicated a matter of some import, Mr. Brannock. May I inquire the nature of your business?"

Virgil waved the cigar with a bluff air of assurance. "I'm here to talk a trade, General Palmer. You have a railroad that's floundering and I have the expertise to save it. In short, we can be of service to one another."

Palmer gave him a blank stare. "What makes you think I need your services?"

"Let's be frank," Virgil replied genially. "There's a financial Armageddon sweeping the country. Every railroad in America is scrambling for construction funds. You're no exception."

"You seem rather well-versed in my financial affairs, Mr. Brannock."

"Well, General," Virgil said modestly, "I've had some experience in that end of the business."

"The word back East," Palmer remarked, "is that you're no longer with the Texas & Pacific. I hear you sold out at a handsome profit."

Virgil smiled. "Good news travels fast."

Palmer removed his glasses and began wiping them with a handkerchief. "Before that, I believe you were with the Denver Pacific." He paused, fixing the glasses on his nose. "I'm told you had a falling out with David Hughes."

Virgil took a long puff on his cigar. His genial expression toughened. "I fail to see the connection."

"I'm also told," Palmer said stolidly, "that you killed Hughes' partner. A man by the name of Luther Evans."

The story was by now part of Denver's folklore. Some eight years past Virgil had been a stockholder as well as the chief fund-raiser for the Denver Pacific. He'd discovered that Hughes, who was president of the line, was bilking the railroad. The ensuing confrontation was aggravated by the fact that Hughes was also the political kingpin of Denver. When Virgil threatened exposure, Hughes had ordered his death.

The upshot was a gunfight between Virgil and his brothers and a gang of hired killers. Having survived that, Virgil represented an even greater threat. He'd gone to the newspaper and revealed the entire story. Afterward, on the street, he'd been braced by Luther Evans and forced into a showdown. Evans drew first and Virgil killed him in self-defense. Still, the shooting had soured Virgil's business prospects in Denver. He sold off his railroad stock, as well as other business ventures, and departed a week later. Had he remained, he would have been assassinated.

"General Palmer," he said now, "I make no apology for killing Luther Evans. A coroner's jury ruled it justifiable homicide."

There was a moment of calculation while Palmer studied him. Virgil stared him straight in the eye, challenging him, and at last the railroad owner nodded.

"There's a rumor," Palmer said with a grim smile, "that you caught Hughes with his hand in the till. Any truth to it?"

Virgil hesitated, as though weighing his words. "I learned a lesson in Denver. When a man has enough political power, he's immune to prosecution. All the same, I've benefited by the experience."

"How is that?"

"I operate on the principle that any politician is corrupt. I've seldom been proved wrong."

Palmer nodded with an approving smile. "I take it that's the basis for your success in Texas. As I recall, you were instrumental in obtaining the charter for the Texas & Pacific."

Virgil laughed, spread his hands. "Just between you and me, several legislators walked away rich men. Nothing gets a politician's attention like the long green."

"You advocate bribery, then?"

"I work within the system, General. As it happens, the system is crooked, top to bottom."

"I regret to say," Palmer observed, "I endorse the sentiment. It's a hell of a way to run a country."

"Or a railroad," Virgil added.

"Well-spoken, Mr. Brannock. I like the way you think."

"From what I've seen, it's the only way that works."

"Something of a paradox, isn't it?"

"A paradox?"

"Nothing less," Palmer said in an orotund voice. "David Hughes is a case in point. However slippery, he nonetheless gave Denver its first railroad. Perhaps the end justifies the means, after all."

Virgil couldn't argue the point. Following his departure from Denver, Hughes had completed the railroad. Stretching northward, the Denver Pacific connected with the Union Pacific at Cheyenne, Wyoming. While the Kansas Pacific arrived in Denver shortly afterward, it in no way detracted from Hughes' accomplishment. He had been the first to link Denver with the outside world.

"I suppose," Virgil mused aloud, "it's an occupational hazard. We become pragmatists, or otherwise we don't build railroads."

"True," Palmer agreed dourly. "But we've strayed off the purpose of your visit. I'm interested to hear how you would save the Denver & Rio Grande."

"As I see it, you've got two major problems: money and time."

"What does time have to do with it?"

"You're in a race, General. Just offhand, I'd say it looks to be a dead heat."

"Spare me your riddles, Mr. Brannock. What race?"

"The Santa Fe."

A stony expression settled on Palmer's features. The Santa Fe Railroad was building west from Kansas. Only recently the line had crossed the Colorado border, angling southward. As yet, the location of their intended terminus remained unknown.

"You seem very well-informed, Mr. Brannock."

"General," Virgil said in a measured tone, "how would you like to know where the Santa Fe's headed?"

Palmer squinted at him. "Are you saying you know?"

"For a fact," Virgil affirmed. "They've surveyed a line to Pueblo."

"If that's true, then you've already done me a great service. May I ask how you came by the information?"

"Let's just say I have my sources."

"Well, no matter. As you so aptly put it, it's now a horse race."

"All the more so since your next scheduled stop is Pueblo."

"By God!" Palmer laughed harshly. "Who did you bribe in my organization?"

Virgil smiled, not at all offended. "I make it a practice to do my homework. Pays to know your competition."

"Apparently so."

"I also know where the Santa Fe's headed after Pueblo."

Palmer looked at him intently. "I'm afraid to ask."

"New Mexico," Virgil said soberly. "They plan to beat you there and get a lock on the southwestern trade. You can mark it down as gospel, General."

"Jesus," Palmer mumbled. "It's worse than I thought."

Virgil puffed a thick wad of smoke. He let the silence build a moment, then resumed. "There's no prize for coming in second. You know what'll happen if the Santa Fe beats you to New Mexico."

"Of course, I know," Palmer said shortly. "It would finish the Denver & Rio Grande."

"Suppose I could show you a way out?"

Palmer gave him a cool look of appraisal. "In exchange for what?"

"A piece of the railroad."

"You play a rough game, Mr. Brannock."

Virgil made an expansive gesture. "I'm not asking for a free ride. I'll contribute my expertise and a fairly sizable chunk of cash. I doubt you'll get a better offer."

"How much cash?" Palmer asked gruffly.

Virgil sensed victory. Yet he subscribed to the old adage about putting all the eggs in one basket. Part of his windfall from the Texas Pacific would be held in reserve. The balance he was willing to commit to the Denver & Rio Grande.

"Three hundred thousand," he said. "I brought a bank draft with me."

"For God's sake!" Palmer said in disgust. "Three hundred thousand won't build twenty miles of track."

Virgil looked at him without expression. "That's twenty miles closer to Pueblo. And a couple of jumps ahead of the Santa Fe."

"You don't believe in pulling punches, do you?"

"Well, General, you do have an alternative. You could do nothing and lose the whole ball of wax."

Palmer brushed away the suggestion with a quick, impatient gesture. "You're talking a drop in the bucket. It would take ten times that amount—three million dollars—to lay track into New Mexico."

Virgil grinned. "That's where the expertise comes in. It just so happens, I know where I can put my hands on that exact amount."

Palmer eyed him suspiciously. "Where?"

"No soap," Virgil informed him. "When we've got a deal—in writing—I'll tell you all my secrets. Not before."

"How do I know you can deliver?"

"Two reasons," Virgil said equably. "First, I've always delivered in the past. And second, I'll have my own money at stake. I aim to turn a profit."

Palmer's brow seamed. "What sort of deal do you have in mind?"

"Down the middle—fifty-fifty."

"Thunderation," Palmer roared. "That's out-and-out robbery. The line's worth at least ten million!"

"Only on paper, General. As of today, you couldn't sell it for a plugged nickel."

Palmer glared at him. "I'll go twenty percent, and that's it."

"Why haggle?" Virgil said agreeably. "Let's make it forty and shake hands."

"Not on your life. Thirty percent, and that's my last offer."

"You would've made a good horse trader. Tell you what, I'll settle for thirty-five."

"Thirty-three," Palmer said curtly. "Take it or leave it."

"Suppose we split the difference. Thirty-four, and you've got yourself a partner."

Palmer pondered a moment, then nodded. "It's a deal."

Virgil offered his hand and they shook once, a hard up-and-down pump. He sat back, puffing on his cigar, thoroughly pleased with himself. His grin widened. "Now that we're partners, what do I call you besides General?"

"Well . . ." Palmer said, reluctant to surrender his rank. "Close friends call me Will."

"That's fine, Will. And why don't you drop the mister? Folks generally call me Virge."

Virgil gave himself another pat on the back. He'd been willing to settle for a quarter-interest and he had bettered that by nine points. A rough calculation put his share of the Denver & Rio Grande at close to three and a half million. All on paper, of course, but not bad for a day's work.

He thought Jefferson Davis would have approved.

6

EARL AND LON arrived on April Fool's Day. They stepped off the train at Colorado Springs with little more than the clothes they wore. Everything they owned was stuffed into a secondhand carpetbag.

For Lon, there was a storybook quality to their trip. His entire life had been spent in San Francisco, where an inland bay opened onto the ocean. The Rockies, which seemed to touch the clouds, were mystical to behold. His eyes never strayed far from the snowcapped mountains. He was at once awed and fascinated.

Inside the depot, Earl inquired about Virgil. The stationmaster scrutinized man and boy with a critical eye. He wondered what business a couple of deadbeats had with the railroad's new vice president. Earl volunteered no information, and the stationmaster, despite his curiosity, was reluctant to pry. He pointed them in the right direction.

Uptown, they turned north on a side street. Everything in Colorado Springs looked new and freshly painted, and the residential area was no exception. As in most western towns, the better homes were to be found north of the business district. The house they sought was a two-story affair, with gables and cornices and lots of windows. A white picket fence bordered the yard.

Virgil opened the door. He looked from Earl to Lon and

back again. His stunned expression gave way to a nut-cracker grin. He let out a loud whoop.

"Godalmightydamn! Where'd you drop from?"

Earl laughed. "Just got off the train."

Virgil pulled him into a mighty bear hug. A year separated them in age, and the older man's eyes suddenly glistened with emotion. As the eldest brother, he was given to a show of feelings, and today the sentiment ran strong. He finally released Earl and looked down at the boy.

"This must be Lon."

Earl nudged the boy forward. "Say hello to your Uncle Virgil."

Virgil reached for him, intent on another hug. The youngster nodded, shifting away a step, and stuck out his hand. He was clearly embarrassed by the display of emotion.

Forced to shake, Virgil chuckled. "He's the spittin' image of you, Earl. I could pick him out in a crowd."

"Too bad," Earl said, ruffling the boy's hair. "I'd hoped he grow up better-looking than his old man."

Virgil's expression abruptly changed. He became aware that there was something of a ragamuffin about the boy. Then, for the first time, he took stock of his brother. Earl looked curiously worn and threadbare, somehow unkempt. He remembered Earl as a dapper dresser, natty and well-groomed, almost vain. What he saw now was a man who was down and out, oddly haggard in appearance. He felt a sharp twinge of concern.

"It just come to me," he said, trying to hide his shock. "How'd you know I was here? We only moved in yesterday."

"Outhouse luck," Earl replied. "I wired you from Salt Lake. The telegrapher in Dallas was obliging enough to wire back. Told us you'd moved here."

Virgil appeared bemused. "What were you doing in Salt Lake?"

"Well . . ." Earl hesitated, glancing down at the boy. "I was sick a spell."

Before Virgil could respond, Elizabeth swept into the vestibule. Laughing with delight, she moved to Earl and embraced him with genuine affection. As they parted, she saw Lon and scooped him into her arms before he could dodge away. When she let him go, her eyes were misty with tears. She pulled a hanky from the sleeve of her dress and blew her nose.

"Just look at me," she said brightly. "I haven't even greeted you properly."

Earl smiled. "It's welcome enough for me."

Jennifer and Morgan appeared on the staircase to the upper floor. Elizabeth motioned them forward and performed introductions. All they knew of their uncle were the stories they'd heard. Their cousin, who was Jennifer's age, was even more a stranger. They eyed him with polite interest.

Lon was strangely silent. He seemed to withdraw, avoiding their stares with a solemn look that belied his age. Observing him, Elizabeth thought he was shy and perhaps a little frightened. She hadn't yet heard him speak a word and he appeared ready to bolt out the door. She moved quickly to put him at ease.

"Lon," she said pleasantly, "we have a big room upstairs for you and your father. Would you like to see it?"

The boy darted a glance at his father. Earl nodded, indicating he should go along. Elizabeth held out her hand, smiling warmly, and he took it. He followed her up the stairs like a rebellious child being led to the woodhouse. Jennifer and Morgan tagged along.

Virgil steered Earl into the parlor. He noticed that Earl had lost a good deal of weight, and his concern deepened. Cartons, still half-unpacked, were scattered about the room. Virgil motioned to a sofa and two overstuffed chairs positioned before the fireplace. After they were seated, he produced cigars and struck a match.

Earl accepted a light, then sat back in his chair. "Guess you're wondering about Lon and me."

"Hell's bells," Virgil said. "I'm just glad to see you. It's been a while since you wrote."

"Nothing to write," Earl said in a remote voice. "Nothing good, anyway."

"I figured as much. It must've been rough on you, what with Monte and all."

There was a stark silence. Earl didn't reply for several moments, idly rolling the cigar between thumb and forefinger. When he spoke, there was an echoing sadness in his words. "She went out like a trouper, Virge. Never complained, never thought of herself. Happy right to the very end."

Virgil nodded soberly. "Monte was a fine woman. I always admired her."

"She deserved better," Earl said. "The last month or so, she went through pure hell."

"How'd the boy take it?"

"Lon doesn't say much. Besides, he was too busy worrying about me."

"What do you mean?"

"After she . . ." Earl stopped, began again. "When it was over, I sort of went off the deep end. Got my head stuck in a bottle."

"Sounds bad," Virgil allowed softly.

"Worse than that," Earl said. "I stayed drunk day and night. Only time I stopped was when I passed out."

"Were you still gamblin', then?"

"You might call it that. I lost every cent I had in less than three months."

Virgil shook his head. "What was the boy doing all that time?"

"Looking after me," Earl confessed. "It got to be a full-time job."

"Way you describe it," Virgil said, watching his drawn features, "the boy's got plenty of spunk."

Earl laughed hollowly. "Except for him, I'd be dead myself. He pulled me out of every gutter in Frisco."

Virgil studied his downcast face. "Are you off the bottle now?"

"After a fashion," Earl noted wryly. "We got as far as Salt Lake before it hit me. I holed up in a hotel room and dried myself out."

"That's what you meant about being 'sick a spell?' "

Earl bobbed his head. "There for a while, I thought I was gonna croak. Lon nursed me along till I was back on my feet." He paused, staring at the cigar. "Hell of a thing for a kid to go through."

Virgil was aware that he'd been placed in the role of father confessor. Earl felt some compulsion to unburden himself, purge his mind of guilt. He was not unlike a penitent seeking absolution for past wrongs. As in their youth, he'd chosen his older brother to hear him out. He could have said these things to no other human.

"What counts," Virgil said at last, "is that you've got yourself straightened out. Anything else is water under the bridge."

Earl got to his feet. He walked to the parlor window and stood staring out into the street. His eyes were unfocused and he seemed unaware that the cigar had gone cold in his hand. A long beat of silence passed before he spoke.

"In Salt Lake," he said in a dead monotone, "I made myself a promise. One way or another, I'm gonna make it up to Lon. I've just about stole his childhood away from him."

Elizabeth entered in time to hear the remark. From the somber look on Virgil's face, she knew the men had been discussing something too personal to bear repeating. Yet she intuitively sensed that Earl's remark represented a turning point. Whatever he and his son had been through, he'd put it behind him. His thoughts were now trained on the future.

Earl turned from the window. He searched her face as she seated herself on the sofa. "How are the kids getting along?"

"Fine," she said gaily. "Of course, Jennifer's in a bit of a snit. Morgan took Lon off to see his army of toy soldiers. She feels slightly left out."

"Toy soldiers," Earl repeated vacantly. "I don't remember the last time I bought him a toy. Funny, the things you forget."

Virgil and Elizabeth exchanged a glance. His eyes cautioned her to silence and she acknowledged with an imperceptible nod. He drew on his cigar, puffed a cottony wad of smoke.

"I was just about to offer Earl a job."

"That's marvelous," she said happily.

Earl took a step away from the window. "I hadn't even thought to ask what you're doing in Colorado Springs. Are you still with the railroad?"

"Same song, different verse," Virgil said amiably. "I've bought part of the Denver & Rio Grande. We're building south, into New Mexico."

"No joke?" Earl asked, grinning. "That's where I'm headed."

"New Mexico?" Virgil said, taken aback.

"Santa Fe," Earl informed him. "I got to talking with a fellow while we were in Salt Lake. He told me it's ripe pickings in Santa Fe. Lots of money when the Missouri traders hit town."

Virgil frowned. "Why go back to gambling? I could arrange a good job with the railroad, and top dollar, too. You'd be a big help to me."

"Gambling's what I know," Earl said, walking back to his chair. "Besides, what would I do on a railroad? I'm too old to change my spots."

"You'd do lots better than you would in Santa Fe. We

spent the night there on the way from Dallas. It put me in mind of a raw mining camp—only wilder.''

"Sounds made to order."

"I would've thought you'd had enough of the sporting life. It hasn't given you much in return."

"Everybody whistles a different tune, Virge. I'm not suited to anything else."

Virgil looked at him seriously. "You told me you were broke. How will you get started?"

"Nothing simpler," Earl said raffishly. "You're gonna stake me."

"What makes you think I'd do a damnfool thing like that?"

"I've got a hunch you won't turn me down."

"Awful sure of yourself, aren't you?"

"No," Earl said with a slow grin. "I'm sure of you, though."

Virgil winced. "I don't know if I like the sound of that. Anybody would think I'm an easy touch."

"Why, hell, Virge, you always were."

Earl laughed and Virgil's sober look gave way to a muted chuckle. For a moment it was like old times, and Earl lit his cigar with a flourish. Then, as the laughter faded, Elizabeth joined the conversation.

"What about Lon?"

Earl looked across at her. "What about him?"

"Oh, I was just thinking," she said quietly. "Is the sporting life what you want for him?"

"I suppose any man wants a better life for his son. That's only natural."

"I'm not talking about when he's grown. I'm talking about now."

"Now?" Earl paused, gave her a bewildered look. "What are you driving at?"

She stared at him. "You're determined to go to Santa Fe, aren't you?"

Earl made an empty gesture with his hands. "What else

would I do? I'm not cut out to be a train conductor or work in an office.''

"We're discussing Lon . . . not you."

"Look, Beth, I'm no good at drawing-room conversation. Why don't you just say what you're trying to say."

Elizabeth took a deep breath. "You may think me a busybody—"

"No," Earl interrupted. "Go on and say it."

"All right," she replied, sitting straighter. "Lon has never known a normal life. He's been raised in a sinkhole of iniquity and evil. Unless something changes, he'll be trapped in the life you've led."

"Maybe he would," Earl said, then shrugged. "So what would you have me do?"

"Leave him here," she said firmly. "Don't take him to Santa Fe."

Earl fixed her with a terrible look. "You're talking about my son, Beth. You want me to just walk off and leave him with strangers?"

"We're not strangers," she countered, "we're family. And right now, he desperately needs that, Earl. A family, with children his own age—all the things he's never known."

"I couldn't," Earl said in a raspy voice. "How does a man walk away from his son?"

"Not permanently! Goodness' sakes, a boy needs his father. But a month or so might do him a world of good. Meanwhile, you'll have a chance to look things over in Santa Fe."

"You ask a lot," Earl said heavily. "Lon and me, we've never been apart . . . not once."

She met the hurt look in his eyes. "Stop and think about it. He'd have a decent home and proper meals, and he'd be attending school." She paused, smiling gently. "Isn't that what you want for him?"

Earl leaned forward, elbows on his knees. He pressed his fingers against his temples and tried to focus his thoughts.

His concentration splintered when he imagined being separated from the boy. But reason slowly prevailed, and with an effort he pulled himself together. His voice was strained and strangely tortured.

"You understand," he said, "it would only be for a little while. Just till I get my feet on the ground."

Elizabeth heard the pain in his voice. "Of course we understand, Earl. We're only offering to help you through a difficult period. Isn't that so, Virgil?"

Virgil seemed astounded by his wife's resolute manner. Caught unawares by the question, he hastily cleared his throat. "She's right, Earl. It's the best thing for the boy."

"All right," Earl said slowly. "I'll leave him with you."

"No!"

The sharp exclamation jolted them erect. They turned and saw Lon standing in the parlor entryway. His features were twisted in an ugly grimace. Before they could move, he whirled back into the vestibule. The front door slammed like a cannon shot.

Earl bounded out of his chair. As he emerged from the house, he saw Lon fumbling with the latch on the picket-fence gate. He hurried forward and took the youngster by the shoulders. Lon went rigid under his hands.

"Listen to me," Earl said, turning the boy around. "You've got it all wrong. It's not like it sounds."

Lon's features were pale and furious. He looked on the verge of tears. "You're lyin'! I heard you. You're gonna dump me—with them!"

"No, I'm not," Earl said sternly. "It's only until I get settled, sort things out."

Tears welled up in the boy's eyes. "I don't believe you. It's just a trick to get rid of me."

"You don't really think that. Why, damnation, sport, I couldn't get along without you."

"Yeah, you could! You've wanted shed of me ever since Ma died. You think I didn't know?"

Earl saw an odd kind of defiance in the youngster's eyes
and a look he couldn't quite fathom. He struggled to keep
his voice under control.

"You're all I've got," he said. "I'd cut my arm off
before I'd lose you. I mean it, son."

"No, you don't," Lon said in a tight, hurt voice. "If
you did, you wouldn't go off and leave me."

"It's not forever," Earl patiently explained. "We'll be
back together before you know it."

"I don't care. I'll run off or somethin'. I won't stay
here."

"C'mon now, sport. You could do lots worse. There's
Jennifer and Morg to chum around with. And you'll get
some regular schooling for a change. Why, you'll have
yourself a whale of a time."

Lon's chin jutted defiantly. "Who needs 'em? Him and
his dumb toy soldiers. And she's not no better! They're a
couple of ninnies."

Earl felt as though his ears had come unplugged. He
suddenly understood that the boy was envious of Jennifer
and Morgan. But beneath the envy lay something far
worse. Lon saw himself as the poor relation, a charity case
and therefore inferior.

More than ever Earl grasped the wisdom of Elizabeth's
suggestion. She had seen in Lon what he saw now. A boy
with no sense of his own worth, no pride in himself. A
boy with no mother and a rummy for a father. He resolved
to turn it around, start fresh today. His son deserved a
chance.

"Lookit here," he said, commanding the boy's attention. "Have I ever lied to you before?"

Lon gave him a hangdog look. "No."

"Then I want you to trust me in what I'm saying to you
now. I won't leave you here any longer than I have to.
You've got my word on it."

"No bull?" Lon asked with a child's directness. "You'll
come back for me?"

"For a fact," Earl promised. "You and me, we're a team, regular matched pair. Nothing's gonna change that."

The boy sniffled, brushing back tears. The defiance went out of his eyes and he smiled an upside-down smile. Earl thought it was the saddest smile he'd ever seen, and a lump formed in his throat. Unable to speak, he laid an arm around the youngster's shoulders and drew him close.

They walked back toward the house.

7

FORT CLARK was 125 miles west of San Antonio. Some fifty miles south lay the Rio Grande and, on the opposite shore, Mexico. In between, there was nothing.

The country around Fort Clark was a hardscrabble land, inhospitable in any season. The rolling prairie was dotted with patches of sand and cactus and dense thickets of chaparral. Interspersed among the naked thorns of the chaparral were mesquite trees and an occasional wild briar. The land was populated largely by rattlesnakes, scorpions, and lobo wolves.

On a Monday morning, Clint rode in by way of the San Antonio road. He passed first through Brackettville, the small town outside the post. A sleepy Texican village, the buildings were a mix of adobe and rough-sawn lumber. He got the impression that it existed solely to serve the needs of the army. Fully half the structures were busthead saloons and hurdy-gurdy dance halls.

The heat was unlike anything Clint had ever known. His shirt was plastered to his back and he felt drenched in his own sweat. On the high plains of Wyoming, as well as the prairies of Kansas, he'd endured many brutal summers. But none of that compared with the parched and sweltering land spread out before him now. He wondered if he'd somehow entered the back door of hell.

The garrison was situated on a limestone ridge beside

the waters of Las Moras Creek. Along the winding shore-
line were shaded clusters of live oaks, towering over the
flat terrain. Where the creek made a lazy dogleg, there was
a large split-rail corral flanked by outbuildings and a double row of stables. Nearby were the enlisted men's barracks and quarters for ranking noncommissioned officers.
Shanty houses for unattached launderesses, known quaintly
as Suds Row, were a short distance away.

The sutler's store was located beside the main gate. To
the immediate front was the parade ground and, beyond
that, the regimental headquarters. Close by were the hospital and the quartermaster's depot, and farther on the quarters for married officers. All the buildings were neat-looking
and substantial, constructed of native stone from a local
quarry. The garrison gave the appearance of sturdy permanence, as though it had been built to last. Everything
looked spruce and well-tended, orderly.

Clint rode past a squad of guardhouse inmates busy
policing the area around the sutler's store. Off in the
distance, he saw men working outside the stables and
another contingent grooming horses. On the parade ground,
a company of sweating troopers was being put through
close-order drill. To a man, they looked wilted and ready
to drop in their tracks. Clint was reminded that the army
had invented some exquisite forms of torture. Foot drill for
horse soldiers seemed to him an asinine exercise.

Outside regimental headquarters, he left the gelding tied
to a hitching post. When he entered, it took a moment for
his eyes to adjust to the dim interior. The orderly room
gleamed with whitewash, and two desks were positioned
to guard an inner office. One desk was empty and behind
the other sat a burly man with stripes covering the sleeves
of his shirt. He had a square tough face and a huge walrus
mustache. Stocky and barrel-chested, the vestiges of a
violent youth were written on his features. He looked
vaguely like a prizefighter in uniform.

Looking up, he nodded. "Good mornin' to you."

" 'Morning," Clint said. "I'd like to see Colonel Mackenzie."

"And what might your name be?"

"Clint Brannock. I'm the new chief of scouts."

"Are you indeed? Well, I'm Seargeant Major Michael O'Hara, and proud to make your acquaintance."

O'Hara shook his hand with a beaming smile and an ore-crusher grip. Clint's hand was numb to the wrist when he finally got it back. He decided the sergeant major was no man to have for an enemy.

"Well, now," O'Hara said genially, "you've just missed himself. He's attending sick call."

"Something wrong with the colonel?"

"No, no," O'Hara said. "It's just that he can't abide malingerers. A walk through the hospital performs miracles."

Clint smiled. "Sounds like a stickler."

"A saint of a man!" O'Hara boomed. "He's hard on the troops but harder on himself. You'll never serve under a better commander, Mr. Brannock."

Clint considered a moment. "I've heard he's no book soldier. Any truth to it?"

"By the Christ," O'Hara said with a graveled chuckle. "Never was a truer word spoken. Spit-and-polish is not what he values, Mr. Brannock. He trains men to fight the heathen redsticks. And none does it better."

"I take it you've been with him awhile?"

"I have indeed. Going on fourteen years, it is."

Sergeant Major O'Hara had ridden with Mackenzie since the start of the Civil War. With little prompting, he related the story of the man he still called "Gen'ral." He told it with simple eloquence.

A West Pointer, Mackenzie had graduated at the top of his class. During the Great Rebellion, he earned his first brevet at the Second Battle of Manassas. In all, he was wounded four times and promoted seven times in the course of the war. By the time he joined Sheridan's command in the Shenandoah campaign, he had risen to the rank of Brevet Major General. At Appomattox, Ulysses S. Grant personally charged him with overseeing the surrender of Lee's army. He was twenty-five years old when the war ended.

In 1870, after serving as a staff officer, Mackenzie had been posted to the western frontier. There he garnered a reputation as the best Indian fighter in the army. With an innovative mind, he had adapted Civil War tactics to the treeless plains. He employed the cavalry as a long-ranging strike force, the most effective of all measures against the hostiles' guerrilla tactics. He was cold and taciturn, seldom touched by emotion. Some men called him a "monk in boots," and it was meant as a compliment. He was a soldier's soldier, devoted to his men and the service.

"There's none like him," O'Hara concluded. "He stands head and shoulders above Custer and all the rest."

"Glad to hear it," Clint commented. "I served with Custer till the summer of '71."

"So I've been told." O'Hara cocked his head at a quizzical angle. "And what was your opinion of the Boy General?"

Clint flipped a hand back and forth. "One day he'll get himself in a tight fix—and he won't get out."

O'Hara roared laughter. "God's blood! I think you'll do nicely, Mr. Brannock. Very nicely indeed."

A footstep sounded outside. The man who entered the doorway was of medium height. He was lean and muscular, with chiseled features and a sweeping handlebar mustache. His presence was commanding, and he gave the appearance of solidity and iron will. His tunic bore the insignia of a full colonel and he wore a battered campaign hat. He crossed the orderly room with a slight limp.

Clint would learn later that the limp was the result of a Comanche arrow. In the battle of Blanco Canyon, Mackenzie had taken a barbed shaft in the leg and refused treatment until the hostiles had been dispersed. The wound healed poorly and he now lived in a state of constant pain. Some attributed his abrasive manner to the torment of his game leg. Yet no one questioned the example he set for those under his command. He refused to acknowledge physical infirmity.

O'Hara snapped to attention. "Gen'ral, sir! Permit me to introduce Mr. Brannock. He's just now reported for duty, sir. You'll recall he's our new chief scout."

"Mr. Brannock," Mackenzie said rather formally, "you're a day early."

"Yessir," Clint affirmed. "I made good time."

"Come inside."

There was no offer of a handshake. Mackenzie strode past him and through the door of the inner office. Clint followed along, somewhat amused by the brusque greeting. O'Hara closed the door behind him and he halted before a scarred desk. The office, like the man, was utilitarian. The sole decorations were the national flag and the regimental flag, draped from standards anchored to the floor.

Mackenzie motioned him to a wooden armchair. Clint removed his hat and took a seat. He pulled out the makings and began rolling a smoke. Halting behind the desk, Mackenzie stood with his hands clasped behind his back. His attitude was somehow austere and cool.

"You come highly recommended, Mr. Brannock. General Sheridan gave you his personal stamp of approval."

Clint struck a sulfurhead. As he lit the cigarette, it occurred to him that there was something more behind the lukewarm greeting. He snuffed the match.

"Something bothering you, Colonel?"

"Let's say I have certain reservations about your being posted here."

'Oh? How's that?"

Mackenzie's eyes were marblelike, piercing. "I believe you served with the Confederate army. Is that correct?"

"General Pemberton's command," Clint said without inflection. "I was captured in the Vicksburg campaign."

"Indeed?" Mackenzie arched one eyebrow in question. "How would you feel about serving with coloreds?"

"I thought the Fourth was a white regiment."

"So it is," Mackenzie noted. "I refer to our scouts. For the most part, they're half-breed Seminoles. One half being Negro."

Clint took a deep drag, exhaling little spurts of smoke. "I never owned any slaves, Colonel. Before the war, my family was farmers, not plantation owners."

"You still haven't answered my question."

"I've got nothing against mixed bloods. So long as a man does his job, we'll get along fine."

"Very reasonable, Mr. Brannock. I'll adopt the same attitude toward you."

"Wouldn't expect any less, Colonel."

Mackenzie smiled humorlessly. "One other thing concerns me. You've never campaigned against the Comanche."

"No, sir," Clint said impassively. "Sioux and Cheyenne, and most lately the Kiowa. 'Course, you've read all that in my service record."

"No criticism intended," Mackenzie said crisply. "However, it may hinder you when we take the field."

"Injuns are Injuns, Colonel."

"No, Mr. Brannock," Mackenzie informed him. "The Comanche are something else entirely. General Sheridan has called them the finest light cavalry in the world. I can attest to the truth of the statement."

There was reason for concern. Fort Clark lay astride the Comanche Trace, the ancient war trail from *Comanchería* into Texas and Old Mexico. At the height of the raiding season, bands of horseback warriors were constantly moving through the countryside. Seldom a week passed without a skirmish against Comanche hostiles.

"For the moment," Mackenzie went on, "we have a

more immediate problem. You're familiar with the Kickapoo tribe, Mr. Brannock?"

"Only by reputation," Clint said. "I heard they were run out of Texas some years ago. Way I got it, they took sanctuary below the border."

"An apt term," Mackenzie observed bitterly. "They raid into Texas and then hightail it back to Mexico. A month ago they burned out a ranch west of here." He paused and his eyes went cold. "The family—women and children included—were butchered."

"How about the Mexican army? Won't they lend a hand?"

Mackenzie seemed to look through him. "The Mexican authorities have declined to take action. Despite repeated requests from Washington, they evidence no interest in the death of *gringos*."

"Guess it figures," Clint remarked. "They've got no love for Texicans."

"Well, no matter," Mackenzie said. "It seems you've arrived just in time, Mr. Brannock. I've been ordered to cross the Rio Grande."

Clint stared at him, astonished. "You're taking the regiment into Mexico?"

"Indeed, I am. We march in two days."

"Won't the Mexicans get their bowels in an uproar? Sounds like a violation of the international boundary."

"Perhaps," Mackenzie said indifferently. "The fact remains, I have direct orders from General Sheridan. In his words, we're to wage a 'campaign of annihilation' against the Kickapoos."

Clint's mouth lifted in a tight grin. "The general don't believe in half-measures, does he?"

"Neither do I, Mr. Brannock."

Mackenzie took a riding crop from the desk. He walked to a large map mounted on the wall. Southern Texas and the northern states of Mexico were displayed on the map. With the crop as a pointer, he indicated a spot some thirty miles into Mexico. In bold lettering, it was identified as *Terreno Desconocido*, the unknown land.

"Somewhere in that vicinity," he said, "we will find the Kickapoo village. I have it on good authority that it's located a few miles outside the town of Remolino."

"Any idea the size of the village?"

"Nothing concrete," Mackenzie told him. "I will expect you and your scouts to reconnoiter ahead of the column. We should be in a position to attack at dawn, three days from now."

"Quick work," Clint replied. "You must be planning a forced march."

"All the more reason for you to get to work, Mr. Brannock. I suggest you meet with your scouts without delay."

Mackenzie indicated that he was dismissed. In the orderly room, Clint stopped for a word with O'Hara. The sergeant major informed him that the former chief of scouts, Frank Bullis, had retired due to ill health. The Seminole Negro scouts, who had served under him for three years, were devoted to Bullis. O'Hara was of the opinion that Clint had a rather large pair of boots to fill.

When asked, O'Hara gladly obliged with a brief history of the half-breed scouts. He began more than forty years past, in the tangled swamplands of Florida. There, in 1832, the Seminole war chief Osceola had led his people against American forces. Runaway Negro slaves, who had fled to the mangrove swamps, joined the Seminoles in the fight. Ultimately, an army led by General Zachary Taylor had defeated the coalition of tribesmen and slaves. Yet it had cost the lives of 1500 soldiers to subdue less than 3000 warriors.

By 1842, the Seminoles had been removed over the Trail of Tears to Indian Territory. Through the years, the former slaves had intermarried into the tribe, creating a generation of half-breeds. In 1851, unhappy with their lot, the Seminoles bolted Indian Territory and sought a new life in Mexico. John Horse, their Seminole Negro chief, led them south and negotiated a peace treaty with the Mexican government. For two decades, living free below the Rio Grande, they were a forgotten race.

Early in 1870, the U.S. Army went looking for them again. The military high command was convinced that the best scouts to use against Indians were other Indians, and they remembered the Seminoles. Frank Bullis was dispatched to Mexico and began talks with Chief John Horse. All Seminoles who enlisted as army scouts would receive rations and the pay of a regular soldier. Further, when their enlistment expired, they would be awarded land grants in Texas. The final inducement was a promise of U.S. citizenship.

A treaty was signed and the Seminole Negroes returned to American soil. The tribesmen were assigned, with their families, to a string of military garrisons along the Rio Grande. Twenty scouts, led by a subchief named Elijah Daniel, were posted to Fort Clark. There, under Frank Bullis, they had served for the past three years. They spoke English and Spanish, as well as some Indian dialects. Their endurance and their tracking skills proved to be far superior to that of any white man. As well, they were fierce fighters, easily the equal of the dread Comanche. Their reputation in battle had earned the respect of the entire regiment.

Clint left the orderly room in a thoughtful mood. After listening to O'Hara, he was forced to a grudging conclusion: the Seminole scouts were unlikely to accept him at face value. Like Mackenzie, they would not be overly impressed with his service record. Until he proved himself— earned their respect in the field—there was little reason to expect either loyalty or trust. O'Hara's assessment hit the mark dead center. He had a large pair of boots to fill.

The scouts were quartered along a distant stretch of Las Moras Creek. Their homes were small, built of adobe bricks, and grouped close together. Behind each house was a garden, and the women were busy weeding rows of corn and squash. Children played along the edge of the creekbank and their laughter carried on a warm breeze. The men, who hunted and fished when not on patrol, lazed about under the shade of live oaks. Warriors, even those on the army rolls, were not expected to do menial labor.

From a distance, Clint spotted Elijah Daniel. He was powerfully built, with a pockmarked face and curly black hair. His skin was dusky black mixed with a faint ocher tint. He was easily identified, for he stood like a black-maned lion guarding his pride. If there was any doubt, the other men provided silent affirmation. They watched for Daniel's reaction as Clint approached.

"I'm Brannock," Clint said, halting a pace away. "If I read the sign right, you're Elijah Daniel."

Daniel nodded. "You read it right."

"There's no secrets on an army post, so you know who I am and why I'm here. I've just finished talking with Colonel Mackenzie."

"Ain't that nice? What's the colonel got to say for hisself today?"

Clint's eyes were very pale and direct. "He says I won't get any respect around here till I've whipped your black ass."

Daniel studied him with a steady, uncompromising gaze. There was a long pause while the men around them watched in tense silence. Finally, the Seminole leader let go a low chuff of mirth.

"You're funnin' me, ain't you?"

Clint smiled. "Figured I'd let you call the shot. 'Course, given my choice, I'd sooner talk than fight."

"What'd you like to talk about?"

"The Kickapoos," Clint said. "Mackenzie aims to pay 'em a surprise visit."

Daniel's eyes went round. "No shit!"

"Got it straight from the horse's mouth."

"When we leave?"

8

THREE DAYS AFTER Easter, Virgil stepped off the train in Washington. A porter collected his luggage and led him outside the depot, where a line of horse-drawn cabs waited. He instructed the hackman to take him to Willard's Hotel.

By 1873, the nation's capital was a burgeoning city. Yet, for all its sophisticated pretensions, it retained the look of a country town. For the most part, the streets were still unpaved and there was no municipal water supply or sewage system. A local joke had it that the stench of the city reflected the ethics of the politicians. President Grant's administration, which was riddled with corruption, demonstrated that truth was the wellspring of humor. Not a week passed without some new and titillating scandal.

Lafayette Square, which fronted the White House, was in the center of the city. The main thoroughfare, Pennsylvania Avenue, was paved with cobblestone and constantly in need of repair. On the south side of the street was Center Market, a hodgepodge of vendor's sheds that was backed by a noxious smelling canal. On the north side was the focal point of the capital's social life. There, within a few blocks, were the upper-class shops, hotels, and restaurants. By European standards, they were still considered rather provincial.

As the hack rolled past the White House, Virgil was reminded of Washington's unsavory reputation. The nation's Centennial, celebrating the founding of the republic, was only three years away. Yet in less than a hundred years the Washington bureaucracy had grown at a pace a thousand times greater than the country's population. Congress, as well as several recent presidents, had discovered the benefits of creating empires. These domains vastly increased their political power, not to mention their personal wealth. The bureaucrats, as though stamped from a cookie cutter, never deviated from expanding their own empires. They joined with Congress and the executive branch in fleecing an unwary and politically naïve populace.

The motto around Washington was "quid pro quo." A rough translation was "one hand washes the other." Congress served not its constituency but rather the vested interests, most notably the railroads and the banking industry. The bureaucrats, forever dependent on Congress for funding, obediently followed the dictates of the politicians. It was a smarmy arrangement, breeding graft and bribes and back-room conspiracy. For the common man, the same fraudulent tactics would have resulted in a long prison term. For politicians and bureaucrats, it was simply business as usual.

Virgil thought the Founding Fathers would have suffered mass apoplexy. Still, for all his personal distaste, it was the only game in town. Anyone seeking favors had no choice but to join in the skulduggery and political machinations. As he'd told Palmer, railroads were built by working within the system. Following his own advice, he had traveled eastward with that very purpose in mind. He had an appointment with two of the most influential Western politicians in Washington. Experience had taught him the language they spoke most fluently.

Willard's Hotel resembled a Grecian structure bastardized by the colonials. For all its odd appearance, it was nonetheless the most prestigious address in Washington. All the high muckamucks of business and industry stayed there, not to mention foreign dignitaries and visiting roy-

alty. The rooms were spacious and handsomely appointed,
and an overnight sojourn went for a king's ransom. By
advance telegram, Virgil had reserved an elegant suite
overlooking Pennsylvania Avenue.

Cleve Suggs and Henry Musgrave appeared late that
afternoon. Suggs was the congressional delegate from Colorado Territory and Musgrave was his counterpart from
New Mexico. By law, neither of the men was allowed a
floor vote in Congress. The peculiar nature of their office
stemmed from the stingy and covetous attitude of the
eastern power structure. Older states were reluctant to
share their political clout with western upstarts.

As enacted by Congress, the territorial system authorized the president to appoint a governor and three federal
judges in each western territory. Once the population of a
territory reached five thousand male voters, they were
allowed to elect a territorial legislature. In turn, the legislature elected a nonvoting delegate to represent the territory
in Congress. The territorial delegates, inevitably were long-
standing cronies of the politicos back home.

The ostensible purpose of the system was to transform
the western territories into states. When the population
exceeded sixty thousand, a territory was permitted to apply
for admission to the Union. Yet nothing in Washington
was as it appeared on the surface. Congress retained legislative supremacy unto itself, and no territory easily achieved
statehood. Still, there was ever a quid pro quo among
reasonable men. East and West met on a common ground of
avarice, forever susceptible to temptation. In Washington,
the long green spoke loudest.

Suggs was shrunken and stooped and looked vaguely
like a toad. Musgrave was a heavyset man with an oval
face and small, beady eyes. However dissimilar in appearance, they shared a trait prized along the Potomac: they
were both crooked as snakes.

Virgil welcomed them with warm cordiality. After taking
their hats, he got them seated in the suite's rather ostenta-

tious parlor. He then poured them drinks, stuffed fine
cigars in their mouths, and flattered them on their ascension in the political hierarchy.

When the small talk was exhausted, Virgil went straight
to the point. He sat back, one leg casually draped over the
other, and waved his cigar. "Gentlemen, suppose we get
down to cases. I'm here to discuss the future of the Denver
& Rio Grande."

Suggs and Musgrave nodded in unison. The railroad
lobby was big business in Washington, and they kept
themselves informed on the current state of affairs. For a
week or more, they had known that General William Palmer
had a new partner. They waited to hear more.

"As you're aware," Virgil went on, "construction money
is tight these days. I'm here to enlist your aid in raising
funds."

"When you say funds," Musgrave asked, "what do
you mean, precisely?"

Virgil smiled. "I want a federal guarantee on a new
bond issue. With that in hand, I propose to raise three
million through New York financial institutions."

Suggs gave him a walleyed look. "That's the damnedest
thing I ever heard. Do you realize a federal guarantee
would take an act of Congress?"

"Naturally," Virgil said. "I'm confident you gentlemen
can arrange it for me."

Musgrave shook his head. "You're asking the impossible. We haven't the influence to pull that off."

"Maybe not," Virgil agreed. "But Samuel Gilchrist
does."

"Gilchrist," Suggs said with sudden agitation. "What's
a Texas senator got to do with this?"

"The Denver & Rio Grande will terminate in El Paso."

Suggs looked worried. "You'll have to spell that out."

Virgil's voice was firm. "Quite simply, I want you
gentlemen to intercede with Gilchrist. Bringing another
railroad to Texas would be a feather in his cap."

"Even so," Musgrave said crossly, "why should he listen to us?"

"I happen to know," Virgil said in a flat monotone, "that you've done him favors in the past. Specifically, I'm referring to military supply contracts for beef. Fort Lyon in Colorado and Fort Stanton in New Mexico. I want you to call the debt."

Suggs angled his head critically. "How'd you find out about that?"

"I never reveal a source. The point is, the information's correct."

"Judas Priest," Musgrave said in a reedy voice. "You're asking us to call in a very large marker."

Virgil shrugged. "Sam Gilchrist carries a lot of weight in the Senate. I need his support to put it across."

Musgrave eyed him, considering. "Suppose we agreed to talk with him on your behalf. What's in it for us?"

"Two things," Virgil said pointedly. "First, a railroad line extending through southern Colorado and into New Mexico. That should be worth a lot of votes with the folks back home."

Suggs raised an eyebrow. "I believe Henry was thinking of something a bit more practical. What's the second reason?"

"A finder's fee," Virgil said dryly. "I'll arrange to have five hundred shares of Denver & Rio Grande stock transferred to each of your wives. No one will be the wiser."

Musgrave fixed him with a reproachful look. "We'd have to wait till doomsday before that stock paid off. We know it and you know it."

"Quite the contrary," Virgil said. "The minute we lay track into New Mexico the price will double. You'll make a fortune."

"I don't know," Suggs said skeptically. "You want a favor now for a payoff down the line. Sounds like a pretty poor swap to me."

Virgil smiled without warmth. "How would it sound if word got out you'd refused to help? No railroad for southern Colorado and the same for New Mexico." He paused, spread his hands. "Politically, I suspect your names would be mud."

A thick silence settled over the room. Suggs eyed him with a baleful stare and Musgrave let out his breath with a deep sigh. At last, they exchanged a look and once again nodded in unison.

"Thank you, gentlemen," Virgil said, rising from his chair. "Tell Senator Gilchrist I'll look forward to seeing him tomorrow afternoon."

When they were gone, Virgil lit a fresh cigar. He poured a drink and toasted himself with considerable relish. It was, in the back rooms of Washington, the best of all deals.

A favor bought with no money down.

The message arrived late the next morning. Signed by Henry Musgrave, it confirmed a one-o'clock appointment with Senator Gilchrist. Short and discreet, the note made no reference to the Denver & Rio Grande. Still, it seemed apparent that Suggs and Musgrave had done their job.

At noontime, Virgil dined alone in the hotel restaurant. The tables were crowded with fashionably dressed men who conversed in low tones. As he ate, Virgil speculated on what manner of business was being conducted. Government contractors and lobbyists often preferred to make their pitch in an informal atmosphere. Good food and a bottle of wine usually put the listener in a receptive frame of mind. Politicians, as well as bureaucrats, responded favorably to cordial treatment.

Watching them, Virgil was struck by a curious thought. Yesterday's meeting, and today's appointment with Gilchrist, represented a milestone of sorts. Previously, his shady dealings had been limited to legislators at the state level. Now, he was hobnobbing with national figures, men who had access to the White House itself. Their discussion entailed an act of Congress and federal guarantees on corporate bonds. None of which served the public interest quite so much as his own. He wondered if he'd joined the ranks of the Robber Barons.

One thought triggered another. He was reminded of a swindle that had assumed the aura of legend. Orchestrated by James J. Hill, it involved the St. Paul & Pacific, which had fallen into bankruptcy. The bondholders were Dutch financiers, who had limited knowledge of the railroad's long-range potential. Hill, who was an aspiring Robber Baron, determined that the road's land grants alone were worth $18 million dollars. Whoever gained control of the line stood to reap a bonanza.

With the deft touch of a bunco artist, Hill convinced the Dutch investors that the defunct railroad was worthless. Several million dollars, he assured them, would be required to resurrect the line and return it to profitable operation. Hesitant to throw good money after bad, the Dutch financiers accepted from Hill a promissory note for a million dollars against a total purchase price of five million. Without spending a nickel, Hill acquired control of a railroad with 565 miles of track and almost four million acres in land grants.

To pay off the $5 million, Hill unloaded $8 million in new bonds on an unwary public. He then worked a fast deal with land speculators and sold off the road's land grant for $13 million. At that point, Hill and his associates split $15 million in company stock among themselves. Shortly the railroad was back in operation and dividends on the stock were $140 a share. In the end, having executed an extraordinary flimflam, Hill realized profits of $5 million. Among railroad men, the story was told with almost reverent gusto. It was considered a classic, and Hill was forthwith inducted into the fraternity of Robber Barons.

Over coffee and dessert, Virgil pondered where today would lead. Whether or not he would become another

James J. Hill seemed a reasonable question. Outright fraud was not all that far removed from shady politics and under-the-table bribes. A thin line separated a clever entrepreneur from an underhanded swindler.

He warned himself to bear the distinction in mind.

On the stroke of the clock, Virgil walked through the door. A man named Joe Urschel, who introduced himself as the senator's aide, was waiting in the anteroom. He took Virgil's hat and escorted him into the inner sanctum.

Senator Gilchrist's private office was paneled in dark wood, with ornately carved furniture and a Persian carpet covering the floor. The senator himself was an imposing man, with a leonine head and a shock of snow-white hair. He was impeccably dressed in a tweed suit, and his muttonchop whiskers were trimmed to perfection. As his aide closed the door, he rose from behind his desk and beckoned Virgil forward. His features were wreathed in good humor.

"So nice to see you, Mr. Brannock."

"The pleasure's all mine, Senator."

After a warm handshake, they seated themselves. Gilchrist leaned back in his judge's chair, nodding affably. "Henry Musgrave and Cleve Suggs called on me yesterday. I must say, they're great admirers of yours, Mr. Brannock."

"It's mutual," Virgil said with a straight face. "They're a credit to westerners everywhere."

"Just so," Gilchrist said with cheery vigor. "And we westerners have to stick together in the wilds of Washington. Too often, we're given short shrift by our eastern brethren."

"Senator, that's exactly why I'm here. The Denver & Rio Grande needs someone of your prominence to act as its sponsor."

"The boys explained your predicament. I have to tell you, it's a tall order, Mr. Brannock. Legislation of that sort requires a lot of horse-trading."

Virgil appeared properly impressed. "All the more reason to have your support, Senator. I've been told you're a man who gets things done."

"Well, now," Gilchrist replied loftily, "I suppose I do have a certain influence. Of course, you realize the bill would have to originate in the House?"

"I think we can depend on Suggs and Musgrave to arrange that. What I'm concerned about is approval by the Senate."

"A shrewd assessment, Mr. Brannock. The Senate represents your major hurdle."

Virgil looked at him with utter directness. "Can I rely on you to push it through?"

"Hmmm." Gilchrist considered a moment. "Where will you be later tonight?"

"I'm staying at the Willard's."

"Fine. I'll send someone around with my answer."

For an instant, Virgil thought he'd lost the game. Then, abruptly, he realized there was a final hand yet to be dealt. Gilchrist showed him to the door, scrupulously polite, and sent him off with a hearty slap on the back. Their discussion had lasted less than five minutes.

Virgil got his answer shortly after ten that evening. There was a knock on the door of his hotel room. When he opened it, Joe Urschel was standing in the hallway. He motioned the aide inside and closed the door.

Urschel was a frail man, with a pursed smile and round moist eyes. He nodded agreeably. "The senator asked me to have a talk with you. He believes he might be able to help you."

"Might?" Virgil repeated. "That sounds a little indefinite."

"These things require a certain finesse, Mr. Brannock. Some members of the Senate aren't persuaded by words alone."

A slight, ironic smile touched Virgil's mouth. "I get the feeling your boss heads the list."

"Well . . ." Urschel lifted his hands, shrugged. "I'm only the messenger, Mr. Brannock."

"Messenger or bagman?"

"Your choice of words, not mine."

"How much persuasion is required?"

Urschel instinctively lowered his voice. "Ten thousand dollars."

"All right," Virgil said. "I'll wire Colorado and have the funds transferred."

"No bank drafts," Urschel said quickly. "It has to be cash."

"Your boss is a careful man."

"Discretion works to everyone's benefit, Mr. Brannock."

"Tell the senator I'll expect fast action. No delays and no excuses. Understood?"

"You needn't worry about Senator Gilchrist. His word is his bond."

"Good night, Mr. Urschel. I'll let you know when I have the money."

When he was alone, Virgil reflected on it with sardonic amusement. He had every confidence that the senator's word was his bond. He thought it an offshoot of an older and even more revealing axiom, one that was part and parcel of Washington politics.

Honor among thieves.

9

THE STAGECOACH pulled into Santa Fe shortly before the noon hour. The driver brought his six-horse team to a halt before the express office and kicked the brake lever. A band of street urchins gathered around as the station agent hurried outside, cursing them in broken Spanish. The young-sters scattered with hoots of laughter.

Earl was the first passenger to step down from the coach. Dusting himself off, he moved into the shade of the office portico. There he waited while the other passengers climbed out and began stretching their legs. When the luggage was unloaded from the boot, he gave one of the Mexican *golfillos* a dollar to run his bag over to the hotel. Lighting a cheroot, he stood for a moment and surveyed the town.

Santa Fe was located on the banks of a stream that flowed southwesterly from the snowcapped Sangre de Cristos. Surrounded by mountain ranges, the town itself was at an altitude above seven thousand feet. A broad plaza, dominated by a cathedral and the old governor's palace, was the center of activity. The place was crowded with shops and businesses and several open-air markets. The architecture was adobe, and the scene had a quaint atmosphere. For all its growth, Santa Fe still retained much of its native charm.

The town looked to be everything Earl had heard. Built

on enterprise and politics, the territorial capital was the major trade center between Mexico and the United States. As the terminus for the Santa Fe Trail, trade goods were off-loaded there for transshipment to all points of the compass. South of the town, the Chihuahua Trail joined with the old Camino Real and served as an artery of trade into Mexico. By any standard, Santa Fe was the focal point of southwestern commerce.

All the way from Colorado Earl had examined various possibilities for the future. He was a gambler by trade, and that seemed the logical place to start. Yet he was now determined to make something more of himself. One way or another, he intended to follow Virgil's example and explore the world of business. Santa Fe would experience boom times when the railroad arrived, perhaps within the next two or three years. Overnight fortunes would be made by those with the foresight to plan ahead. He intended to keep his eye open for a promising business venture, or some sort of real-estate investment. For once, he meant to stake his claim before the boom got under way.

The change in attitude had little to do with his own welfare. He was thinking instead of the boy he'd left behind. Upon reflection, he had decided that the sporting life was not what he wanted for his son. Lon deserved something better, something stable and more dependable. A gambler was forever on the move, always looking toward the next El Dorado. Worse, a gambler's existence was one of feast or famine, flush one day and broke the next. It was the life Earl had chosen for himself and it suited him. But it was no life for a father to impose on his son. He believed Santa Fe was the place to wipe the slate clean and start fresh. For Lon's sake, he was determined to make it work.

The plaza was bustling with activity. At the northwest corner of the square, under a stand of cottonwood trees, peddlers hawked their wares. All manner of fruit and vegetables were for sale, and freshly butchered mutton hung from the tree limbs. Carts pulled by oxen were laden with sacks of grain, and a string of burros, packing piñon firewood, was being led into town. Stores and shops were busy, and crowds of New Mexicans moved in a steady stream around the square. In the exact center of the plaza stood a tall, monolithic sundial. Chiseled on its stone face was the inscription "Life fleeth as a shadow."

Crossing the plaza, Earl walked toward the hotel. He was reminded that the first of the Missouri traders would not arrive until early summer. The arduous journey across the plains began in late spring, after the mud season had passed. Only then was the fabled road westward a passable route for the freight wagons hauled by yoked oxen. With summer, however, the plaza would become a vast market-place, often jammed with a hundred or more wagons. Their arrival was signaled by tolling of the bells in the cathedral tower.

The trade route to Santa Fe had been blazed some fifty years past. The jump-off point, where traders were outfit-ted for the trek westward, was Independence, Missouri. The initial leg of the journey led across boundless prairies to where the trail forded the Arkansas River. From there, it meandered on to Bent's Fort and then dropped into New Mexico through Raton Pass. By 1824 caravans of freight wagons were crossing the plains. Fully half the goods hauled overland were funneled through Santa Fe and on into Old Mexico.

In 1846, with the advent of the Mexican War, Santa Fe became a frontier outpost of the United States. The volume of business along the trail increased enormously as freight-ers rushed to supply the military with contract goods. After the war, there was an upsurge in private trading companies as new markets were opened throughout territories under the American flag. The huge Conestoga wagons carried upward of five thousand pounds of merchandise. Cargoes included cotton and yard goods, hardware and cutlery, and a wide assortment of glassware. On the return journey, the traders hauled back hides and pelts, gold and silver bullion, and blankets woven of native wool. The trade was immensely profitable, both outwardbound and on the return trek eastward. Santa Fe, as the hub of the activity, prospered the year round.

Approaching the Capitol Hotel, Earl felt a kindling of optimism. He had a sense of being in the right place at the right time, as though great things were somehow destined. Unlike Frisco and the mining camps he'd worked in the past, gambling would be nothing more than a means to an end. He envisioned a time when he would own some legitimate enterprise and become a respected member of the community. A time when he provided a home for Lon and the chance for a decent education. All the things a man owed his son.

The thought of it put a spring in Earl's step. He entered the hotel whistling a cheery tune under his breath. He figured he couldn't be beat.

An overhead lamp cast a fuzzy glow across the poker table. Apart from Earl there were three players seated in the game. One was a nattily attired fat man who owned a local mercantile. Beside him was a drummer who sold ladies' notions and patent medicines. The last man was a teamster who smelled strongly of mules.

A large share of the money on the table was heaped in front of Earl. Since the game began he'd enjoyed an unchecked winning streak. In some measure, it was attributable to good cards and a run of luck. But the greater reason was his uncanny skill at reading the other players. An hour into the game, he had catalogued all their quirks and mannerisms. After that, he knew when to hold and when to fold. He pretended amazement at his phenomenal good fortune.

The saloon was located several doors from the hotel. After supper he'd toured the plaza, inspecting various establishments with gaming facilities. When he found a poker game already in progress, he had taken a seat. The limit was ten dollars and most of the players favored five-card stud. They were also partial to cutthroat poker, which made it legal to check and raise. It was a rough game, but one that Earl played with seasoned skill. Three hours after taking a chair he was ahead by nearly four hundred dollars.

Shortly before ten o'clock his attention was drawn to the door. While there were other Mexicans in the saloon, the two who entered now were an oddly matched pair. The man in the lead was lithe and muscular, with high cheekbones and hawklike features. He was dressed in a short *charro* jacket, boots with roweled spurs, and a wide-brimmed hat. A nickel-plated pistol was holstered at his side.

The other man was a vast-shouldered hunchback. He was a full head shorter than his companion and walked with a peculiar shuffling gait. His massive head and abnormally long arms gave him the appearance of a gorilla. The impression was enhanced by his bark-dark skin and his misshapen features. A jagged scar twisted his mouth in a gargoyle grimace.

When they entered, Earl's attention had strayed from the game. He had just folded a bad hand and was in the process of lighting a fresh cheroot. He watched as the two men halted at the end of the bar and ordered drinks. Then, for no apparent reason, his gaze was drawn to three men farther down the bar. They too were Mexican and they seemed to stiffen, their drinks abruptly forgotten. The one in the middle pushed away from the counter, staring toward the front of the room. His companions moved to flank him on either side.

"Guerra!"

The leader of the threesome spat the name in a whip-crack voice. At the end of the bar, the man in *charro* clothes looked up without expression. Beside him, the hunchback went immobile, glowering at the three Mexicans. All along the bar men quickly vacated their spots, moving to a safer distance. Conversation ceased and an electric tension fell over the saloon.

"*¡Hijo de puta!*"

The insult crackled with rage. Even as he spoke, the leader of the three men pulled a gun. The other two were only a beat behind as they clawed at holstered revolvers. The hawk-faced man and the hunchback reacted in the same instant. A staccato roar hammered the saloon as four shots blended into one.

As though chopped down, the Mexican leader and one of his men were knocked off their feet by the impact of heavy slugs. The third man, his gun extended at arm's length, drew a bead on the lean figure in *charro* clothes. Earl had no recollection of drawing his pistol. His hand dipped inside his coat and reappeared with a cocked bellygun. He fired as the barrel cleared the table.

The Mexican jerked upright as a bloodburst splattered his shirtfront. A surprised look came over his face and the gun dropped from his hand. His mouth worked but no sound came out and he slowly corkscrewed to his knees. He slumped dead on the floor.

There was a moment of stark silence. Gunsmoke hung in the air and everyone in the saloon stared at the bodies. Finally, the hawk-faced man turned and looked at Earl. His expression was one of blank astonishment, somehow questioning. He crossed the room, followed by the hunchback. Halting at the poker table, he nodded.

"*Gracias, señor*," he said with grave courtesy. "I am in your debt."

Earl kept his tone light. "Think nothing of it, *señor*. I just didn't care for the odds."

"I am Ramón Guerra." He held out his hand and smiled with considerable charm. "I would be honored if you joined me in a drink."

Earl saw no way to decline the offer. He pocketed his winnings, nodding to the other players. Guerra led the way to an empty table and they sat down. The hunchback took a seat facing the door.

"Allow me," Guerra said, indicating the other man. "This is my *compañero*, Ignacio Zarate. And you are . . . ?"

"Brannock," Earl said. "Earl Brannock."

Zarate gave him a strange crooked smile. One side of the hunchback's mouth curled upward while the other remained frozen by the deep scar. Earl had the eerie sensation that behind the man's eyes there was nothing but an elemental cruelty. Zarate made no offer of a handshake.

A waiter materialized with a bottle of tequila and three glasses. Without being told, Zarate poured the glasses brimful. Guerra lifted his glass in toast to Earl.

"*Salud*, Mr. Brannock."

"Your health, Señor Guerra."

Guerra laughed out loud. "I owe my health to you. Had you not acted, I would surely be a dead man."

"Who knows?" Earl ventured a smile. "Perhaps you would have done the same for me."

Guerra looked faintly amused. "You are new to Santa Fe, *señor*?"

"Just arrived this morning."

"*Madre mía!*" Guerra uttered a low chuckle. "Your first day here and already you've killed a man. God is truly a jester."

Earl wondered at Guerra's precise command of English. Over the rim of his glass he studied the man closer. Guerra was handsome in a rough sort of way, with hooded eyes and a vaguely sinister look. There was an air of magnetism about him, some sense of restless vitality and understated confidence. Earl was reminded of a Spanish term he'd once heard. He thought the man was the perfect image of a *pistolero*.

Zarate tensed as the front door swung open. Guerra glanced around as a large, thickset man with a badge on his chest entered the saloon. His gaze shifted to the hunchback and an undercurrent of something unspoken passed between them. Zarate grunted coarsely and rose from his chair. He lumbered across the room.

"Our town marshal," Guerra said casually. "Ignacio will advise him of what occurred. You have no reason for concern."

When Earl remained silent, Guerra went on. "What happened here tonight was a private matter. Those *cabrones* took exception to my conduct of certain business affairs. The law takes little interest in such disputes."

"I understand," Earl said with an aimless shrug. "A man's business is a man's business."

Guerra nodded sagely. "Would it offend if I asked your line of business?"

"Not at all," Earl said. "I'm a gambler."

"So?" Guerra said with an evaluating glance. "You hope to make your fortune in Santa Fe. ¿*Verdad*?"

"Not at gambling," Earl replied. "I'm looking for an investment of some sort. Anything that'll turn a steady profit."

"Have you something particular in mind?"

"No, not really. I'm just on the lookout."

Guerra took a sip of tequila. His eyes narrowed in thought and he smiled a lazy catlike smile. He looked across the table. "May I call you Earl?"

"Of course."

"Excellent," Guerra said amiably. "And you must call me Ramón. I insist."

"I'm not much on formality myself."

"Good." Guerra lit a cigarillo, exhaled smoke. "You have done me a great service tonight, Earl. In fact, you quite probably saved my life."

"Forget it," Earl said with a wave of his hand. "You don't owe me anything."

"Please, *compadre*! I consider it a debt of honor. I would like to assist in your search of a fortune."

Earl looked faintly surprised. "I don't understand."

Guerra leaned closer, his voice low and confidential. "I

have a way for you to double your money and double it again. Would you be interested?"

"Maybe," Earl said slowly. "Depends on what it involves."

"A moment ago," Guerra said with a half-smile, "you mentioned profits. Those who know me well know that I am in the most profitable business of all. I'm an Indian trader."

Earl swirled the opaque liquid in his glass. "I've heard that's not altogether legitimate."

Guerra's smile was cryptic. "I have a certain influence with the authorities. No one observes my activities too closely."

Earl detected no braggadocio in the statement. He thought it unlikely that anyone would meddle in Ramón Guerra's affairs. A moment passed, then he nodded. "What is it you're suggesting?"

"What else?" Guerra spread his hands in a bland gesture. "I'm offering you a share in my venture. It's the least I can do."

Earl sounded uncertain. "All because I took a hand in the fight?"

Guerra grinned, as if sharing a private joke with himself. "We Mexicans make a great thing of honor. A debt unpaid soon becomes a moral burden." He paused, staring at Earl. "I make the offer in earnest."

Earl examined the notion. A complex of gut instinct and gambler's hunch told him the man could be trusted. On sudden impulse, he decided to accept. "How do we go about it?"

Zarate approached the table. He rattled something in Spanish, motioning to the town marshal. Guerra frowned and slowly got to his feet. He looked down at Earl.

"Excuse me, *compadre*. The marshal requires a written statement. We will talk more another time. *Hasta luego*."

Guerra turned away, followed by the hunchback. At the door, they joined the lawman and walked from the saloon.

A bartender, assisted by several customers, dragged the bodies out onto the street. Within moments, the atmosphere in the room had returned to normal.

A girl appeared at Earl's elbow. Earlier he'd noticed her at the bar, laughing and talking with customers. She was smallish and compact, with an olive complexion and hair dark as obsidian. Her waist was tiny and her breasts spilled over the top of her low-cut blouse. He thought she had the most provocative eyes he'd ever seen on a woman.

"*Buenas tardes*," she said in a sultry voice. "I am Guadalupe Ríos. May I join you?"

"Good idea," Earl said, offering her a chair. "You can help me with this bottle of tequila."

"But of course," she said, a devilish glint in her eye. "That is my job, entertaining men."

"Worked here long?"

She laughed a deep, throaty laugh. "All my life."

"Then you must know Ramón Guerra?"

"*Sí, señor*. Everyone knows El Alacrán."

"Sorry, I don't speak Spanish."

She smiled. "He is called the Scorpion. You saw why tonight" Her voice suddenly turned light and mocking. "I think you too have a sting, *señor*."

Earl chuckled. "Anybody that takes me for a gunfighter would miss the mark. I'm a gambler by trade."

"We have many of those in Santa Fe."

"Well . . ." Earl hesitated, watching her closely. "You might say it's only temporary. I'm going into business with Señor Guerra."

"No!" she breathed. "Truly?"

Earl paused, alert to her reaction. "Says he's gonna make an Indian trader of me."

"I think it is something more than that, *señor*. A great deal more."

"How so?"

A vixen look touched her eyes. "Have you not heard of the *Comancheros*?"

"Not that I recall. Who are they?"

She laughed and tossed her head. "I sometimes talk too much, *señor*. Perhaps you should ask El Alacrán that question."

Earl let it drop. He called for a fresh glass and poured her a drink. She flirted openly with him and their talk turned to more personal matters. He was reminded that a long while had passed since he'd been with a woman. The prospect of spending the night with Guadalupe Ríos seemed to him an idea worth exploring.

Yet, even as they talked, a corner of his mind was still on Guerra. It occurred to him that a man was not called the Scorpion without good reason. Several questions needed asking, and he decided to ask them soon. The one that intrigued him most was the one that left him vaguely uneasy. He silently repeated it to himself.

The *Comancheros*.

10

THE INDIGO of dusk settled over the land. Beyond the mountains, the purple blemish of last light faded into darkness. A dog yipped mournfully in the valley below.

Clint and Elijah Daniel were shadowed apparitions in the quickening gloom. Flat on their bellies, they peered over a rocky outcropping. Below, not a half-mile away, were the lodges of the Kickapoo village. A faint scent of wood smoke carried on the evening breeze.

Early that afternoon, they had crossed the Rio Grande. Mackenzie had elected to hold the column on the north bank while Clint and the Seminole Negro scouts reconnoitered ahead. With Daniel and two more scouts, Clint had set a course through the foothills of the Santa Rosa Mountains. By midafternoon they were deep in the heart of *Terreno Desconocido*, the unknown land.

An hour before sunset they had skirted the Mexican village of Remolino. Then, not twenty minutes later, they topped a rise and spotted the Indian encampment. Clint and Daniel went forward while the other scouts remained behind with the horses. For the past quarter-hour, the two men had scanned the village below. Not a word was spoken and yet they read one another's thoughts perfectly.

Clint tapped the scout's arm. Daniel nodded and eased back off the outcropping. With a last look at the village, Clint wormed around and rose to a half-crouch. Turning downslope, they made their way to a darkened arroyo. There, all but invisible in the deepening night, the other scouts stood beside the horses. They waited silently as the two men approached.

When Clint halted, Daniel and the scouts crowded around him. His voice was barely audible, little more than a whisper. He looked at the Seminole leader.

"I make it about seventy lodges, Elijah. What was your count?"

"Closer to eighty," Daniel said. "Some of 'em was blocked by a patch of mesquite."

"How many warriors you reckon they've got?"

"I always figgers a couple to a lodge."

"So by rough count we're talking at least a hundred and fifty. Would you say that's a fair estimate?"

"Well, that's just the men. Some of their women will fight, too. Squaws ain't bashful when it comes to killin'."

"All right," Clint allowed. "We'll round it off at two hundred. Where the colonel's concerned, the more the merrier."

Daniel grunted sharply. "You right there. That man got a powerful hate for Injuns."

"No," Clint said softly. "I doubt that he hates them. He just figures they're less trouble dead than alive."

Daniel grinned ferociously. "Then I 'spect we're gonna make him happy tonight."

"I'd make bank on it, Elijah."

Clint took the gelding's reins from one of the scouts. Grasping the pommel, he swung aboard and settled himself in the saddle. With a nod to the other men, he pulled the gelding around and took a sighting on the North Star. They rode toward the Rio Grande.

The regiment was encamped a mile north of the river. No fires were permitted, and a mealy, weblike darkness screened the position. Every precaution had been taken to avoid detection by the Mexican authorities.

Earlier that day the regiment had ridden out of Fort Clark. Four troops of cavalry, totaling four hundred men, comprised the force. A supply train of twenty pack mules carried rations for three days, including sufficient grain for the horses. The march to the Rio Grande, some fifty miles, had been timed almost to the minute. Between dusk and dark the regiment had ridden into the holding area.

Supper was hardtack washed down with water. The horses were grained and picketed, forced to await the river crossing before being watered. After supper, the men were ordered to clean weapons and look to their gear. Their carbines were single-shot breechloaders, the 1866 Springfield .50-70 government issue. Their sidearms were Colt .44 revolvers converted from cap-and-ball to cartridge. The saber, made obsolete by the saddle carbine, was no longer carried in the field. Swords were now relegated to ceremonial functions.

The encampment was spread over a large area dotted with mesquite and chaparral. The companies formed a boxlike square, essentially a defensive position. Regimental headquarters, located in the center of the square, was staffed by one officer and several runners. Along the outer perimeter, pickets were posted to provide security and act as listening posts. The balance of the Seminole Negro scouts were positioned near regimental headquarters.

A short while before midnight one of the southernmost pickets challenged Clint and his three scouts. After identifying themselves, they were passed through the company lines. Elijah Daniel and the other two men rejoined the scouts, who were sprawled on the ground near their horses. Clint dismounted in the headquarters area, handing the reins to a runner who stepped forward. He found Mackenzie seated on a folding campstool, waiting with considerable impatience. The colonel's voice was abrupt.

"You're overdue, Mr. Brannock."

"Figured our horses deserved a breather, Colonel. We've still got a far piece to go tonight."

Mackenzie looked at him. "I assume you found the Kickapoo village?"

"Yessir," Clint acknowledged. "Near about a mile outside Remolino."

"So the information I had was correct, after all."

"I'd say you got the straight goods."

"Did you encounter any trouble?"

"Went smooth as silk. We got in and out with nobody the wiser."

Mackenzie nodded. "How close were you to their camp?"

"A half-mile or so."

"Describe the terrain."

Clint briefed him on the layout of the land. Mackenzie asked several questions about location of the village in relation to prominent terrain features. They then discussed what Clint thought to be the best approach for mounted troops.

Mackenzie pondered it a moment. At length, as though thinking out loud, he went on. "What is your estimate of their strength, Mr. Brannock?"

"Give or take a few, I'd judge it to be about a hundred and seventy."

"Your judgment alone"—Mackenzie hesitated, staring at him—"or does Daniel agree?"

Clint's expression was wooden. "Elijah figured some of the women will fight, too. He put it at closer to two hundred."

"What's your opinion?"

"Well, sir, I don't think it matters a whole helluva lot. I've never yet seen squaws turn the tide against cavalry."

Mackenzie grunted. "So you wouldn't recommend attacking on foot?"

"No, sir, I wouldn't. I'd sweep through there and make them fight on foot. Take an Injun off his horse and he's already half-whipped."

Mackenzie was silent, considering. "Where is their horse herd located?"

"Off on the south edge of the village."

"How many head?"

"Four hundred or thereabouts."

Mackenzie gazed off into the darkness. He looked like a grizzled philosopher contemplating some profound abstraction. He finally glanced around. "How far to the encampment?"

"Give or take a mile," Clint said deliberately, "I'd call it thirty miles."

"Thank you, Mr. Brannock. I suggest you and your men see to your horses. We'll depart within the hour."

As Clint walked away, runners were dispatched to the company areas. A few minutes later the four captains commanding the cavalry troops appeared out of the darkness. They gathered silently before Mackenzie, who was still seated on the campstool. He got to his feet, looking from one to the other. His tone was quite military.

"Gentlemen, I want to be across the Rio Grande by oh-one-hundred. Order of march will remain the same as followed earlier."

Mackenzie paused, staring at them. When he spoke again, the timbre of his voice was charged with vigor. "I expect stiff resistance. Mr. Brannock informs me that we will be met by a force of almost two hundred braves. You needn't be told that they will fight well."

The four captains returned his stare, quietly attentive. Mackenzie seemed to stand taller and his eyes burned with sudden intensity. "I am not interested in killing women and children. Instruct your men to concentrate on the warriors. As usual, no quarter will be given."

Captain Amon Carter cleared his throat. "What about prisoners, Colonel? Are we to take them or not?"

Mackenzie's hand balled into a raised fist. "Strike them down, Captain. Our business is to punish, not reform. Do I make myself clear?"

"Yes, sir."

"Good," Mackenzie said, steel underlying his voice.

"Order of battle will be the same as order of march. B Troop will go in first. Any questions?"

No one spoke. Mackenzie searched their faces a moment, then nodded. "Be prepared to mount in ten minutes."

The officers saluted, then turned away into the darkness.

Mackenzie sat down on the campstool with a heavy sigh. He stretched out his left leg and began rubbing it with both hands. His features were stoic, registering nothing.

A faint blush of dawn lighted the sky. Clint and Elijah Daniel once again stared down into the valley. Their features were cold and hard in the sallow overcast.

The Seminole Negro scouts were ranged behind them, mounted and waiting. To their immediate right, on the reverse slope of the hill, was B Troop. Farther away, stretched out on line, the other three troops were visible through the haze of first light. Horses and men appeared frozen in a stilled tableau.

To the west, at the bottom of the hill, was a narrow stream. On the far bank were clustered the lodges of the Kickapoo village. There was no one about and no sign of morning cook fires. The only movement was from the horse herd, perhaps a hundred yards south of the encampment. The ponies grazed on sparse grasses bordered by chaparral.

The scouts were somewhat disgruntled with their orders. They were assigned the task of stampeding the horse herd and driving it off from the village. By doing so, they would separate the Indians from their ponies and eliminate any chance of swift flight. For all its importance, the assignment nonetheless left the scouts in a sullen mood. There was little glory to be gained in chasing horses.

Mackenzie rode to the crest of the hill. He sat for a long moment, gazing down at the village without expression. No bugle calls would sound the attack, for he was intent on retaining the element of surprise. Instead, he raised his arm overhead, looking first at the scouts and then toward the commander of B Troop. He dropped his arm like a falling lance.

Clint booted the gelding. With the scouts swarming behind him, he cleared the top of the hill and went barreling down the forward slope. On his right flank, B Troop drove straight toward the center of the village. The second company on line swung at an oblique angle behind B Troop and rode toward the southern edge of the encampment. The last two companies fanned out to the north in an encircling movement. Mackenzie and his headquarters staff galloped in the immediate wake of B Troop.

Crossing the stream, the scouts suddenly shattered the morning stillness. Their voices rose in a howling screech of war whoops and yipping shouts. Thundering forward in a wedge, they skirted the village and rode headlong toward the horse herd. Their ululating cries stampeded the skittish ponies and sent them hurtling southward. The ground rumbled under the drumbeat of hooves, and a dense swirl of dust erupted behind the herd. Terrified, the ponies fled before the pack of whooping centaurs.

To the immediate front, Clint caught sight of two Indians as they stepped from a patch of mesquite. They were young, apparently posted as night guards, but determined to protect the herd. One shouldered an ancient muzzleloader and the other raised a drawn bow. The rifle belched smoke and a lead ball whistled past Clint's head. He extended the Colt .44 and fired even as the second Indian loosed a feathered shaft. The scouts opened fire with their carbines, and bullets snicked past him like furious bees. As though winnowed down, the young night guards were blown off their feet.

A mile from the village the scouts brought the herd to a halt. Once turned, the ponies milled in wild-eyed confusion, encircled by the men. In the distance, there was a rattle of gunfire from the village, interspersed with shouts and the steady pounding of hoofbeats. Turning in his saddle, Clint saw women and children fleeing toward the western foothills. Fighting a rear-guard action, what appeared to be a hundred or more warriors covered their retreat. The encampment was already overrun and cavalry troops converged on the line of braves. The gunfire abruptly swelled in intensity.

Clint's attention was diverted by a hoarse shout. He turned and saw two scouts assisting Elijah Daniel down from his horse. An arrow protruded from his shoulder, and his teeth were gritted against the pain. Clint recalled the night guard with the bow, aware now that the shaft had found its mark. He swung down from the saddle and hurried toward the dismounted scouts. Halting, he dropped to one knee beside the Seminole leader. A quick examination revealed the worst.

The shaft had not gone all the way through. Below the collarbone, the arrowhead was buried in a mass of muscle and flesh. Clint exchanged a look with Daniel, whose face was ashen. Before either of them could speak, a regimental messenger galloped in from the direction of the village. The trooper slid his horse to a halt in a swirl of dust, sawing at the reins. His eyes were wild with excitement.

"We licked 'em!" he shouted. "Killed a whole slew of the bastards and drove the rest into the hills."

"Glad to hear it," Clint said, rising to his feet. "The colonel send you down here to tell me that?"

"Naw," the trooper said, laughing. "He's ordered the village burned to the ground. Says to tell you we're pulling out in fifteen minutes."

"What the hell's the rush?"

"Colonel wants to get back across the Rio Grande. He's almighty skittish about tangling with the Mex army."

"Goddammit," Clint cursed, "we've got a wounded man here. He needs medical attention."

"We got some wounded, too. The colonel ordered them to be transported the best way possible."

"Jesus Christ," Clint said hotly.

"Almost forgot," the trooper told him. "The colonel

wants them Injun ponies shot. Says to get it done
lickety-split."

"Shot?" Clint repeated. "All of them?"

"Ever' last one. He ain't leavin' the redsticks nothin'
that walks on four legs."

The trooper reined his horse about and rode off. Clint
stood their a moment, his mouth set in a grim line. Finally, he looked down at Daniel.

"How about it, Elijah?" he asked. "Think you can
ride?"

"Got no choice," Daniel muttered. "Orders is orders."

"Looks that way, don't it?" Clint pulled his bowie
knife and knelt down. Gingerly, working slowly, he notched
a ring around the arrow shaft. When he finished, he gave
Daniel an apologetic look and snapped the shaft off three
inches above the shoulder.

Daniel grunted sharply, beads of sweat dotting his forehead. He slumped back on the ground.

Standing, Clint sheathed the bowie knife. He nodded to
the two scouts. "Spread the word to the others. Let's get
to killing horses."

Within minutes, the scouts began firing. They formed a
ring around the herd, their carbines barking as fast as they
could eject and load. The earth turned red with the blood
of thrashing horses. A sweet stench of death settled over
the land.

Unwilling to watch, Clint turned and looked north. The
village was ablaze with fiery lodges.

A searing noonday sun stood fixed in the sky. The 4th
Cavalry forded the Rio Grande shortly before one o'clock.
Their pace had been slowed by concern for the wounded.

The mood of the column was buoyant. The raid had
been conducted with tactical precision and absolute secrecy. Apart from the slaughtered ponies, they had destroyed an entire village and killed thirty-one hostile warriors.
Somewhat miraculously, they had suffered only four

wounded and none killed. Nor had they encountered the Mexican army below the border. Of such campaigns were legends built.

The regiment had been in the field slightly more than thirty hours. In that time, the men had not slept and they had been in the saddle almost twenty-four hours total. They were haggard with fatigue and their horses were spent. The column was halted where they had bivouacked the night before. After the horses were cooled down and grained, the men were allowed to kindle fires. They had their first hot meal since departing Fort Clark.

A field hospital was set up near regimental headquarters. Major Albert Mizner, the surgeon, was a slender man with quick movements and an abrupt manner. He ordered a wide tarpaulin spread out on the ground and had the wounded laid side by side. Examination revealed that the most urgent case was the scout, Elijah Daniel. Mizner dosed the scout with laudanum, an opiate sedative, and prepared to operate immediately. He delayed only until the sedative took effect.

Clint and the scouts watched from a short distance away. Assisted by a corpsman, Mizner first cleansed the wound with alcohol. The operation was complicated by the fact that war arrowheads were purposely barbed, which made extraction doubly dangerous. Using a thin probe to clear a path, Mizner inserted a length of stiff wire, with a loop on the end, into the wound. By manipulating the wire, he was finally able to engage the arrowhead in the loop. Holding the shaft in one hand and pulling the wire with the other, he slowly worked the arrowhead out. A gout of dark blood jetted from the wound.

Swiftly, by applying pressure, the flow of blood was slowed to a trickle. While the corpsman dressed the wound, Mizner moved on to a trooper who had a bullet lodged in his thigh. As he worked, he glanced up at Clint. He nodded owlishly.

"Where did you learn to leave part of the shaft in the wound?"

"Up north," Clint said. "I saw what happens when men try to jerk an arrowhead out. Generally makes a helluva mess."

"Not to mention killing the patient. For what it's worth, you probably saved Daniel's life."

Clint made no reply. As the surgeon returned to his work, the scouts eyed Clint with new respect. They bobbed their heads, smiling, open admiration written across their faces. Somewhat embarrassed, Clint nodded and walked toward the headquarters area. He found Mackenzie seated on the campstool, swigging coffee from a tin cup. He halted, jerking a thumb over his shoulder.

"Looks like Daniel will pull through."

"That's good news," Mackenzie said, staring at him a moment. "You seem to have earned the respect of your scouts, Mr. Brannock. In itself that says a great deal."

Clint realized he'd just passed muster. The compliment was understated, but nonetheless meant to convey a message. He shrugged it off with a smile. "All in a day's work, Colonel."

"Hardly that," Mackenzie said gravely. "We rewrote the rule book today, Mr. Brannock. I daresay the hostiles will have second thoughts about Mexico as a sanctuary."

"How about the Mexicans?" Clint asked carefully. "You expect any trouble from them?"

Mackenzie permitted himself a grim smile. "No doubt they'll lodge formal protests in Washington. All of which, as Shakespeare so aptly put it, amounts to 'sound and fury signifying nothing.' "

Clint nodded thoughtfully. "Wonder what we'd do if a Mex regiment crossed into Texas? I wager it'd be a damn sight more than 'sound and fury.' "

"Indeed it would," Mackenzie said with a hard grin. "Ulysses Grant would probably take the field himself. Just think of it, Mr. Brannock! We'd have ourselves a proper war, then.''

Clint easily read between the lines. Professional soldiers like Mackenzie and Sheridan considered Indian-fighting a distasteful task. It was somehow beneath them to do battle with what they termed "horseback barbarians." Yet, in the same breath, they dubbed the Comanche the finest light cavalry in the world. One seemed to Clint wholly at odds with the other.

All the more so since the Plains tribes were still making war. After thirty years and countless battles, the hostiles hadn't yet called it quits. He thought the army had a lot to learn.

11

On a drowsy Sunday afternoon a faint breeze stirred the parlor curtains. Through the windows, the mountains seemed to shimmer beneath a brilliant April sun. The greenery of spring was only just appearing on the studded slopes of the Rockies.

Virgil sat slumped in his easychair. The local newspaper, which was published every Saturday, was draped across his lap. Beside his chair lay the *Rocky Mountain News*, which was published in Denver and circulated throughout the territory. He religiously kept himself apprised of business and political events within Colorado, as well as the ever-shifting winds in Washington. Nothing of consequence escaped his attention.

A fortnight past he had returned from the East. With Senator Samuel Gilchrist's support, the bond guarantee had moved through Congress without serious opposition. Afterward, he had entrained for New York, where he'd called on several of the leading financial institutions. The weight of federal guarantees, which spoke well of his political connections, had proved persuasive. Upon departing Wall Street, he had commitments for $3 million in construction funds. The Denver & Rio Grande resumed building toward Pueblo.

Outside, a burst of laughter broke his concentration. The children were playing in the yard and he listened a moment to their shrill voices. As usual, Lon was bossing Jennifer and Morgan, assuming the role of leader. Virgil sometimes worried about the boy, whose upbringing had given him a worldliness beyond his years. Lon seemed to him a schemer, bold and manipulative, and slyly aggressive. So far, the youngster's schoolwork was passable, and his behavior, if unusual for a seven-year-old, was largely tolerable. Nonetheless concerned, Virgil wondered how long it would last.

Distracted from his newspaper, he glanced across at Elizabeth. She was seated in a cane-bottomed rocker, her hands busily engaged in crocheting a bedspread. Earlier, with the whole family togged out in their Sunday finery, they had attended morning church services. The noon meal, traditionally the most elaborate of the week, had left them surfeited with good food. Then, while the children went outside to play, Virgil and Elizabeth had fallen into their Sunday-afternoon ritual. He read the papers and she crocheted.

Elizabeth caught his look. She glanced up and her hands paused momentarily. "Finished with your paper, dear?"

"No," Virgil said. "Just resting my eyes."

"Good." She resumed crocheting. "While you have a moment, I'd like to discuss something. Actually, it's about something I read in the Denver paper."

"Oh, what's that?"

"Susan B. Anthony will be in Denver on Tuesday. She's addressing the territorial legislature."

"Anthony," Virgil repeated slowly. "Isn't she that eastern—what's the word?"

"Suffragette," Elizabeth commented. "In fact, she's the guiding force behind the suffrage movement. Some people consider her the most influential woman in America."

Virgil appeared somewhat bemused. Like most men, he considered suffragettes to be a hybrid mix of radicals and revolutionaries. The tone of the conversation left him vaguely disturbed. "I wasn't aware you had any interest in the suffrage movement."

"Don't be silly," she said seriously. "Every woman with an iota of sense supports universal suffrage."

"Well . . ." Virgil hesitated, suddenly perplexed. "Are you saying women should have the vote?"

"Among other things," she observed. "The right to vote is more or less a starting point. Women are entitled to far more, and deservedly so."

"Beth, I'm the least bit confused. Where is this conversation leading?"

Her crochet needle stopped. She looked at him directly. "For some time, I've been a subscriber to *The Revolution*. Are you familiar with it?"

Virgil frowned. "You're talking about that radical newspaper? The one published in New York?"

"Not radical," she corrected him. "It's merely feminist in viewpoint. A viewpoint I advocate."

Virgil looked stunned. "I've never seen it around the house. What've you done, kept it hidden?"

"Until now," she admitted. "I've decided that's not only deceitful but rather cowardly. I want you to know how I feel."

Virgil glanced down at the *Rocky Mountain News*. He tugged at his mustache, met her gaze. "This has something to do with the article on Susan Anthony, doesn't it?"

"Yes, it does," she said mildly. "I thought I might take the train to Denver tomorrow."

"I see." Virgil nodded, silent a moment. "You want to hear her address the legislature, is that it?"

"Yes, partly. I also want to meet her, talk with her personally. I might never have another chance."

"To what purpose?"

Elizabeth stared at him with a faint smile. "I'm seriously considering joining the suffrage movement. I believe it's time I got involved."

"Involved!" Virgil groaned. "Just what the hell does that mean?"

Elizabeth hesitated only an instant. She had lived with

Virgil too long to misjudge him now. Her husband was open-minded and scrupulously fair, unburdened by strong prejudices. She was convinced he would not feel threatened by what she planned. She prayed she was right.

"Be honest," she said frankly. "Do you think I could be trusted with the vote?"

Virgil knew her to be a levelheaded woman. He respected her intelligence as well as her intuitive wisdom. "Of course I do," he said honestly. "On the other hand, I wouldn't say the same for most women. They'd tend to vote with their hearts and not with their heads."

Her eyes demanded truth. "Wouldn't you agree that most men vote the same way? Aren't they swayed as much by the candidate as the issues?"

"Yeah, I suppose so. But men are more experienced in these things. They're realistic about politicians."

"Then, you tell me," she asked simply. "How will women become experienced—and realistic—unless they have the vote?"

Virgil sensed she was right. There was no rational way to overturn an argument grounded in truth. "Let's say I agree," he conceded. "What's that got to do with you and the suffrage movement?"

A smile softened her look. "All your life," she said, "you've followed your conscience. I believe I must follow mine, too."

"You're talking about getting actively engaged. Marches and demonstrations, that sort of thing?"

"Yes," she said quietly, "that sort of thing."

Virgil considered only a moment. "All right," he said, nodding. "You do what your conscience tells you. Just don't expect me to get involved."

"I won't," she promised. "All I want is your support . . . and your approval."

"On one condition." Virgil suddenly grinned. "Once you get the vote, we have to stick together. No splitting along party lines."

"We'll see," she said merrily. "After all, I do have to follow my conscience."

Virgil chuckled, slowly shook his head. "One thing I won't do is put on an apron and wipe noses. What happens to the kids while you're gone?"

"I'll take Jennifer and Morgan with me. They've never met their grandfather and it's the perfect opportunity. Daddy would be hurt if I didn't bring them along."

"That still leaves Lon."

Her eyes brightened with laughter. "I've hired a housekeeper," she replied airily. "A widow woman, with children of her own. She starts tomorrow."

"Great thunderin' cannonballs!" Virgil grumbled. "You had the whole thing rigged and ready to go. How'd you know I wouldn't turn thumbs down?"

She blew him a kiss. "Because, my dear, you always vote your conscience. It's why I married you."

Virgil grumped something under his breath. He rattled the newspaper and went back to reading. Yet his mind was more on her than on the printed word. She was clever and calculating and ever a mystery. A sprightly chameleon.

He thought her the most desirable woman he'd ever known.

Denver was a place of bittersweet memories. It was there Elizabeth had met and married a promising young businessman. There, too, her husband had killed and almost been killed. She returned with mixed emotions.

After an absence of almost eight years, she felt herself a stranger. The city had doubled in size and there was a curiously cosmopolitan flavor about Colorado's capital. Larimer Street, the main thoroughfare, was now paved, and trolleycars clanged through the business district. The buildings were taller, the people were smartly dressed, and everywhere there was a sense of bustling growth. On the whole, it seemed to her a foreign land.

Perhaps the personal changes affected her most. In her

absence, her mother had died following a lingering illness. She was shocked to discover that the experience had visibly altered her father. As the town's leading banker, Walter Tisdale had been a man of vigor and unstinting enterprise. He was still prosperous, still active in community affairs, but clearly changed by his wife's death. He seemed to have aged twenty years, suddenly grown old.

Tisdale proved to be a doting grandfather. After a teary-eyed reunion, he largely ignored Elizabeth throughout their first evening in town. At dinner, he directed his conversation to the children, seemingly fascinated by their every response. Jennifer and Morgan were quickly won over, and their presence acted as a restorative on his spirits. Only later, when they had been put to bed, was he able to concentrate on Elizabeth. By then, she knew she'd done the right thing in bringing the children.

In the parlor, Tisdale poured a brandy for himself and a sherry for Elizabeth. He evidenced little surprise when she explained the reason for her visit. While he was opposed to the suffrage movement, he knew his daughter to be a headstrong and willful woman. Yet he wisely kept his opinion to himself, for he had no wish to spoil the reunion. He turned the converstion instead to Virgil.

"Your last letter," he began, "indicated that Virgil had obtained financing. How are things progressing?"

"Fabulously well," she replied. "I understand they're laying a half-mile of track a day. Just imagine!"

"Virgil and General Palmer are still getting along?"

"Why, of course they are. Honestly, Daddy, where would the Denver & Rio Grande be without Virgil? He literally saved it from extinction."

"Perhaps," Tisdale mused aloud. "Then, again, I understand the Santa Fe has designs on that southern route. I suspect Virgil still has a fight on his hands."

"Oh, he'll win," she said with some conviction. "You may recall, he's a very determined man."

"So are the men behind the Santa Fe."

She gave him an odd look. "What is it you're trying to say?"

"Well . . ." Tisdale stopped, his mouth curled in a sheepish smile. "I was just thinking, it would be nice to have you and my grandchildren nearby. Should Virgil's plans not work out . . ."

"Yes?"

"In that event, you might consider moving back to Denver. I'm getting on in years and there's really no one to replace me. I've always thought Virgil would make an excellent banker."

She stared at him astonished. "Have you forgotten why we left Denver? Virgil was almost assassinated—twice!"

The statement spoke for itself. David Hughes, the political czar of Denver, had put a price on Virgil's head. Only a last-minute truce had forestalled further bloodshed.

"Haven't you heard?" Tisdale asked, chortling out loud. "There's a reform movement spreading through Denver. Hughes is on his way out."

"Is he indeed?" she said somewhat skeptically. "What about the other one—Ed Case?"

Tisdale fidgeted, averting his eyes. Ed Case was the boss of Denver's sporting district, and an integral part of Hughes' political machine. His hostility toward the Brannocks—Clint and Earl as well as Virgil—was public knowledge.

"With Hughes out," Tisdale said, smiling weakly, "the problem no longer exists. Ed Case will do what he's told."

Her expression was doubtful. "I wish I shared your confidence. Where politics are concerned, I suppose some of Virgil's cynicism has rubbed off on me."

"Come now, my dear! I've just told you that the reformers will virtually control City Hall."

"Only until Ed Case corrupts them. There is simply too much money in vice, Daddy. Even reformers learn the temptations of graft."

Tisdale scowled. "Cynicism doesn't become you. Nor your husband, I might add. He was always a bit quixotic for my tastes."

She laughed softly. "We all tilt at our own windmills, don't we, Daddy? After all, why else am I here?"

Tisdale sipped his brandy. The thought occurred that his daughter had married the wrong man. Virgil Brannock encouraged her rebellious nature, abetted it even. She was now beyond any hope of redemption.

He silently wished she'd married a ribbon clerk.

The gallery was packed with an overflow crowd. Below, the territorial legislators slowly filed into chambers. As befitted the occasion, their faces were properly solemn.

Today, the Colorado legislature was to be addressed by Susan B. Anthony. The honor accorded her was all the greater in that she was of the female persuasion. Far from making a speech, no woman had ever before been allowed on the floor of the legislative chambers. Nor would one have been allowed there today except for her name. She represented a groundswell movement that no lawmaker could ignore.

Susan B. Anthony was a former schoolteacher. In 1869, working in concert with other female activists, she had formed the National Woman Suffrage Association. As publisher of *The Revolution* and nationwide lecturer on women's rights, she was the acknowledged leader of the movement. No one questioned her dedication, or the fact that she had devoted her life to the cause. So strong was her commitment that she had been arrested for illegally casting a ballot in the 1872 presidential election.

Apart from the vote, the fundamental principle at issue was the right to own property. No married woman could buy or sell anything without her husband's permission. Nor could she make contracts or sue in court or retain any portion of a family inheritance. All she had, including her clothing and household goods, belonged to her husband.

Upon his death, unless otherwise directed in his will, she
inherited one-third of her husband's estate, with the balance going to the children. Only as a widow was she free
to manage her own affairs.

Suffragettes sought to overturn what was essentially a
man's world. They demanded the right to own property,
equal opportunity in commerce and education, and the
right to vote. Understandably, the movement encountered
resistance from a male-dominated establishment. Yet, oddly
enough, the suffragettes had achieved some measure of
success in the western territories. In 1869, women were
given the vote in Wyoming and the process was repeated
in Utah in early 1870. No other state or territory in the
Union had even come close to the passage of such
enactments.

Colorado was the most hotly contested battleground.
Bordering Utah and Wyoming, Colorado had witnessed
improvements directly attributable to women's votes. For
one thing, the right to vote had attracted women to areas
where males outnumbered females by a margin of five-to-
one. No man could ignore the advantages of enticing
decent, marriageable women to migrate westward. Nor
were they blind to the civilizing influence that women
brought to the frontier. Legislators, as well as male voters,
were aware that an influx of women quickened the establishment of law and order. Families and children and
schools transformed raw frontier towns into stable commu-
nities. Hard as it was to swallow, few men would deny the
good wrought by women's votes.

From the gallery Elizabeth looked on as the legislators
seated themselves. To the rear of the chamber Susan B.
Anthony entered through a door, escorted by the lieutenant
governor. There was a buzz of conversation as she took a
chair near the speaker's podium. In token honor, the lieutenant governor made a brief introduction. Then, stepping
aside, he bowed to the suffragette leader.

A hush fell over the chamber as Susan Anthony walked

to the podium. She was a plain woman, with solemn features, her hair pulled back in a tight chignon. She wore a simple black dress, with a white lace collar and a brooch at the throat. Her carriage was dignified and she stood for a moment staring intently at the assemblage. When she spoke, her voice was firm and assured. Her eyes burned with hypnotic fervor.

"Gentlemen of the Colorado legislature. Today I wish to speak with you of inequity and injustice."

She paused, underscoring the challenge of her words. Hands on the podium, her gaze seemed to touch every legislator in the chamber. The silence was absolute when she resumed.

"Because universal suffrage is a political subject, it has often been said that women have nothing to do with its passage. So I ask you to ask yourselves these questions. Are women aliens, lesser than even the newest immigrant, simply because we are women? Are we bereft of citizenship because we are mothers, wives, and daughters? Have women no country—no interest in the public good—no partnership in our nation's destiny? Have we no voice in our own destiny?"

She stopped, letting the words ring through the chamber. Then, with mounting force, she went on. "To borrow from our Constitution, I hold these truths to be self-evident. American women have to do with universal suffrage not only because it is moral and just, but because it is a political subject. We are citizens of this republic! Our lives, our liberty, and our well-being are unalterably bound to government and laws—and politics!"

The speech lasted not quite an hour. There was nothing vitriolic or polemical in what Susan Anthony advocated. Nor was there any logical argument by which her remarks could be rebutted. When she finished, the legislators responded with polite applause. No one seriously believed that a bill would be introduced, much less passed. Her appearance before the lawmakers had changed nothing.

Later, outside the capitol building, Elizabeth introduced herself to the suffragette leader. Several other women were waiting as well, and Susan Anthony invited them back to her hotel. There she elaborated further on the movement, holding them spellbound with her vision of the future. When she asked for recruits, only a few of the women volunteered. The others, intrigued but fearful, requested time to consider. They departed one by one.

Except for Elizabeth, all of those who volunteered were from Denver. The meeting lasted through the afternoon and into early evening. Susan Anthony discussed the organization of suffrage groups as well as methods of drawing public attention to their cause. Of all the women there, she seemed most impressed by Elizabeth. No one took offense when she invited Elizabeth to join her for supper.

Some hours later Elizabeth emerged from the hotel. As the doorman assisted her into a cab, she felt drunk with exhilaration. Only moments before she had been appointed chairwoman of southern Colorado. Her immediate goal was to organize the women of Colorado Springs.

By fate or fluke, some days alter the course of many lives. She knew that nothing in her life would ever again be the same.

12

A VAST EMPTY land stretched eastward from New Mexico into the western fringes of the Texas Panhandle. The Spaniards centuries before, had named it *Llano Estacado*, the Staked Plains. Flat and treeless, the plains were covered with buffalo grass and broken by an occasional canyon. No man ventured there except through alliance with the Comanche.

Earl and Ramón Guerra rode at the head of a dusty column. Strung out behind was a small caravan of rickety Mexican *carretas*. These lumbering, oversize carts were constructed entirely of rawhide and wood. The wheels were made from enormous logs, sawed crosswise and fashioned into crude disks.

Lashed on top the wagon frames were huge basketlike cargo carriers, covered with canvas and piled high with trade goods. The *carretas* were drawn by yoked oxen, while drivers with popping whips walked alongside. In turn, the drivers were prodded along by the hunchback, Ignacio Zarate.

Guerra had made a proposition too tempting to resist. For every dollar Earl invested in trade goods he was guaranteed two dollars in return. In time, should their arrangement prove satisfactory, Guerra had hinted at an even larger share of the profits. By any measure, it was a generous offer, clearly prompted by what Guerra considered a debt of honor.

Earl had accepted with visions of doubling and redoubling his money, ultimately transforming a modest stake into a small fortune. Yet he had entered into the arrangement with certain qualms, all too aware that they were trading in illicit goods. Four days on the trail had done nothing to dispel his initial concern. Bit by bit, Guerra had told him of an informal and rather loose-knit organization: an order of men known as the *Comancheros*, a Spanish term.

The *Comancheros* were men who dealt with the horseback tribes. The trade originated with Mexican hunters who ventured onto the plains to kill buffalo. The first expeditions were begun in the 1760s and their purpose was to harvest meat for sale in the New Mexico settlements. Inevitably, the hunters came into contact with the Comanche, who ruled the Staked Plains. Over the years a mutual trust developed and the hunters became the Indians' prime source of trade goods. Thereafter, they were known as the *Comancheros*.

For years the commerce was principally an exchange of buffalo robes for trade goods. With time, however, the Comanche learned that stolen horses could be bartered for muskets and gunpowder. Afterward, the ranches of Texas and the *haciendas* of northern Mexico were routinely plundered of livestock. As the trade developed into contraband, it shifted away from the settlements and farther onto *Llano Estacado*. Before long, commerce with the Indians was dominated by a small band of men who headquartered in Santa Fe.

From Mexican Gulf ports the trade goods were carted over a tortuous inland route. The trail wound through central Mexico and up the Rio Grande to Santa Fe. After resale to the *Comancheros*, the goods were transported by *carreta* to the southern reaches of the Texas plains. The cargo was eventually enlarged to include muskets and pistols, beads and knives, and quantities of cheap whiskey carried in gourd containers. The smaller traders packed their goods eastward with strings of overloaded burros. The more prosperous *Comancheros* organized caravans of oxen-drawn *carretas*.

Early Spanish settlers learned that the Comanche were accomplished horse thieves. In later years, these lords of the Staked Plains turned their talent to cattle rustling. When buffalo were scarce, they found that cows were a suitable, albeit less tasty, substitute. All the more significant, they discovered that the *Comancheros* considered cattle a valuable medium of exchange. Shortly before the Civil War, the theft of horses and cows began in wholesale measure. The stolen livestock was driven to the badlands at the foot of the Staked Plains, where entire herds were bartered away. By the early 1870s, it was estimated that some 300,000 head of cattle and more than 100,000 horses had disappeared into *Llano Estacado*. New Mexican ranchers, who seldom asked for a bill of sale, bought entire herds from the *Comancheros*.

There were three trails from New Mexico into the uncharted wilderness of *Comanchería*. The upper trail led northeast to the Canadian River and forked near the Texas line. One fork branched off downstream and the other turned southeast toward *Puerto de los Rivajenos*, the Door of the Plains. The name derived from a natural opening in the Cap Rock, which was part of the towering escarpment guarding the Staked Plains. From the Cap Rock, the trail continued on to the Valley of Tongues, so called because various tribes gathered there to trade. Farther north was *Valle de las Lágrimas*, the Valley of Tears. Aptly named, it was the place where Texican mothers and children were brought after being taken captive in raids. The fortunate ones were bought by *Comancheros* and later ransomed back to their families.

The trail followed by Ramón Guerra's party led eastward from the Pecos to a canyon along the upper Brazos.

Known as *Las Casas Amarillas*, the Yellow Houses, it was a distinctive landmark. At the head of the canyon was an alkaline lake, bordered by high bluffs of a yellowish hue. From a distance, the sheer bluffs, which were pocked with caves, gave the appearance of a walled city. Below the lake was a clear stream sheltered by tall cottonwoods. Spread along the creek bank were the lodges of the Quahadi.

The Comanche Nation was composed of five major bands. The Quahadi, who ruled the Staked Plains, were considered the fiercest warriors of the tribe. Led by Quanah, their war chief, they swept down out of *Comancheria* to plunder the Texas settlements and raid northern Mexico. Their domain was a mystery to white men, unmapped and as yet unexplored. Other tribes, even the other Comanche bands, roamed *Llano Estacado* at their sufferance. The Quahadi jealously guarded what they claimed as their ancestral lands.

Comancheria was a vast land mass encompassing eastern New Mexico, the Texas Panhandle, and distant stretches of the west Texas plains. Westward was the *Llano Estacado*, rising like a palisaded barrier, forming a high wall north and south. From these escarpments the land sloped eastward, crisscrossed by barren prairies and a latticework of rivers. These streams were fertile oases, lined with cottonwood trees, their sandy banks covered with wild plums and persimmon bushes. There, sustaining themselves on the great buffalo herds, the Quahadi reigned supreme.

The *Comancheros*, unlike most outsiders, were always welcome in Quahadi territory. The traders were allowed freedom of passage under an informal, mutually beneficial truce. In exchange for stolen livestock, the Quahadi got trade goods that could be obtained from no other source. The Mexicans, for their part, were assured a safe journey upon departing *Comancheria*. An element of trust was essential, for the traders were four hundred miles from the

New Mexico settlements. Their lives, in large measure, were dependent on the goodwill of the Quahadi.

Early in June the trading party rode into the Quahadi village. Guerra and Earl, who rode in the lead, were instantly surrounded by clamoring children and barking dogs. Spirals of smoke curled skyward from cook fires and women paused to watch as the *carretas* rolled to a halt. Warriors stood before their lodges, solemn-faced and observant, offering no sign of welcome. The noisy children went silent as Guerra stepped down from his saddle.

Earl dismounted, holding the reins loosely in one hand. Apart from tame Indians, he'd never had any dealings with the horseback tribes. The Quahadi, standing all around him now, seemed somehow wilder than he'd expected. He was uncomfortably aware of the smell peculiar to Indians, that pungent blend of wood smoke, tallow, and old buffalo robes. Their closeness, combined with their lukewarm reception, gave him second thoughts. He wondered why he had listened to Guerra.

A tall, imposing figure emerged from one of the lodges. He was light-skinned for a Comanche, clearly of mixed blood. His features were aquiline, with high cheekbones and a wide brow. He strode directly to Guerra and stopped, nodding slightly. His eyes were friendly.

"*Buenos días*," he said in perfect Spanish. "Welcome to our camp."

"*Gracias, jefe*," Guerra said formally. "I come to trade with the great Quanah and his people."

"The Quahadi have prepared for your visit. Observe what we have gathered from the *tejanos*."

Quanah motioned with a grand gesture. Across the stream, a herd of some five hundred longhorns grazed on an open prairie. Horsemen, mounted on fleet buffalo ponies, held the cattle bunched near the stream.

Guerra laughed appreciatively. "You have been busy, Great Chief. The *tejanos* no doubt mourn their loss."

"So they should," Quanah said with a wolfish smile. "We raided in the Leaf Moon and caught them asleep. They still have not learned to fight."

The remark brought a murmur of amused contempt from the tribesmen. For the Comanche, there were two distinct and very different breeds of white men. One was an *americano*—or in the Comanche tongue, *tahbay-boh*, a general term for white man. The other was a *tejano*, anyone who lived between the Red River and the Rio Grande. The *tejanos* were invaders, encroaching on ancient tribal lands, and deserved no mercy. Stealing their cattle seemed to the Quahadi a rough form of justice.

To Earl's surprise, the trading did not commence immediately. Quanah, acting the part of host, first invited the *Comancheros* to relieve their hunger. From throughout the village women brought stewed buffalo meat and served a meal outside Quanah's lodge. Afterward, a ceremonial pipe, carved from dark-hued stone, was produced. Filled with kinnikinnick, a mixture of tobacco and aromatic herbs, the pipe was offered to the four winds. Then, after being lit by Quanah, it was presented to the *Comanchero* leader. Guerra puffed smoke with the solemnity demanded by the occasion.

When the pipe was returned to Quanah, he addressed a question to Guerra. Their conversation was conducted in Spanish, and Quanah occasionally directed a glance at Earl. At last, when the Quahadi chief seemed to lose interest, Guerra looked around. He spoke to Earl in English.

"Quanah asks why I bring a white man into his camp. I told him how you saved my life and became my friend."

Earl nodded slowly. "What was his reply?"

"A rough translation," Guerra said with a sly grin, "would be that a friend of mine is welcome here. He expresses some doubt that you will ever become a *Comanchero*."

"Why is that?"

"Your color," Guerra said, and chuckled. "He says all white men are thieves. I vouched for your honesty."

"And he accepted your word?"

"Of course, *compadre*! I am too valuable for him to do otherwise."

The statement was no idle boast. When the trading got under way, Guerra's men first unloaded the usual assortment of beads and calico and cheap knives. Quanah, who acted as spokesman for the band, proved to be a sharp trader. Even when the gourds of whiskey were produced, he continued to haggle like a veteran fishmonger. He bargained the *tejano* longhorns away one cow at a time.

The reason shortly became apparent. Unloaded last from the *carretas* were four wooden crates. One contained a dozen lever-action Henry carbines, chambered for .44 caliber. Still another was packed with Colt and Remington revolvers, all of them the outmoded cap-and-ball variety. The remaining two crates were filled with cartridges for the carbines and molded balls for the pistols.

The trading now began in earnest. Guerra demanded, and eventually got, twenty cows for each of the Henry carbines. The crate of revolvers fetched a total of two hundred head, which reduced the cattle herd to practically nothing. In order to get the ammunition, Quanah grudgingly threw in thirty horses, stolen in the recent raid. Even then, Guerra still had one wagon of trade goods held in reserve.

The Quahadi chief refused to part with more horses. Finally, with some reluctance, he mentioned that a Kiowa raiding party would return shortly to *Las Casas Amarillas*. Since the Kiowa were considered allies, it was agreed that Guerra could await their return. Quanah, who evidenced a certain humor, even permitted himself a smile. He noted that it would be a joke of sorts on the Kiowa. All the carbines and pistols were now in the hands of the Quahadi.

Earl failed to see the humor. Until the crates were unloaded, he hadn't known about the firearms. It bothered

him that repeating carbines would be used in raids on
Texas settlers. Yet, even as he wrestled with his conscience, he sensed there was nothing to be done. The
Comancheros dealt in supply and demand, and modern
weapons were much in demand by hostiles. No one, the
army included, would put a halt to such a lucrative trade.
He told himself what he'd been hesitant to admit since
leaving Santa Fe.

Beyond the Staked Plains, there was a term for men
such as himself. Worse than *Comanchero*, it was a term
reserved for white men who bartered with hostile tribes.
He was now an Anglo renegade.

A pale sickle moon hung suspended in the sky. Starlight
rippled off the yellow bluffs, casting an eerie glow over
the valley. The night seemed bathed in flickering shadow.

Earl and Guerra sat crosslegged beside Quanah. Flanking them on either side were the council elders and several
warriors of prominent rank. They were seated outside
Quanah's lodge, which was positioned in the center of the
village. Before them a blazing fire showered the night with
sparks.

The evening had proved an eye-opener for Earl. At
dusk, women had piled fresh wood on fires throughout the
village. As dark approached, a carnival spirit seemed to
infect every member of the band. To his great amazement,
the sober-faced braves and their women became laughing
pranksters. He was quickly disabused of the notion most
white men had about Indians. Far from the stoic savage,
they were filled with a rollicking, sportive humor.

Before long, he learned as well that they were inveterate
gamblers. Outside a nearby lodge, Zarate and the other
Comancheros were playing the button game with a group
of warriors. The "button" was a small piece of wood that
could be hidden in the hand, and score was kept with a
pile of tally sticks. One team attempted to deceive the
other by passing the button from man to man. The decep-

tion came about when a team member retained the button and pretended to pass it along. Tally sticks were won or lost by guessing which man actually held the button. The stakes were trade good geegaws wagered against tanned pelts.

Throughout the camp, the gourds of whiskey were being consumed at a prodigious rate. Some warriors were already drunk and even the sobersided elders were flush with good cheer. Around the main fire, some thirty men and women had formed a dance circle. Several skin-covered drums provided a thumping beat, accompanied by hand rattles made of dried buffalo scrotums. The dance circle contracted and expanded, while the men chanted and the women sang a shrill intonation. Occasionally the dancers formed a snakelike parade and shuffled around the fire.

Earl took more than a casual interest in the dancers. Warmed by whiskey, he fixed his attention on one of the younger women. Her face was alive and expressive and her eyes were like matched black pearls. She moved with light-footed grace, and beneath her doeskin dress, her figure was rounded and shapely. Her complexion was dusky gold, and in accordance with Comanche custom, her hair was cropped short. As she danced, she watched Earl with a veiled but searching look. He thought he saw invitation in her eyes.

Toward midevening, the first group of dancers was replaced by another group from the throng of spectators. As the girl moved away from the fire, she looked directly at Earl. Her head dipped in an imperceptible nod and she cut her eyes in the direction of the stream. Easing through the crowd, she disappeared from sight.

After a moment, Earl got to his feet. Guerra shot him a warning look, but the liquor had dulled his instincts. He grinned and walked off through the village. His eyes were stoned with lust and his only thought was for the bold invitation he'd seen in the girl's face. He headed toward the stream.

A short time later he found her waiting beneath the cottonwoods. She laughed and tossed her head, leading him deeper into the shadows. He held out his arms, and without a word being spoken, she stepped into his embrace. Her hands went behind his neck and she responded to his kiss with a fierce, passionate urgency. His arms tightened, strong and demanding, and her breath quickened. She moaned low in her throat.

Entwined, their mouths joined, they slowly sank to their knees. He lowered her onto the ground.

Late the next morning Earl was summoned to Quanah's lodge. Stooping through the door hole, he found Ramón Guerra seated beside the Comanche chief. Off to one side, the girl stood with her head bowed, a splotchy bruise covering one cheek. An older man, short and chunky, dressed in leggings and breechclout, stood with her.

Guerra looked up, his face troubled. "We have a problem, *compadre*. You are accused of taking this girl to the bushes."

"Guilty as charged," Earl said with a waggish grin. "She gave me the high sign and I accepted. Why is that a problem?"

"Because, my friend, you are the wrong color."

Guerra briefly explained. By American standards, Comanches took a liberal attitude toward such things. There was no taboo on sex before marriage, and casual mating was tolerated by parents. Older girls often initiated young boys into sex, and such affairs were regarded with rough good humor. Still, sex with a white man was another matter entirely. No *tahbay-boh* had ever been permitted to marry into the tribe.

Earl blinked. "Who said anything about marriage?"

"Her father," Guerra said in a low voice. "Allow me to introduce you to Spotted Dog. He beat the truth out of her."

Spotted Dog's face looked adzed from dark hardwood.

An evil light danced in his eyes as he stared at Earl. Guerra went on, his tone flat and guarded.

"The girl is twenty-two winters old. She is a widow, with no children. Her man was killed in a raid on the Apaches."

"What's your point?" Earl asked.

Guerra's look betrayed nothing. "She's considered old for a Comanche woman. Even worse, she might be barren, since she's had no children. No man wants a barren woman, and there have been no offers of a remarriage. She has become a burden to her father."

Earl was thoughtful a moment. "So he figures to push her off on me?"

"Precisely."

"And if I refuse?"

"You won't," Guerra said with chilling simplicity. "For if you do, they will roast you headdown over a slow fire."

A smile froze on Earl's face. "What changed their minds about a white man marrying into the tribe?"

"I did," Guerra growled, half under his breath. "I convinced Quanah that it will benefit his people. A *Comanchero* in the band will serve their interests."

"Are you saying I'm now a *Comanchero*?"

"For the rest of your life, *compadre*. As we say among ourselves, once in, never out."

Earl received the news with surpassing calm. He found himself unaccountably resigned to both the marriage and his forced induction into the *Comancheros*. All the more so since the alternative in either instance was death.

"What the hell?" he mugged, hands outstretched. "I guess there's no honey without stings. What's the bride's name?"

"Little Raven," Guerra replied. "On your behalf, I have offered her father a marriage price of ten horses. I will deduct it from your share of our profits."

Earl uttered a jocular bark of laughter. "What happens now?"

Guerra, switching to Spanish, spoke to Quanah. The chief, in turn, addressed the girl's father in the Comanche tongue. Spotted Dog grunted, glancing at Earl with a humorless, yellow-toothed smile. He stepped forward and held out a square, stubby-fingered hand. Earl pumped his arm a couple of times and let go.

"Congratulations," Guerra informed him dryly. "You are now married."

"That's it?" Earl said. "No ceremony or nothing?"

Guerra smiled, blessing him with the sign of the cross. "*Vaya con Dios, compadre.*"

Earl shook his head ruefully. He turned and found Little Raven staring at him with open adoration. Her mouth curved in a kittenish smile.

The thought occurred that he was now a squaw man, as well as a *Comanchero*. Then, suddenly, his mind went back to Santa Fe and a comment made by Ramón Guerra. A jest at the time, it seemed a great truth today.

God was indeed a jokester.

13

THE SUTLER'S STORE was unusually quiet. With payday come and gone, few soldiers had the price of a drink. Tonight, with the exception of a lone sergeant, the place was empty.

Clint emerged from the enlisted men's tavern room. After supper he had stopped by for his customary whiskey. But now, with the drink under his belt, he had nowhere to go. He halted on the porch and rolled himself a smoke.

For no particular reason, it occurred to him that he'd grown to like Fort Clark. He supposed it had more to do with the Seminole Negro scouts than the army. Over the past month the regiment had beeen involved in several engagements with hostiles. In one, a brief skirmish with a Comanche war party, his horse had been shot from beneath him. Pinned under the dying roan, he'd looked up to see a yipping warrior riding him down. Elijah Daniel had saved him with a quick snapshot and afterward refused his thanks. Like the other scouts, Daniel now thought of him as one of their own.

Only three days ago they had jumped a Kiowa raiding party. On routine patrol with D Troop, they crossed fresh sign some miles west of the fort. Clint and five scouts ranged ahead of the troop, tracking the hostiles throughout the day. At sundown, they overtook the Kiowas, who had stopped to make camp. Outnumbered two-to-one, they charged with pistols, and the Kiowas scattered after a brief fight. One scout suffered a minor wound while four Kiowa braves were killed in the engagement. Word got around the post that Clint was "double wolf on guts and savvy." The troopers, no less than the scouts, valued coolness in a tight situation.

Studying on it now, Clint thought the same remark applied to Ranald Mackenzie. The colonel was a tough campaigner, and he'd recently gathered a few kudos of his own. In the aftermath of their raid across the border, the Mexican government had lodged a formal complaint with Washington. Still, despite the diplomatic repercussions, the president and General Sherman had publicly supported Mackenzie. Texans lauded the action, and the state legislature passed a resolution commending the colonel and his regiment. The only sour note for Clint was that no one mentioned the Seminole Negro scouts. Texicans, on the face of it, weren't about to waste their praise on coloreds.

The absurdity of it still stuck in Clint's craw. Stepping off the porch, he walked along the road bordering the parade ground. The post was lighted by a mellow half-moon, and he saw a sentry standing outside the guardhouse. As he approached, he spotted a trooper "bucked and gagged," one of the military's harsher forms of punishment. The man was seated on the ground, feet flat and knees bent. His wrists were bound tight, with his forearms locked across his lower legs. A short pole had been thrust beneath his knees and wedged across the bend of his arms. He was gagged with a bandanna and looked to be in considerable discomfort.

" 'Evenin', Lancaster." Clint paused, nodding to the sentry. "Who you got here?"

"Private Mulvaney, C Troop. The dumb bastard only reported in day before yesterday."

"What'd he do?"

Lancaster snorted. "Insubordination to an officer. He's got a smart mouth on him."

"Who'd he get smart with?"

"Lieutenant Greer hisself. As you might imagine, it put the lieutenant's nose out of joint."

Clint stared down at the man a moment. "How long will he stay trussed up?"

"Till reveille," Lancaster said. "He'll likely never again get his legs straightened out."

Clint ground his cigarette underfoot. "I'll have to watch myself around Lieutenant Greer."

"Indeed you had, Mr. Brannock. Him being a proper West Pointer and all."

Walking away, Clint was reminded that the military was no life for a faintheart. Any breech of discipline brought swift and uncompromising punishment. Careless saddling of a horse, which caused the animal's back to gall, bought a trooper four hours on the parade ground, carrying a fully packed saddle as he marched. For drunk and disorderly, a trooper was required to dig a hole ten feet square by ten feet deep. Then, having dug it, he was forced to fill it in. The experience was a lesson in the virtue of sobriety.

Based on observation, Clint pegged most discipline problems to boredom. Garrison duty, particularly for men in the ranks, was a dull existence. The troopers' daily routine of drill, guard duty, and fatigue detail exerted a grinding tedium. There was nothing glamorous or romantic about cleaning horse stalls, chopping firewood, and scrubbing barracks' floors. For many men, the sheer monotony of army life was maddening beyond endurance. Every year, almost 30 percent of those who enlisted simply deserted, vanishing without a trace. So many deserted, in fact, that the army made only a token effort to track them down. They were replaced, instead, by raw recruits.

To a large extent, the regular army was a mercenary force. Fighting wild Indians attracted few patriots, and only a small percentage of those in the service were native-born Americans. Volunteers for military service were generally immigrants, with the majority fresh off a boat from Ireland. The recruits were signed up for a three-year hitch and paid the princely sum of thirteen dollars a month. Some joined the army because jobs were scarce and their background suited them for little besides menial labor. Others saw the service as an escape from the drudgery of farm life, or in many instances a refuge from the law. For a variety of reasons, many men enlisted under false names.

Promotion for men in the ranks was painfully slow. Usually it took several enlistments to make sergeant, and even then the pay was a paltry eighteen dollars a month. Apart from low pay, living conditions on frontier garrisons were hardly more than tolerable. The barracks were often crude and uncomfortable, hot in the summer and cold in the winter. The food consisted of salt pork and tinned beef, rice and beans, and lots of coffee. Nor were health conditions on western outposts any better. Constant exposure to the elements crippled many soldiers with severe rheumatism. Disease and lack of sanitation produced illness and an unusually high death rate. The toll from natural causes was greater than for those killed by the hostiles.

Officers fared little better than the enlisted men. The dangers were the same, they endured the same monotony and forlorn surroundings. While many officers were married, the presence of wives and families only partially relieved the tedium. Still, the greater burden for most officers was that they shared no camaraderie with their men. The frontier army operated on a caste system, and tradition ruthlessly eliminated any hint of equality. The personal isolation, compounded by all the other problems, was often too much. Loneliness and boredom drove many in the officer corps to alcoholism.

Yet, for all the obstacles, the army proved itself equal to the mission. One reason was that the enlisted men were physically tough and generally made the best of a bad situation. Training and rigid discipline prepared them for the hardships of frontier campaigns. Their attitudes were straightforward, and they rightfully assumed that in any normal engagement they would be outnumbered. Moreover, they understood that capture by the horseback tribes meant torture and an agonizingly slow death. So they fought with determination and a sense of abandon, seeking survival through victory. Their world was one in which mercy had no place, and they behaved accordingly. The worst of the lot took his trade seriously and fought to win.

Still another reason for the army's record on the frontier was the professionalism of the officer corps. Overall, despite the stiff-necked attitude of many officers, the army was well-led. Fully half the officers on the western plains were graduates of West Point. Their training in the tactics and logistics of warfare made them the equal of any officer corps in the world. As for the balance of the officers, most of them were seasoned veterans of the Civil War. The end result was that there were few glory-seekers, and even fewer incompetents, on the frontier. However stern their leadership, it was tempered by professionalism. Their men might hate them, but few questioned their judgment in battle.

Tonight, reflecting on it as he skirted the parade ground, Clint found little to criticize. While the system was by no means perfect, commanders such as Mackenzie made it function with brutal efficiency. The men, who were a hard lot themselves, accepted the need for rigorous discipline. A soldier's life was no tea party, but it was the life all of them, officers and men alike, had chosen. For the most part, they pulled together and somehow got the job done. No one could ask for more.

On past the parade ground, Clint turned toward his own quarters. He'd been billeted in a one-room affair tacked onto the end of noncoms row. In all, there were eight stone dwellings, wedged side by side, for married noncommissioned officers. As he turned down the lane, he saw Sergeant Major O'Hara seated outside the largest of the houses. By now, they were on familiar terms and shared a degree of mutual respect. But O'Hara was a soldier of the old school and a stickler for formality. No one, including the post commander, dealt with him on a first-name basis.

"Well, now," he called in high good humor. "Out for a stroll, are you, Mr. Brannock?"

"Not exactly," Clint said. "Stopped off at the sutler's for a drink."

O'Hara motioned to a vacant chair beside his own. As Clint took a seat, the sergeant major pulled out an oilskin pouch and tamped tobacco into an ancient pipe. Clint rolled himself a cigarette and they lit up on one match. O'Hara puffed a thick wad of smoke.

"Could I offer you something?" he said genially. "I've an idea the missus still has coffee on the stove. Or perhaps you'd prefer a touch of spirits?"

"I'm fine," Clint said. "One drink wets my whistle. Any more puts me in a mood not to stop."

"Truer words never spoken," O'Hara said with a wide peg-toothed grin. "Like any god-fearin' Irishman, I'm partial to the stuff myself. I'd sooner have none than one."

"Guess the sutler will never get rich off us."

O'Hara smoked in silence for a time. "Perhaps you've not heard," he said at length, "but the colonel thinks highly of your work. He told me so himself."

"Glad to hear it," Clint said with a measured smile. "You suppose he'll ever say it to my face?"

O'Hara laughed a loud, booming laugh. "Your guess on that's as good as mine, Mr. Brannock. Still, I can say he was mightily impressed with your last engagement. How many heathens was it you killed?"

"Four," Clint said, flicking ash off his cigarette. " 'Course, the scouts deserve the credit. Elijah and his boys love a good fight."

"Hmmm." O'Hara nodded thoughtfully. "I'm trying to recall your report. Kiowas, weren't they?"

"Yeah," Clint said. "Whole bunch of Kiowas."

"And you've had only the one brush with Comanches. Isn't that so?"

Clint gave him a sideways look. "What makes you ask?"

"Nothing special," O'Hara said absently. "Just wondering how you would rate them with the Kiowa."

"Hard to say," Clint told him. "Except that the Comanche killed my horse. I reckon that's a point for them."

"I noticed you're riding a sorrel now. Looks to be a good mount."

"No complaints so far."

O'Hara's gaze drifted out across the parade ground. "It's an odd thing," he said as though thinking aloud. "I've fought all manner of Indians in my time. But I hold an abiding respect for the Comanche."

"Why is that?"

"Are you being polite, Mr. Brannock? Or would you be interested in an old trooper's opinion?"

Clint cracked a smile. "I always listen when the sergeant major talks."

"God's blood!" O'Hara said in his rolling voice. "I'm the one to give you an earful, then."

Puffing his pipe, O'Hara launched into a tale that bedeviled all cavalrymen. The Comanche, he noted, were creatures of an unknown land, the Staked Plains. On military maps it was a vast blank, the course of rivers and streams still a mystery. Only a few Anglos, mostly Texas Rangers, had dared to probe the badlands guarding *Llano Estacado*. Those who returned evidenced no wish to go there again. One trip into *Comanchería* seemed enough for any man.

For the cavalry, it was a grisly game of hide-and-seek. Comanche war parties rode down from the Staked Plains

with little fear of reprisal. On the trail scouts were de-
ployed ahead of the main party by several hours. They
selected campsites for the night and were constantly vigi-
lant for army patrols. By full dark, the party was encamped
on high ground, with lookouts on guard. No one approached their position undetected.

Highly organized, a war party established a base of
operations once the raiding area was reached. Spare mounts
were left in camp, heavily guarded, while scouts fanned
out to survey likely targets. Their purpose was always
threefold: to kill settlers, steal horses and cattle, and take
tejano women and children captive. There was nothing
random about the raid, and oftentimes it lasted for several
days. Before the first blow was struck, every detail had
been worked out in advance.

The raids generally began on the full moon. With good
reason, Texicans called it the Comanche Moon. The war
party split into small groups and staged their raids over a
wide area. Settlers were slaughtered, their cabins burned
and plundered, and livestock was driven off. Captives
were lashed to stolen horses and became the personal
property of individual warriors. Then, as the moon waned,
livestock and captives were herded back to the base camp.
Night after night the process was repeated throughout the
surrounding countryside. The raids halted only when a
cavalry patrol stumbled upon the carnage or an alarm was
somehow sounded. By then, the war party was generally
on its way back to *Comanchería*.

Following a raid, warriors drove their horses to exhaus-
tion, often riding a day or more without stop. When one
horse collapsed, they switched to a fresh mount; captives
who could not maintain the grueling pace were killed and
left at trailside. When pursued by cavalry troops, the war
party scattered to the winds, later regrouping at a prear-
ranged rendezvous. To throw off pursuers, a route was
selected over wasteland terrain, avoiding streams and

waterholes. The raiders' water supply, carried in animal-gut bags, was conserved for their own wounded. As a last resort, the warriors had with them an on-the-hoof source of liquid. They thought nothing of drinking warm blood from horses already spent and about to be abandoned.

On one occasion, Mackenzie's regiment had been attacked by the Quahadi band. The engagement took place in the Texas Panhandle, and the warriors were led by Quanah, their principal war chief. Mackenzie soon learned that the Comanche employed different tactics against a military force. The initial onslaught, relying on the element of surprise, quickly separated into a double ring of warriors. Horsemen in one circle loosed a barrage of arrows and lead, hanging low over their fleet ponies. They then maneuvered outward, reloading while the second circle closed to attack. Another lesson learned was the Comanche will never meet a cavalry charge in a head-on clash. The warriors simply splinter apart and envelop the charging troopers by counterattacking on both flanks. Against mounted tribesmen, the classic cavalry charge became an exercise in futility and death.

"Nothing like 'em," O'Hara concluded. "They're tricky buggers, cunning and sly. Damn good fighters."

Clint rubbed his jaw reflectively. "I recollect General Sheridan called them the best light cavalry in the world. From what you say, it's a fair statement."

"Never underestimate the bastards, Mr. Brannock. Your first mistake would almost certainly be your last. They're murderous, God-cursed heathens—red devils!"

Clint looked at him curiously. "Why do I get the feeling you're telling me all this for a reason?"

"By the Jesus!" O'Hara laughed shortly. "I'll answer your question with a question. Would you prefer to learn it the hard way?"

"No," Clint said, raising an uncertain eyebrow. "I'm just wondering if I should read between the lines."

"Are you, now?" O'Hara said bluffly. "And what is it you think I'm trying to say?"

"Without saying it," Clint observed, "maybe you're telling me there's a campaign in the wind. Are we going after the Comanche, Sergeant Major?"

O'Hara's rough features mirrored wry amusement. "Sooner or later we'll take the field, Mr. Brannock. Whether it's sooner than some might think isn't for me to say."

"One thing's for damn sure," Clint informed him. "You leave a man scratching his head."

O'Hara studied him with mock gravity. "You know what troubles me most about the Comanche?"

"What's that?"

"Why do the dirty heathens steal cattle? You think on it a moment, Mr. Brannock. What does a wild, horseback Indian do with cows?"

Clint shook his head from side to side. "I've asked myself the same question. So far I haven't come up with an answer."

"Ask yourself another." O'Hara paused, regarding him with a dour look. "All the tribes steal horses. But only the Comanche and the Kiowa steal cattle. Why do you think it's so?"

"You tell me."

"By all that's holy I wish I could. Just thinkin' on it keeps me awake nights."

"Have you discussed it with the colonel?"

"Oh, aye, indeed I have. He's no less mystified than myself."

"What's his best guess?"

"Not a guess," O'Hara said, "but still another question. Why is it the Comanche have so many repeating rifles?"

When Clint made no reply, O'Hara went on. "All the more worrisome, Mr. Brannock—where do they get 'em?"

"Yeah," Clint said with soft wonder. "Where the hell does an Injun buy rifles?"

O'Hara's voice dropped. "I've an idea it's a place we've never been, Mr. Brannock. A place we've avoided too long now . . . the Staked Plains."

"What Indian trader would have the nerve to go there?"

"By the lord God almighty, there's a question!"

A silence settled over them. They sat and smoked, pondering the question. Neither of them ventured an answer.

14

"WELCOME BACK."

"Good to be home, Will."

"How was Santa Fe?"

Virgil laughed. "Hotter than hell's attic!"

Palmer chuffed a good-natured chuckle. He motioned Virgil to a chair and opened a humidor on top his desk. After selecting cigars, they nipped off the tips and lit up in a dense cloud of smoke. A moment elapsed while they puffed in silence.

"Well?" Palmer said, eyeing him keenly. "Don't keep me in suspense. What happened?"

"I regret to say," Virgil replied, "that New Mexico politicians aren't any different than the rest. It surely tests your faith in mankind."

"In short, they're a bunch of crooks. Is that what you're saying?"

"The same old three Cs. Crooked, crafty, and corrupt."

"So there were no surprises?"

"Nooo," Virgil acknowledged. "Although I'll have to say they're slippery as a barrelful of eels. I didn't get a straight answer the whole time I was there."

Palmer's brow puckered in a frown. "You mean you came back without a deal?"

"I mean they wouldn't say yes and they wouldn't say

no. What they said was 'maybe' and 'probably' and 'let us think about it.' They want some time to think it over.''

"Think what over?'' Palmer rasped. ''We're offering them a railroad!''

"So's the Santa Fe crowd.''

"*What*?''

"Gospel fact,'' Virgil said soberly. ''A fellow named John Tanner was through there last week. Claimed he was the official representative of the Atchison, Topeka & Santa Fe.

"I never heard of him.''

"Neither have I,'' Virgil noted. ''But he's apparently a smooth talker.''

While in Santa Fe, Virgil had attempted to locate Earl. He thought perhaps his brother would have heard local rumors about the politicos' meeting with John Tanner. The mailing address he had for Earl was a second-rate hotel near the Mexican quarter. Upon inquiring, he was informed that his brother was out of town, even though the room had been paid a month in advance. He went away confused and vaguely troubled. He couldn't imagine where Earl had gone, or why.

"One thing's for sure,'' he said now. ''We'll have to go some to outdo this fellow Tanner.''

Palmer's worry lines deepened. ''What was he doing in Santa Fe?''

"Same thing we were,'' Virgil said with a faint smile. ''Trying to buy a railroad charter.''

"Christ,'' Palmer muttered. ''You were right all along. They've got their eye on New Mexico.''

"I'd judge it's more than an eye. From what I was told, they're committed to a southern route.''

Palmer puffed furiously on his cigar. He stared across the desk through a milky haze of smoke. ''How much did this Tanner offer them?''

Virgil shrugged. ''That's a tough one, Will. The boys in

Santa Fe played it real cagey. They said, and I quote, 'It's a substantial amount.' ''

"Goddamn politicians! Every dangblasted one of them was hatched under the same rock."

"Amen to that."

"Am I correct in assuming they intend to play us off against the Santa Fe crowd?"

"On the nose," Virgil affirmed. "We've got ourselves involved in a down-and-dirty auction. The charter goes to the highest bidder."

Palmer munched his cigar. "How much did you offer them?"

"Not a dime."

"What—?"

"Hold your horses, Will. They'd like nothing better than to get us into a bidding war. Before you know it, they'd have the price jacked up sky-high."

"Surely to God you made some sort of counteroffer?"

"Yes, I did," Virgil said hesitantly. "You'll probably blow your stack—"

"Get to it," Palmer interrupted. "How much?"

"No specific dollar figure. I simply assured them that we would top any offer made by the Santa Fe."

"You're mad! That could cost us a fortune—ruin us!"

Virgil wagged his head. "I figure Tanner told them pretty much the same thing. Otherwise, they would have quoted me a figure on the spot."

Palmer glared at him. "So now they'll get a price from the Santa Fe and ask us to top it. Is that what you're saying?"

"Exactly."

"How will we know if they're telling the truth? For Chrissake, they could pick a figure out of thin air."

"Never happen," Virgil said confidently. "What they'll do is boost the Santa Fe's price by about ten percent. We'll better that by another five percent."

"What makes you so all-fired certain?"

"Will, I've had tons of experience with politicians. They're crooks one and all, but they're not dummies. Simply put, they won't bite the hand that feeds them."

Palmer looked doubtful. "Would you care to spell that out?"

"Of course," Virgil said agreeably. "The bigger payoff comes when we start operating in New Mexico. Land grants and right-of-ways provide unlimited possibilities for graft."

"Are you saying we've got them in our pocket?"

"Nothing's a lead-pipe cinch. You pays your money and you takes your chances."

Palmer scowled with stuffed-animal ferocity. "You're awfully damn flippant about it."

"I'm telling you to relax, Will. One way or another, we'll get the charter."

"For all our sakes, I hope you're right. We're fast approaching the sink-or-swim stage."

Palmer's statement was a blunt truth. Construction had been delayed in May by a massive rockslide. Only last week an unseasonable rainstorm had washed out a bridge over a normally dry gully. The repairs in both instances had proved a costly setback in time. Their projected construction schedule had been pushed back by almost two weeks.

Pueblo, which was the next proposed terminus, lay some thirty miles south of Colorado Springs. From there, it was another hundred miles to Raton Pass, the only natural byway through the mountains. Beyond the mountains was New Mexico Territory, and a fortune to be reaped in southwestern rail traffic. Yet they were approaching the middle of June, and their ultimate goal, El Paso, remained a distant mirage. Time had suddenly become an unreplenishable resource.

The problem was critical, even though their tracklaying crews were within ten miles of Pueblo. While stalled by construction delays, they had watched helplessly as the

Santa Fe closed the gap. The latest reports indicated that
Santa Fe workcrews were within fifteen miles of Pueblo
and driving hard. Raton Pass was the crucial objective, but
there was no denying the importance of Pueblo. A supply
depot there would provide a jump-off for the next stage
of construction.

"While you were away," Palmer said now, "I've been
toying with an idea. I believe you've just pushed me into a
decision."

"Oh?" Virgil said, suddenly leery. "What's that?"

A wintry smile lighted Palmer's eyes. "We're going to
hire more men and go to double shifts. I intend to reach
Pueblo no later than two weeks from today."

"You're out of your mind. That would double our
construction costs."

"Damn the cost! We cannot allow the Santa Fe to beat
us to Pueblo. That would jeopardize all our future plans."

"How do you propose to pay for it?" Virgil asked
reasonably. "We're budgeted down to the last nickel."

Palmer gave him a hard wise look. "I propose for the
town of Pueblo to foot the bill. Bright and early tomorrow
morning, I want you to hotfoot it down there and have a
talk with the local muckamucks." He paused, gesturing
with his cigar. "Tell them we want to float a bond issue—
one hundred thousand dollars."

"You're begging trouble," Virgil said darkly. "Why
should they pay our freight? All they have to do is wait for
the Santa Fe to pull into town. So far as they're concerned,
one railroad's as good as another."

"Hardly," Palmer said in a cold dry manner. "Unless
they pay, I'll bypass Pueblo entirely. We'll make a straight
run for Raton Pass."

"What about a new supply depot?"

"We'll locate it somewhere outside Pueblo. Perhaps
start a whole new town."

Virgil looked at him. "Like you started Colorado
Springs?"

"Precisely." Palmer grinned through bluish cigar smoke. "What worked here will work equally well there."

"And if we bypass them, they lose an outlet to the Southwest. Isn't that the gist of it?"

"Virgil, you've just made our case. I have no doubt you'll persuade them easily enough."

"Thanks, but no, thanks."

"I beg your pardon?"

"Well, it's like this," Virgil said coolly. "I'll make deals with crooked politicians, but I won't sandbag a whole town. You do your own dirty work."

Palmer's voice was clipped, incisive. "I commend your Christian attitude. However, I believe you've overlooked the salient point."

"What might that be?"

"Quite simply, you're a minority shareholder. Your position as vice president depends solely on my goodwill. Either you follow orders or you're out of a job."

Virgil's mouth set in a hard line. "You wouldn't fire me, Will. I'm the pipeline between you and the moneymen."

"On the contrary," Palmer advised him. "You've arranged all the finances we're likely to obtain. I could do without you very nicely."

A moment elapsed while the two men stared at each other. "I've met some cold bastards," Virgil said finally, "but you take the prize hands down."

Palmer laughed cynically. "The army spoiled me, Virgil. I became accustomed to being obeyed. You'll have to indulge me, I'm afraid."

Virgil managed a strained smile. "Do I have to call you general, too?"

Palmer ignored the gibe. "Let's understand one another. We're 'partners' only so long as you follow my wishes. Otherwise, you can retire and collect dividends on your stock. Do I make myself clear?"

"Crystal-clear." Virgil uncoiled from his chair. "I'll leave for Pueblo in the morning."

On his way out, Virgil slammed the door. Palmer took a puff on his cigar, slowly assessed the situation. He realized he'd played his trump card and made an enemy in the bargain. An enemy who would neither forgive nor forget.

He began considering ways that he might rid himself of Virgil Brannock.

Pueblo was situated in the southern foothills of the Rockies. The surrounding landscape was arid, despite the proximity of the Arkansas River to the town. Eastward lay a vista of broken plains, and to the west there was a panorama of jutting mountains.

The town had a history of settlement. In 1806 Zebulon Pike camped with his expedition at the confluence of Fountain Creek with the Arkansas. Forty years later a band of Mormons settled there briefly on their way to Utah. A trading post was established shortly after their departure, and the original townsite was laid out in 1859. Stage service to Denver began in 1862.

Unlike much of Colorado, there were no gold strikes in Pueblo. The population, after fourteen years of settlement, hovered around the thousand mark. Apart from hardscrabble farms, the only source of livelihood was the coalfields located outside town. Development was slow, and the community seemed mired in the backwaters of economic progress. The town leaders saw it as a form of stagnation, erosion rather than growth. They anxiously awaited the arrival of the railroad.

Virgil stepped off the stage early the next afternoon. His first stop was the town's one hotel, where he registered for the night. In his room, he penned notes to Pueblo's mayor and the local banker. He requested a meeting, alluding to a matter of interest involving the Denver & Rio Grande. The hotel owner arranged to have the notes delivered and there was an immediate response from both men. The meeting was set for three o'clock.

As usual, Virgil had done his homework. Through contacts in Colorado Springs, he had gathered a dossier on the two most influential men in Pueblo. Ned Wagner, the mayor, was one of the original settlers. In addition to operating a hardware store, he owned some farmland and a piece of the livery stable. The local banker, Chester Oldham, was heavily invested in the coalfields and held title to a tract of land on the outskirts of town. Oldham, in Virgil's view, was the key to floating a bond issue.

Today, Virgil was not so punctual. He emerged from the hotel at ten minutes after three and sauntered along the town's main street. His tardiness was calculated, designed to put the men on edge. He meant to keep them off balance and uncertain by making them wait. Further, he intended to establish an order of dominance from the outset. His job here was personally repugnant, the sort of tactic he associated with unscrupulous railroad builders. Yet, for all his reluctance, he thought it could be handled with a degree of fairness. To that end, he wanted Oldham and Wagner to understand that their options wavered between slim and none. For Pueblo, the Denver & Rio Grande was it.

The bookkeeper ushered Virgil into Oldham's private office. A sturdy man, the banker's beard was dappled with gray and his hair was thinning out above a craggy forehead. Ned Wagner was almost cadaverous in build, with watery brown eyes and a reedy voice. He sat as if nailed to his chair, hands clasped tightly across his stomach. Virgil walked into the office all beaming geniality.

"Mr. Brannock!" Oldham bounced out of his chair. "A pleasure sir."

Virgil accepted his handshake. "I appreciate your making time, Mr. Oldham."

"Not at all," Oldham said jovially. "Let me introduce our mayor, Ned Wagner."

Wagner unfolded from his chair like a slim accordion.

His handshake was moist and limp. "Pleased to meet you, Mr. Brannock."

At Oldham's request, Virgil took a wooden armchair. Wagner resumed his seat and the banker sat down behind the desk. There was a moment of oppressive silence while the two men stared expectantly at Virgil. Finally, Oldham found his voice.

"Well now, Mr. Brannock, your note was most intriguing. I gather you're here on railroad business?"

Virgil spread his hands. "That depends on you gentlemen, Mr. Oldham. I'm here seeking an accommodation."

"Accommodation?" Oldham echoed, as though testing the word. "I'm not sure I understand."

"As you know, the Denver & Rio Grande has surveyed a line to Pueblo. We thought to make it our next terminus."

"Yes," Oldham said eagerly. "Please go on."

Virgil spoke in a carefully measured voice. "I'll be frank with you, gentlemen. We feel your town should be more actively involved in the venture." He paused, allowed the idea to percolate an instant. "We'd like you to put through a bond issue, to show good faith. Something on the order of a hundred thousand."

There was a moment of stunned silence. Then, sputtering hoarsely, Oldham recovered. "Dollars?" he said, pop-eyed with shock. "A hundred thousand dollars?"

Virgil nodded. "We consider it a reasonable gesture."

"Horsefeathers!" Wagner spat angrily. "It's highway robbery, pure and simple."

"Worse than that," Oldham added, "it's out-and-out extortion. We will not pay it. Never!"

"Sorry to hear it," Virgil announced. "No bond issue, no railroad, and it's just that simple. We'll bypass Pueblo altogether."

"You're bluffing," Wagner snapped.

"No, Mr. Mayor, I'm dead-serious. We're prepared to lay out a whole new town north of here. You'll recall that's how Colorado Springs came about."

Oldham's mouth went tight and bloodless. "You've conveniently forgotten the Santa Fe, Mr. Brannock. Their representative, John Tanner, stopped by here day before yesterday. He assured me their tracks will hit town before the end of the month."

Virgil wasn't at all surprised. He marked again that John Tanner was an adversary worthy of respect. In Santa Fe, and now again in Pueblo, the man had beaten him to the punch. He wondered when their trails would actually cross.

"Let's be realistic," he said, looking at Oldham. "If we build a town north of here, the Santa Fe won't save you. We'll control the access route from Denver, and that's that." He hesitated, underscoring the thought. "Pueblo would wither on the vine."

"Very clever," Oldham said, jaws clenched. "We go with you or we go to hell. Is that it?"

"The Denver & Rio Grande prefers a harmonious relationship, Mr. Oldham. Suppose I could make it worth your while to support the bond issue?"

Oldham looked at him blankly. "I don't follow you."

Virgil kept his gaze level. "I'm told you own a parcel of land on the edge of town. It so happens, we'll need land for our depot and railyards. Do you follow me now?"

Oldham's eyes did a slow roll. "By gravy, I think I do, Mr. Brannock. Assuming, of course, we're talking a decent price."

Thumbs hooked in his vest, Virgil grinned broadly. "One thing you can always count on. The Denver & Rio Grande treats its friends real generously."

"Goddarnit!" Wagner suddenly broke in. "When do we get my irons in this here fire? I'd think the mayor of the town deserves something, too."

"Well, naturally," Virgil said vigorously. "Suppose we contract with your hardware store to supply our work gangs and repair shop. How does that sound?"

"Juicy," Wagner cackled. "Plumb juicy."

"Gentlemen, I think we're in business. I'll expect you to move right along on the bond issue."

After mutual assurances and a round of handshakes, Virgil walked from the bank. He was by no means proud of himself, but neither was he contrite. All things considered, it was an equitable and rather cozy arrangement. The town fathers got a little richer and the town got not one, but two railroads. As for the bond issue and the hike in tax rates, it was the same old tune.

The people, as usual, got stiffed.

15

THE KIOWA war party rode into camp on a blazing summer afternoon. There were some twenty warriors, hazing along a large herd of longhorn cattle. Guarded closely were three captives, one boy and two young girls.

While awaiting their arrival, Earl had heard a good deal about the Kiowa. At night, seated around the campfire, Ramón Guerra had spoken of them at length. His tone was one of respect, for he considered the Kiowa somewhat more advanced than the Comanche. He evidenced as well a curious mix of fear and admiration.

"Take care," he'd said one night. "Never allow yourself to be taken prisoner by the Kiowa."

"Why is that?" Earl asked.

"Because they enjoy torture. Compared to Kiowas, the Comanche are merciful."

"I always heard the worst torturers were the Apache."

"¡Caramba!" Guerra laughed. "You have much to learn, *compadre*. The Kiowa are masters of the art— *bárbaros*!"

Earl seemed puzzled. "Sounds to me like a contradiction. You said before they're fairly civilized."

"Not civilized," Guerra corrected. "Their ways are perhaps more enlightened than other *indios*. But that makes them no less savage."

The *Comanchero* leader went on to explain. The tribal culture of the Kiowa was the most elaborate on the south-

ern Plains. Their religion was rich in pageantry and folklore, centered around *taime* dolls. These were sacred idols,
stone images handed down from ancient times. Holy men,
somewhat like priests, were entrusted as the keepers of the
taime figures. No greater honor could be bestowed on a
member of the tribe.

Kiowa rituals were also more elaborate. They revered
the sun, and their bands gathered every year to perform a
dance and worship before the Sun Doll. Unlike the
Comanche, they possessed a sense of tribal history. Older
men, too aged for the war trail, kept detailed calendars,
tanned hides painted with pictographs of memorable events.
Of all the Plains tribes, only the Kiowa accepted the
concept of lineage and hierarchy.

A society composed of the ten greatest warriors formed
a military aristocracy. In the Kiowa tongue they were the
Koh-eet-senko, the Society of the Ten Bravest. These men
were sworn to lead in battle, always fighting at the forefront, until they were victorious or struck dead. Their
leader wore a black elkskin sash that trailed down to the
ground, and custom dictated that he take the vanguard in
battle. There, he pinned the sash to the ground with a
ceremonial arrow and stood fast while the battle swirled
around him. No leader of the *Koh-eet-senko* had ever been
known to retreat.

For all that, the Comanche nonetheless looked upon the
Kiowa as an inferior people. The two nations were bound
together by an ancient alliance; but the Comanche considered themselves the stronger tribe and greater warriors in
battle. While the Kiowa were the more accomplished
torturers, the Comanche were shrewder tacticians and bolder
in their approach to warfare. As in times past, when the
Comanche led the way against the Spanish, they now
carried the fight to the Anglos. Over the generations the
Kiowa had adopted the role of tolerated vassals.

The war party that rode into the village today was no
different. Tall Bear, their leader, was a member of the

Koh-eet-senko. His valor in battle was beyond question, and no man would heedlessly challenge him to a fight. Yet his entrance into camp went largely unnoticed, for a Kiowa, whatever his fame, was accorded no honors in *Comanchería*. The feeling was deepened by the fact that Tall Bear's band usually wintered on the reservation. The Quahadi frowned on anyone, Comanche or Kiowa, who took handouts from the *americanos*.

Tall Bear and his warriors had jumped the reservation a month past. Their raid had taken them deep into Texas, almost to the Rio Grande. A clash with pony soldier scouts, half-breed *negritos* led by a white man, had turned them northward again. With the herd of longhorns, they had ridden toward the canyon of Yellow Houses, hopeful of meeting the *Comancheros*. That hope was compounded by the fact that they had taken three young *tejanos* captive. The risk of returning to the reservation with white children was considered too great. Tall Bear planned to exchange them for trade goods.

As negotiations got under way, Earl looked on with simmering anger. He paid little attention to the haggling that went on between Guerra and Tall Bear. His thoughts, instead, were on the boy and the two girls. They appeared to be seven or eight years old and thoroughly terrified of their captors. Worn and bedraggled, they looked drained by the long ride northward. Yet, oddly enough, there was no sign that they had been abused or mistreated. The Kiowa apparently hoped to fetch a better price by presenting them in decent shape.

Earl felt a strong tug of conscience. Still, nothing he could do or say would stop the tribes from taking captives. In fact, his guilt was alleviated somewhat by his role in such affairs. As a *Comanchero*, he would be instrumental in ransoming captives and returning them to their families. He tried not to think about Guerra, who would demand a profit on the exchange. Nor would he allow himself to dwell on those captives who were never offered for trade.

The Quahadi, in particular, were often reluctant to barter away captives. They adopted them instead, as a means of infusing new blood into the band. Several times, walking through the village, Earl had seen both Anglo and Mexican youngsters who were content with their lot. The wild life seemed to agree with them, and Guerra had told him that few of them would willingly return to their former lives. To make his point, Guerra had related the story of Quanah, who was actually a half-breed. Quanah's mother, Cynthia Ann Parker, had been taken captive as a nine-year-old. Some twenty-five years later she was captured by an army patrol and returned to her family in Texas. After several attempts to escape, she finally starved herself to death. Among the Comanche, it was said she died of a broken heart.

Earl was inclined to agree. Only a short time in camp had greatly affected his thinking. He found himself unaccountably fascinated by these horseback barbarians. Their life on the plains was harsh, and the cruelty imposed on their enemies was revolting to behold. But they enjoyed a freedom beyond anything a white man might imagine. No warrior was bound to accept the orders, or the dictates, of another Comanche. Even a great leader such as Quanah was followed by those who chose to follow. So far as Earl could see, it was an undiluted form of democracy. A Comanche, for the most part, did as he damn well pleased.

As for the women, they were far less bound than white women. They were respected members of the band, valued for their ability to tan robes and feed and clothe their families. Seldom submissive, they ruled their lodges and demanded a certain equality with their warrior husbands. As well, they encouraged their men to take a number of wives. Their chores were easier when divided among several women, and the arrangement rarely fostered jealousy. Often as not, a woman's husband chose her younger sisters to share the lodge.

The idea had no great appeal for Earl. While he was

fond of Little Raven, one Indian wife seemed to him
enough. She was affectionate and delighted in spoiling him,
and he found himself returning the sentiment. What he felt
for her was hardly the depth of emotion he'd shared with
Monte. But he enjoyed her company, and all in all it
seemed a congenial arrangement. He was free to come and
go, and the marriage imposed no bonds outside *Comanchería*.
He sometimes thought he had the best of both worlds.

Guerra shortly concluded his talk with Tall Bear. The
longhorn herd and the three young captives were exchanged
for a wagonload of trade goods. The Kiowa leader appeared pleased with himself, and Guerra, as usual, had got
the best of the bargain. Upon his return to Santa Fe, he
would collect double the price of the trade goods for the
children alone. The cattle would boost his profits several-
fold more.

With a final handshake, Guerra walked away from Tall
Bear. He motioned to Zarate and Earl, and they fell in
beside him. He seemed in excellent humor.

"We've done well," he said expansively, nodding to
Zarate. "There will be something extra for you and the
men."

"*Gracias, patrón*," Zarate replied. "They will be pleased
by your generosity."

Guerra glanced at Earl. "And you, *compadre*? Are you
satisfied with your first venture as a *Comanchero*?"

"Yeah, I am," Earl said smiling. "It's like a license to
print money."

"So it is," Guerra agreed genially. "What will you do
with your profits?"

"I'd thought to reinvest the whole works. Double it and
double it again."

"A wise decision, my friend. We will settle accounts
when we reach Santa Fe."

"Well, as to that . . . ." Earl hesitated, then went on. "I
figured I might stick around a while longer. Spotted Dog
has invited me to join a buffalo hunt."

Guerra exchanged a look with the hunchback. Zarate's expression was unreadable, but he uttered a low grunt. After a moment, the *Comanchero* leader fixed Earl with an inquiring gaze.

"This invitation from your father-in-law . . . how was it extended?"

"I've picked up some Spanish and Little Raven's been teaching me sign language. Between the two, I'm able to make myself understood."

"Is it merely the buffalo hunt"—Guerra paused, eyeing him quizzically—"or have you some wish to remain with the Comanche?"

"Nothing permanent," Earl said easily. "Guess I'm just curious because it's all new. I'd like to hang around another week or so."

Guerra was silent, thoughtful. "You would never find your way back to Santa Fe alone. I will leave a man to act as your guide."

"Good idea," Earl said. "I'm obliged."

"Perhaps you will also take some advice?"

"Why, sure thing. What's that?"

"The Comanche way of life is not for us, *compadre*. Do not let yourself be lured into thinking otherwise. I've seen good men ruined once they turned Indian."

"Indian?" Earl echoed. "What makes you think I'd do a fool thing like that?"

Guerra shrugged. "Consider it a friendly warning. Temptation comes in many forms."

The *Comancheros* departed early next morning. Earl stood outside his lodge, watching until the herd of longhorns was a distant speck on the plains. He told himself that Guerra's warning, however genuine, was a tad far-fetched. The idea of him turning Indian was preposterous.

Chuckling to himself, he ducked through the door hole of the lodge. Little Raven, who always slept naked, held out her arms with seductive innocence. He dropped down beside her on their bedrobes.

* * *

A tawny sun stood high in the sky. Four men comprised
the hunting party, with Spotted Dog and Earl in the lead.
They were mounted on fleet war ponies.

Before them, a herd of buffalo grazed placidly on a
verdant plain. The shaggy beasts took no notice of the
horsemen, who proceeded forward at a slow walk. Some
distance to the rear, Little Raven waited with the women
of the other warriors. Like the men, they were mounted on
sturdy ponies.

To the Comanche, a horse was almost a sacred object.
In their language, which was often highly symbolic, the
term for horse was "god dog." Wealth was determined by
the number of horses a warrior owned, and adept horse-
stealing was considered proof of manhood. A nomadic
people, constantly on the move, their lives centered around
horses. For them, the god dog was as indispensable as the
earth itself.

Unlike many tribes, the Comanche were also skilled
horse-breeders. They stole fine livestock from the *tejanos*
and periodically captured wild horses from the herds that
roamed *Llano Estacado*. The bloodlines were then mixed,
and the result was war ponies bred for speed and stamina.
While the women and older men used saddles, warriors
invariably rode bareback. For a bridle, they used a braided
rawhide thong, looped over the horse's lower jaw. In war,
as in the hunt, their ponies were trained to respond to knee
commands. Thus a man's hands could be freed from the
bridle and devoted instead to his weapons.

Today, Earl saw a demonstration of the fabled Comanche
horsemanship. Spotted Dog and the other two warriors
kneed their ponies into a gallop and charged the buffalo
herd. Thundering along behind them, he watched as the
buffalo stampeded in headlong flight. The warriors carried
stout bows, constructed of *bois d'arc*, and their hunting
arrows were tipped with iron broadheads. Drawing abreast

of the herd, they each selected an animal and nudged their ponies closer. At a distance of mere feet, they loosed the feathered shafts.

Spotted Dog, perhaps to impress his *tahbay-boh* son-in-law, had selected a huge buffalo bull. As his bowstring twanged, his pony instantly swerved aside, trained to avoid the hook and slash of deadly horns. The arrow penetrated behind the short rib and went clean through the bull, embedding itself in the ground. Snorting blood, the bull lumbered on for perhaps another hundred yards. Then, like a monolith brought to earth, the great animal collapsed in midstride. Spotted Dog raised his bow overhead in an exultant roar.

Not to be outdone, Earl rode up alongside a buffalo cow. He extended his pistol and placed three shots within a handspan below the shoulder. The cow slowed, drifting off to one side, and crumpled to her knees. A gout of blood jetted from her nostrils, and her hindquarters suddenly buckled. She dropped to the ground, one leg jerking in afterdeath, and then lay still. Earl spun his pony about and looked back at Spotted Dog. The old warrior nodded approval and allowed himself a wide grin. Later, seated around the campfire, he would tell the story of his son-in-law's first kill.

The herd rumbled off across the flat grassland. As the women rode forward, the men dismounted and unsheathed their knives. In short order, the downed buffalo were skinned out and the robes set aside. The women then undertook the job of butchering, their knives flashing red in the sunlight. Little Raven offered Earl one of the delicacies of the kill, a slice of hot liver smeared with juice from the gall bladder. He found it surprisingly tasty, but he declined another choice morsel. Somewhat awed, he watched as she lopped off a section of warm gut and stripped it between her teeth.

That evening they feasted on hump steak and ribs. The

meat was cooked over a bed of fiery coals, emerging charred on the outside and blood-red within. Other sections of meat would be stewed in metal pots, acquired from the *Comancheros* and much prized by the women. Fully half the meat taken in the day's hunt was passed along to the aged ones of the band. No Quahadi went hungry when there was fresh meat in the camp.

After the meal, Little Raven busied herself around the lodge. Earl seated himself on the ground outside and lit a slim cheroot. He felt gorged on meat and thoroughly content with the moment. He stared out across the village, aware of a serenity unlike anything he'd ever known. Somewhere a child laughed and outside nearby lodges warriors and their families lazed around low fires bright with embers. He thought it a good life, a full life. He idly reflected on all he'd learned about the Comanche.

What impressed him most was the distribution of work within the band. By tradition, everyone was assigned specific tasks, and the system was immensely practical. Warriors defended the village against enemy attack and periodically raided below the Red River. While in camp, they broke and trained horses, and attended to their war gear. Fashioning arrowheads occupied a good deal of their time, and they were masters of the craft. Scraps of iron, cut from barrel hoops and old frying pans, were heated in a fire and then hammered into shape. Once tempered in cold water, the arrowheads were filed to a keen edge. Firearms were much coveted, but no warrior was ever without his bow and a bullhide quiver of arrows.

When camp was moved, the women displayed one of their principal crafts. The typical lodge consisted of tanned buffalo hides sewn together with sinew and fitted over a framework of supple poles. Usually fourteen feet in diameter, it was large enough to accommodate five to eight people. In the winter it could withstand the most violent blizzards, and in the summer, with the sides rolled up, it was shady and cool. The lodge could be set up by a woman in fifteen minutes or less, and taken down in five. An entire camp, with all its belongings, could be packed and on the move in twenty minutes.

Once a camp was established, the women never lacked for chores. They sewed colorful buckskin dresses, which were decorated with glass beads and fringe. For their men, they fashioned breechclouts and leggings, which was a moccasin-boot that stretched from foot to hip. Winter boots were sewn of bison wool, and for outerwear, furry robes rather than blankets were preferred during cold weather. Aside from sewing and cooking, part of each day was spent gathering wild berries, nuts, and a variety of roots. All these supplemented a diet that consisted largely of buffalo meat and antelope. A special treat for children was a form of candy made from mesquite beans and bone marrow.

To Earl, it seemed an idyllic existence. The Comanche lived in harmony with the earth and all its creatures. Great herds of buffalo provided food and shelter, and the tribe killed only what was needed to subsist. Apart from *tejanos* and their ancient enemies, the Apache, they also lived in harmony with man. They were proud and perhaps a bit arrogant, but nonetheless generous in spirit. On *Llano Estacado*, where they roamed free as the wind, they were at peace with their world. He thought white men might learn much from their example.

Some inner voice abruptly mocked him. As though from afar, he heard again Ramón Guerra's warning. All his woolgathering about the Comanche suddenly seemed a danger signal. He told himself to beware, for it was apparent that a man could grow comfortable with such a life. Soon, within a fortnight or so, he would have to return to his own world. While happenstance had made him a *Comanchero*, it was foolhardy to think of himself as a Comanche. He was, in the end, what he would always remain, a *tahbay-boh*.

The realization saddened him. But then, his mind drifted back to Santa Fe and a slow smile touched his mouth. A squaw here and a *señorita* there was hardly reason for complaint.

Perhaps, after all, he would have the best of both worlds. The more he considered it, the better the idea sounded. He puffed his cheroot and dreamed awhile longer.

16

THE JULY FOURTH celebration began at sundown. Enlisted men, except for those unfortunate enough to draw guard duty, were allowed to leave the post. Virtually en masse they trooped into Brackettville.

The officers' Grand Ball was held in the headquarters building. The ballroom, which normally served as the officers' mess, had been cleared of furniture earlier that day. Patriotic bunting and flags were then draped from the walls, and paper lanterns, aglow with tiny candles, hung from the ceiling. A crystal punch bowl, centered on a long table, was flanked by cold meats, bread, and an assortment of desserts. Whiskey for the officers and sherry for their ladies was dispensed by three privates impersonating bartenders.

Across the parade ground, a similar function was under way for the noncommissioned officers. A large room in the hospital had been cleared for the night and decorated in a patriotic manner. Several inmates from the guardhouse had spent the afternoon waxing the floor, until it shone like mirrored glass. Unlike the officers, the noncoms' punch bowl was lightly laced with spirits. Stronger libations were served by the drink, with the unstated admonition that no man would exceed his limit.

As darkness fell, two separate parades slowly formed. From officers' row, the officers and their wives streamed toward the regimental headquarters. The bachelor officers, who were in a majority, ensured that none of the ladies would sit out a dance during the evening. From the opposite direction, the noncoms and their wives strolled toward the hospital. While their finery was not as fine as the officers' wives, they were nonetheless resplendent in their best gowns.

Neither group passed within speaking distance of the other, which was another of those unwritten military customs. Officers' wives, unless forced to it, seldom spoke to the women of noncoms' row.

Seated outside his quarters, Clint watched the proceedings with sardonic amusement. The army's caste system seemed to him a humorous and somewhat stodgy institution. His years as a scout had taught him that people were people, whether they wore chevrons or stars. The officers were perhaps better educated and their ladies were generally more refined. Yet it was the noncoms who actually ran the army, often bypassing regulations and officers alike. As for their women, he much preferred them to officers' wives, who were overly impressed by rank. A woman with her nose in the air struck him as a farce in skirts.

Oddly enough, many of the noncoms' wives had started out on officers' row. Unmarried girls, hired as cooks and servants, were imported through employment agencies back East. An eligible female who arrived at a western garrison shortly found herself besieged by lonely soldiers. However homely—and many were downright unattractive—they were quickly swamped with proposals. The officers' wives complained and attempted to bribe them, but all to no avail. A new girl was usually married and ensconced on noncoms' row within a month after reaching the post.

The problem was solved, in part, by reverting to an old army custom. To pacify their wives, many officers hired soldiers from the ranks as family servants. In military parlance they were called strikers, and earned five or ten dollars a month extra pay. As a rule, they were relieved of routine duties, which made it a highly coveted job. The practice had been outlawed in 1870, but western outposts were far from Washington. Officers of every rank ignored the regulation in an effort to quiet their wives. A striker, unlike imported servant girls, rarely got involved in matrimony. At Fort Clark, as at other garrisons, the custom flourished.

In other respects, the women on a post were remarkably alike. To relieve the boredom of army life, they organized all manner of social activities. Tonight's formal balls, celebrating the nation's independence, were but one example. The officers' ladies and their counterparts on noncoms' row were continually engaged in tea parties, sewing bees, and gala dinners. Musicales were popular, and on occasion they pestered their husbands into accepting roles in amateur theatrical plays. Outdoor activities, such as horseback riding and picnics, were sporadic, rarely held during the hostiles' raiding season. Any excuse would do for a soiree, however, and there was a steady round of such affairs.

While social events were rigidly separated, the caste system broke down at other times. When the bugle sounded officers' call, Judy O'Grady and the captain's lady shared the anxiety of all army wives. They waited in quiet dread whenever the company commanders were summoned to the colonel's office for marching orders. Then, later, as the troops rode out and the regimental band played a lively air, they struggled to smile bravely and suppress their tears. Where their men were concerned, they were very much sisters under the skin. All too often, without regard to rank, the army made widows of them.

Clint felt little envy toward married men. Home-cooked meals and someone to wash and iron seemed to him a poor bargain in exchange for freedom. All of his adult life he'd been afflicted with itchy feet and a severe case of wander-

lust. What lay over the next hill was far more important
than the companionship of a good woman. Nor was he
struck by any great urge to sire another generation in his
likeness. He thought Virgil and Earl had extended the
Brannock bloodline aplenty. By choice, he'd made his
own life a roll of the dice. He never looked back and he
seldom wondered about the future. One day at a time
suited him just fine.

Across the way, he heard the opening dance numbers.
Half the regimental band was at the officers' ball and the
other half was playing for the noncoms. Unofficially, as
chief of scouts, he was welcome at either affair. Yet the
caste system extended to civilian scouts as well as the
enlisted men. No one had bothered to invite him to the
officers' ball, and his appearance there would have proved
a minor embarrassment. As for the noncoms, he had received a verbal invitation from the sergeant major himself.
No dancer, and admittedly poor at small talk, he was
reluctant to attend. Still, the invitation was an honor of
sorts and not to be taken lightly. He decided to drop by for
a couple of minutes.

Earlier, he had washed and shaved and changed into a
clean shirt. Hardly formal attire, it was the best he could
manage, since he hadn't owned a suit in years. Yet, as he
entered the hospital ballroom, he felt like a poorly groomed
hayseed. The ladies wore colorful gowns, their hair coiffed
and teased, and the men were tricked out in full-dress
uniforms. Sergeant Major Michael O'Hara was the most
resplendent of the lot. Stiffly elegant in the dark-blue
tunic, he wore a high collar, and his cuff tabs were trimmed
in gold and his chest glittered with medals. The piping on
his trousers was also gold, and the sleeves of his tunic
were a sunburst of chevrons. He looked like he'd stepped
out of the pages of a Prussian military manual.

"Mr. Brannock," he said jovially. "We're glad you
could join us."

Clint nodded absently. "Quite a turnout. Guess everybody's here."

"They are indeed!" O'Hara boomed. "Not a one would dare to stay away. After all, we're celebrating independence from bloody King George."

Clint smiled. "Spoken like a true Irishman."

"Aye, and proud of it. Though prouder still to be an American. We've built ourselves a grand country, Mr. Brannock."

"No argument there," Clint said with a good-humored shrug. "Fact is, I'm almost glad the Confederacy lost. 'Dixie' wouldn't make much of a national anthem."

O'Hara burst out laughing. "Well now, I never thought I'd hear that from a Johnny Reb such as yourself. By the sweet Jesus, let's drink on it!"

Beaming a wide grin, O'Hara led him to the refreshment table. Several company sergeants greeted Clint and warmly shook his hand. He noted their festive mood and shortly understood why they weren't on the dance floor. A private, serving tonight as bartender, set out two glasses and poured drinks from a square bottle. Clint studied the amber liquid.

"Irish whiskey," O'Hara informed him. "We saved it special for the occasion."

Clint lifted his glass. "Here's mud in your eye, Sergeant Major."

"And your very good health, Mr. Brannock."

Clinking glasses, they knocked back their drinks. O'Hara smacked his lips appreciatively and swiped his mustache with a thorny finger. Clint took a moment to catch his breath before attempting to speak.

"Got a nice bite, doesn't it?"

O'Hara chortled out loud. "There's much to be said for the old country, Mr. Brannock. Kentucky bourbon doesn't hold a candle to good Irish whiskey. Damn me if it's not a fact!"

"I'm a Missourian myself," Clint said without irony.

"So I won't come to the defense of the Kaintucks or their bourbon. Personally, I've always been partial to white lightning."

"White lightning, you say? And what might that be?"

"A dab of this and a dab of that. Usually corn-mash whiskey made in a backwoods still. Guaranteed to snap your suspenders."

"By the saints," O'Hara said, suddenly brimming with patriotism. "That's what makes it such a glorious country. Every man free to choose what suits him best. Have you ever wondered on it, Mr. Brannock?"

Clint looked bemused. He'd never considered liquor in the same light as freedom of speech and other constitutional guarantees. But on the Fourth of July, coming from an Irishman turned American, it made perfect sense. He thought it rather sage observation.

Mary Margaret O'Hara appeared at her husband's elbow. She was short and plump, wisps of gray starting to show in her flame-red hair. She sniffed the sergeant major's breath and her corseted bosoms heaved. Her brow wrinkled in a tiny frown.

"Aren't you one to be setting the example, Mr. O'Hara? Would you have the men so drunk they're not able to dance?"

"Hush, woman," O'Hara said gruffly. "We've only one bottle of the good stuff, and that near gone. Allow us to finish it in peace."

"Humph!" Mrs. O'Hara snorted. "For all your fancy braid, you're still a trooper at heart. And you've not danced with me once tonight."

O'Hara brightened with sudden inspiration. "You remember the missus," he said, clamping Clint's arm in a viselock grip. "Be a good lad and show her some of your fancy footwork. She's a marvelous dancer, light as a feather!"

Clint's protest was cut short as the sergeant major propelled him forward. Mrs. O'Hara shot her husband a waspish look and then stepped into Clint's arms with a beatific smile. Across the room, the bandleader gave a downbeat and the musicians thumped into a waltz.

Feeling somewhat like a plowboy, Clint tried to get his feet in harness with the tempo. Mrs. O'Hara, who was a head shorter and strong as a stevedore, clung to him with all her might. Trying to make the best of it, he shoved her around the polished dance floor, steering a path through the other couples. His one hope was to finish the number without stomping her toes.

The waltz ended mercifully soon. As the band segued into a sprightly reel, Clint walked Mrs. O'Hara back to the refreshment table. The sergeant major accepted his wife's hand with a look of amiable resignation. She hauled him onto the dance floor and he swept into the reel with surprising agility for a man his size. Clint watched until they were lost in the crowd, then turned and beat a hasty retreat. He figured he'd paid his respects for the night.

Outside, he paused to roll a smoke. After lighting up, he tugged his hat down and started across the parade ground. A quick walk brought him to the sutler's store and there he turned onto the road toward town. The one drink had whetted his thirst and he thought he might organize a celebration of his own. He knew a place where no one would ask him to dance.

The sky was flecked with stars. As he ambled along in the pale light, his mind went back to the conversation with O'Hara. It occurred to him that men who had emigrated from distant shores were often more patriotic than native-born Americans. Or perhaps they were simply more outspoken about the freedoms that most people took for granted. Either way, it was a curiosity he'd noted on army posts across the West. The newcomers, whatever their nationality, were inevitably the most zealous.

Clint was not an introspective man. Still, as he reflected

on it, he saw something he'd never quite fathomed before.
Sherman and Sheridan, not to mention Ulysses S. Grant,
believed in the righteousness of westward expansion. Their
cause was God-ordained, predestined that they should open
wild and bountiful land to settlement. They saw themselves as superior to the horseback tribes, armed mission-
aries opposed by murderous heathens. The Indians, in their
view, were no more than expendable savages.

The attitudes of the generals were reflected throughout
the officer corps. Even Mackenzie, who respected the
Comanches' fighting ability, held the Indians in contempt.
It was both understandable and natural that these same
attitudes would filter down through the ranks. Like a
contagion, it spread from the sergeant major to the lowliest
enlisted man. Because the men in the ranks were mostly
foreign-born, the God-ordained attitude joined hands with
their zealous patriotism. The result was an explosive force
waiting to be unleashed.

Suddenly, as though a fog had lifted, Clint saw the
future. The Comanche and all the other hostile tribes were
living on borrowed time. One day soon, when the government's peace policy failed, the army juggernaut would be
loosed. Then, with terrible swiftness, the hostiles would be
run to ground and destroyed.

Clint found it a sobering vision. All the more so because
the defeat of the wild tribes would end his life as a scout.
For men such as himself the final campaign loomed as a
last hurrah.

The Oriental Saloon was owned by an émigré Dutch-
man. The name of the dive was somewhat misleading, a
figment of his imagination. There was nothing Oriental or
even vaguely exotic about the establishment.

Tonight, like most of the joints in Brackettville, the
Oriental was packed. A regiment of troopers, out celebrating the Fourth of July, jammed every saloon and hurdy-

gurdy dance hall along the town's main street. By dawn, a good many of them would be sleeping it off in the guardhouse.

Clint shouldered himself a spot at the end of the bar. All the tables were full, and along the opposite wall a couple of faro dealers were doing a brisk business. At the rear of the room was a platform stage, with a fiddler and a piano player. The main attraction was a curvaceous singer by the name of Lottie Hall. Local rumor had it that she'd acquired the name because she was a "lot of woman." Her voice, which was a sultry alto, did nothing to dispel the myth.

The saloon was quiet as a church as she rendered the last lines of an Irish ballad. When the final note faded, the spellbound troopers broke out in wild cheers and applause. After taking several bows, she stepped off the stage and threaded her way through the crowd. Unlike the bar girls, she never worked the back-room cribs, where passion sold for a dollar. She was an entertainer who bestowed her favors on a select clientele. Few troopers, apart from well-heeled sergeants, had ever visited her room upstairs. The price was roughly equivalent to a week's pay.

For all that, every man in the saloon lusted after Lottie Hall. She was a vest-pocket Venus, with a stemlike waist, jutting breasts, and perfectly rounded hips. Her features were attractive, with creamy skin and a lush coral mouth that accentuated her high cheekbones. Onstage or off, she was every soldier's fantasy. She seemed to them a bawdy nymph, eminently desirable but unattainable. The memory of her conjured dreams on still nights in the barracks.

She made her way to the end of the bar. With a small wave, she parted the troopers standing three deep and wedged in beside Clint. Over the past few months they had gotten to know one another on an informal, though rather intimate basis. She liked his company and found him somewhat more gallant than her usual customers. She also derived a perverse thrill in the knowledge that other men considered him dangerous. On an average of once a week he slept over in her room upstairs.

"Hello, there," she greeted him. "Where have you been keeping yourself?"

Clint smiled a lazy smile. "Just got back off a patrol yesterday. Figured I'd wait till tonight to drop by."

Her voice was light and mocking. "Aren't you sure of yourself! How'd you know I wouldn't be busy?"

"Simple," Clint said in a jesting tone. "All your 'regulars' are at the noncoms ball. I doubt they'll make it into town."

A naughty smile played at the corners of her mouth. "So you thought you'd have me all to yourself?"

"Yeah, something like that. Why, have you got other plans?"

"That's for me to know and you to find out. I'd say it all depends."

"On what?"

"On whether or not I get a better offer."

Clint pretended to search the room. He shook his head with a wry grin. "I don't see anybody man enough to fill my boots."

She wrinkled her nose. "You are a bastard, aren't you? I might just fool you one of these days."

"You might," Clint allowed. "But it'd sure spoil a good thing. I'd be hard to replace."

"Says you!" She vamped him with a look. "Of course, I'm willing to be convinced . . . if you've got all night."

Clint laughed. "You must've read my mind."

She gave him a bright, theatrical smile. "I have to sing the soldier boys another song. Don't go away."

"Wouldn't dream of it."

She walked off, blink-blinking her hips as she sashayed through the crowd. A round of applause erupted from the troopers as she once more mounted the stage. She nodded to the piano player and he led the fiddler into "Sweet

Betsy from Pike." Skirts lifted high, she belted out the bouncy tune.

From the bar, Clint admired her shapely legs. The thought of a night with her improved his spirits enormously. He forgot the Comanche and his earlier vision of an era drawing to a close. Sipping his drink, he told himself what was by now his personal credo. The one thing in life he believed with certainty:

Tomorrow would take care of itself.

17

THE CANTINA was dim and cool. A wayward shaft of sunlight filtered through the fly-specked window fronting the plaza. Outside, Santa Fe sweltered in the midday heat of late July.

Earl sat with Guadalupe at one of the rear tables. They were drinking *cerveza*, bottled native beer chilled in spring water. She watched as he polished off a large plate of *frijoles* and *tortillas*. Her expression was that of a woman who appreciates a man with a hearty appetite.

At the bar, Ignacio Zarate stood nursing a bottle of beer. The hunchback was a solitary drinker, seemingly a man without friends. Even his relationship with Guerra was that of *segundo* and *patrón*. He never indulged in pleasantries or small talk and apparently had no need of companionship. The other men at the bar wisely left him to himself.

For Earl, it was a matter of no great concern. He considered Zarate a brutish thug, with no redeeming qualities. Apart from loyalty to Guerra, the man had all the social instincts of an adder. Earl neither trusted him nor liked him, and was content not to be bothered by his company. They were on nodding terms and seldom spoke except on matters of business. Whenever possible, Earl simply avoided him.

"Another beer?" Guadalupe asked. "It's no trouble to get it."

"*Gracias, no,*" Earl said, pushing his empty plate away. "I've had all I want."

She looked at him with an odd smile. "Are you upset about something?"

"Why do you ask that?"

"Oh, I don't know. You just seem so quiet."

Earl sipped his beer. "Guess I've got things on my mind."

"You know what I think?"

When he shook his head, she went on in a soft voice. "I think you miss your little boy. Is it not true?"

"Yeah, I do. I spend a lot of time wondering how he's doing."

Every week or so a letter would arrive from Virgil and Elizabeth. Enclosed, there was always a note from Lon, short and laboriously written. From the sound of it, Lon was happy and doing well in school. But Earl worried about him nonetheless and sometimes regretted the decision to leave the boy behind. Colorado Springs seemed as distant as the moon.

"You shouldn't concern yourself," Guadalupe said at length. "You've told me he has a fine home with your brother."

"Not the same," Earl said grumpily. "Not for him, and especially not for me."

"Why not go visit him, then? Perhaps it would do you both good."

"I intend to," Earl said. "'Course, it'll have to wait till the end of the trading season. I couldn't get away now."

She touched his arm. "Even though it's your son, I don't want you to go, anyway. Does that sound selfish of me, *querido*?"

Her intimate tone somehow bothered Earl. Some three weeks past he had returned with his guide from *Comanchería*. Since then, Guadalupe had hardly let him out of her sight. She was darkly vivacious and compellingly attractive, and he should have been pleased by the attention. But his feeling about her veered wildly, and within the last few days he'd turned moody. His mind drifted constantly to that faraway land, *Llano Estacado*.

Unaccountably, he found himself lost in long reveries about Little Raven and the Quahadi band. He missed lazing around the lodge, listening to her chatter with the other women as they performed their chores. Even more, he missed their rough lovemaking and her fiery uninhibited passion. Guadalupe was no less passionate, and insofar as looks were concerned, she was considerably more attractive. Still, even when they were locked in fierce embrace, his thoughts inevitably centered on Little Raven. Her memory was like a haunt, unbidden and ever present.

Yet there was more to it than the woman he'd taken to wife. The thing he missed most was a way of life, that unbounded freedom found only on the plains. For a professional gambler, which was how he'd always thought of himself, it was absurd. Try as he might, however, he couldn't deny that his whole life had been turned topsy-turvy. He was somehow different, almost as though his inner compass had been knocked askew. He felt himself drawn to that more elemental existence, the harsh but carefree ways of the Quahadi. And like it or not, *Comanchería* was where his spirit now dwelled. He had to return.

Guadalupe's voice intruded on his thoughts. He realized he'd drifted off again, deaf to whatever it was she had asked. She was watching him with a quizzical expression.

"Sorry," he said apologetically. "Guess I was day-dreaming."

"You seem far, far away. Do I bore you so?"

"It's not you," Earl assured her. "I'm just thoughtful, that's all."

She shook a roguish finger at him. "I better not catch you looking at another woman. I'll scratch her eyes out. And yours, too."

Earl marked again the secrecy of the *Comancheros*.

Were it any other group of men, word of his Indian wife would have been common gossip by now. But Guadalupe and everyone else in Santa Fe had yet to hear the news. The reason none of the men had talked was standing at the bar, sipping beer. Ignacio Zarate, at Guerra's order, would have cut their tongues out.

Guadalupe was awaiting a response. On the verge of lying, Earl was suddenly spared the effort. A large raw-boned man dressed in rough clothes and mule-eared boots stopped before the table. His mustache was dark as lamp-black and his features were windburned from weeks on the prairie. He was almost certainly a Missouri trader.

"'Afternoon," he said. "Would you be Earl Brannock?"

"I'm afraid you have the advantage of me."

"The name's Josh Bishop."

Earl detected something antagonistic in the man's tone. He noted as well that Bishop was armed wtih a pistol and a bowie knife. "What can I do for you, Mr. Bishop?"

"I'd like to talk to you."

"Go right ahead."

"In private," Bishop said roughly. "It's a personal matter."

"Look here—"

"I don't mind," Guadalupe interrupted hastily. "I'll get you another beer."

Earl made no move to stop her. He waited as she rose from her chair and walked toward the bar. His gaze was fixed on Bishop, but he saw her pause and whisper something to Zarate. The hunchback turned slightly and looked toward the table. His brow knotted in a frown.

"Speak your piece," Earl said. "I haven't got all day."

Bishop pulled out a chair and sat down. "I've been told," he said slowly, "that you might be able to give me some information."

"What sort of information?"

"I'm a trader," Bishop replied vaguely. "Brought nine wagons in from Missouri day before yesterday."

"So—?" Earl said impatiently.

"No sooner got here," Bishop observed, "and I started hearin' stories about three white children. Some greaser had bought 'em off the hostiles and was willin' to turn 'em over for a price." He paused, staring across the table. "Everybody thought his price was too high."

Earl was familiar with the story. Ramón Guerra had set a price of a thousand dollars on the boy and two girls brought back from *Comanchería*. While he waited for someone to pay the ransom, the children were kept hidden somewhere in Santa Fe. Working through intermediaries, Guerra never became involved in the negotiations. His name was unknown to the authorities.

"Let me guess," Earl said at last. "You paid the price and got the children."

"About an hour ago," Bishop acknowledged. "A couple of greasers handed 'em over to me outside of town. Then they skedaddled *muy pronto*."

Earl recalled that Zarate had entered the cantina not quite a half-hour ago. He knew the hunchback would never have been a party to the actual exchange of captives. Yet he had no doubt that the man seated opposite him was known to Zarate. He returned Bishop's gaze levelly.

"Glad things worked out," he said. "What's it got to do with me?"

Bishop leaned forward, elbows on the table. "I've been talking to the other traders. They say those greasers belong to an outfit called the *Comancheros*." He hesitated, eyes narrowed. "Ever hear of them?"

"Not that I recollect," Earl said, straight-faced. "Who are they?"

"Way I hear it, they trade with the Comanches. It's not the first time they've ransomed off white captives."

"Sounds like they're doing everybody concerned a favor."

"Gawddamn vultures, that's what they are! I aim to see 'em caught and strung up."

"Maybe you ought to talk to the authorities."

"Already have," Bishop snorted. "Claimed they don't know nothin' about nothin'. Told me to ask around the plaza, talk to the Mex shopkeepers."

Earl nodded. "I take it they weren't too helpful?"

"Everybody's scared shitless. You mention *Comancheros* and they get a sudden case of lockjaw. I never saw anything like it."

"So what brings you to me?"

"I heard you're pals with a big-shot greaser. Somebody by the name of Ramón Guerra."

A fleeting look of puzzlement crossed Earl's face, then his expression became flat and guarded. "Who told you that?"

"What's the difference?" Bishop growled. "You know him or not?"

"Suppose I do," Earl said. "Where's that get you?"

"I'd like to talk to him. The word's out he knows everything worth knowin' where Mexicans are concerned."

"You're wasting your time. Guerra wouldn't tell you anything you haven't already heard."

"You speak for him, do you?"

"I'm just offering you some friendly advice."

"One white man to another . . . is that it?"

"Call it whatever you want."

Bishop fixed him with a dour look. "Appears to me you're awful thick with the greasers. Maybe your own hands aren't so clean."

"Say what you're trying to say."

"Hell, who knows?" Bishop eyed him with open suspicion. "I've heard of renegade white men before. Maybe you're a *Comanchero* youself."

Earl's mouth hardened. "Get up and walk out of here, Mr. Bishop. If you don't, you'll force me to kill you." His voice dropped. "Go on, get moving."

Bishop glowered at him a moment. Then, slamming his chair back, the trader rose and walked away from the table. As he neared the bar, Zarate casually turned, a beer bottle in his hand. They collided and the bottle crashed to the floor, shattering on impact. The hunchback's face twisted in a grimace.

"*¡Gringo cabrón!*"

"Hold on," Bishop said quickly. "It was an accident. I'll buy you another beer."

"*Hijo de puta*," Zarate snarled.

"Listen, you gawddamn greaser! Watch who you're callin' names."

A cold tinsel glitter surfaced in Zarate's eyes. He took a step closer and backhanded the trader across the mouth. All the blood leeched out of Bishop's features and his face went chalky with rage. He clawed at the gun on his hip.

Zarate was a beat faster. From the sheath at his belt, he pulled a broad-bladed *sacatripas*, the knife favored by *Comancheros*. He struck out in a shadowy movement and buried the blade to the haft in Bishop's chest. The trader stood stock-still, the knife handle jutting out just below his breastbone. Suddenly he choked and vomited a great gout of blood down across his shirtfront. His eyes rolled back in his head and his knees collapsed. He dropped dead at Zarate's feet.

An oppressive stillness settled over the cantina. The bartender and his customers, all of them Mexican, were immobilized. Farther down the bar, Guadalupe appeared stunned by the swiftness of the trader's death. None of them moved as Zarate stooped down and jerked his knife free.

The hunchback pulled a bandanna from his pocket. As he began wiping the blade, his gaze shifted across the room to Earl. His eyes were alive with a light akin to madness and his mouth zigzagged in a cruel smile. He slowly shook his head.

Under Zarate's ugly stare, Earl could scarcely mistake the message. He was being warned to play along and keep his mouth shut. The alternative, though unspoken, was equally obvious.

*   *   *

Ramón Guerra arrived a short time later. One of the bar patrons had been dispatched to his home and he'd hurried uptown. He immediately ordered the cantina closed to business.

The bartender, along with Guadalupe and the other customers, were told not to leave. Guerra nodded to Earl and led him down a short hallway at the rear of the building. Zarate stayed behind, ordering the bartender to serve a round of drinks. The body was still sprawled on the floor.

Followed by Earl, the *Comanchero* chief led the way to Guadalupe's room. Hardly larger than a monk's cell, the room was furnished with a narrow bed, one straight-back chair, and a washstand. The girl's clothes hung from wall pegs and a wooden cross was mounted over the head of the bed. A barred window looked out onto the alley.

"Well, *compadre*," he began quietly, "I thought we should talk before I send for the marshal. *¿Quién sabe?*"

"What's to savvy?" Earl replied. "You want me to back Zarate's story . . . right?"

Guerra regarded him with great calmness. "You will say that Bishop started the argument, pulled a gun. Zarate killed only to protect himself. Is that clear?"

"How about the others? Will they go along?"

"No Mexican would take the part of a *gringo*. You need not concern yourself with them."

"Still won't wash," Earl said woodenly. "By now, everyone knows that Bishop ransomed those children. What's worse, he was asking around town about the *Comancheros*."

Guerra's laugh was scratchy, abrasive. "What does that have to do with you and Zarate. Neither of you are *Comancheros*. *¿Verdad?*"

"All the same," Earl persisted. "Word will get out that Bishop was looking for me. How do we explain that?"

"Quite easily," Guerra said with a sourly amused look. "You were fellow Missourians and he wanted to meet you. What could be more natural?"

"Sounds kind of thin, don't you think?"

"Who's to dispute it? Your conversation was conducted in private and Bishop is dead. You are your own witness."

Earl kept his gaze level and cool. "You knew Bishop was hunting for me, didn't you?"

Guerra shrugged. "To be truthful, I hoped you would kill him. It would have been simpler that way."

"But since I didn't" Earl said angrily, "you had the hunchback on tap. That's why he showed up here, wasn't it?"

Guerra's face was hard, implacable. "Bishop should have stopped when he had the children. He was a foolish man."

"Well, he's an object lesson now. Don't poke your nose into *Comanchero* business. Isn't that the message?"

"You sound offended." Guerra said with a flare of annoyance. "I wasn't aware you placed such value on life."

"There's a difference between killing and cold-blooded murder. Zarate's nothing but an assassin!"

A moment elapsed while they stared at one another. When Guerra spoke, his voice was ominously quiet. "I would remind you that you are a *Comanchero*. Perhaps you need to think on that."

Earl gave him a bitter grin. "Once in, never out. Wasn't that how you put it?"

Guerra's eyes hooded. "A priest's vows are no less sacred, *compadre*. You would do well to take it seriously."

"Don't worry," Earl said in a flat voice. "I'll back Zarate's story."

"I never expected you wouldn't."

Guerra walked from the room. When the door closed, Earl slumped forward in his chair. There was a leaden feeling in his chest and he realized with dark fatalism that he would get his wish. All his life, he would return again and again to *Llano Estacado*. For his vows, unlike those of a priest, could never be renounced. No one quit the *Comancheros.*

Guadalupe stepped through the door. She saw the anguish in his face and she quickly crossed the room. She stopped before him, and without rising from the chair, he put his arms around her waist. She drew his head to her breast and held him close. Her voice was husky and her eyes misted with tears.

"*Mi amor, querido. Mi amor.*"

18

VIRGIL SAT with his hands locked behind his head. Feet propped on the desk, he was tilted back in his swivel chair. His gaze was fixed on a wall calendar.

The date was August 10. His eyes skipped ahead to the end of the month and he mentally ticked on the first two weeks in September. A frown line creased his forehead as he weighed time and distance. He thought it looked to be a dead heat.

The bond issue in Pueblo had gone through without problems. As he'd promised, the mayor and the town's banker were allowed to share in the windfall. Working double shifts, the Denver & Rio Grande had crossed the town line ahead of schedule. Still, for all the finagling, it had been a short-lived victory. The Santa Fe tracklayers reached Pueblo barely a week later.

By then, Virgil was working still another deal. The town of Trinidad, which was some seventy miles south of Pueblo, was slated as the next terminus. At William Palmer's insistence, he had sandbagged the community leaders into floating a bond issue. But the funds obtained were inadequate to maintain an expanded construction schedule. The money disappeared like pouring water down a rat hole.

A few miles south of Pueblo the proceeds of the bond issue ran out. The Denver & Rio Grande was forced to lay

off the extra crew and return to a single shift. The Santa
Fe, on the other hand, was not hamstrung by financial
difficulties. Operating a double shift, Santa Fe tracklayers
had now closed the gap to within four working days.

Staring at the calendar, Virgil foresaw what lay ahead.
Raton Pass, the critical objective for both railroads, lay ten
miles south of Trinidad. By early September, there was
little doubt that Santa Fe work gangs would overtake the
Denver & Rio Grande. Surveyors for the rival company
had already been sighted a mile or so beyond end-of-track.
Their route roughly paralleled the Denver & Rio Grande's
survey line.

No crystal ball was needed to predict the outcome.
Barring a drastic change, the Santa Fe would be the first to
surmount Raton Pass. Should that happen, all the future
plans of the Denver & Rio Grande would be placed in
jeopardy. New Mexico Territory, and revenues from southwestern rail traffic, would represent a substantial loss. So
great a loss, in fact, that the drive southward could be
forestalled completely. The Denver & Rio Grande might
never reach El Paso.

Virgil hardly needed a reminder that the situation was
critical. Yet, less than an hour ago, Palmer had ordered
him to unearth a new source of financing. Since then, his
mind in a funk, he'd sat with his eyes glued to the calendar. He hadn't the foggiest notion of where additional
funds might be raised. There was nothing to be gained in
approaching eastern moneylenders for construction loans.
Denver & Rio Grande stock, under the circumstances,
would not be acceptable as collateral. Nor was there another town between Trinidad and Raton Pass to be blud-
geoned into a bond issue. From any angle, the prospects
looked bleak.

To compound matters, Virgil's personal prospects were
in a ticklish state. His working relationship with Palmer
had steadily eroded over the past two months. Their meet-

ings had taken on an adversarial tone, invariably ending
with harsh words. Palmer was demanding, even dictatorial
at times, and seemingly impossible to please. While he
had no actual proof, Virgil saw the deterioration in their
partnership as a warning signal. He thought it entirely
likely that Palmer meant to force him out of the company.
As yet, however, he had devised no plan to protect himself. His position as minority stockholder severely limited
his options.

A knock sounded at the door. Art Vogel, the chief
bookkeeper, stepped into the office. He jerked a thumb
over his shoulder.

"You have callers," he said. "Jeff Dawson and Arnold
Hecht."

Virgil looked puzzled. "What do they want?"

"Search me," Vogel replied. "I didn't ask."

"All right, show them in."

The two men came through the door a moment later.
Dawson was completely bald, his oval face peppered with
liver spots. His companion, Arnold Hecht, was a small
bespectacled man with a bony nose and thinning hair.
Among the first to settle in Colorado Springs, they were
both respected members of the town council. Neither of
them had previously had dealings with the railroad.

"Gentlemen," Virgil greeted them politely. "What can
I do for you?"

Hecht took the lead. "We're here on a personal matter,
Mr. Brannock."

"I see," Virgil said, even more perplexed. "Won't
you have a seat?"

The men settled themselves in wooden armchairs. Virgil
resumed his seat behind the desk, and there was a moment
of strained silence. Finally, he looked from one to the
other.

"I'm a bit in the dark, gentlemen. Are we discussing
your personal affairs or mine?"

"Yours," Hecht said bluntly. "We want to talk to you about your wife."

"Elizabeth?" Virgil said, astounded. "What about her?"

Dawson took in the whole of Colorado Springs with a baroque sweep of his arm. "She's disrupting the community, that's what about her. The town council wants it brought to a halt."

Virgil cocked his head, studied them thoughtfully. "Are you talking about her activities as a suffragette?"

"Yessir, we are," Hecht said in a peevish voice. "Now, I wouldn't want you to misunderstand. Mrs. Brannock is a fine, Christian woman. None better."

"But . . . ?" Virgil prompted him.

"But she's too damn outspoken about this equality nonsense. Too militant!"

"And radical," Dawson added with stern disapproval. "She's got everybody in town stirred up with that tomfoolery."

"When you say 'everybody,'" Virgil inquired, "are you talking about the women?"

"Mostly," Dawson admitted. "She's been making speeches at sewing bees and church socials. Not that God ever intended females to hear such talk."

"I wasn't aware," Virgil said in a neutral voice, "that God had taken a position on suffrage. Or did I miss that in the scriptures?"

"Look here," Hecht temporized. "Couldn't we just talk about this man to man? We're all rowing the same boat, you know."

"Oh?" Virgil said. "What boat is that?"

Dawson, obviously disgruntled, leveled a finger. "Up the creek without a paddle if the women ever get the vote. We'd have a revolution on our hands."

"Jeff's right," Hecht observed loftily. "We've got a rebellion brewing, Mr. Brannock. And much as I hate to say it, your wife's the leading activist."

Virgil eyed them with studied calm. "I'll be frank with you," he said. "I'm out of town a good deal of the time and my wife doesn't tell me everything." He paused, seemingly confounded. "What's she done to cause such a ruckus?"

With an unpleasant grunt, Dawson pulled a sheet of paper from his coat pocket. He handed it across to Virgil, who unfolded it and found himself looking at a printed flyer. To all appearances, it was a standard handout supplied by the suffragettes' national headquarters. The tone was vitriolic and the wordage was classic hyperbole. Virgil was hard-pressed not to smile.

"She's passing those out," Dawson complained. "Every dangblasted woman in town has read it by now. And it's billy-blue-hell on men!"

"So I see," Virgil said, concentrating on the flyer. "What's the reaction so far?"

"Not good," Hecht said in a voice webby with phlegm. "It's got the women talking, and that's a bad sign. They're liable to believe that claptrap."

"What's worse," Dawson said with asperity, "your wife is egging them on to form a local chapter of the National, uh . . ."

Virgil held up the flyer. "National Woman Suffrage Association. Says here they're headquartered in New York."

"Anarchists!" Hecht invested the word with scorn. "A hotbed of radicals and frustrated females. They even publish a newspaper."

"Lord God," Dawson groaned. "To read that rag you'd think men were the ruination of the earth."

"I might add," Hecht said crossly, "your wife is selling subscriptions to the paper. And for your information, the masthead reads *The Revolution*. That ought to tell you a lot right there."

"Sounds sinister," Virgil said, suppressing a smile.

"I'm amazed the government allows it to be sent through the mails."

"Exactly!" Dawson rapped the desktop with his knuckles. "If the Founding Fathers meant for women to have the vote, they would've written it into the Constitution. You'll recollect it said 'all men are created equal'—not *women*."

Virgil nodded vigorously. "You said the town council wants all this stopped. Does that include the mayor as well?"

"Of course it does," Hecht affirmed. "Mayor Gentry knows trouble when he sees it. Only a crackpot would side with the women."

"On top of that," Dawson chimed in, "we've got county elections next month. Somebody might decide to put this suffrage nonsense to a referendum vote. Then we'd be in a helluva fix."

"By Judas!" Hecht said hotly. "We'd be the laughing-stock of Colorado if that ever happened. Who knows where it would lead?"

Virgil looked at them for a long moment. "Where there's smoke, there's fire, no doubt of that. What would you have me do?"

Hecht swelled with sudden importance. "We're not here to tell you how to run your home life. On the other hand, a tight rein never hurt any marriage. Do you take my meaning?"

"What he's saying," Dawson noted crisply, "is that it's your responsibility. Nobody can put the quietus on your wife but you."

"Maybe," Virgil said without conviction. " 'Course, you boys don't know my wife. She's got a mind of her own."

Hecht shook his head firmly. "These things require a strong hand, and the sooner the better. You owe it to the men of the town."

Virgil opened his hands, shrugged. "I'm not all that certain she'd listen to me. I wonder . . ."

His voice trailed off and Hecht urged him on. "Go ahead and say it. Whatever's on your mind."

"Well, it occurs to me that she might listen to someone else. Would you gentlemen consider talking to her?"

Dawson studied him with a glassy expression. "Let me understand this. You want us to talk turkey to your wife?"

"Would you?" Virgil asked with a shamefaced smile. "After all, it's for the good of the town."

Hecht appeared pleased by the prospect. "By thunder, he's right! We men have to stick together. I'm for it."

"What the hell," Dawson said gamely. "We're the appointed spokesmen for the town council. I guess that makes it official."

"Thank you, gentlemen," Virgil said, rising from his chair. "Suppose you drop by the house tonight after suppertime. Say around seven?"

After seeing them to the door, Virgil returned to his chair. What he had in mind would doubtless brand him a traitor among the town's male fraternity. But he detested pomposity and he allowed no man to lecture him on personal matters. Hecht and Dawson needed to be taught a lesson.

As for the suffrage movement, Virgil still had mixed feelings. He was neither for it nor against it, but somewhere in the middle. On one thing, however, his conviction never wavered. Freedom of speech was the cornerstone of liberty, an inalienable right. No one should be silenced for his—or her—views.

He wasn't about to muzzle his own wife.

Dawson and Hecht arrived promptly at seven. Virgil admitted them and led the way into the parlor. The men appeared to be brimming with confidence and eager to get on with their mission. As a pair, they looked positively righteous.

Elizabeth joined them shortly. She greeted both men

civilly, with perhaps more charm than they had expected. Acting the good wife, she explained that the children were in their rooms, under strict orders to stay there. Nothing would intrude on the serious nature of tonight's discussion.

Before either of the men could open their mouths, someone knocked at the front door. Elizabeth excused herself, darting Virgil a quick glance, and left the room. The sound of women's voices, low and somewhat indistinguishable, carried from the vestibule. A moment later Elizabeth returned, beaming a dazzling smile. With her were Amanda Dawson and Margaret Hecht.

The two merchants sprang from their chairs. For an instant, their faces were frozen in a curious attitude of sullen disbelief. Then, almost in unison, they looked at Virgil with the sideways suspicion of kicked dogs. Arnold Hecht was the first to recover his wits.

"What's the meaning of this?" he demanded. "Why weren't we told our wives would be here?"

"Actually," Elizabeth said with mock innocence, "I invited them. It seemed only fair that they be a party to our discussion."

"Consarn it!" Dawson huffed. "I'm not gonna be bullyragged by a—"

"Oh, shut up, Jeffrey," his wife scolded. "Sit down and try to act like a gentleman."

Amanda Dawson was a plain-faced woman with eyes bright as berries and a stinging voice. No less imposing, Margaret Hecht was stout and gray-haired, with rosy cheeks and a wise mouth. Together, they made a formidable combination, and their husbands quickly adopted discretion as the better part of valor. The men resumed their chairs and the women settled onto a slipcovered sofa.

An air of hushed expectancy fell over the parlor as Elizabeth marched to the fireplace. She paused before the mantel, took a deep breath to steady herself, and then turned to face them. Her voice was strong and she stared intently at the men. Hardly drawing a breath, she spoke for ten minutes straight. She addressed the issues of a society governed by male tyranny and women compelled to submit to laws that made them subservient to their husbands. She spoke eloquently of the different moral codes for men and women and the inequity of the courts when a woman attempted to redress the slightest wrong. She concluded with a question for the two merchants.

"I ask you, gentlemen," she said with a guileless smile, "is justice served when your wives are denied access to the courts?"

Hecht squirmed in his chair. "Haven't you overstated the case somewhat, Mrs. Brannock?"

"I think not," Elizabeth said with great relish. "Are you aware that all household goods, the furniture and the bedding and the utensils—even your wife's clothing—belong to you?"

Hecht shook his head as though a fly had buzzed his ear. "I can't rightly say I ever thought about it before."

"Perhaps you should," Elizabeth said, her chin tilted. "Are you aware, Mr. Dawson, that a single lady has most of the rights of a man? Although she can't vote, she can make contracts, acquire property, accumulate land holdings. Why are those rights denied a married woman?"

"How would I know?" Dawson looked like he'd just bitten his tongue. "I'm a storekeeper, not a lawyer."

"Hallelujah!" Amanda Dawson crowed. "All the lawyers are men and every last one dabbles in politics. They're the weasels who write the laws."

"Not only that," Margaret Hecht added, glaring at her husband. "You took the inheritance from my father and poured it into your mercantile. But the law says I own no part of the store. How's that for justice?"

"C'mon, Maggie," Hecht said, his voice clogged. "You know it's as much yours as it is mine."

She stabbed out at him with a bony finger. "What's yours is yours, and what's mine is yours too!"

"Hold on a minute," Dawson interrupted. "I thought we were here to talk about suffrage and the women's vote and all that."

"In good time," Elizabeth told him with a short emphatic nod. "Tonight we're here to form a chapter of the National Woman Suffrage Association. I'm delighted to announce that your wives have volunteered to serve as members of the board."

Dawson's jaw dropped open. Hecht slumped back in his chair, his face doughy and stunned. So complete was their astonishment that they stared at her like blind men. She smiled sweetly.

"Gentlemen, we earnestly solicit your support. We intend to put Colorado Springs on the map."

Hecht coughed raggedly. "Are we to assume you'll be the president of this—organization?"

"Chairwoman," Elizabeth corrected with a dignified nod. "I've been appointed by Susan B. Anthony herself."

"God save us," Dawson moaned. "We're ruined."

"Not entirely," Elizabeth said, mimicking his dour look. "Whether or not you support us is a matter between you and your conscience. All we require is that you do not oppose us."

Dawson frowned. "That sounds like an ultimatum. What happens if we don't go along?"

"Separate bedrooms," Amanda Dawson announced in an iron voice. "And I'll personally inform all your cronies on the town council. Lord love us, you'd never live it down."

The meeting adjourned. Dawson was reduced to tongue-tied silence and Hecht departed with a doglike dumbfounded expression. Their wives followed them out the door, intoxicated with the night's triumph. No one spoke as the foursome trudged off down the street.

When Elizabeth and Virgil were alone, he looked at her with open admiration. "I'm proud of you," he said genuinely. "You brought it off without a hitch."

"Why, thank you, sir. I'm rather proud of myself."

"One thing, though," Virgil said, holding out his arms. "No separate bedrooms for us—ever."

"Never ever, no matter what."

She stepped into his arms. He pulled her into a tight hug and gently kissed the top of her head. She snugggled close against his chest.

19

SOME DAYS REMAIN with a man all his life. A scent of wood smoke or a tree silhouetted against the sky evokes sharp memories. Certain days, no matter how a man tries, are impossible to purge from the mind.

For Earl, it was a day in late September. The Comanche called it the Yellow Leaves Moon, the month that frost first settled over *Llano Estacado*. Their camp was stretched out along Tule Canyon, south of the Cap Rock. Warm days and cold nights had already touched the trees bordering the river, and leaves were dabbed with color. All the signs pointed to an early winter.

The *Comancheros* had arrived only two days past. Quanah and his Quahadi band had greeted them with the usual reserve, hardly pausing as the *carretas* rolled into camp. Yet there was an undercurrent of excitement throughout the village, for this would be the last rendezvous of the trading season. All across the Staked Plains similar gatherings were underway between the horseback tribes and other groups of *Comancheros*. The traders would not return until the following spring.

To Earl, it was a homecoming of sorts. He was weary of Santa Fe and anxious once again to be among the Quahadi. His bond with the *Comancheros* seemed to him a pretext, an excuse to return to *Llano Estacado*. Forgotten now was the murder of the Missouri trader and the strain that had

developed between himself and Ramón Guerra. On the
outbound trip their easy camaraderie had been rekindled,
their past differences put aside. Even more, there was a
quickening sense of anticipation as they neared Tule Canyon. Guerra and his men were invigorated by the prospects
of great profits. Earl's thoughts were on Little Raven.

The first night in camp had been a time of celebration.
A feast was held in honor of the *Comancheros* and drums
throbbed as dancers shuffled around an enormous bonfire.
Later, when the festivities ended, Earl and Little Raven
had retired to their lodge. Away from the curious eyes of
her people, she had at last greeted him as a wife. Their
long separation had inflamed her passion and dawn purpled the skies before they finally slept. Never before had
he felt so welcome, or so wanted.

Trading got underway the next morning. Throughout
the summer months raiding parties had savaged the Texas
frontier. A herd of longhorns, numbering more than a
thousand head, was gathered on rolling grassland near the
mouth of the canyon. There too was a herd of some three
hundred horses, stolen from *tejano* ranchers and settlers.
Guerra and Quanah haggled until long into the afternoon,
slowly exchanging the contents of the *carretas* for horses
and cows. Apart from the usual trade goods, the Quahadis
came away with several crates of repeating rifles and a
supply of ammunition. When the day ended, every wagon
in the *Comanchero* caravan had been emptied.

Upon returning to his lodge, Earl was in high spirits.
His share of the profits represented a fourfold return on his
original investment, all accomplished within a matter of
five months. By the end of next trading season, he envisioned himself as a man of considerable means. His idea
of investing in Santa Fe business property no longer seemed
farfetched. He saw a time, not too far away, when all he'd
dreamed would become reality. A *Comanchero*, he told
himself, could still engage in legitimate enterprise. No one
asked a man's credentials when he had hard cash to invest.

Little Raven had a surprise of her own. She had purposely waited, knowing he would be in a good mood following the trading session. With her limited Spanish and a great deal of sign language, she told him the news. When he still looked confused, she took his hand and placed it on her stomach. He felt a slight bulge and suddenly it registered on him that she was heavier than when he'd last seen her. Watching him, her almond eyes were apprehensive as she awaited a reaction. A moment passed before the full realization hit him. Abruptly, his features split in a wide grin.

"*Bebe.*" He laughed, patting her stomach, and pointed at her. "*¿Mamacita?*"

She nodded rapidly and he tapped himself on the chest. "*Papá.* I'm gonna be a daddy!"

Her eyes brimmed with happiness and she threw herself into his arms. Earl caught her, whirling her around, and lifted her high overhead. Then he brought her down and kissed her soundly on the mouth. Her face was radiant with joy and she hugged him fiercely around the neck. He whooped a great shout of laughter.

"Jesus H. Christ! Wait till I tell Ramón."

There was an even wilder celebration that night. With the trading done, the Quahadi had reason to congratulate themselves. A summer of raiding had brought wealth to their lodges.

Fires blazed throughout the village. Warriors drunk on trade whiskey retold stories of their victories. From time to time, one would leap to his feet and reenact a moment of prowess in battle. Women and children ganged around, laughing and nodding appreciatively, waiting for the drums to start. No one would sleep tonight.

Outside Quanah's lodge, Guerra and Earl were seated with the chief. Assisted by Little Raven, Quanah's three wives had served the men a gluttonous meal. As the women cleared away the scraps, Earl extracted long black

cheroots from inside his jacket. He handed one to Quanah
and another to Guerra and kept one for himself. Leaning
forward, he took a glowing stick from the fire and passed
it around. When they were all puffing contentedly, he
waved his cheroot in a grand gesture. He smiled broadly,
nodding to Guerra.

"Among Anglos," he said, "passing out cigars has a
special meaning. Are you familiar with the custom?"

"No, *compadre*. What does it mean?"

Earl drew himself up proudly. "It means congratulations are in order. I'm going to be a father."

"*Sangre de Cristo*," Guerra said, looking at him. "Are
you certain?"

"Why, sure, I'm certain. What makes you ask?"

"Your woman was thought to be barren. No one believed her capable of bearing children."

"Well, she's going to bear mine. I'd judge she's about
four months along."

Quanah addressed Guerra in Spanish. They spoke at
length, with the *Comanchero* leader answering several
questions. Finally, nodding to Earl, Quanah rattled off a
quick speech. He motioned for Guerra to translate.

"Our host," Guerra noted, "says you are *muy hombre*.
He's pleased that your seed is strong. The Quahadi need
children."

Earl's expression betrayed nothing. "Sounds like he's
trying to tell me something."

"Listen closely," Guerra said without a flicker of emotion. "Your blood means nothing. The child will be a
Comanche, a member of the Quahadi band. Do you
understand?"

"Yeah, I think so," Earl said slowly. "You're saying
they'll never let the child leave the band. Whether I like it
or not, I've fathered a Comanche."

"Precisely."

Guerra went on to explain. Quahadi women seldom bore
more than two children, and many of them bore none. The

band's nomadic wanderings and a lifetime spent on horse-back caused countless miscarriages. As a result, the Quahadi prized their children, even those of mixed blood. No one who valued his life would attempt to take a child from *Comanchería*.

Earl was silent for a time. He felt Quanah's gaze boring into him, and he knew that the warning, however subtly stated, was meant in earnest. At last, he nodded to Guerra.

"A child belongs with his own people. Tell Quanah he has no need to worry."

The reply apparently pleased Quanah. He grunted, puffing on his cheroot, and allowed the subject to drop. Guerra glanced back at Earl.

"I should have mentioned it earlier, *compadre*. We have been asked to delay our departure by a few days."

"Oh?" Earl asked. "Why so?"

Guerra's voice was toneless. "A war party returns from Mexico tomorrow. We have been invited to witness the celebration."

"What sort of celebration?"

"I am told they have a prisoner."

"A Mexican?"

"Yes," Guerra said quietly. "He killed one of their warriors. For that, he will die a slow death."

Earl frowned. "You're saying they plan to torture him."

"Nothing less."

"How does Quanah know when they'll get here?"

Guerra shrugged. "I presume someone rode ahead. Does it matter how he knows?"

"I suppose not."

Earl took a long draw on his cheroot. He'd killed several men in his lifetime and he was by no means squeamish. But the thought of watching someone put to torture gave him an uneasy moment. All the more so since he had no choice in the matter.

Quanah's invitation, clearly, was not to be refused. They were to be the honored guests at another man's death.

* * *

A flush of gold dusted the eastern horizon. The silhouettes of cottonwoods stood bold against the sky, and tendrils of smoke drifted from overnight fires inside the lodges. Dawn marked the day that would remain with Earl forever.

The war party rode into camp shortly after sunup. Buffalo Hump, their leader, sat astride a magnificent black-and-white pinto. Behind him, mounted on a captured horse, was a Mexican in his late twenties. The man was stark-naked, haggard from exposure and the long ride. Otherwise, curiously enough, he had not been abused. He was lean and muscular and appeared in excellent health.

A month past, eight warriors had elected to follow Buffalo Hump on a raid. Today, only seven warriors followed him back into camp. One of their number had been killed in a horse-stealing raid, shot down by the vaquero guarding the herd. The vaquero had been overpowered and captured, and the dead warrior had been buried beside the trail. Custom dictated that the warrior's widow must give away all his earthly possessions. To salve her grief, Buffalo Hump had brought her the Mexican.

Lodges throughout the camp emptied as the Quahadi gathered to greet the war party. Buffalo Hump wore a war helmet made of the topknot and spiked horns of a bull buffalo. The warriors' features, hideously painted, were daubed with broad black stripes across the face and forehead. As they halted in the center of the village, a woman screamed and rushed from the throng of people. Her man was not among the returning warriors and she ran toward the Mexican, cursing him in a shrill voice. Several women hurried to restrain her.

Earl stood with Little Raven outside their lodge. She nodded toward the vaquero, and then, holding both hands against her body, she motioned down and under with her left hand. It was the sign for death, and Earl understood that the Mexican's ordeal would not end quickly. The outrage and sorrow of the widow would be washed away in the act of torture, almost as if she had been freed from torment and could begin life anew. Further, the Comanche believed that a mutilated enemy could not cross over into the land of afterlife. The vaquero's doomed spirit would wander forever in a void of lost souls.

A sharp scream attracted Earl's attention. He saw the dead warrior's widow break loose from the women holding her. She ran to her lodge and emerged a moment later with a butcher knife. As the other women watched stoically, she slashed her arms and legs in a frenzy of grief. Then, dripping blood, she placed her left hand on the edge of a cast-iron pot and chopped off her forefinger. She held the grisly stump to the sky and loosed a keening, guttural cry. Quickly, as though on unspoken command, the other women surrounded her and removed the knife from her hand. She was led back inside the lodge.

The Mexican was jerked from his horse by the warriors. His hands were tied behind his back and he was shoved forward to where a heavy stake had been anchored in the ground. One end of a long rawhide cord was lashed to his bound hands and the other end was secured to the post. The warriors led their horses away and within moments the vaquero stood alone in the center of the camp. He clumsily lowered himself to the ground as the crowd drifted back to their lodges. His features were set in a look of utter resignation.

Little Raven explained what would happen. In broken Spanish, she told Earl the Mexican would not be mistreated during the day. He would be left tied to the stake until nightfall, allowed to contemplate his fate. Custom required that he be kept physically fit for the ordeal ahead, able to withstand the widow's vengeance. No one wanted to see him die easily, or swiftly.

She turned and entered the lodge. After watching the vaquero a moment longer, Earl followed her inside. He suddenly longed to see Santa Fe.

*   *   *

The sun sank lower, smothering in a bed of copper beyond the distant plains. A group of women began building a huge fire near the bound Mexican. None of them looked at him or spoke a word.

By nightfall the flames leapt skyward in a towering blaze. The Quahadi slowly gathered in a massed circle, crowding closer for a better view. Quanah and Buffalo Hump were seated, the members of the war party ranged behind them. Off to one side, Earl and Little Raven stood with Guerra and the other *Comancheros*. The naked Mexican was on his feet, staring wildly around at the crush of onlookers. His expression was one of silent terror.

On Quanah's command, the crowd went eerily quiet. A group of women, led by the widow, detached themselves from the throng. They walked forward and bodily hurled the vaquero to the ground, holding him down. With one stroke of her butcher knife, the widow severed the Mexican's penis and scrotum. The striken man screamed, his eyes distended with pain, and broke loose from their grip. He rolled over on the ground, knees bent double, squeezing the raw stump between his legs. The spectators hooted with savage delight as the widow pranced around the fire. She held his manhood aloft for all to see.

One of the women snatched a long slender stick from the fire. She whipped it through the air, extinguishing the flames, until she held a glowing spike. The Mexican was still on his knees, face in the dirt, his legs locked tight in agony. Stepping forward, the woman spread his buttocks wide and rammed the fiery point straight up his rectum. With a hair-raising shriek, the vaquero exploded off the ground. He crow-hopped around the post, moaning pitifully, tossing his backside as he tried to shake the stick loose. The crowd went hysterical, clutching their sides with laughter at his wild antics.

Still stomping his ghastly dance, the Mexican suddenly found himself encircled by the women. They each held a sizzling firebrand and he backed away, the stick in his rump forgotten. One of the squaws lunged, driving the cherry-red point of her spike into his chest. He lurched backwards, slamming into the stake, and the women from behind jabbed him in the legs and shoulders. He dodged around the post in a frenzied, shambling run, and suddenly another woman drove her orange-tipped spike into the bloody stump of his penis. Jerking away, he lost his footing and fell heavily to the ground. A squaw darted forward and thrust a searing tip of fire straight into his eyeball.

The vaquero's scream was unearthly, a cry of anguish beyond mortal suffering. Like magpies swarming over warm meat, the women crowded around and began poking with their sticks. One jabbed him in the ear and another jammed a fiery spike deep inside his open mouth. Still others burned his chest and the soles of his feet and his buttocks. They grunted and shoved and kept on jabbing, none of them uttering so much as a curse. Yet their eyes glistened as the glowing firebrands hissed and smoked wherever his skin was touched. A look of atavistic jubilation crossed their faces as his body recoiled in spastic convulsions.

At last, the Mexican ceased to move. The women poked at him a minute then dropped their sticks and backed away. Walking forward the widow grabbed him by the hair and leaned down with her butcher knife. She made a clean, quick cut around the base of his topknot and yanked upward. His scalp tore loose with a squishy snap, and his features, no longer supported by the hairline, sagged down over his cheekbones. As the widow stepped away with her grisly trophy, the vaquero's eyes opened in a numbed glaze. On all fours, he crawled to the post, muttering crazed gibberish. He somehow pushed himself erect and stood staring sightlessly into the night.

The women closed on him once more. Grabbing arms and legs, they lifted him high overhead. The widow cut the rawhide cord binding him to the post and the women marched to the fire. There, with a mighty heave, they tossed him bodily into the roaring flames. The Mexican seemed to melt before the onlookers' eyes. His skin burst and peeled back, and the globular tissue beneath crackled like dripping fat over an open spit. Sparks showered skyward and he was suddenly consumed in a sizzling ball of fire. As the body shriveled into a hard blackened knot, the stench of charred flesh drifted over the encampment. For an instant, there was absolute silence.

Whooping shrilly, the widow paraded one last time before the spectators. She held the vaquero's penis in one hand and his gory topknot in the other, waving them triumphantly overhead. The sight seemingly jarred the Quahadi out of their trance and they surged forward. Laughing and shouting, their howls split the night as they crowded around the widow. Abruptly, as though on signal, the drums began to throb with a pulsing beat. Buffalo Hump and the members of his war party moved forward and formed a shuffling circle around the fire. Their heads arched skyward in victory cries and the earth shuddered beneath the stomp of their feet.

Watching them, Earl wanted to gag. His stomach was queasy and there was a bitter taste of bile in his throat. Yet he pulled himself together and somehow managed to keep a dispassionate expression on his face. Little Raven held onto his arm tightly and her touch seemed to sear through his shirt. He couldn't trust himself to look at her.

Beside him, Ramón Guerra muttered something under his breath. Earl glanced around and for a moment their eyes locked. Neither of them spoke, but words were unnecessary. A single thought passed between them.

It was time to leave *Comanchería*.

20

THE SKY WAS like dull pewter. A brisk October wind whipped through Colorado Springs, scattering dust and grit. Townsmen walked with their heads bowed and their hats tugged low.

Earl stepped down off the northbound train. He'd traveled by stage from Santa Fe to Pueblo, where he had transferred to the Denver & Rio Grande. With his old carpetbag in hand, he followed the other passengers across the depot platform. On the street, he turned uptown.

Some three weeks past he had put *Llano Estacado* behind him. His parting with Little Raven was bittersweet, for he wouldn't see her again until spring. Even as he departed, the Quahadi were preparing to move to their winter camp in Palo Duro Canyon. There they would remain while howling blizzards savaged the plains.

By the time he returned, Little Raven would have given birth to their child. At first, he'd felt a nagging guilt that he wouldn't be with her. But then, after a brief stopover in Santa Fe, his thoughts had turned northward. Close to six months had passed since he'd seen Lon, and the boy's latest letter had left him vaguely disturbed. Something between the lines told him that all was not well in Colorado Springs.

Twilight turned to dark as he approached the house. The windows glowed with lamplight and he saw a shadowy figure move through the parlor. He knocked, and when the door opened, he knew his instinct hadn't played him false. Virgil's face was etched with worry.

"Come in," he said shortly. "Sorry to sound abrupt, but we've got problems. The boy's in a bad way."

"Lon?" Earl asked, stepping past him.

"No, it's Morg. The doctor's with him now."

"What's wrong?"

"Pleurisy," Virgil said in a low voice. "He's running a godawful fever."

Earl dropped his carpetbag on the floor. "Where are they?"

"In the kitchen. The doc's trying—"

He stopped as the kitchen door opened. Elizabeth walked forward through the hallway. Her eyes were hollow and her face was drained of color. A stout man with his sleeves rolled up followed her into the vestibule. She smiled wanly at Earl and halted with her arms wrapped around her waist. Virgil introduced the man as Doc Granby.

"No luck," Granby said quietly. "A syringe just won't draw that pus out. I'll have to operate."

"Now?" Virgil said. "Here?"

"On the kitchen table," Granby told him. "It's better done here than in my office. I've already dosed him with laudanum."

Virgil looked stunned. "How much risk is there?"

"I won't lie to you," Granby said. "Your son's condition isn't good. We'll just have to take our chances."

"But—" Virgil paused, shook his head. "Can you do it by yourself?"

"Mrs. Brannock has agreed to assist me."

Virgil glanced at her. "I don't know about that, Beth. Are you up to it?"

"I have to be," Elizabeth said firmly. "There's no one else."

"Don't worry," Granby added quickly. "She's already proved herself a very capable nurse."

With a nod, the physician turned and walked back toward the kitchen. Elizabeth delayed a moment, squeezing Virgil's hand, then hurried off down the hallway. She disappeared through the door.

The brothers stood there a moment, wrapped in silence. Virgil's gaze was fixed on the kitchen door and he seemed lost in thought. When Earl finally spoke, his voice was unnaturally loud in the stillness.

"Where's Lon?"

"Upstairs," Virgil said. "I told him and Jennifer to stay in their rooms."

"Well—" Earl hesitated, then moved toward the stairs. "I'll go up and let him know I'm here."

Virgil appeared to collect himself. "We'd better have a talk before you see the boy."

"What about?"

"Lon's been expelled from school."

Virgil turned and walked toward the parlor. Somewhat reluctantly, Earl followed him through the entranceway. They took chairs before the fireplace.

Claude Granby bent over his patient. He checked the boy's eyes, satisfying himself that Morgan was below the threshold of consciousness. With his stethoscope, he then took a final sounding of the chest and lungs. The youngster's breathing was slow and labored.

Elizabeth looked on with mounting apprehension. Not quite two weeks past Morg had taken a bad chest cold. She had treated it with mustard plaster and other home remedies, but to no avail. The cold quickly developed into pneumonia, with a raging fever and intermittent bouts of delirium. Even with the physician in attendance, the boy survived largely due to his stout constitution.

Still, the ordeal had yet to run its course. As the pneumonia diminished, pleurisy rapidly spread throughout the youngster's system. Inflammation of the pleura membrane created an enormous deposit of pus in the right lung and the chest cavity. The deposit expanded to the point that it was squeezing Morg's heart against his left lung. Efforts to remove the pus with a syringe had proved futile. There was now no alternative but to operate.

"We'll proceed," Granby said, finished with his examination. "Help me roll him onto his stomach."

The boy's features were pallid. He groaned as they gently turned him on the kitchen table, which was covered with a clean bedsheet. Another sheet covered him from the waist down, leaving the upper half of his body exposed. Granby rotated the youngster's head to one side, listening a moment to the irregular breathing pattern. Then he looked at Elizabeth.

"You won't faint on me, will you?"

"No," she said softly. "I won't faint."

"Good," Granby said with a reassuring smile. "Now, there's going to be a lot of bleeding. What I want you to do is keep it soaked up with gauze."

When Elizabeth nodded, he went on. "Don't wait for me to ask you. Just do it, and do it quickly. I have to be able to see what I'm about."

"I understand."

"All right, let's get to work."

A tray of surgical instruments was positioned at the head of the table. Granby selected a scalpel and leaned forward over the boy. He made two quick incisions on the back, laying bare the upper rear of the rib cage. Standing on the opposite side of the table Elizabeth quickly swabbed blood away with a wad of gauze. Another stroke of the scalpel freed one of the rib bones from surrounding tissue.

As Elizabeth swabbed, the doctor took a narrow-bladed saw from the instrument tray. Her breath caught in her throat when he gingerly grasped the exposed rib between thumb and forefinger. For an instant, as the teeth of the saw grated on bone, she felt giddy and curiously light-headed. Then, from somewhere inside herself, she summoned a reservoir of strength. Avoiding his hands, she continued to dab blood from the gaping incision.

Granby dropped the saw on the table. As he lifted the severed rib bone out, a noxious fountain of pus erupted with explosive force. The thick yellowish liquid spurted across his forearms and soaked his shirtfront. When the drainage slowed, he motioned for Elizabeth to swab the wound. Bending closer, he peered into his handiwork and grunted with satisfaction. He glanced up at her.

"I think that does it. Let's get this boy stitched back together."

"Will he be all right?"

"Unless I miss my guess," Granby said jovially, "he'll be up and around in no time. He's a strong lad."

"Thank God," Elizabeth whispered.

"You're no weak-sister yourself, Mrs. Brannock. I've seen grown men keel over at less."

Granby chuckled at his own humor. He cleansed the youngster's back and then deftly threaded a surgical needle. Humming softly to himself, he began closing the incision.

"What the hell happened?"

"No one thing," Virgil said morosely. "Lon's teachers just can't control him. He's constantly in trouble."

Earl frowned. "What sort of trouble?"

"Skipping school heads the list. Course, that wasn't what got him expelled. Yesterday he beat the holy bejesus out of another boy."

"Why?" Earl demanded. "He must have had a reason."

Virgil's face was serious. "The boy's got a short fuse. Here lately, he loses his temper over nothing."

Earl shook his head. "That's not like Lon. He was always pretty easygoing."

"We thought so, too," Virgil said. "But the last month or so, he's been hell on wheels. Nobody can talk to him, either. He just stares a hole through you."

"Well, something brought it on. Haven't you at least got a clue?"

"Yeah, but you might not want to hear it."

"Try me and see."

Virgil stared into the fireplace. His features were limned in the amber glow of the flames. "When you left here," he said, "you told him it wouldn't be for long. That was almost six months ago."

"I know," Earl said lamely. "One thing led to another and I couldn't get away. Hell, Virgil, you know how it is! Sometimes business comes first."

"Not to a kid," Virgil observed. "Way I see it, he figures you deserted him. He's hurt and he's mad."

"So he's taking it out on the rest of the world?"

"Something like that," Virgil said, nodding slowly. "Anybody that's hurt bad enough will strike out at the nearest thing handy. The boy he whipped yesterday wasn't the first one."

Earl looked up, sharply concerned. "You're not saying he took it out on Morg?"

"No, I'm not," Virgil replied. "For the most part, he ignores Morg and Jennifer both. He's turned into a loner."

Virgil suddenly stared past him. Footsteps sounded in the hallway and a moment later Elizabeth entered the parlor. She crossed the room, halting beside Virgil's chair. Her voice trembled between laughter and tears.

"It's over," she said. "He's going to be all right."

Virgil searched her eyes. "Doc Granby said that? Those very words?"

She smiled happily. "Ask him yourself. He's getting ready to leave."

"Leave!" Virgil jackknifed to his feet. "Shouldn't he stay here to look after the boy?"

"There's no need," she said confidently. "We can't move him until in the morning, but he's doing fine. I'll sit with him tonight."

"We'll both sit with him." Virgil grinned and put his arm around her shoulders. "You're not the only nurse in this family."

Earl rose from his chair. "Anything I can do?"

"Not really," Elizabeth said. "We have a housekeeper who comes in every morning. She can relieve us after we've moved Morg to his room. I wouldn't sleep till then, anyway."

"Go talk to Lon," Virgil advised him. "You two need to get acquainted again. He's liable to be a bit snippy."

"Don't worry, I'll bring him around."

Earl followed them out of the parlor. As they turned toward the kitchen, he slowly mounted the stairs. He felt far less confident than he'd sounded a moment ago. He hadn't the least idea of where to begin. Or what to say.

Lon was stretched out on the bed. He was still dressed and appeared lost in some deep rumination. As Earl entered the bedroom, a spark of boyish exuberance flared briefly. But then the look faded and he slowly rolled out of bed, standing slouch-shouldered. His expression was coolly impersonal.

"Hello, sport," Earl said smiling. "How's tricks?"

"Okay," Lon said indifferently.

"C'mon now, that's not much of a greeting."

Earl reached out to hug him. The boy twisted away and stumped across to the window. He stood staring out into the night, hands stuffed in his pockets. A moment passed, then Earl sat down on the edge of the bed.

"Guess you're mad at me, huh?"

Lon shrugged. "Who cares?"

'I do." Earl tried to keep his tone light. "Sort of figured you'd be glad to see me."

Turning from the window, Lon drew himself up stiffly. His face was pinched around the mouth. "Only waited till you come back so I could tell you myself. I'm fixin' to leave for Frisco."

Earl saw the hurt in his eyes. "Why Frisco?"

"I got friends there."

"You have family here," Earl said. "Believe it or not, they're your friends too."

"Who needs 'em?" Lon said, suddenly tight-lipped. "I'll get along awright on my own."

Earl realized they were at an impasse. Nothing he might say would change the youngster's mind. Forced to stay in Colorado Springs, the boy was almost certain to run away. He knew his son too well to believe otherwise.

"Sorry to hear it," Earl said, almost to himself. "I had an idea we might get back together."

Lon fidgeted uncomfortably. "What d'ya mean?"

"Well, I thought you might like to see Santa Fe. It's got things you won't find in Frisco."

"Like what?"

"Oh, wild Indians and cowboys, lots of Mexicans. Stuff like that."

"C'mon," Lon said, squinting at him. "Who ever heard of Injuns in a big city?"

Earl chortled softly. "You've got it all wrong, sport. Santa Fe's wild and woolly, regular frontier outpost. It makes Frisco look tame."

The boy looked torn between anguish and anxiety. He stared back at his father with a searching expression. "You're not just funnin'?" he asked in a hushed voice. "You really want me to come along?"

"Bet your boots!" Earl said with a jocular air. "I told you once before we're a team. We've got to stick together."

"Would I hafta go to school?"

"Damn right," Earl said with mock severity. "None of this nonsense about getting expelled, either. I'd expect you to toe the mark."

"Nothin' to that," Lon said eagerly. "I could make my grades with my eyes closed."

"Guess that settles it, then. Now, how about a hug for your old man? I've come a long way to get one."

Lon approached a step at a time. Then, as Earl held out his arms, the boy took the last few steps in a rush. He flung himself on his father and they held one another, rocking back and forth. Neither of them was able to say what was in their hearts.

* * *

Later, when the boy fell asleep, Earl went downstairs for a smoke. He found Virgil slumped in one of the easychairs, puffing a cigar. After lighting a cheroot, he seated himself on the opposite side of the fireplace.

"How's Morg?" he asked. "Any change?"

"All for the better," Virgil said genially. "His breathing's pretty near back to normal."

Earl nodded, quiet a moment. "You must be proud of Beth. She's quite a woman."

"I've got lots to say grace over, and that's a fact. I ought to count my blessings more often."

When Earl smiled, saying nothing, his expression turned quizzical. "How'd it go with Lon?"

A strange inner look settled on Earl's face. "Guess it's time to count my blessings, too. I'm taking him back to Santa Fe with me."

Virgil stared off into some thoughtful distance. "Maybe it's for the best. We tried, but he's just not happy here. I suppose a boy needs his father."

"Yeah, he does," Earl agreed. "Especially in his case. I'm all he's got."

"Knowing you, I'd say it works both ways. You weren't cut out to be a loner, either."

"Speaking of loners, what do you hear from Clint? I haven't had a letter from him in a couple of months."

"Neither have we," Virgil grumped. "Last I heard, he was still down at Fort Clark. Wish he'd find himself another occupation."

"What the hell," Earl said, grinning. "Clint courts trouble the way most men court women. He won't settle down till he's got one foot in the grave."

"That reminds me," Virgil remarked. "Earlier you said something about business keeping you in Santa Fe. What sort of business?"

Earl laughed. "You're not gonna believe it, Virge. I quit the sporting life the day I got there. I'm an Indian trader now."

"Indian trader?" Virgil repeated as if he couldn't have heard correctly. "How'd that come about?"

Too late, Earl wished he'd kept his mouth shut. There was no reasonable way to explain his involvement with the *Comancheros*. Nor was he willing to reveal the illicit nature of his activities.

"Outhouse luck," he said cheerfully. "I made friends with a wealthy Mexican. He let me buy into his trading company."

"I understood trading with Indians was against the law."

"Only the hostiles." Earl waved his cheroot, dismissing the thought. "We trade with the peaceful tribes—Navajo and the like."

Virgil looked at him strangely. "What would a Navajo have that's worth trading?"

An indirection came into Earl's eyes. "Oh, they tan pelts and some of them raise horses. Nothing grand, not like your railroad. But it's profitable enough for me."

"And it's all aboveboard . . . legitimate?"

"I hope to tell you!" Earl said too loudly. "We're licensed by the federal government."

A sense of foreboding settled over Virgil. He had a strong suspicion that Earl was lying. Yet there was nothing to be gained in pursuing it further. Whatever the truth, it wouldn't be spoken here tonight.

A cone of silence enveloped them. Quietly smoking, they stared into the crackling fireplace. Virgil made a mental note to write his friends in Washington. He seemed to recall there was an agency responsible for the western tribes.

An agency that licensed Indian traders.

21

ON THE FIRST Saturday in November, Clint departed Fort Clark. Civilian scouts, unlike regular army personnel, were not entitled to military furlough. Still, after submitting a formal request, he'd been granted a month's leave. He planned to spend Thanksgiving with Virgil and Beth.

Colonel Mackenzie was not adverse to granting his request. With the onrush of winter, the horseback tribes had all but vanished from sight. Most were camped on the reservations, where they would draw supplies from the Quaker agents. The Quahadi Comanche, as was their custom, simply disappeared into the vastness of *Llano Estacado*. The raids would not commence again until late spring.

Added to all that, President Grant's administration was attempting one last effort at a peaceful solution. Under pressure from religious groups, the president had agreed to negotiate with the tribes. Government agents were instructed to offer amnesty to all hostiles who agreed to permanent settlement on the reservations. Sherman and Sheridan, much to their disgust, were ordered to forgo a winter campaign. The peace policy was to be allowed a last-ditch chance.

Clint thought it was a pipe dream. His view was shared by the officers and men of Fort Clark, as well as knowledgeable Texans. Only naïve Easterners, who had never seen the aftermath of a Comanche raid, were advocates of offering the olive branch to warlike tribes. Yet, from a personal standpoint, Clint was not altogether displeased by the move. He hadn't taken an actual furlough in nearly two years, which was a large chunk out of any man's life. He figured he was overdue to spend some time with his family.

By stagecoach, he traveled from Brackettville to Dallas. From there, he took a roundabout train ride to Kansas and then hopped a westbound for Colorado. He pulled into Pueblo aboard a Santa Fe passenger coach, where he wired ahead and told Virgil to expect him. Early the next morning, he caught the Denver & Rio Grande to Colorado Springs. For the distance he'd covered, it seemed to him a miracle of the modern age. The entire trip had consumed less than a week.

At the house, he was treated to a hero's welcome. Virgil wrung his hand and Elizabeth kissed him so soundly he blushed like a schoolboy. Hardly before he had his hat off, Jennifer and Morg began peppering him with questions about his exploits on the Mexican border. Even the housekeeper, a woman introduced as Mrs. Murphy, fussed over him as though he'd just returned from some distant and exotic land. He was embarrassed, but not entirely uncomfortable with the attention. He thought a man could grow to like it.

Dinner was a lavish affair. Under the impression that an army scout rarely ate well, Elizabeth and Mrs. Murphy set a table that would have done justice to a boardinghouse. Between mouthfuls, Clint was brought up to date on the family's activities. Somewhat astounded, he listened as Elizabeth related her derring-do as a suffragette. Before he could digest that, Morg launched into a graphic tale of his missing rib bone. Jennifer added a laundered version of her cousin Lon's assault on the local school system. The meal, along with the marathon conversation, left Clint's head buzzing. He wondered if he would last through the Thanksgiving holiday.

After supper, the men retired to the parlor. Clint rolled himself a cigarette while Virgil fired up a cigar. Their talk turned to the Denver & Rio Grande, and Virgil recounted the perils of being a railroader. When the topic had exhausted itself, Virgil steered the conversation onto Earl's recent visit. His tone was subdued and he gradually worked around to what was clearly troubling him. Quoting from memory, he reconstructed the discussion about Earl's business venture. He concluded on a somber note.

"Earl lied to me. I only suspected it when he was here. I know it for a fact now."

Clint looked at him. "What makes you so sure?"

"I checked it out," Virgil said in a grave voice. "I wrote one of my congressman friends in Washington. He spoke with the people at the Bureau of Indian Affairs. Earl doesn't have a license as a trader."

"What about his partner?" Clint asked. "Maybe he's the only one licensed."

"Won't wash," Virgil said. "Earl told me his partner's a Mexican. Nobody with a Spanish surname has a license to trade in New Mexico."

Clint smoked in silence a moment. "You're right, it's not like Earl. Why would he lie to you?"

"Good question," Virgil commented. "I wish I had an answer."

"But you've got an opinion—don't you?"

"I do indeed," Virgil said grimly. "I think he's involved in something illegal. Or to put the worst possible face on it, something criminal."

Clint shook his head ruefully. "I'd hate like hell to believe it. That would mean he's trading with the hostiles."

"Exactly," Virgil grumbled. "And that would make him the worst kind of renegade."

"I hope you're wrong. You might recollect, they hang renegades."

Virgil nodded, suddenly very tired, and slumped down in his chair. "What in God's name possessed him? Why would he get involved in such a thing?"

"Who knows?" Clint frowned, thinking aloud. "Maybe the boy's at the bottom of it. Earl might've done it for him."

"If that's true, then I'm partially to blame. I read Earl the riot act when he and Lon first showed up here."

"You think you were too hard on him?"

"It's possible." Virgil shrugged, eyebrows raised. "I thought I was doing the right thing. He needed somebody to bring him to his senses."

Clint took a slow drag on his cigarette. He studied the fiery tip a moment, his expression abstracted. "Could be a case of a leopard trying to change his spots. Earl always looked up to you."

"I don't take your meaning."

"Well, try to put yourself in his boots. You've got a big house and a big job. Your family's livin' on easy street. And he shows up here busted flat . . . a deadbeat."

Virgil looked at him with dulled eyes. "Clint, I tried my damndest to fix him up with a job. He downright refused."

" 'Course, he did," Clint said. "To him, that would've been a handout."

"At least it would have been honest work."

"Sometimes a man's too proud for his own good."

"I'd judge he's not all that proud of himself now. Otherwise, why would he lie to me?"

Clint's voice was thoughtful. "Maybe he saw a chance to make a quick killing. Figured he'd finally do right by the boy."

"Then God help him," Virgil said. "He's on the road straight to hell."

"I doubt that God's gonna save his bacon."

Virgil felt unaccountably chilled. A sudden impulse told him that Clint would not let it rest here. He stared across at the younger man. "What are you thinking?"

"I'm thinking I won't be able to stick around for Thanksgiving."

"Why not?"

Clint smiled. "Let's say I've got a yen to see Santa Fe."

"I'll go with you," Virgil said quickly. "Maybe between us we can convince him to quit."

"No." Clint's headshake was slow and emphatic. "I'll have enough to worry about with Earl. You'd just cramp my style."

"That sounds like you expect trouble."

"Trouble comes when you least expect it. I've got to where I keep a sharp lookout."

Virgil's expression darkened. "You think he's involved with a bunch of cutthroats, don't you? That's why you don't want me along."

"Tell me," Clint said, ignoring the question. "What's the best way from here to Santa Fe?"

Virgil realized it was hopeless. Nothing he could say would alter Clint's decision. Still, were he to pick a man for the job, Clint would have been his choice. No one he knew was better suited to handling trouble.

He began explaining the route to Santa Fe.

Upon arriving in Santa Fe, Clint went directly to the hotel. There he was informed that Earl could be found in a cantina down the street. The desk clerk imparted the information with a ring of certainty. He seemed well-versed on Earl's daily routine.

Outside, Clint stood for a moment inspecting the plaza. Winter was the slow season and many of the vendors' stalls were closed. He saw few people about and hardly any of them were Anglos. The thought occurred that Santa Fe was still largely Mexican in custom and character. He reminded himself to watch his step.

The cantina was about what he'd expected. Several Mexicans were ranged along a rough bar, and off to the other side were the tables. Looking closer, he spotted Earl seated at a table, playing solitaire. A bottle and glass were at his elbow, and he appeared to have changed little in the eight years since they'd last met. A slight graying at the temples was the only noticeable difference.

Clint halted before the table. "That a private game or can anybody sit in?"

Earl glanced up, startled. His face went slack with surprise and he dropped the cards. "Clint—!"

"Nobody else."

Hitching his chair back, Earl scrambled to his feet. He grabbed Clint's hand and laughed. "Where'd you come from? What the devil are you doing here?"

"Whoa, hoss," Clint said, grinning. "Aren't you gonna offer me a drink?"

"Hell, yes! Here, sit down."

Earl signaled the barkeep for another glass. When they were alone, he poured from the bottle of tequilia. He hoisted his own glass in a toast. "Here's to the old days."

Clint clinked glasses and took a tentative sip. "Where'd you get a taste for the local firewater?"

"It's an acquired habit," Earl said easily. "C'mon now, what's the lowdown? How'd you get here?"

"By way of Colorado Springs. I stopped off to visit Virge and Beth. Figured you were next on the list."

"Well, I'm damned glad to see you. It's been too long since the last time."

"Lot of water under the bridge," Clint agreed. "How are things with your boy?"

"Aces high," Earl said with a wide grin. "You'll meet him when school lets out. He's smart as a whip."

"So Virge told me. He said you and Lon are a pair and a half."

"Virge was mighty good to the boy, and Beth treated him like one of her own. How are they doing?"

"Well . . ." Clint paused, concern in his voice. "Tell

you the truth, Virge is the reason I'm here. He's worried about you.''

A shadow crossed Earl's face. "Why would he worry about me?''

"Mostly because you lied to him.''

"*What*—!''

"You know Virge," Clint said in an offhand manner. "Once he gets his teeth into something, he's like a bulldog. He had your story checked out.''

"I don't follow you. What story?''

"You're not licensed as an Indian trader. Neither is your partner, assuming you have one. Nobody in Washington ever heard of you.''

"Jesus Christ," Earl said in disbelief. "Virgil wrote to Washington?''

"Got all the wrong answers, too.''

Earl brooded on it a moment. "Goddammit, he's got no right poking around in my business.''

"Yeah, he does," Clint said simply, "and so do I. We're your brothers.''

"So what?" Earl snapped. "I'm full-grown.''

Clint looked him directly in the eye. "Suppose you stop dancing around and just level with me. Are you trading with the hostiles?''

Earl stiffened, averting his eyes. He toyed with his glass, clearly groping for a way out. Finally, he sighed heavily and nodded. "I just sort of fell into it. One thing led to another.''

"Tell me about it.''

Haltingly, Earl related the story. He left nothing out concerning Guerra and the *Comancheros*. Yet, on the spur of the moment, he omitted any mention of Little Raven. He saw no reason to touch on personal matters.

When he finished, there was a marked silence. Clint's gaze was faraway and clouded, an unsettled look. At last, shaking his head in wonder, he spoke in a stilled voice.

"The *Comancheros* explains a lot. We never understood how the hostiles were getting hold of repeating rifles."

"We?" Earl said questioningly. "Are you talking about the army?"

Clint stared at him. "Those repeaters have killed a lot of good soldiers."

"I guess you'll be conscience-bound to inform the authorities?"

"Course, I will," Clint said harshly. "We've got to put a stop to it."

"Not likely," Earl told him. "Guerra and the other *Comancheros* have big political connections. Nobody in New Mexico will touch them."

"How do you know that?"

"Guerra likes to brag," Earl said. "Offhand, I'd say he's got good reason. Ask yourself why no one in Texas ever heard of the *Comancheros*."

"They will shortly," Clint promised. "I'll see to that personal."

"What about me?" Earl asked. "You'll put my neck in a noose, too."

Clint wagged his head. "I want you long gone before then. Get Lon and hightail it out of here."

Earl didn't answer for a moment. He forced a wry smile, but his expression was one of absolute resignation. His voice sounded like it was trapped deep in his throat. "I can't quit," he said. "Not just yet, anyway. I married a Comanche woman and she's going to have my baby in the spring. I have to go back."

"You've got rocks in your head. Nobody marries a squaw for real. Any preacher will tell you that."

"Save your breath. A regular church wedding wouldn't have tied the knot any tighter. So far as I'm concerned, we're married."

"Goddammit, Earl, that's plumb loco."

"Maybe so," Earl said, trying to ease the tension with a smile. "But I've got two rules I never break. I don't cheat at cards and I don't run out on my women. Loco or not, she's my wife."

Clint saw that it was useless to argue. Earl had his own twisted sense of honor, and words alone would never persuade him. Something more was needed.

Earl suddenly tensed. His eyes narrowed as Zarate came through the door and walked toward the table. He spoke to Clint in a low voice.

"We're about to have a visitor. Watch what you say or you're liable to get us both killed. He's Guerra's pet rattlesnake."

Clint assessed the hunchback at a glance. On impulse, he abruptly decided to force Earl's hand. He steeled himself to seize the moment.

Zarate halted at the table. His gaze touched on Clint, then shifted to Earl. "Who's your friend?"

"Tell me," Clint broke in, "is it true what people say? Are you *un hombre muy malo*?"

Zarate fixed him with a puzzled scowl. "What concern is that of yours?"

Earl started to interrupt, but Clint silenced him with an upraised palm. "Stay out of it," he said, still staring at Zarate. "I want to hear what this freak has to say."

"Careful, *gringo*," Zarate bridled. "One more word and I'll cut your tongue out."

"Try it and you'll learn the greatest truth of all."

"What truth is that?"

Clint smiled. "The grave straightens out hunchbacks."

"*¡Chinga tu madre!*" Zarate moved even as he spat the obscene curse. He pulled his broad-bladed knife and slashed crosswise, going for the throat.

Clint twisted away, hitching his chair back as the razor tip sliced past his jugular. Then, in one fluid motion, he stood and drew his pistol. He thumbed the hammer as the Colt cleared leather, and fired.

A crimson dot appeared on Zarate's chest. The impact of the slug straightened him up, and for an instant the hump on his back seemed to flatten. He teetered there a moment, then the knife clattered to the floor and he slowly slumped forward. He went down with a jarring crash and lay still.

An oppressive quiet settled over the cantina. Clint shifted slightly and brought the Colt to bear on the men at the bar. Their eyes were fastened on the snout of the pistol, and none of them moved. He glanced down at Earl, who was still seated.

"Let's go," he said. "I've just burned all your bridges."

"Sorry to disappoint you," Earl replied, "but this doesn't change a thing. I'm staying."

"Don't act the fool. How would you explain it to Guerra?"

"I'll think of something. For the moment, we have to worry about you. The *Comancheros* have their own brand of justice."

"You're saying Guerra would have me backshot?"

Earl nodded. "There's a livery stable a block down the street. You'll find a mouse-colored dun in the last stall on the right. Take him and get out of town."

"It won't solve anything," Clint said. "Even if I don't mention your name, I'll still have to make a report. I couldn't do otherwise."

"Go on," Earl told him. "shake a leg. I'll hold these gents till you're on your way."

The men at the bar were straining to hear the muttered conversation. Their expressions remained blank as Earl rose from his chair and pulled his gun. He kept them covered, watching closely while Clint walked to the door. At the last moment, Clint turned and looked back.

Earl smiled, motioning with an idle gesture. A long beat passed before Clint holstered his Colt and stepped outside. When the door swung shut, Earl felt a peculiar sense of loss. He knew a part of his life had ended.

Later, Earl concocted a plausible story. He told the town marshal that he'd been approached by a stranger. The man had identified himself as the brother of the Missouri trader killed by Ignacio Zarate.

As though ordained, Earl went on, Zarate had walked into the cantina. Words were exchanged, and after Zarate pulled a knife, the stranger had shot him. As for his own actions, Earl had a reasonable explanation. He'd held the other customers at gunpoint rather than see the Missourian mobbed. Had he done otherwise, there would have been even more bloodshed.

Ramón Guerra accepted the story at face value. He understood vengeance, and the Missourian, in seeking retribution, had acted as any honorable man would. What he didn't understand was why Earl had given the man a horse, enabling him to escape. To that, Earl replied with blunt directness.

"Sooner or later," he said, "I would have killed Zarate myself. The Missourian saved me the trouble."

Guerra seemed disinclined to pursue it further. While he regretted the loss of his *segundo*, he couldn't fault Earl's part in the affair. He told himself that a man could not be blamed for acting in his own best interests.

The discussion ended there.

22

WINTER PASSED with spectacular grandeur. Heavy snowfall blanketed the mountains and sometimes spread a hoary mantle across the distant plains. The world seemed locked in an arctic tableau.

For a good part of the winter, the Denver & Rio Grande was at a standstill. Construction proceeded in fits and starts, depending on the weather. Some days the numbing cold alone idled me and machines, and frostbite was a constant problem. The track gangs spent much of the time in their bunkcars, huddled around potbellied stoves.

Virgil had but one consolation. The harsh winter stalled the Santa Fe's work crews as well. Before first snowfall, the rival line had overtaken the Denver & Rio Grande. Thereafter, the drive southward had become a neck-and-neck race, with the competition slowly pulling ahead. Unhindered by finances, the Santa Fe was still working double shifts.

In a large measure, Virgil dreaded the end of winter. Once good weather returned construction would resume at the normal pace. He foresaw the Denver & Rio Grande falling farther and farther behind, until it was no longer a contest. Throughout the early months of 1874, winter had been his ally. Yet, as spring approached, the advantage eroded along with the melting snow. Fair weather loomed like some sinister deadfall.

As the days grew longer, Virgil's mood steadily worsened. By letter as well as personal contacts, he had put out feelers over the last several months. None of the eastern banks or financial institutions had offered so much as a scintilla of hope. Having lost its dominant position in Southern Colorado, the Denver & Rio Grande was a railroad with tarnished prospects. The likelihood of obtaining added construction funds seemed increasingly remote.

On a personal note, the news was hardly more encouraging. Virgil had received letters from both Clint and Earl shortly before Christmas. When placed side by side, the letters told highly conflicting stories. Clint's version, which seemed the most believable, merely reaffirmed Virgil's worst fears. Their brother was involved in a perilous game and heedlessly ignoring the danger. The revelation that Earl had married a Comanche woman left Virgil mired in gloom. He thought it a portent of darker days ahead.

Elizabeth was more concerned with the here and now. She watched as Virgil's mood went from despair to impassive melancholy. The mix of business problems and personal worries was sapping his vitality as well as his spirit. She knew him to be a man of endurance and great emotional strength. Yet, because he confided in her, she saw that he was nearing the limit of what was tolerable. Quietly, she took steps to remove part of his burden. She told him nothing, for she was all too aware that he was ruled by stubborn pride. She simply went ahead and hoped for the best.

Walter Tisdale arrived in early April. Ostensibly, at Elizabeth's invitation, he was there to visit his grandchildren. Jennifer and Morgan, remembering how he'd doted on them in Denver, greeted him with noisy exuberance. Virgil's reception was at first somewhat restrained. He hadn't seen his father-in-law in eight years, and his own memories of Denver were hardly pleasant. Still, by the second day of Tisdale's visit, he had thawed noticeably. He seemed genuinely cordial at the dinner table that night.

After supper, Elizabeth insisted that the children help with the dishes. Over their objections, she placed them in charge of Mrs. Murphy, who normally left before the evening meal was served. Virgil was surprised by her adamant manner, for the children were seldom required to perform kitchen chores when the housekeeper worked nights. He was still pondering on it when Elizabeth led the way into the parlor.

Virgil poured brandy for himself and Tisdale, and sherry for Elizabeth. She took a seat on the sofa as the men settled into armchairs. She sat with her hands folded in her lap, curiously attentive and suddenly very quiet. A moment passed while the men busied themselves lighting cigars. Then, with a glance at his daughter, Tisdale addressed Virgil.

"Has Elizabeth told you the latest on David Hughes?"

Virgil frowned at the mention of his old enemy. Hughes was the reason he continued to avoid Denver. "No," he said flatly. "She hasn't told me anything."

"Indeed?" Tisdale gestured with his cigar. "Well, then, I'm the bearer of good tidings. Hughes has departed Denver bag and baggage."

"For good?" Virgil asked.

"Forever!" Tisdale announced jovially. "The reformers overthrew his political machine and hounded him out of town. We've seen the last of David Hughes."

Virgil was visibly impressed. "I take my hat off to them. Hughes was a tough cookie."

"Well, he's past history now. He even sold his interests in the Denver Pacific."

"You're joking!"

"A banker never jokes about money. Hughes was paid a princely sum to divest himself of his railroad holdings."

"Who bought him out?"

"I did," Tisdale said amiably. "Or to be more precise, the bank and a consortium of investors raised the necessary capital. I now control thirty percent of the outstanding stock.''

"Congratulations," Virgil said heartily. "I assume you're on the board of directors as well?"

"Oh, of course," Tisdale replied. "As a matter of fact, that's one reason for my visit. I have a proposition to offer you."

"What sort of proposition?"

"We would like you to take over as president of the Denver Pacific."

Virgil glanced at Elizabeth. She was watching him intently, her mouth curved in a faint smile. She was obviously aware that her father intended to make the offer. Nor was there any doubt that Virgil would find it a tempting notion. He had been one of the original founders of the Denver Pacific.

"I'll have to pass," he said, looking back at Tisdale. "For one thing, I wouldn't consider returning to Denver. That's a closed book and I prefer to leave it that way."

Tisdale puffed a wad of smoke. "I gather there's something more?"

Virgil nodded. "Whoever gets into New Mexico first will make millions on the southwest trade. I'm betting the Denver & Rio Grande will pull it off."

"Perhaps," Tisdale said, eyeing him keenly. "On the other hand, I understand you're strapped for funds."

"We are, temporarily. I'll find the money somewhere."

Tisdale raised a speculative eyebrow. "Suppose I could arrange a loan. Would you be interested?"

"I'll be a monkey's uncle!" Virgil threw back his head and laughed hard. His gaze shifted to Elizabeth with a look of open amusement. "You planned out this whole thing, didn't you? You knew I'd never move back to Denver."

"You have a very suspicious mind, Mr. Brannock."

"And you have a gift for conspiracy, Mrs. Brannock."

She smiled, pleased with herself. With a saucy look, she rose and placed her sherry glass on a nearby table. "I'll leave you to discuss business. I have to check on the children."

Virgil watched as she walked briskly from the room. He shook his head with admiration, still grinning. Then he looked his father-in-law straight in the eye. "All right, Walter," he said, "tell me what you and my wife have cooked up."

Tisdale chuckled slyly. "I understand from Elizabeth that you need a half-million dollars."

"You understand correctly," Virgil said, stuffing the cigar in his mouth. "The question is, what do you want in return?"

"Half the rail traffic from New Mexico. In effect, the Denver Pacific would act as a freight carrier for the Denver & Rio Grande."

"How long are we talking about?"

Tisdale leaned forward, very earnest now. "We've no assurance that your line will beat the Santa Fe into New Mexico. To make it worth the risk, I would require a ten-year contract."

"Forget it," Virgil said emphatically. "There's no way I'd ever sell that to Palmer."

"I'm open to a counterproposal. What would you suggest?"

Virgil kneaded the back of his neck. "The best I could go would be a five-year contract. Even then, you've made yourself quite a deal."

"It's a losing deal," Tisdale pointed out, "unless you get to Raton Pass first."

"We'll get there," Virgil said with conviction. "Otherwise I wouldn't take your half-million."

Tisdale nodded sagely. "When can you talk with Palmer?"

"First thing tomorrow morning."

Virgil neglected to mention what he'd already formulated in his mind. There would be no deal for the Denver

& Rio Grande until he had one for himself. He meant to make William Palmer pay a stiff price.

Early next morning, Virgil rapped on the door of Palmer's office. A muffled voice sounded from within and he moved through the doorway. He nodded as Palmer looked up from his desk.

" 'Morning, Will."

"Good morning."

"Got a minute?"

"Only if it won't wait."

Virgil took a chair. "Would a half-million dollars get your attention?"

Palmer stopped writing. He returned his pen to the inkwell and set the unfinished letter aside. "You have my undivided attention."

"Yesterday," Virgil said affably, "I turned up a source of new financing. Under the circumstances, it's liable to be the last one we'll find."

Palmer peered at him, one eye sharp and gleaming, like a watchful animal. "Who's the lender?"

Virgil smiled. "Before we get to that, I need some assurances myself."

"What are you talking about?"

"Simply put," Virgil said, "I won't work at your sufferance any longer. I want a contract."

"Contract?" Palmer echoed. "What sort of contract?"

"An ironclad, unbreakable, lifetime contract. You'll appoint me senior vice president and agree that I cannot be terminated for any reason."

"The hell I will!" Palmer huffed. "You're out of your mind."

"Don't be too hasty," Virgil advised him. "The alternative would be the construction schedule we're stuck with now. Without the money, we'll never go back to working a double shift."

A crafty look came over Palmer's face. "You wouldn't

risk letting the Santa Fe beat us to Raton Pass. You'd lose everything!"

Virgil met his gaze steadily. "Without a contract, I'll lose anyway. You planned to fire me the day we enter New Mexico."

"That's ridiculous," Palmer objected. "Why would I fire you?"

"Because you're a no-good horse's ass. I wouldn't trust you any farther than I can spit."

The two men stared at each other in silent assessment. Palmer's face was masked by anger and his mouth went tight and bloodless. Several moments elapsed before he was able to collect himself. "All right," he conceded, "you'll have your contract. Now, who's the lender?"

Virgil nodded to the inkwell. "I'll dictate and you write. Then we'll discuss the details."

"Hold on." Palmer's eyes veiled with caution. "How do I know you've made a reasonable deal? What have you pledged in return for this half-million?"

"Let's just say I've mortgaged the future. Everything is contingent on our reaching New Mexico."

"That sounds a little vague."

"Do you want the money or not?"

Palmer hesitated, then dipped his pen in the inkwell. Virgil dictated a contract so irrevocable that it was all but carved in stone. When it was finished, complete with Palmer's signature, he tucked it away in his coat pocket.

Quickly, with no great elaboration, Virgil then explained the deal. Palmer's look of skepticism slowly dissolved into a smirky grin. He shook his head with grudging admiration.

"Virge, whatever else you are, you're a shrewd bastard. That's a no-lose proposition."

"I thought you'd like it." Virgil rose and walked from the office.

On a warm afternoon late in April, the people of Colorado Springs gathered to celebrate Founders Day. It was a

community function held every year outside the county
courthouse. The town's main street was draped with bunting and flags, and by high noon nearly a thousand people
jammed the boardwalks along the business district.

The festivities were elaborate and well-organized. A
parade, sponsored by local merchants, would feature the
volunteer fire department and a marching band from the
Good Fellows League. There were to be speeches and
street dancing, and late that afternoon, a barbecue supper
courtesy of the town fathers. It promised to be a momen-
tous day, honoring both the founders of Colorado Springs
and the homesteaders who had settled the countryside.

The courthouse was an imposing stone structure located
in the heart of town. A speakers' platform had been hammered together and festooned with patriotic decorations.
As one o'clock approached, the crowd began congregating
on the street outside the courthouse. The festivities were to
be opened by remarks from the Honorable Wallace Gentry, mayor of Colorado Springs. Following speeches by
local notables, the parade was scheduled to get under way.
Saloons were doing a brisk trade, and half the men in the
throng of spectators were already fortified for the occasion. By nightfall, only churchmen and teetotalers would
pass the test for sobriety.

On the speakers' platform was an assemblage of the
town's big augers. Among the politicos were the mayor
and several county officials, including the sheriff. Arnold
Hecht and Jeff Dawson, as members of the town council,
were relegated to chairs in the back row. The guest of
honor was the president of the Denver & Rio Grande,
General William Palmer. In large degree, he was the
founder of both the railroad and the town. Politicians and
businessmen buzzed around him like vassals paying hom-
age to their liege lord. No one questioned his influence
within the power structure of Colorado Springs.

Virgil was seated on the last chair in the first row. As
senior vice president of the railroad, his position in the

community was second only to Palmer. His political connections, particularly at the federal level, commanded the respect of every man on the speakers' platform. Yet he avoided involvement in local affairs and took little interest in the town's politics. His presence today was a matter of courtesy rather than a sense of civic responsibility. He watched with sardonic amusement as the officialdom of Colorado Springs swirled around William Palmer.

Presently everyone took their seats. Mayor Gentry, who was attired in a stovepipe hat and hammertail coat, walked to the speakers' podium. A murmur ran through the crowd as he raised his arms for silence. Then the noise subsided and the mayor removed his hat, gazing out across the upturned faces. His voice carried all along the street.

"Good friends and neighbors! Allow me to welcome you to our annual Founders Day. Not long ago, where you're standing at this very moment was a barren wasteland. Today, we're blessed with prosperity and a town that's only begun to grow. We are truly the—"

A loud thumping sound cut short his speech. As he halted in midsentence, the onlookers turned and stared upstreet. From the direction of the main intersection, the thumping sound slowly swelled to the beat of a bass drum. Voices raised in song, all of them feminine, gradually became distinct. The words were the familiar standard of crusaders everywhere, "Onward Christian Soldiers."

Elizabeth marched at the head of the column. Arrayed behind her was a phalanx of some twenty women, striding along two abreast. In the first rank, with the drum strapped over her ample bosoms, Amanda Dawson pounded a steady marching beat. All the other women carried cardboard placards attached to poles. Emblazoned on the placards were slogans advocating the rights of women and universal suffrage.

The crowd parted as the little band of suffragettes angled toward the speakers' platform. The women sang louder, waving their placards, oblivious to the catcalls and heck-

ling in their wake. Farmers and townsmen slapped one
another across the shoulders, laughing and shouting as
they pointed their fingers in ridicule. With a final drumbeat, the song ended and the column halted. An instant of
leaden silence slipped past, then Elizabeth stepped forward.

"Mr. Mayor—"

Scattered boos and sullen curses drowned out whatever
she was about to say. A knot of men grouped before the
platform were the loudest of the lot. Fueled on alcohol,
they abruptly charged into the women. One roughly shoved
Elizabeth aside and another put his fist through the bass
drum. Others began grabbing the placards, trying to wrest
them away from the women. Sudden pandemonium swept
through the crowd.

Virgil vaulted over the platform railing. He landed in
the middle of the fray just as Elizabeth stormed toward the
man who had shoved her. Brushing past her, Virgil hit the
man with a sharp chopping blow that knocked him to the
ground. Another man turned on Virgil and they squared
off with fists raised. All around them the women were
shrieking and pounding their assailants with the placards,
which by now were reduced to tatters and shreds. Following Virgil's example, several men stepped forward from
the crowd to join the fight.

Sheriff Odell Johnson fired his pistol into the air. The roar
of the gunshot brought the scuffle to an abrupt standstill.
The drunks separated from the suffragettes and a sudden
hush fell over the onlookers. Everyone craned for a better
view of the sheriff, who was standing at the edge of the
speakers' platform. He nodded politely to Elizabeth.

"Mrs. Brannock, I think you ladies have made your
point. I'd hate to arrest you for disorderly conduct and
breaking the peace. So you'll oblige me by clearing the
street without further incident."

Elizabeth stared at him for a long moment. Then, to the
delight of the spectators, she kissed Virgil soundly on the
mouth. Without a word, she signaled her bedraggled fol-

lowers and they marched off through the crowd. Their backs were ramrod-straight and their heads were held high with pride. Behind, they left a shattered drum and a pile of broken placards.

Dusting himself off, Virgil walked to the steps at the end of the platform. Several men pounded him on the back and their women followed him with admiring glances. As he resumed his seat, he exchanged a look with William Palmer. The railroader frowned and wagged his head in disgust. Virgil smiled, listening as the suffragettes once again raised their voices in song.

Onward Christian soldiers, marching as to war . . .

23

EARLY IN JUNE the *Comancheros* ventured once again onto the Staked Plains. Ramón Guerra led his dusty column of *carretas* along the ancient trail stretching from the Pecos to the Brazos. Their destination was *Las Casas Amarillos*, the Canyon of Yellow Houses.

No stranger now to *Llano Estacado*, Earl rode out front of the wagons. He approached the new trading season with a sense of unconcerned fatalism. Whether or not the army was searching for the *Comancheros* seemed to him a matter of supreme indifference. He believed that any such campaign would be restricted to the eastern badlands, well south of the Cap Rock. Never before had the military dared a deeper probe into *Comancheria*.

Confident of his own assessment, Earl had gone a step farther. There were no secrets between himself and Lon, and the boy had badgered him incessantly to be taken along on the trip. Certain that no danger would befall the youngster, he had finally relented. A contributing factor was his reluctance to leave Lon alone in Santa Fe. Then, too, he felt it only appropriate that the boy should meet Little Raven. By now she would have given birth to a child, which meant Lon had either a half-brother or a half-sister. An introduction seemed in order.

Guerra offered only mild objections. While he wouldn't bring a child of his own onto the Staked Plains, he saw no reasonable way to deny Earl. So Lon was fitted out with trail clothes and a gentle saddlehorse and allowed to come along. From the outset, as though born to it, he displayed a natural affinity for the outdoor life. He reveled in the vastness of the plains and the easy camaraderie around the campfire. Before long the *Comancheros* were calling him *hombrecito*, the little man.

Upon arriving at the Quahadi village, Earl discovered that he had a new son. Little Raven had given birth to a boy child some three months past, while the band was still encamped at Palo Duro Canyon. The baby was lighter than his mother, clearly a half-breed, but with a shock of black hair. Like all Comanche males, he would not receive a formal name until he'd grown to a small boy. Earl, for want of a better name, decided to call him Hank.

Lon evidenced only passing curiosity about his stepbrother. He looked Little Raven over with a critical eye and apparently thought she passed inspection. To Earl's relief, he displayed no signs of jealousy toward either the mother or the baby. Instead, he seemed content the moment he stepped into the lodge, accepting it as his new home. He allowed Little Raven to fuss over him and wolfed down a bowl of buffalo stew with hungry gusto. By early evening, he was fast asleep on a furry robe.

Later, when the lodge was dark, Earl and Little Raven crawled into their bed robes. Their long separation had kindled within her a fiery passion and she came to him like a minx in season. They coupled quickly and he was amazed by the depth of his own emotion. Afterward, as they lay quietly in each other's arms, he realized that his loyalty had not been misguided. She was his wife, the mother of his child, and the one woman he truly needed. He felt like a wanderer who had returned at last to the place called home.

Little Raven snuggled closer. Her voice was soft and

warm, but somehow troubled. She spoke to him in halting Spanish. "I am concerned for the boy."

"Lon?"

She bobbed her head. "Because he is your son, the elders will accept him. The children will not."

Earl lay very still. "What will happen?"

"To the children, he is a blue-eyed intruder. He will be taunted and forced to endure abuse. They will treat him harshly."

"Are you saying he will never be accepted?"

"No." She hesitated, searching for words. "They will test him and try to break his spirit. How he behaves will show what he is inside."

"I see," Earl said slowly. "They believe him to be a coward, unworthy of acceptance. He must prove himself somehow—prove them wrong."

"Yes, my husband. But all will be against him; no child would dare take his side. And there is another thing."

"What is that?"

She rose up on one elbow. Even in the dark, her eyes seemed to glow with intensity. "The boy must stand alone. You cannot interfere or show your concern. To do so would bring dishonor on all in our lodge."

Earl mulled it over for a long while. He was faced with a clear choice, one that evolved from centuries of Comanche custom. He could keep Lon at his side throughout their visit, thereby preventing any confrontation with the village children. On the other hand, he could allow the boy to be subjected to a harsh test of character. For an eight-year-old, neither of the options was pleasant to contemplate.

Just for a moment Earl wished he hadn't brought the youngster along. But then, upon deeper reflection, he realized he was shortchanging the boy. Lon was a scrapper, mentally tough and accustomed to hard knocks. He'd been raised on the Barbary Coast and he had held his own with street hooligans and teenage thugs. All the more significant, he was wise beyond his years. Any attempt to shield him would be obvious, and bitterly resented. His pride simply wouldn't allow it.

"I won't interfere," Earl said at length. "A boy must find his own way in life. Only then will he become a man."

Little Raven nestled her head on his shoulder. "I trust your judgment, my husband. After all, the boy is his father's son."

"Even more, he's a Brannock. And mark my word, we're not quitters."

In subsequent days, the statement proved to be prophetic. Lon was given the run of the village and he quickly encountered the hostility reserved for "blue-eyed devils." At first, the antagonism took the form of taunts and jeers. Wherever he went, the village children ganged around, mocking him with laughter and shouts of derision. When he ignored them, they were provoked to harsher measures. The boys began crowding him, jostling and shoving, growing progressively rougher. Their insults assumed a feral tone.

His chief tormentor was a youngster about his own age. The boy's name was White Bear, and the other children seemed to have appointed him as their leader. On Lon's third day in the village, White Bear blocked his path as he walked toward the stream. Too quick to counter, the Comanche youngster hooked a heel behind his leg and shoved him to the ground. Everyone within sight stopped what they were doing to watch. Indian children practiced a rough-and-tumble form of wrestling and it was the accepted way to settle disputes. White Bear had just issued a challenge.

Climbing to his feet, Lon cocked his fists. White Bear stared at him quizzically, then suddenly grabbed for an armlock. Lon popped him in the nose and followed with a haymaker right to the jaw. Staggered by the blows, White

Bear went down on the seat of his breechclout. Game but groggy, he levered himself off the ground and got to his feet.

In rapid succession, Lon knocked him down four times. Finally, his nose bloodied and his lip split, White Bear failed to rise. After a moment, Lon stepped forward and assisted him off the ground. They took one another's measure and Lon silently extended his hand in friendship. The gesture was at once magnanimous and unexpected. Swallowing his pride, White Bear grinned and accepted the handshake.

Word spread through the camp within minutes. The Comanche had never seen anyone—man or boy—who fought with his fists. The concept was alien and thought by some to be another form of *tahbay-boh* trickery. Yet the Quahadi admired a winner, and they revered bravery above all attributes. By nightfall, one of the elders had dubbed Lon with a tribal name. A literal translation meant "he who strikes with both hands." Because that was too cumbersome, the people shortened it to something more manageable. Lon was thereafter known as Strikes Both Ways.

White Bear and Strikes Both Ways became inseparable. Before long, Lon was togged out in breechclout and moccasins and tanned brown as bark. He taught White Bear the rudiments of fisticuffs, and their sparring sessions never failed to draw a crowd. In turn, White Bear taught him the bow and arrow and how to ride horseback at a full gallop. Mounted on buffalo ponies, they were like young centaurs, riding on the wind. Nothing seemed beyond them, no dare too great.

Watching them, Earl experienced mixed feelings. He was proud of Lon, the pride of a father whose son has taken the first step on the passage to manhood. By not interfering, by allowing the boy to fight his own battles, he had himself garnered considerable honor. Quanah and the men of the band now treated him more like a Comanche than a *Comanchero*. He had taken a Quahadi woman to wife and sired a Quahadi son, and the actions of his blue-eyed son proved the strength of his seed. The elders thought it only fitting that he be honored with a Quahadi name. He was now called Stone Bull.

For all that, Earl still had misgivings. The boy known as Strikes Both Ways was fast being transformed into a young savage. As he'd done last summer, Earl had elected to stay behind when Guerra and the *Comancheros* returned to Santa Fe. A fornight had passed since their departure and each day saw Lon draw closer to the Quahadi way of life. The boy was already mastering the Comanche tongue, and apart from his blue eyes and sun-bleached hair, he seemed much like the other youngsters. No longer was Earl surprised that captive children were so easily converted to horseback barbarians. He saw it happening to his own son.

By the third week in June, Earl began searching for excuses to return to Santa Fe. Nothing clever or particularly believable occurred to him until other tribes started drifting into camp. He heard talk of a shaman called Eeshatai and rumors of a Sun Dance. As well, there was talk of war on the buffalo-killers, the *tahbay-boh* with long guns. A war to halt the slaughter of the herds.

He decided, once again, that it was time to leave *Comanchería*.

For the last month, Quahadi hunters had returned to camp with a stark message. On a scout of three days' sleep they found mile upon mile of rotting carcasses and whitening bones. The plains were soaked with the blood of buffalo.

Listening to the men talk, Earl was hardly surprised by the reports. Hide-hunting was big business and had been for the past four years. The slaughter began in earnest in 1870, when eastern tanneries discovered a process for converting buffalo hides to commercial leather. During the previous hunting season, Dodge City alone had shipped more than a million hides eastward. At three dollars or better a hide, there was a fortune to be made on the western plains.

Estimates of the great herds placed the numbers of buffalo somewhere between sixty million and a hundred million. Whatever the true figure, the herds had been reduced by tens of millions in only four short years. Some hunters killed upward of two hundred beasts a day, and kept a crew of hide-skinners busy from morning till night. There were hundreds of such operations on the plains, and wagons filled with bloody hides rumbled into distant rail-heads from early spring until late fall. There was profit in butchery and no dirth of men eager to take part in the slaughter.

No legal means existed for halting the bloodbath. Nor was the government concerned with the extermination of the herds. From a practical standpoint, the army looked upon the hide-hunters as allies. General Sherman argued that to oppose the extermination of buffalo was to impede the advance of civilization. His western commander, Phil Sheridan, applauded the hunters for destroying the Indians' "commissary." Without buffalo, the specter of starvation would soon force the Plains tribes onto the reservations. The killing, with the tacit approval of the government, went on unabated.

By treaty, the Comanche and other horseback tribes were guaranteed the sanctity of the southern herd. A regulation, in effect since 1867, strictly forbade hide-hunters from operating below the Arkansas River. Yet the army routinely ignored their activities, and cavalry patrols, by unwritten order, made no effort to turn them back. Emboldened by their alliance with the military, the hunters went farther and farther afield. For the first time, in the spring of 1873, they invaded the high plains of the Texas Panhandle. Their pursuit of the great southern herd brought them at last to *Comanchería.*

A week ago one of the Quahadi scouting parties returned with a disturbing report. The buffalo-killers had advanced farther westward than ever before, and their numbers were growing. At the site of an abandoned trading post called Adobe Walls, they had established a base camp. From there, they ranged out over the plains with their long guns and their wagons, slaughtering a thousand or more buffalo every day. The scouts reported that the buffalo-killers numbered almost thirty, and with them was one woman. Nowhere within a day's ride was there any sign of a pony soldier patrol.

After listening to the scouts, Quanah conferred with the council elders. Then he sent swift-riding messengers to summon all the tribes encamped in *Comanchería*. To the disgust of every Quahadi, only scattered members of the four Comanche bands were to be found. But other horseback tribes, those with their warrior spirit still intact, had left the reservations in the Leaf Bud Moon. Among them were the Quahadi's allies, the Kiowa, as well as the Arapaho and the Southern Cheyenne. All agreed to meet with Quanah and smoke the pipe of war.

Earl and Lon departed the day the war council began. Except for Little Raven, hardly anyone took notice of their leaving. The reason was a great excitement surrounding the appearance of Eeshatai, the Comanche *puhakut*. A mystic and healer, Eeshatai was acknowledged as the most powerful of all tribal shamans. He was believed to have brought back the dead and there was talk that he had ascended to the land beyond and communed with the spirit forces. Only a winter past he had predicted that a comet would light the skies and signal a summer of drought. As he foretold, so it had happened.

The spirits were thought to be capricious as well as merciful. Every Comanche warrior sought supernatural power, the gift called *puha*, or medicine. Yet it was known that the spirits favored certain individuals, granting them stronger medicine and magical powers. These men, the _puhakut_, were capable of overcoming illness as well as casting death spells on the healthy. Their blessing was widely sought by war parties, and the power of their _puha_ was believed to make warriors victorious in battle. Among all the Comanche _puhakuts_, Eeshatai was considered the one true voice of the spirits.

A prophet before, he now proclaimed himself a messiah. At the vast gathering of the Quahadi and the other tribes, he told of a vision quest lasting four days and four nights. The spirits had spoken to him and revealed that the time of deliverance from the evil _tahbay-boh_ was near. The tribes were to be brought together in one encampment and there the spirits ordered that they perform the sacred Sun Dance. When the dance was over, the warriors would fall upon the buffalo-killers and annihilate them. The victory would signal a war of extermination, one in which the _tejanos_ would be driven from the land. Then, with the tribes united, their world would be as it had been in ancient times. The _tahbay-boh_, once gone, would never return.

Eeshatai's message inflamed the vast assemblage. At sundown, the drums throbbed and the women began to chant. Fires were lighted and the warriors formed in one great mass, stomping and shuffling in unison until the earth itself shook. Gathered there were seven hundred horseback tribesmen, Comanche and Kiowa, Arapaho and Cheyenne, all bonded by a single blood oath. They performed the Sun Dance for three days, spurred on by the chants and the drums, the eerie sigh of rattles and eagle-bone whistles. Finally, as dawn rose on the fourth day, Eeshatai declared that the spirits were appeased. He proclaimed a blessing on all who rode against the buffalo-killers.

Quanah was appointed war chief by acclamation. With Eeshatai riding at his side, he led the horde of mounted warriors southward onto the high plains. Just before dawn of the following day, the massed war party reined to a halt atop a knoll overlooking Adobe Walls. The ponies stamped and pawed, tossing their heads in the ghostly twilight of impending sunrise. Eeshatai, who had stripped naked and painted his body yellow, sat staring at the trading post for a long moment. Then, finally, he turned to the Quahadi leader and nodded. Quanah raised his arm and dropped it, signaling the attack. Their voices raised in a thunderous roar, the warriors rode down off the ridge.

Eeshatai's *puha* proved to be flawed. By chance, two of the hide-hunters were already awake, standing outside the main building. They gave the alarm even as Quanah signaled the attack, and the element of surprise was lost. The hunters quickly forted up in the old trading post and a nearby outbuilding. Superb marksmen, the defenders were armed with .50-caliber Sharps rifles, capable of dropping a buffalo at a thousand yards. Firing from behind cover, they smashed back the assault with volley after deadly volley. The war party retreated to the distant ridge.

For three days, the horseback warriors laid siege to the trading post. Yet their attacks were blunted by the heavy Sharps, and they were unable to overrun the buildings. At long range their carbines were no match for the buffalo guns, and their casualties steadily mounted. Fifteen warriors were killed, as opposed to three hunters, and Quanah narrowly escaped death when his horse was shot from beneath him. Finally, late on the third day, Eeshatai's magic was destroyed for all time. A warrior mounted beside him on the ridge was blown off his horse. The shot had carried almost a mile and even Quanah accepted it as an omen. The horde turned and rode away from Adobe Walls.

With Eeshatai's downfall, the alliance forged by Quanah quickly shattered. Comanche and Kiowa, Arapaho and Cheyenne rode their separate ways under a hot June sun. Yet the war against the *tahbay-boh* was by no means ended on the rolling prairie outside Adobe Walls. The

24

By EARLY August, there was a general uprising among the Plains tribes. The Kiowa, as well as members of the four Comanche bands, jumped the reservation after being ordered to assemble at Fort Sill. They joined Quanah and his Quahadi on the Staked Plains.

The raids were widespread and particularly vengeful in nature. The Arapaho and Cheyenne rode north and west, pillaging Kansas and Colorado. Texans were subjected to unrelenting terror by their ancient enemies, the Comanche and Kiowa. The death toll mounted steadily, with almost two hundred Anglos butchered beyond recognition. Settlers everywhere abandoned their homesteads and sought refuge at the nearest army post.

The uprising ultimately brought a backlash of public opinion. As newspapers reported on the "atrocities," the arguments of humanitarians were lost in a storm of outrage. Public revulsion led to political expediency, and the attitude in Washington swung full circle. The Quaker Peace Policy was abruptly terminated, and President Grant ordered the army to "subdue all Indians who offer resistance to constituted authority." All restrictions were lifted from the military, and Indian Territory was no longer to be treated as a sanctuary. Any tribes caught off the reservations were to be considered hostile.

The change in policy was not limited to the southern

plains. There was to be a general pacification of all the western tribes. The Sioux and the other northern tribes were to be treated no differently than the Comanche. Never again were the Indians to be permitted to wander at will or terrorize Anglo settlers. Those who surrendered were to be considered prisoners of war and herded onto the reservations. Those who resisted were to be attacked and pursued and destroyed. No amnesty was to be offered to anyone, including women and children.

There was little opposition to what constituted a declaration of war. Editorials throughout the country supported the government, advocating the advance of civilization over the "rights of a few aborigines." The Comanche, in particular, were vilified by the press. Quanah and his warlike Quahadi were widely denounced for inciting the other tribes and formenting "a summer of barbaric horror." The protests of eastern religious orders were drowned out by the public outcry for retribution. Peace on the western plains was to be imposed by military force.

Late in August, General Phil Sheridan moved against the southern tribes. He ordered a campaign characterized by bold strategy and absolute ruthlessness. At the core of his military objective was the subjugation of the Quahadi Comanche. A vast sweep of the southern plains was to be conducted, with army units converging from every direction on *Comancheria*. The net was to be drawn ever tighter, and for the first time, troops would penetrate deep into the unknown wastes of *Llano Estacado*. The Comanche and Kiowa were to be pursued and hounded without letup, even if the campaign extended into winter. Those who refused to submit were to be hunted down and killed.

From Fort Dodge, Colonel Nelson Miles was ordered south with eight troops of the 6th Cavalry and four companies of the 5th Infantry. Colonel John Davidson was to advance westward from Fort Sill with six troops of the 10th Cavalry and two companies of the 11th Infantry. From northern Texas, Colonel George Buell was to pro-

ceed northwesterly with six troops of the 9th and 10th
Cavalry and two companies of infantry. Major William
Price, with four troops of the 8th Cavalry, was to sweep
eastward from Fort Bascom, New Mexico.

The 4th Cavalry was designated the Southern Column.
Mackenzie was ordered to push northward from Fort Clark
toward the headwaters of the Red River. His command
would be comprised of some six hundred men, with eight
troops of cavalry and five infantry companies detached
from Fort Concho. The infantry was to act as escort for his
supply train and guard a base camp to be established on
the Freshwater Fork of the Brazos River. Because Sheridan
admired his aggressive style, Mackenzie was awarded the
pivotal mission. His orders were to probe *Llano Estacado*
and locate the Quahadi band. He was to kill, or capture,
the war chief Quanah.

On August 22, the campaign was prematurely touched
off. A band of Nakoni Comanche, returning from a raid
into Texas, sought sanctuary in Indian Territory. Operating
out of Fort Sill, Colonel Davidson and his 10th Cavalry
tangled with the band of hostiles. After a stiff fight, with
the Comanche joined by a band of Kiowa, the combined
force of hostiles fled westward. Farther north, Colonel
Miles and the 6th Cavalry engaged in a running battle with
some two hundred Cheyenne warriors. Finally, after five
hours of bitter fighting, the Cheyenne retreated southward
onto the Staked Plains. Far from solving anything, the skirmish merely drove another warlike band into *Comanchería*.

A few days later, Mackenzie summoned the troop commanders to regimental headquarters. All summer the men
of the 4th had chased raiding parties up and down the
border. Several clashes had resulted, but none of the engagements was of a conclusive nature. The warriors were
constantly on the move, with no permanent camps, and the
opportunity to deliver a decisive blow simply hadn't materialized. But now, there were rumors of a massive campaign, being orchestrated by Sheridan himself. As yet

Mackenzie had confided in no one, and the officers therefore hoped that today might be the day. To a man, they
thought the time for a major offensive was long overdue.

Clint was summoned along with the officers. As chief of
scouts, he was critical to the success of any mission.
Today, the role of his Seminole scouts suddenly assumed a
mantle of grave significance. Mackenzie's opening statement riveted the attention of everyone in the room.

"Gentlemen, I have good news. We have been ordered
to proceed forthwith to the Staked Plains. Our mission is
to capture—or destroy—the Quahadi Comanche."

The officers appeared stunned. No cavalry unit had ever
penetrated the uncharted wilderness of *Llano Estacado.*
Clint's reaction was one of troubled uneasiness, mixed
with lingering guilt. Week by week, since his return from
Santa Fe, he had put off reporting on the *Comancheros.*
He saw no way of exposing the traders without incriminat-
ing his own brother. Until now he had justified his silence
with the fact that army patrols always stopped short of the
Staked Plains. That excuse abruptly ceased to exist.

"The campaign," Mackenzie went on, "has but one
purpose. The hostiles are to be pacified and driven onto
the reservations. Those who resist will be shown no mercy."

Using his riding crop as a pointer, Mackenzie turned to a
large map on the wall. He quickly briefed them on the
coordinated effort, indicating the five army columns that
would converse on *Comanchería.* Then, with a cold
smile, he informed them that Indian Territory would no
longer serve as a sanctuary. Any hostile band could be
tracked down, and attacked, wherever the trail might lead.

A murmur of approval rippled through the officers.
Mackenzie waited for them to quiet before he resumed. On
his fingers he ticked off certain crucial points. There was a
thrum of iron in his voice.

"Hostiles will not be allowed to surrender to Indian
agents. They will be taken into custody by an army unit—or
forced to fight.

"The women and children of hostile bands, along with their old people, will be turned away from the agencies. As a result, the warriors will be slowed down by their families and forced to hunt—or go hungry.

"All hostiles taken captive will be treated as prisoners of war. They will be disarmed, their horses will be confiscated, and they will be marched—on foot—to the reservations."

Mackenzie paused, his eyes like ball bearings. "We will not allow the Comanche time to hunt winter meat. We will harass them, keep them on the move, and destroy their camps wherever found. If necessary, we will resupply ourselves in the field and campaign into winter."

No one moved as he stood there a moment, staring at them. His voice took on an ominous note. "We will pursue Quanah and the Quahadi and bring them to bay. When they turn to fight, I want it understood throughout this command—no quarter will be given."

The officers understood completely. Quanah and his band would be pursued relentlessly. Their camps would be destroyed and their food supplies exhausted. Their women would tire, and the old people and children would weaken from hunger. The campaign would be one of attrition and surrender, or extermination.

"Any questions?" Mackenzie asked.

"Yes, sir," Captain Carter replied. "We know nothing about the Staked Plains. Without maps, we'll be operating in the dark. How do you propose to find Quanah?"

"I'll leave that to Mr. Brannock and his scouts. Somewhere out there, I'm confident we'll cut sign. When we do, we'll follow it till doomsday."

"Colonel, what happens if we don't cut sign? There's thousands of square miles of empty land out there."

The question was foremost on the mind of every officer present. Like all rational men, they had an innate dread of the unknown. To die in battle was a soldier's lot, an occupational hazard. To die of thirst on barren plains was another matter entirely.

Mackenzie slapped his open palm with the riding crop. He stared hard at Carter. "Have I ever led you wrong before, Captain?"

"No, sir!"

"Then accept my word and pass it along to the men under your command. We *will* find the Quahadi."

"Yes, sir."

"We march in three days, gentlemen. I suggest you be about your business."

The officers snapped to attention, saluting smartly. Mackenzie returned their salute and sat down as they trooped out of the office. When the door closed, Clint was still standing before the desk.

Mackenzie looked up. "Something more, Mr. Brannock?"

"Yessir." Clint shuffled uneasily, staring down at the floor. "I've got something to tell you, Colonel. You're not gonna like it."

"Indeed?" Mackenzie eyed him obliquely. "Please go on, Mr. Brannock. I'm listening."

Clint squared himself up. "Have you ever heard of a bunch called the *Comancheros*?"

"No, I don't believe I have. What does the term mean?"

"A rough translation would be 'those who trade with the Comanche.' "

Mackenzie fixed him with a piercing look. "What sort of trade?"

"The usual geegaws," Clint said, "along with some whiskey. The worst part's the guns—repeating rifles and cartridges."

Mackenzie sat there a moment, his face pale with anger. When he spoke, his voice was very low. "I believe you had best explain yourself, Mr. Brannock."

Clint's expression was stoic. Touching on salient details, he outlined the system of trade that existed between the hostiles and the *Comancheros*. He noted that the *Comancheros* were headquartered in Santa Fe and bartered their goods across the far-flung regions of *Llano Estacado*.

While loosely organized, he observed, their political connections greatly reduced the risk of exposure. The one thing he omitted was any mention of Earl's involvement.

Mackenzie listened without interruption or comment. His eyes narrowed in concentration, and when Clint finished, he pondered it at length. Finally, he shook his head.

"Why have you waited until now to tell me?"

"Personal reasons," Clint said, meeting his gaze. "That's as much as I care to say."

"No, by God!" Mackenzie's voice cracked like a whiplash. "Personal reasons won't hold when a state of war exists. I'll have an answer, Mr. Brannock."

Clint seemed turned to stone. His eyes took on a haunted look and he was silent for a long while. At last, his shoulders lifted in a resigned shrug.

"One of my brothers lives in Santa Fe. When I was through there last fall, he told me the whole story. He somehow got himself involved with the *Comancheros*."

"I see," Mackenzie said in a precise voice. "Out of concern for your brother, you failed to report what you'd learned. Is that correct?"

"Yessir," Clint admitted. "Course, after today, I had to speak up. Figured you ought to know before you took off after Quanah."

Mackenzie nodded, thoughtful. "Well, at least we know how they obtain repeating weapons. I only wish you had come to me sooner."

"Yeah, me too," Clint mumbled. "Am I under arrest or will you let me resign?"

"When I want your resignation, I'll ask for it. Understood?"

"Colonel, you need a scout you can trust. How do you know I won't warn my brother?"

"To what purpose?" Mackenzie inquired. "A cavalry regiment tends to draw attention, Mr. Brannock. Quanah's own scouts will alert him long before he hears it from the *Comancheros*."

"Maybe so," Clint conceded. "But that still doesn't answer the question. Why would you want me to stay on?"

"I can think of two reasons. First, you've earned the respect of the Seminoles and we'll need you on the campaign. As for the second, let's just say you've earned my respect as well. You didn't have to tell me about the *Comancheros*."

"Well . . ." Clint seemed stumped for words. "I halfway figured you'd want my head."

Mackenzie dismissed the thought with a brusque gesture. "What I want are more details, Mr. Brannock. As an example, you mentioned the stolen livestock only in passing. What happens to all those horses and cows?"

"The way I understand it, they're sold to ranchers in New Mexico. I reckon nobody's too concerned with a bill of sale."

"What about brands? Wouldn't that cause people to ask questions?"

"When the price is right, folks tend to overlook the particulars. Besides, New Mexicans never had much love for Texans anyway."

Mackenzie studied him a moment. "What we're talking about is a rather widespread conspiracy. No one questions that the livestock is stolen. Yet, at the same time, no one reports it either."

"Sounds like there's enough profit to go around."

"Enough for everyone," Mackenzie agreed. "The politicians, the local authorities, the ranchers—perhaps even the army."

Clint looked surprised. "How would the army get involved?"

"The quartermaster on every post buys remount horses. Wouldn't you think they'd be interested in brands?"

"Yeah, I would," Clint said thoughtfully. "All the more so if those brands had been altered with a running iron."

"I suspect you've done the army a great service, Mr. Brannock. One day soon, we'll have to take a closer look at these *Comancheros*."

"But not now," Clint said evenly. "Or did I hear wrong?"

Mackenzie laughed shortly. "For the moment, we'll concern ourselves with the hostiles. After that, I've no doubt the renegades will come under scrutiny."

On his way out the door, Clint was struck by a random thought. Because of the upcoming campaign, the *Comancheros* had been given a reprieve of sorts. He hoped Earl would use it to put distance between himself and Santa Fe.

O'Hara stopped him in the orderly room. The sergeant major vaguely resembled an overgrown leprechaun, albeit one with a pugilist's flattened nose. There was a curious glint in his eye, laughter hardly contained.

"Well, now," he said in a jocular voice, "all good things come to him who waits. I told you we'd go after the bloody redsticks one of these days."

"So you did," Clint acknowledged. "And high time, too."

"Aye," O'Hara rumbled. "They've had themselves a merry summer. But I'm thinking we'll soon put a stop to that."

"From what I just heard, that's an understatement. The whole goddamn army plans to take the field."

"All the same, General Sheridan has given us the plum assignment. No other regiment would stand a chance of running Quanah to ground."

"Probably not," Clint allowed. "What does your crystal ball tell you about our chances? Will we catch him?"

O'Hara burst out laughing. "If it's a prediction you want, I'll give you one. That heathen devil won't last out the winter. We'll have him in a ball and chain—or dead."

"Either way sounds good to me."

"Given a choice, Mr. Brannock, I'd take the ghost over mortal flesh. A dead man would never again lead them off the reservation."

The statement was revealing. As Clint crossed the parade ground, he thought O'Hara's attitude reflected the wishes of the army high command. Sherman and Sheridan would clearly prefer to see Quanah dead and buried and forgotten. It all had the faint sound of a death sentence.

Clint walked on toward the creek. He found Elijah Daniel seated under a tall cottonwood, behind the row of adobe houses. The Seminole leader listened impassively as Clint related details of the forthcoming campaign. His dark features twisted in a scowl at the mention of *Llano Estacado*.

"Lemme ask you," he said finally. "You a superstitious man, Mr. Brannock?"

"Clint gave him a quick, intent look. "What's superstition got to do with it?"

"Ain't we headed where angels fear to tread?"

"Are you talking about the Staked Plains?"

"Lordy mercy!" Daniel groaned. "I dunno which is worst—bein' half-nigger or half-Injun."

"C'mon, Elijah," Clint demanded. "What the hell are you trying to say?"

Daniel let go a harsh bark of laughter. "Why, I'm tryin' to choose, Mr. Brannock. Should I fix myself some juju magic or do a war dance for the Great Spirit." His eyes twinkled. "What d'you think?"

"I think you're pulling my leg."

"No," Daniel said, suddenly serious. "We're headed where no man was meant to go, leastways white or black. Sorta gives you a funny feelin'."

Clint merely nodded. While he wasn't superstitious, he nonetheless shared the sentiment. *Llano Estacado* was an enigma, unexplored and unknown.

He wondered what juju a white man might take along.

25

BY EARLY September, the Denver & Rio Grande was within ten miles of Raton Pass. The land had grown progressively rougher and steeper, climbing gradually into mountainous terrain. Tracklaying had slowed to less than a half-mile a day.

With the loan from Walter Tisdale's bank, the operation was once again working double shifts. Yet the race with the Santa Fe was still very much a toss-up. One day the Denver & Rio Grande was slightly ahead and the next found their rival inching into the lead. No one was laying odds on the outcome.

For all that, Virgil remained doggedly confident. Every obstacle along the way had been surmounted and turned to advantage. He believed himself capable of handling any problem that arose, and thus far he hadn't been proved wrong. He believed as well that the man who anticipated troublesome situations already had half the battle won. So it was that his attention turned to the matter of Raton Pass.

At an elevation of almost eight thousand feet, there was a natural bypass through the mountains. First discovered by fur trappers, it had served for decades as the gateway from Colorado into New Mexico. By the late 1820s, one branch of the Santa Fe Trail wound through the pass, serving as an artery of commerce for the Missouri traders. But then, in 1866, Raton Pass became the domain of a single man. His name was Dick Wootton.

Understandably, Virgil had done his homework on the man who controlled the right-of-way through Raton Pass. A Virginian, Wootton had migrated west at the age of twenty. After a short stint as an Indian trader, he joined a party of fur trappers. In 1838, he organized a two-year hunt that took them across the Rockies and northwestward to Fort Vancouver. From Oregon, he traveled south through California and then turned east into Utah, once more crossing the Continental Divide. For several years he traded with the Ute and the other tribes, and in 1847 he served as a scout in the Mexican War.

Later still, Wootton became a Missouri trader, freighting goods over the Santa Fe Trail. In the 1850s he established a trading post in Denver, which evolved into a saloon and hotel. A rabid southern sympathizer, he sold out when Denver went pro-Union during the Civil War. After acting as a guide for Oregon-bound wagon trains, he hatched the one great scheme of his life. He finagled a charter from the legislators of Colorado and New Mexico authorizing him to operate a toll road through Raton Pass. There he graded a twenty-seven-mile road and built an inn atop the summit. For the past eight years, he had prospered by collecting tolls and furnishing lodging for travelers. He was, in a rather literal sense, King of the Mountain.

From his investigation, Virgil gleaned two nuggets of noteworthy value. First, Dick Wootton was a man of audacity and tough-minded enterprise, one of the old-breed pioneers. No less significant, while he was a westerner, he remained a Virginian and a dyed-in-the-wool Confederate. Virgil believed he could turn both points to advantage in negotiations with Wootton. His plan was to acquire right-of-way through Raton Pass and thereby close the gateway to the rival line. He had delayed until now, confident that the Santa Fe would have already made an offer. He thought Wootton would be receptive to a counteroffer, perhaps a bit of dickering. Especially from a former comrade in arms.

On a bright September afternoon, Virgil arrived in a buckboard drawn by a matched pair of grays. A cool breeze whipped through the pass as he stepped down and hitched the team. The inn was a ramshackle affair, constructed of logs and mortar and native stone. Farther along the road, he saw a column of freight wagons halted before a toll gate. It occurred to him that Wootton's bonanza was about to peter out. Even the King of the Mountain had to make way for progress.

The door of the inn cracked open. The man who stepped out was on the sundown side of fifty, with a shock of white hair and fierce sapphire eyes under thick snowy brows. He was shambling and unkempt, but formidable in size and still blessed with a ruddy complexion. He looked somehow cantankerous, and the perception was immediately borne out. His manner was at once irascible and abrasive.

"Who might you be?"

"Are you Mr. Wootton?"

"Sonny, you ought to learn yourself some manners. I asked first."

"No offense intended," Virgil said. "The name's Brannock—Virgil Brannock."

"Huh!" Wootton grunted. "You by God took your own sweet time gettin' here."

"You were expecting me?"

"Ain't you with the Denver & Rio Grande?"

"Yes, I am."

"There you are, then," Wootton said gruffly. "Tanner told me you'd be along by the bye."

"John Tanner," Virgil asked, "with the Santa Fe?"

"Yep, that's the one. Told me you could lie your way out of a locked safe. Any truth to it?"

Virgil smiled. "Depends on whether or not you'd believe a Yankee."

"I suppose you're gonna tell me you was a Johnny Reb?"

"Army of Northern Virginia," Virgil said casually. "Served under General Gordon at Appomattox."

Wootton pulled a plug of tobacco from his shirt pocket. He bit off a large chaw and worked it into a gummy cud. One eye on Virgil, he spat a brownish jet and splattered a nearby rock. When he spoke, there was something close to mockery in his voice.

"I always thought Lee was a gawddamn quitter. Too bad Stonewall Jackson didn't live to see Appomattox. He would've told Grant to shove them surrender papers."

"I suspect you're right," Virgil said diplomatically. "Jackson was a staunch champion of the Confederacy."

"Well, it don't make no nevermind now. You're here to hornswoggle me outta everything I've slaved to build. Ain't that so?"

"I'm here to talk about the right-of-way, Mr. Wootton. Federal law says you have to sell it—not me."

"By jiggers," Wootton said sullenly. "Tanner told me you was slicker'n greased owlshit. Way you talk, he was plumb right."

Virgil realized he'd made a mistake. Allowing Tanner first crack at the old reprobate had been a serious miscalculation. The Santa Fe representative was too skilled an adversary, and versed in the art of slander as well. He reminded himself to settle the score at the first opportunity.

Still tactful, he managed a strained smile. "I assume the Santa Fe made you an offer. We'd like a chance to better it."

Wootton's eyes seemed to glitter with secret amusement. "Well, now, let's see. What they offered me was a ton of money and a lifetime pension and no hocus-pocus. You figger to better that, slick?"

Virgil felt his temper slip a notch. He took a tight grip on himself. "All we ask," he said without inflection, "is the chance to negotiate fairly. How much was their offer in total?"

"None of your business," Wootton said in a vinegary tone. "Besides, it wouldn't do you no good if I told you anyhow."

"Why not?"

" 'Cause I don't deal with turncoats, that's why not!"

"Are you calling me a turncoat?"

"You work for General High and Mighty Palmer, don't you?"

Virgil looked baffled. "What's that got to do with anything?"

'Gawdalmightydamn!" Wootton howled. "He's the Yankee sonovabitch that helped crucify Ol' Jeff Davis. And you call yourself a Reb!"

Virgil studied him with a thoughtful frown. "Has it occurred to you that Tanner and the Santa Fe crowd are all Yankees? Aren't you dealing with them?"

Wootton laughed a wild braying laugh. "Hell's bells, I ain't just dealin' with 'em! I'm robbin' the bastards blind."

"Well, fair's fair. Why not try robbing us?"

"I done give you my reason. Go on back and tell Palmer to shove it up his ass sideways."

Wootton turned on his heel and walked toward the inn. As the door slammed shut, Virgil wearily hefted himself into the buckboard. He felt like a man who had just visited an asylum. Nothing about it seemed real or sane.

He drove north out of Raton Pass.

Trinidad was a small town situated along the banks of the Purgatoire River. Settled in 1859, it was little more than a crossroads until the arrival of the Denver & Rio Grande. Raton Pass lay some ten miles south of the town line.

Early that afternoon Virgil sighted end-of-track. On first glance a tracklaying operation looked like organized chaos. Out front, with mule-drawn scrapers, the grading crew transformed rough earth into level roadbed. Behind them another work gang laid the ties, followed by the iron men, who spiked parallel rails to the cross-timbers. Farther back were the gandy dancers and the filler crew and the track liners, advancing rail by rail in a frenzy of construction.

The commotion was steadily punctuated by the metallic whang of sledgehammers on steel.

Uptrack from the work gangs was the construction train. Every mile of track required forty carloads of supplies, plus food and water for the men and animals. For all intents and purposes, the construction train was a town on wheels. Hauled by one locomotive and pushed by another, it was a ponderous collection of freight cars and flatbeds, several three-decker rolling bunkhouses, and one entire boxcar devoted to the mess kitchen. While one shift slept, the other worked, and all the parts somehow meshed. Far from chaos, it was a highly synchronized operation.

William Palmer visited end-of-track once or twice a week. His inspection tours generally involved an overnight stay and he brought along his own accommodations. Like most railroad barons, he maintained a private car that was both office and living quarters. The car was lavishly appointed, with a bedroom to the rear and a spacious parlor area in the center section. Toward the front was a dining area and small kitchen, attended by a manservant. A mahogany desk, just off the forward companionway, served as an office.

In Virgil's opinion, the private car was a monument to one man's vanity. He thought the money would have been better spent on the tracklaying operation. Still, as he mounted the steps on the front platform, his mind was engaged with more immediate problems. The manservant answered his knock and ushered him through the narrow companionway. He found Palmer seated at the dining table, enjoying a leisurely noonday meal. Fine linen covered the table, with an array of glittering silver and bone-white china. He marked again that the railroader believed in living in style.

"Quick trip," Palmer said by way of greeting. "Would you care for a cup of coffee?"

"No, thanks."

Palmer dismissed the manservant with a wave. He dabbed his mouth with a napkin and rose from the table. Nodding to Virgil, he led the way to the parlor, where they seated themselves in leather armchairs. His expression was at once inquisitive and concerned.

"How did it go with Wootton?"

"Not good," Virgil said, his eyes grave. "As of now, the Santa Fe owns Raton Pass."

"I told you," Palmer raged. "All along I said you shouldn't allow them to make the first offer. But you wouldn't listen. You never listen!"

Virgil wagged his head. "Wouldn't have mattered one way or the other. Wootton won't deal with the Denver & Rio Grande."

"Won't deal?" Palmer repeated. "Why not?"

"Jefferson Davis."

"I beg your pardon?"

Virgil recounted the conversation with Wootton. As he talked, Palmer's anger slowly turned to astonished bewilderment. When he finished, there was a moment of deadened silence. Palmer looked like a man in shock.

"For God's sake, it was wartime! I was a soldier following orders. How could he hold that against me?"

Virgil shrugged. "He blames you for the capture of Jeff Davis. In his words—and I quote—you're a 'Yankee sonovabitch.' "

"So are the Santa Fe crowd!"

"With one notable difference. None of them helped imprison the Father of the Confederacy."

Palmer got to his feet. He walked to a wide window at the side of the car and stood staring out at the bleak landscape. A time passed and he seemed to regain control of himself. He turned back to Virgil.

"To be frank," he said in a toneless voice, "I expected some sort of underhanded scheme. Through a confidential source, I was informed that the Santa Fe has hired a professional gunman."

A startled expression crossed Virgil's face. "Why would they hire a gunman?"

"I wondered that myself. After what you've told me I understand their reasoning."

"Suppose you explain it to me."

Palmer's mouth went tight, scornful. "Apparently they're not all that confident they can hold Raton Pass. They mean to protect their interests with force."

Virgil scrutinized him closely. "Are you saying they think we'd try to take the pass by force?"

"So it appears," Palmer commented. "The man they've hired is known as Doc Sontag. Ever heard of him?"

"No," Virgil said. "Who is he?"

"I gather he was a marshal in one of those Kansas cow towns. I've been informed he's recruiting some of his old friends—other gunmen."

"That sounds like they're preparing for a siege. Why else would they hire a bunch of mercenaries?"

"Offhand, I'd say they know their opponent. I don't intend to take this lying down."

"What's the alternative?" Virgil inquired. "They've got Wootton in their pocket."

Palmer shook his head in exasperation. "I'm not above using force myself. I will not be denied passage into New Mexico."

"Come off it, Will. We're building a railroad, not fighting a war."

"Indeed?" Palmer demanded churlishly. "Either we fight or we lose everything. What other choice do we have?"

"Aren't you forgetting something? The right-of-way belongs to them now. Wootton's already signed it over."

"To hell with them," Palmer said vindictively. "Possession is nine points of the law."

"Maybe so," Virgil conceded glumly. "But what happens if we do take it by force? We'd wind up in federal court trying to make it stick."

"Which could take years," Palmer said, and laughed out loud. "Meanwhile, we're into New Mexico and on our way to El Paso. No court could stop us then."

A sudden chill settled over Virgil. He had the sensation of sinking ever deeper in quicksand, and it occurred to him that he had long since passed the point of turning back. His own fortune, as well as the money borrowed from his father-in-law, was tied to Raton Pass. He looked up at Palmer.

"What do you suggest?"

"Why, it's really quite simple, Virge. We need a gun-man of our own."

Central City was thirty miles west of Denver. Foremost among the Colorado mining camps, it was called "the richest square mile on earth." Upward of a hundred thousand dollars a week was gouged from the mountainous terrain.

The town itself was scattered along a gulch some two miles long. Main Street was a hodgepodge of log cabins and frame buildings with false fronts. Saloons and dance halls and gaming dens were liberally scattered among more legitimate businesses. Like all mining camps, the lure of easy money acted as a magnet for cardsharps and whores and men who were windward of the law. No one took notice of the hard cases who constantly drifted through town.

Virgil stepped off the noon stage. Three days had passed since his talk with Palmer, and he was now resigned to fighting fire with fire. Several years ago, he'd got his start in business as a wholesale liquor distributor in the mining camps. He was known throughout the gold fields as a man of honesty and personal integrity, qualities that commanded respect. His hope was that the passage of time had done nothing to dim his reputation. Today, he planned to trade on old friendships.

Crossing the street, he went through the batwing doors of the Metropole. A combination saloon and gaming dive, it was a favorite haunt of the rougher crowd. The bartender, who was standing behind a row of brass beerpulls, wore a candy-striped shirt and red sleeve garters. His name was Dolph Jordan and he greeted Virgil with a wide grin. After reminiscing about the old days, Virgil turned the conversation to more immediate matters. Jordan listened, nodding slowly, and agreed to arrange an introduction. He knew just the man for the job.

A short while later Luther Roebuck walked through the door. He was whipcord-lean, with deep-set onyx eyes and a drooping black mustache. Like an undertaker who has been informed of a death, he looked sober but not really sad. Strapped to his waist in a workmanlike crossdraw holster was a Colt revolver with gutta-percha grips. He halted before Virgil's table.

"I understand you wanted to see me."

"Have a seat," Virgil said, looking him over. "Can I buy you a drink?"

"Never touch it before sundown."

Roebuck took a chair facing the door. He folded his hands across his vest and waited. Virgil decided there was no need for preliminaries. He went straight to the point.

"I have need for a man of your talents, Mr. Roebuck. You come highly recommended."

Roebuck stared at him dead-eyed. "What's the job?"

"A railroad war," Virgil said deliberately. "We're involved in a dispute over a certain piece of real estate. The other side won't turn loose without a fight."

"Why don't you tell me about it?"

Virgil told him. While he talked, the gunman's eyes remained devoid of expression. Only toward the end was there any outward reaction. Roebuck's mouth curled in a cynical, wolfish grin.

"The Santa Fe's sitting on Raton Pass. You want it and they won't let go. Does that about cover it?"

Virgil nodded. "Think you can handle it?"

"Why not?" Roebuck said easily. "Who's the gunhand they hired?"

"A former marshal," Virgil observed. "His name is Doc Sontag."

Roebuck let out his breath in a low whistle. "You got yourself some stiff competition. Sontag's a widowmaker from way back."

Virgil looked at him blandly. "Want to change your mind?"

"Nope," Roebuck said with a tight, mirthless smile. "But it'll cost you a thousand now and a thousand when the job's finished. I get top dollar to go up against somebody like Sontag."

"Agreed," Virgil said quickly. "How many more men will you need?"

"Ten or twelve ought to do it."

"What will that cost?"

"Peanuts," Roebuck said. "Couple of hundred a man."

"I'll leave it to you to make the arrangements. When can you start?"

Roebuck laughed, spread his hands. "When you pay me the thousand."

Virgil pulled a wallet from his inside coat pocket. He counted out the money and pushed it across the table. Roebuck climbed to his feet, folding the wad of bills, and stuffed them into his vest pocket. He nodded pleasantly. "See you in Trinidad, Mr. Brannock."

Neither of them offered to shake hands. Virgil watched him out the door, then poured himself another drink. He downed it neat, with a sharp intake of breath. While he was no stranger to death, hiring a killer was a whole new experience. One that left him uneasy with himself.

He somehow felt soiled.

26

DAWN TORE a jagged line across the horizon. The date was September 27 and the regiment was encamped along the headwaters of the Pease River. Their line of march had brought them at last to *Comanchería*.

The 4th Cavalry had been in the field slightly more than three weeks. Upon departing Fort Clark, they had set a course north by northwest into the Texas Panhandle. On September 24 their base camp had been established on the Clear Fork of the Brazos. There the supply train of some twenty wagons had been formed into a boxlike defensive square. The five infantry companies remained behind to secure the camp.

Freed of the wagons, the cavalry was able to make better time. Their day began at first light and they were in the saddle long before sunrise. The morning's march was generally five hours, ending shortly before noon. At the midday break, which was principally for the benefit of their mounts, the horses were fed and watered. No fires were allowed, since the break was never longer than an hour. After tending to the animals, the men made a hasty meal on hardtack and cold salt pork. Few complained, for the welfare of the horses was their first consideration.

The relationship between a trooper and his mount was highly personal. On the plains, where almost all fighting was done from the saddle, a good horse was essential to survival. Cavalry mounts were trained not to bolt when a carbine or pistol was fired from the saddle; on occasion an animal was used as a living breastwork. By lifting one foreleg and leaning into the shoulder, a trooper could throw his mount to the ground. The horse was trained to stay there while the trooper took cover and fired across the saddle. Somewhat like partners, the trooper and his mount were dependent on each other. And never more so than in a campaign against the horseback tribes.

Unless engaged in pursuit, a cavalry column always halted by late afternoon. Daylight hours were needed for the many chores that went into making an overnight camp. The animals headed the list; after picket lines were strung, the horses were once again fed and watered. Guards were posted around the perimeter and work details were then allowed to gather fuel for cooking fires. Supper was the main meal of the day, generally consisting of beans and fried salt pork, and hardtack grilled in the pork grease. A quart of coffee, laced with a precious spoonful of sugar, finished off the meal. Not long after dark, the fires were extinguished and the men crawled into their bedrolls.

From dawn to dusk, the daily routine seldom varied. The regiment had marched more than four hundred miles since departing Fort Clark. The last 130 miles, roughly the distance between the Brazos and the Pease, had been covered at a faster pace. Clint and the scouts ranged out ahead, looking for any sign of hostiles, and the cavalry troops followed in a mile-long column. Their objective was the Prairie Dog Fork of the Red River, some twenty miles north of the Pease. Somewhere near the headwaters of the Red they would ascend to the high plateau of *Llano Estacado*.

For the past day, the column had been shadowed by mounted warriors. The hostiles kept their distance, clearly intent on scouting the regiment's line of march. Even through binoculars it had been impossible to determine whether the hostiles were Comanche or members of some other tribe. Still, as Mackenzie had predicted, there was little chance of entering *Comanchería* without being detected. Late yesterday, when the column bivouacked for the night, a lone warrior had been spotted on the crest of a distant hill. Their movements, quite obviously, were being watched and reported.

Mackenzie interpreted the surveillance as a hopeful sign. He thought it entirely probable that a hostile camp would be found within a day's march of the Pease. Otherwise, there seemed little reason for the column to be kept under such close scrutiny. Whether the Indians would flee or stand their ground remained to be seen. Yet he'd dealt with the wild tribes too long to accept anything at face value. Under a pale moon, he had ordered extra sentries posted, with instructions to keep a sharp lookout over the horses. Nothing unusual had been reported throughout the long night.

But now, as dawn brightened the sky, a gunshot split the stillness. From a distant ravine, thirty or forty mounted warriors boiled into sight and charged the camp. Whooping and shrieking, firing their carbines at a full gallop, they rode toward the picketed horses. Their intent was to stampede the cavalry mounts and leave the regiment afoot on the plains. As they drew closer, the sentries opened fire with a rattling volley. The warriors veered off, surprised by the unexpected heavy volume of fire. A moment later troops throughout the camp sprang from their bedrolls.

Hauling their ponies about, the warriors hastily retreated toward the ravine. The sentries, joined now by half-dressed troopers, speeded them along with a withering fusillade. Somewhat miraculously, the raiding party made it to the ravine without the loss of a man. There they dismounted and took cover behind the rim of the defile. Shielded from sight, they began popping away at anything that moved. The camp, which was on a stretch of open ground, suddenly buzzed with lead. Horses reared and squealed at the picket lines while troopers hit the dirt.

Oblivious to the snipers, Mackenzie calmly made his way to the far side of camp. There he huddled in a one-sided conversation with Captain Boehm, commander of E Company. Several minutes later, accompanied by Clint and the Seminole scouts, E Company rode out at a gallop. While the rest of the regiment laid down covering fire, Boehm and his troopers swung wide in a flanking maneuver. They hit the ravine from the south and quickly stormed the hostiles' position. A brisk fight ended with mounted warriors streaming westward.

When the firing ceased, the bodies of dead hostiles littered the bottom of the ravine. As the Seminoles set about collecting scalps, Captain Boehm ordered recall and began forming his troop. Clint rode back to camp, swinging down from the saddle before his horse came to a halt. Mackenzie stepped forward to meet him.

"Cleaned 'em out," Clint reported. "Killed fifteen or so and didn't lose a man. Only one trooper got himself winged."

"Good work," Mackenzie said. "Were you able to identify their tribe?"

"Kiowa," Clint said without hesitation. "Not a Comanche in the bunch."

"Where do you think they're headed now?"

Clint scanned a distant rise. The Kiowas who had escaped the ravine were milling around in a swirl of dust. As he watched, they disappeared over the rise and rode westward. He turned back to Mackenzie.

"Colonel, they look to me like decoys. I'd say they're trying to draw us off—away from their camp."

"I agree," Mackenzie said firmly. "Which direction would you take instead, Mr. Brannock?"

"Well . . ." Clint paused, studying on it moment. "I doubt they'll make a run for the reservation. If it was me, I'd have a looksee north of here."

Mackenzie weighed the alternatives. He thought it unlikely that a hostile camp would turn east, toward Indian

Territory and the reservations. With the exception of the
Fort Bascom column, the other regiments were converging
from points eastward. Their movements would exert unrelenting pressure, forcing hostile bands in a westerly direction. Yet, even though the Kiowa war party had fled
westward, he agreed with Clint that it was a hoax. That
left only one point on the compass.

"Very well, Mr. Brannock," he said at length. "We'll
proceed with our original plan. Collect your men and press
northward without delay."

Clint looked at him. "How far ahead should I scout?"

"I'll have the regiment on the move within the hour.
Unless you have something to report, continue on to the
Prairie Dog Fork of the Red. We'll meet there."

"What if I hit a trail?"

"Follow it," Mackenzie ordered. "The only exception
would be a trail headed east. I won't be turned away from
our objective—not now."

"You're talking about the Staked Plains?"

"No," Mackenzie said forcefully. "I'm talking about
the Quahadi and Quanah."

Some ten minutes later Clint rode north with the Seminole scouts. Behind them, dawn turned to day and the
Pease River went molten with sunlight. No breakfast fires
were built and the regiment went without morning coffee.
The men were ordered to water their horses and prepare to
move out.

A mile or so from camp, Clint still couldn't shake the
look on Mackenzie's face. He'd seen it before, that exact
expression, on the faces of other men. Once, in a mirror,
he had seen it on his own face.

It was the look of a hunter who scents the kill.

The brassy dome of the sky shimmered under a mid-
morning sun. High overhead buzzards swooped and cir-
cled, quartering something on the land below. The rolling
plains marched onward into endless distance.

Clint shielded his gaze against the sun. Elijah Daniel rode beside him and the Seminole scouts were halted behind them. They sat motionless, their horses stretching to nibble bunches of grass. Their eyes were fixed on the buzzards.

All morning they had ridden steadily northward. Holding their horses to a walk, constantly on the lookout for sign, they had covered some ten or twelve miles. Until now they had spotted nothing that would indicate a hostile encampment. But the wheeling dark specks in the sky gave them pause.

Buzzards were the talebearers of the plains. Anything dead, whether man or animal, brought them flocking in large numbers. No less attractive to the winged scavengers was a recently deserted Indian village. The Plains tribes always left behind decaying refuse and great piles of animal bones. Drawn by the ripe odor, circling buzzards soon filled the sky.

Warily, Clint and the scouts rode forward. The buzzards were quartering a sector of land a mile or so directly ahead. As the distance closed, they saw that the grassy prairie dropped off abruptly. A worn trail led downward into a shallow canyon that wound westward for perhaps two miles. Stunted trees shaded the canyon floor and a lazy stream trickled off into the distance. Along both banks there were unmistakable signs of a recent encampment.

From moccasin prints and various discarded objects, Clint soon determined that it had been a Kiowa village. The imprints of some thirty lodges were still visible and a sizable herd of horses had been watered at the stream. One of the scouts found a broad trail leading northward, toward the Prairie Dog Fork of the Red. The travois marks were fresh, and piles of horse dung were not yet baked hard by the sun. All the signs indicated that the hostiles had broken camp early that morning.

Elijah Daniel found anther trail leading westward out of the canyon. The tracks were those of a lone horseman and two broad-wheeled carts, drawn by oxen. Footprints left no doubt that the horsemen and the drivers of the carts were wearing boots. A closer inspection revealed that night insects had not crisscrossed the deep wagon tracks. The telltale signs were clear to read, as though a message had been wrought in the earth. The men and wagons had departed the camp hastily, shortly after sunrise. Of still greater significance, they were not Indian.

Clint grasped immediately what the tracks meant. By sheer happenstance, he had stumbled upon a small party of *Comancheros*. Like the Kiowa, the traders had been frightened off by the nearness of cavalry troops. His first inclination was to follow orders and stick closely to the hostiles' trail. Yet some deeper instinct told him to forget the Kiowa and pursue the *Comancheros* instead. A hurried explanation brought quick agreement from Elijah Daniel. They led the scouts westward.

Some two hours later the broad-wheeled *carretas* were sighted. Topping a small rise, Clint spotted them not quite a mile ahead, on a flat stretch of prairie. He motioned the scouts onto line, waiting until they fanned out on either side of him. Then, at a lope, they rode forward.

The Mexican horseman foolishly chose to fight. He unlimbered a saddle carbine and wheeled his mount to face the charge. The *carretta* drivers followed his example, halting their teams and leaping to the ground with rifles in hand. By their reaction, all three preferred a quick death to a hangman's knot.

At a range of a hundred yards, the *Comancheros* opened fire. Their repeaters hammered out a hailstorm of lead, the shots blending into an unbroken roar. Yet their targets were hurtling toward them, bobbing and weaving as hooves churned the earth. Terrified by the Seminoles bloodcurdling war cries, the Mexicans hurried their shots, firing faster, and missed. As the range closed to fifty yards, none of the scouts had been hit.

Clint opened fire with his pistol. An instant later, as

though awaiting his command, Elijah Daniel and the other
scouts let go with their Springfield carbines. All in a split
second Clint's .44 Colt and twenty carbines spat a sizzling
wall of lead. The heavy slugs struck with fearsome impact,
shredding the *carretas* and downing three of the four oxen.
One of the drivers stumbled backward, clutching his gut,
and fell spraddled out in the dust. The other one dropped
like a puppet cut loose from its strings.

The Mexican horseman went down in a tangle of arms
and hooves. His mount died beneath him, bored through
by a Springfield slug. Too late, he tried to kick free of the
stirrups and hit the ground instead with one leg pinned
underneath the horse. The fall jarred his senses and he lay
momentarily stunned. By the time he collected his wits, he
saw that it was futile to resist. His carbine was out of reach
and his leg was trapped by nearly a half-ton of horseflesh.
He ceased struggling with a look of stoic resignation.

The scouts skidded their horses to a dusty halt. Several
of them vaulted from the saddle, their scalping knives
unsheathed, and swarmed the fallen drivers. As they began
squabbling over the topknots, Clint and Elijah Daniel reined
to a stop before the pinned Mexican. He stared up at them
without expression, his eyes empty and lost. Clint grinned
and flipped him an offhand salute.

"*Buenos días, Señor Comanchero.*"

"Ask him where I can find Quanah."
"*¿Donde puede el coronel hallar a Quanah?*"
Elijah Daniel waited a moment. The Mexican, whose hands
were bound behind his back, looked stolidly ahead. He
was a gnarled, lynx-eyed man, with leathery features and a
straight mouth. Daniel finally turned away.

"He ain't gonna talk, Colonel."
Mackenzie studied the *Comanchero* with a corrosive
glare. Clint and several officers stood nearby, watching the
interrogation. Thus far, the prisoner hadn't opened his
mouth.

Earlier, Mackenzie's forward element had happened upon the abandoned Kiowa village. While they were still looking for sign, Clint and the scouts had ridden in with the Mexican. The regiment was now strung out along the canyon, on the opposite side of the stream. The troopers were dismounted, watering their horses.

Mackenzie was silent for a time. When at last he spoke, there was an odd timbre to his voice. "Bring the prisoner along, Elijah."

Daniel took the Mexican by the scruff of the neck. He trailed a pace behind as Mackenzie walked to the stream and halted beneath a tree. Clint and the officers followed along, uncertain as to what the colonel intended. At Mackenzie's command, a length of rope was fetched from one of the pack mules. A sergeant from A Troop waded across the stream and handed the rope to Daniel. As he rejoined his company, a sudden hush fell over the onlookers.

Mackenzie's eyes were steely. He nodded to Daniel and his voice was suddenly edged: "Listen closely, Elijah. I want you to hang the prisoner, but be prepared to let him down on my command. I don't want him killed."

"Yassuh!"

Daniel's mouth split in a ferocious grin. He fashioned a noose in the rope and looped it over the *Comanchero's* head. Stepping back, Daniel tossed the loose end of rope over a low-hanging limb. He then moved to the base of the tree and braced one foot against the stout trunk.

The Mexican looked petrified, his face slack with fear. His lips moved in a monotone prayer.

Hauling back on the rope, Daniel jerked him off the ground. When the noose snapped tight, the Mexican's eyes seemed to burst from their sockets, streaked fiery-eyed with engorged blood vessels. Thrashing and kicking, he danced frantically on air, as though trying to gain a foothold. His face slowly purpled, then grew darker and turned a ghastly shade of blackish amber. His swollen tongue popped out like an onyx snake.

Mackenzie signaled with a quick motion. Daniel let go the rope and the Mexican dropped heavily to the ground. When the noose was loosened, he sucked down great gasps of air. His color gradually returned, but the rope burn around his neck was raw and bloody. A long minute passed before Mackenzie nodded to Daniel.

"Ask him if he wants to live."

"¿Quiere usted vivir, hombre?"

"Sí." The Mexican's voice was a strangled whisper. "Por Dios, mi coronel!"

"Tell him," Mackenzie warned with cold menance, "that he has but one chance. A lie will get him hanged."

As Daniel translated, the Mexican rapidly bobbed his head. "Sí," he blurted with a weak smile. "Lo sé."

The Comanchero talked like an eager sparrow. His name was José Tafoya and he'd been involved in the illicit trade for many years. While he dealt only with the Kiowa, he was familiar with the habits of the Comanche. Some thirty leagues to the northwest, high on Llano Estacado, there was a great canyon called Palo Duro. Quanah and the Quahadi band, he noted, always made their winter encampment in the canyon. He readily agreed to act as guide for the regiment.

When the interrogation ended, Mackenzie turned to Clint. "Well, Mr. Brannock," he said with grim satisfaction, "I believe we're on the right trail at last. Do you agree?"

"Yessir," Clint said, and smiled. "I doubt he'd risk another taste of the rope."

"From your tone, I take it you approve of my methods?"

"Colonel, there's no rules out here. I'd have skinned him alive to make him talk."

Mackenzie seemed to deliberate a moment. "According to Tafoya, we're roughly thirty miles from Palo Duro Canyon. How do you feel about traveling over unfamiliar terrain—at night?"

Clint rubbed the stubble along his jawline. "We'll have

plenty of moonlight and we've got ourselves a guide. I don't see any big problem.''

"Good!''

Mackenzie punched a fist into the palm of his hand. His gaze shifted to the group of officers, who were watching him intently. His eyes hooded and his voice went cold.

"Gentlemen, we attack the Quahadi at dawn.''

27

NEVER BEFORE had so many tribes wintered on *Llano Estacado*. Palo Duro Canyon, for the first time in memory, was crowded with hostile bands. Drawn to *Comanchería* as a last refuge, they had taken a solemn vow. None of them would ever again return to the reservations.

The Quahadi, as was their custom, established camp at the lower end of the canyon. A short distance upstream were remnants of the other Comanche bands. Beyond them were the Kiowa and the southern Cheyenne and the Arapaho. Their combined horse herds totaled several thousand head, and as the Yellow Leaves Moon drew to a close, graze was already becoming sparse. Old men talked of a long winter.

Earl and the *Comancheros* arrived toward the end of the month. Only four days remained in September, and they risked encountering an early storm on their return trip to Santa Fe. Still, with the frontier in turmoil, Ramón Guerra had been forced to postpone the fall rendezvous. All the hostile tribes, including the Quahadi, had been on the move since the fight at Adobe Walls. Unlike past years, their raids were aimed at wreaking vengeance rather than collecting spoils.

Onrushing winter had at last forced them to quit the warpath. The need to organize buffalo hunts and store meat for the hard months ahead could be denied no longer.

Within the last week or so, the horseback tribes had finally begun drifting toward their winter camps. As a result, Guerra and his men arrived at Palo Duro not by choice, but out of necessity. Until now, there had been no chance to rendezvous with Quanah and his people. The Quahadi were too busy taking *tejano* scalps.

On the outbound trip Guerra had talked at length about Palo Duro Canyon. Yet nothing he'd said had prepared Earl and Lon for what they saw that crisp September morning. The canyon floor was nearly two miles wide, bisected by a stream heavily bordered with trees. To the north and south, the canyon walls rose in sheer palisades almost a thousand feet high. Stretching east and west, the vast fissure in the earth extended for a hundred miles, approachable by ancient trails known only to the hostile bands and a small number of *Comancheros*. To all appearances, it was an impregnable fortress, guarded above by *Llano Estacado*.

Entering the canyon, Earl was struck by the gathering of so many different tribes. The sight immediately gave him second thoughts about having brought Lon along. But then, after a moment's reflection, he decided there was no reason for alarm. The youngster was accepted among the Quahadi and even bore a Comanche name, Strikes Both Ways. He was, moreover, the son of Stone Bull, a *Comanchero* who had married into the band and fathered a Quahadi son. As credentials went, Earl decided it sounded pretty impressive. All the more so since the other tribes were wintering in *Comanchería* at the Quahadi's sufferance.

A greater concern was the army. Before leaving Santa Fe, Earl had heard rumors of a sweeping campaign against the hostiles. His first thought had been of Clint, and whether or not the military had been alerted to the existence of the *Comancheros*. But he was soon diverted from that by Ramón Guerra, whose worries were more real than imaginary. Through his political contacts, Guerra had learned that five columns of troops were converging on the Staked

Plains. Their stay in *Comanchería*, Guerra had told him, would therefore be dictated by events. Any sign of cavalry patrols would be the signal to depart Palo Duro Canyon.

Soon after their arrival, Earl put such worries aside. Little Raven greeted him with sunny joy, proudly displaying their son, who had grown strong and chubby-cheeked over the summer. Within minutes, Lon had changed to breechclout and moccasins and hurried off to find his Quahadi friends. While Earl was still admiring the baby, Spotted Dog stepped through the door hole. He seemed genuinely pleased to see his *tahbay-boh* son-in-law and shook hands with a firm grip. Then, seating himself before the fire, he proceeded to expound on his exploits against the *tejanos*.

Little Raven gave Earl a hopeless shrug. But his interest took a sharp uptick when Spotted Dog began talking about the pony soldiers. The Quahadi, through their kinsmen on the reservation, were reliably informed on the army's warlike plans. Already there had been clashes with military patrols involving both the Kiowa and the Cheyenne. These skirmishes had occurred toward the end of the last moon and had amounted to nothing. The pony soldiers, as usual, had inflicted little damage.

Spotted Dog went on to relate that the Quahadi leaders had met in council. There had been much discussion as to measures the band would take to defend itself. But when all the others had spoken, Quanah had chided them for their fears. *Llano Estacado*, Quanah informed them, was all the defense the Quahadi needed. The pony soldiers, based on past actions, would stop short of the high plains. Even if they should enter *Comanchería*, he declared, they would wander in endless circles and doubtless perish of starvation and thirst. None of their leaders, he concluded, was capable of locating the Quahadi's stronghold, Palo Duro Canyon. To a man, the council elders had endorsed Quanah's wisdom. The pony soldiers posed no threat.

Earl was persuaded as well. After listening to Spotted

Dog, his own concern was greatly diminished. He recalled how the Quahadi boasted that Quanah had never been defeated in battle. As a war chief, Quanah was a master of strategy and thought to have powerful medicine. The Quahadi leader had fought dozens of engagements with the pony soldiers, always emerging victorious. For countless raiding seasons, Quahadi war parties had savaged the *tejanos* with virtual impunity. In all that time, the *americano* soldiers had never once ventured onto *Llano Estacado*. No one seriously believed they would be so foolish as to challenge Quanah on his own ground.

Upon reflection, Earl decided his initial fears were groundless. He had allowed himself to become infected with Guerra's misgivings. But now, having heard the other side, it seemed to him that Quanah's assessment was the more realistic. For almost thirty years, the army had confined its probes to the outlying borders of *Comanchería*. There was no reason to believe that the new campaign, however broad in scope, would break the pattern. Nor was it reasonable to believe that the cavalry, even if it should invade the Staked Plains, would somehow stumble across Palo Duro Canyon. Their search, covering thousands of square miles, would end as Quanah had predicted. With the first snows of winter, the pony soldiers would still be riding in circles.

By late morning, Earl had convinced himself that there was nothing to fear. He played with the baby while Little Raven looked on with adoration, content merely to have her man and her man-child under the same lodge. When she finally returned the baby to his cradleboard, Earl felt a tug of emotion unlike anything he'd ever known. On sudden impulse he resolved what until now had been a fanciful daydream. He had no doubt whatever that Lon would approve.

Instead of returning to Santa Fe, they would winter with the Quahadi. Together with his wife and his sons he would reclaim what he'd lost so long ago. A sense of purpose,

and all the more important, a sense of belonging. His own
family.

Guerra insisted that the trading session take place that
afternoon. Quanah voiced no objection, and after smoking a pipe, they set about outfoxing one another. To observ-
ers, there was a certain ritualism in the way they haggled
back and forth.

As the sun dipped westward, the last *carreta* was emptied of trade goods. Guerra, following established practice,
had withheld three crates of firearms to the very end.
When he finally shook hands with Quanah, they both
seemed pleased with themselves. Neither of them thought
the other had been cheated beyond reasonable limits.

Earl was in particularly good spirits. His share of today's profits represented a degree of financial independence. With only four trips to *Comanchería*, he had parlayed
an original investment of two thousand dollars into a very
respectable thirty-two thousand dollars. He invited Guerra
back to his lodge, where he produced a bottle of tequila.
Their profitable venture seemed to him cause for celebration.

Seated outside the lodge, they drank from horn cups.
Guerra joined in toasting their good fortune, obviously
relieved to have the trading behind him. Yet he appeared
somehow distracted, as though his mind were on other
matters. He silently watched Lon and a group of Quahadi
boys down near the stream. They were shooting at a
makeshift target with their miniature bows and arrows.
After a while he glanced at Earl.

"Your son seems at home here. He might yet make a
Comanche."

"No fear of that," Earl said casually. "He's just a kid
playing at being an Indian. It's a game."

"A game," Guerra noted, "that he plays in earnest.
Take care, *compadre*."

"What do you mean?"

"I once warned you that the *indio* way of life can be a

seductive thing. The thought applies to boys as well as men."

"Well, maybe so," Earl said doubtfully. "But it'll never happen to Lon. I've got other plans for him."

"Then perhaps it is just as well that we leave tomorrow."

"Tomorrow?" Earl said, surprised. "What's your rush?"

"I wish to be gone," Guerra said in a musing tone. "I have a bad feeling about this place, *un presentimiento malo*. And a man should obey his instincts."

Earl looked skeptical. "Quanah doesn't agree with you about the army. He says they'll never find this canyon."

Guerra shrugged. "I trust my instincts more than I trust Quanah's judgment. We leave tomorrow."

"Tell you the truth," Earl said with a vague gesture. "I figured to hang around awhile. Thought the boy and me might even spend the winter."

"Madre de dios," Guerra said sharply. "Have you lost your mind?"

"No," Earl replied without inflection. "Way I see it, I'm as much at home here as I am in Santa Fe. What's wrong with that?"

"Tonto!" Guerra said in a disgusted voice. "What you have here is a squaw and an *indio* half-breed. It is their home—not yours."

Earl took a sip from the horn cup. His mouth narrowed in a tight smile. "I'll thank you not to call me a fool. *¿Comprendes?*"

"Then don't talk like one. To spend the winter here would be the act of *un loco*. I tell you plainly, the Quahadi will be forced to fight before the snows melt. I feel it in my bones."

"No offense, but your bones don't convince me. I'll go with Quanah's judgment this time."

"Listen well," Guerra warned, his face darkening. "We are leaving here tomorrow, and that is not a request. It is an order."

Earl gave him a short look. "Sounds like you've got

things a mite bassackwards. We're partners, but that don't make you my *patrón*. I don't take orders from nobody.''

Guerra's gaze suddenly went past him. On the far side of the stream, a group of Kiowa warriors rode into view. Strung out behind them were the women and children of the band, their possessions lashed to travois drag poles pulled by horses. From the direction of their march, they had just descended the eastern trail off the high plains.

As Guerra and Earl watched, one of the warriors separated from the band. He rode directly to Quanah's lodge, where the war chief was distributing trade goods. The Kiowa was immediately surrounded by Quahadi braves, who listened intently as he spoke with Quanah. Gesturing eastward, the Kiowa's voice carried a note of alarm, and cold anger. His words were a mixture of Kiowa and Comanche and Spanish.

Quanah questioned him at length. His answers brought harsh grunts and murmurs of alarm from the Quahadi braves. Finally, with the discussion ended, the Kiowa mounted and rode off to join his people. Quanah issued a guttural burst of orders and the braves abruptly scattered throughout the village. Within a matter of moments, the council elders were seen hurrying toward Quanah's lodge. One by one they disappeared through the door hole, while the crowd outside continued to grow larger. Their faces were etched with worry.

''What's happening?'' Earl asked. ''I only caught a few words here and there.''

Guerra regarded him with an odd, steadfast look. ''It seems my instinct was right after all. The army has come at last to *Llano Estacado*.''

''The Kiowa said that?''

''That and more, my friend. He reports a large column of pony soldiers only one day's march from here. His band managed to elude them this morning.''

''I'll be damned,'' Earl said softly. ''Are they headed in this direction?''

"Who knows?" Guerra said with a listless shrug. "The Kiowa claims that his band covered their trail too well to follow. Perhaps he tells the truth."

"Maybe that's not as bad as it sounds. Between here and there the soldiers could get themselves lost eight ways to Sunday. You told me yourself there's no maps of this country."

"Listen to me," Guerra urged. "For the boy's sake, if not your own, come with me tomorrow. You are not safe here."

"What about Little Raven and the baby?" Are they safe here?"

"Soldiers do not make war on women and children. If you are caught, my friend, you will be hanged. I suggest you think on that a moment."

Guerra placed his cup on the ground. He stood, gazing down at Earl a moment longer, and then walked off through the village. For some reason, Earl had never felt more alone in his life. He downed the last of his tequila.

It was late evening. Stars were scattered to the horizon and a full moon lighted the sky. The earth seemed bathed in a silvery glow.

Earl stepped from his lodge. Only moments before Little Raven had fallen asleep in his arms. Their lovemaking had been long and tender, a reunion of body and spirit. Yet sleep eluded him and he'd waited until she drifted off before slipping from their bedrobes. His mind was a muddle of doubt and uncertainty.

Wearing a heavy mackinaw, he filled his lungs with the chill night air. He stood a moment, hands stuffed in his pockets, staring up at the starry sky. Then, out of the corner of his eye, a tongue of flame caught his attention. He turned and saw Quanah seated before a small fire, a buffalo robe thrown over his shoulders. The Quahadi leader looked curiously like a holy man lost in prayer.

The village was quiet, all the lodges dark. Earl hesitated, reluctant to intrude on the chief's privacy. But then, goaded by the need to talk, he moved toward the fire. He halted a pace away, nodding.

"*Buenas noches, jefe.*"

By now, Earl was fluent in Spanish. He was conversant as well in sign language, the universal language of the Plains tribes. Quanah replied in Spanish, motioning him closer.

"Come, sit with me, Stone Bull. I welcome your company."

Earl lowered himself to a cross-legged position. "I was unable to sleep," he said. "I thought perhaps the air would clear my head."

Quanah nodded solemnly. "Some nights, there is no rest for thoughtful men. While others sleep, we search for newfound wisdom."

"You speak now of the pony soldiers?"

"Tonight, I think of nothing else."

Earl looked him directly in the eyes. "Will they find us here, Great Chief?"

Quanah's features were immobile. "The danger of that is slight. I believe we are safe for the moment."

"And the future?" Earl asked. "What do you see on the path beyond?"

Under the dappled moonlight, Quanah's hands flashed angrily. He extended the fingers on both hands and rapidly jabbed them in unison, one toward the other. His eyes were black pinpoints of hate.

"War to the death," he said coldly. "The *tahbay-boh* will not allow us to live in peace. We are animals to be penned on their reservations."

"A war to the death," Earl remarked, "sometimes has no winners. Are you resigned to fall in battle?"

Quanah tapped himself on the chest with a forefinger. "I have lived long beyond my time. Among the Quahadi, it is said that the brave die young." He spread his hands, shrugged. "Perhaps my day has come."

"And if you should die"—Earl's face was serious—
"what would happen to the People?"

Quanah stared stonily ahead. "The Quahadi will survive
my passing. Whether they will live free on the wind is not
for me to say. I only know they will not perish."

"Even so," Earl observed, "what are the People without a leader?"

"Hear me, Stone Bull," Quanah said with dignity.
"Only the earth and the sun endure forever. A warrior
merely chooses his time to die."

Earl lapsed into a brooding silence. From Quanah's
words, he saw now what had been unclear before. Whether
or not the pony soldiers found Palo Duro Canyon would
change nothing. The tide of events dictated that the horseback tribes would be subdued. If not tomorrow, then a
month from now, or next year. Time was the ally of the
army, and inevitably the Quahadi would be forced to make
a stand. Even on *Llano Estacado* there was no longer a
place to hide.

Suddenly he felt whipsawed from one extreme to the
other. His loyalty to Little Raven and the baby was at odds
with his responsibility to Lon. In good conscience, he
could not endanger the youngster by remaining on in the
Quahadi camp. But neither could he live with himself if he
deserted wife and child. The obvious solution—to spirit
them out of *Comanchería*—was no solution at all. Were
he to try, he had every certainty that Quanah would order
him killed. Or perhaps banished forever to the land of the
tahbay-boh.

Heavy in heart, he bid Quanah good night. Walking
back to the lodge, he undressed and quietly slipped into
the bedrobes. His eyelids felt lead-weighted and a weari-
ness of spirit pulled him slowly toward darkness. His last
waking thought was one of inward loathing.

He cursed the day he'd become a *Comanchero.*

28

THE DAY WAS raw and overcast. A cold wind whistled through Raton Pass and a metallic sky rolled above the mountains. Distant snow-capped peaks were obscured by clouds.

The Denver & Rio Grande had advanced to within three miles of the pass. To the west, the Santa Fe tracks had kept pace virtually rail for rail. Still, as both sides were aware, the contest would not be decided by tracklaying crews. Word had leaked out that the summit was now occupied by an armed force.

Traders and freight-haulers continued to ply the toll road through the pass. From wagon masters, Virgil had learned that a Santa Fe grading crew was hard at work on the summit. Their section of roadbed was pointed northward, clearly intended to connect with the Santa Fe's southbound tracklayers. The wagonmasters advised as well that a gang of armed hardcases was overseeing the operation. No one questioned that their purpose was to protect the grading crew.

Virgil saw it as a tactical problem. The Santa Fe's hired gunhands held the high ground, the summit. Acting as watchdogs for the grading crew was merely a sidelight. Their greater purpose was to deny the Denver & Rio Grande access to Raton Pass. The terrain, which was mountainous on all sides, afforded them a perfect defensive position. There was no practical way to stage a flank attack, and the south entrance to the pass represented still another bottleneck. On balance, there seemed no alternative to a frontal assault.

Early that morning, Virgil mustered his forces. The lead element would be comprised of Luther Roebuck and eleven mounted gunmen, recruited from the mining camps. Behind them would march a gang of some fifty roustabouts armed with ax handles. Teamsters and their mules would bring up the rear, ready to start a grading operation once the pass had been secured. Hardly volunteers, the railroad workers had been enlisted with the promise of double pay.

Virgil's orders to the men were explicit. Their objective was to dislodge the Santa Fe, hopefully without violence. Roebuck and his hired guns were meant to checkmate the opposition's mercenary force. There was to be no shooting, except on his command or in the event the other side opened fire first. The roustabouts were to hold themselves in reserve, joining the action only if the Santa Fe grading crew refused to budge. The idea, Virgil explained, was to gain control of the pass without resorting to bloodshed. His strong show of force was intended as a deterrent and a bargaining lever. He thought the Santa Fe would rather talk than fight.

William Palmer was far less optimistic. In his opinion, the Santa Fe defenders would have to be routed and driven out of the pass. Late last night, after meeting with Virgil, he had departed aboard his private railroad car. He preferred to await results in Colorado Springs, rather than remain at end-of-track. While no one mentioned it, he clearly wanted to distance himself from the site of a potential battlefield. His attitude was like that of a commander-in-chief. He ordered the attack, but he declined to lead the troops.

The three miles from end-of-track to Raton Pass was covered without incident. Virgil and the hired gunmen

rode saddle horses rented from the livery stable in Trinidad. On foot, strung out behind them, were the roustabouts and the teamsters. As they approached the summit,
the Santa Fe grading crew abruptly stopped work. The
roadbed generally followed the line of the toll road and
sloped gently downhill. The terrain was studded with boulders and rocky outcroppings and ascended steeply on either side of the roadbed. Shouldering shovels and pickaxes,
the grading crew gathered in a rough formation.

Posted on the hillsides flanking the roadbed were men
armed with pistols and carbines. By quick count Virgil
placed their number at ten, and suddenly he wished he
were armed with something more than his old Remington
revolver. Farther ahead, he saw Dick Wootton and two
other men step onto the porch of the roadside inn. Wootton
held his position on the porch while the two men walked
forward at an unhurried pace. Virgil raised his hand overhead, halting his column short of the grading crew. He
studied the two men walking toward him.

The shorter one looked like the image of death itself. He
was lean and grizzled, with cold slate-colored eyes and a
soupstrainer mustache. He wore a flat-crowned hat, and
the tail of his greatcoat was pushed back over a holstered
pistol. There seemed little question that he was the Kansas
gunfighter, Doc Sontag. His companion was a tall ferret of
a man, with gaunt features and a gashlike mouth. He was
attired in a vested suit and a townsman's narrow-brimmed
hat.

The men pushed through the grading crew and stopped
at the edge of the roadbed. Some ten yards separated them
from Virgil and Luther Roebuck, who were still mounted.
To the rear, as though on silent command, Roebuck's
hired guns reined their horses onto a ragged line. A moment vanished in a leaden drop of silence. Then the taller
man nodded to Virgil.

"Mr. Brannock" he said pointedly, "I'm John Tanner.
What can we do for you?"

Virgil held his gaze levelly. "Well, we meet at last, Mr. Tanner. I've crossed your trail many times over the past year."

"And I yours," Tanner responded. "Another time and I'd offer to buy you a drink. I've grown to respect you as an adversary."

"In that event, maybe we can come to an understanding here today."

"I'm always willing to listen. What's on your mind?"

Virgil watched him carefully. "The Denver & Rio Grande claims right-of-way through Raton Pass. We'd like you and your men to vacate—now."

"No can do," Tanner said with a look of veiled mockery. "As you're aware, we made a deal with Dick Wootton sometime ago. We're here to stay, Mr. Brannock."

"Either you move," Virgil said calmly, "or we'll have to move you. I'd rather it didn't come to that."

Doc Sontag took another step forward. There was a catlike eagerness in his eyes and he fixed Virgil with a faintly contemptuous smile. "You talk big, but I say it's all wind and no whistle. Anybody gets moved, you're gonna have to start with me."

Before Virgil could reply, Roebuck reined his horse sideways. His gunhand rested on the saddlehorn and his pale eyes glinted coldly. "You must be Doc Sontag."

"That's the name."

"I'm Luther Roebuck."

"So what?"

Roebuck laughed shortly. "So I say you're gonna move, and *muy* damn *pronto*. Unless you want a one-way ticket to the boneyard."

"Or vicey-versay," Sontag told him. "You mess with me and you're the one that'll wind up worm pudding."

"Wanna bet?"

Even as he spoke, Roebuck clawed at the crossdraw holster. Sontag seemed to move not at all. A Colt revolver appeared in his hand and spat a sheet of flame. For a moment, Roebuck sat perfectly still, a great splotch of blood covering his breastbone. Then, like a felled tree, he toppled out of the saddle.

Virgil reacted in the same instant. He pulled his Remington as John Tanner turned and ran toward the distant inn. Before he could clear leather, Sontag fired a quick snapshot. The slug plucked at the sleeve of Virgil's coat even as he aligned the sights on Sontag. He touched the trigger and the pistol belched a cloud of smoke. The bullet took Sontag in the throat and his mouth opened in soundless amazement. He shuffled forward a couple of steps and then the amazement went out of his face. He fell dead.

The gunfire suddenly became general. From the hillsides, the spitting bark of carbines increased at a steady beat. The riflemen concentrated at first on Virgil, who was out front and badly exposed. Slugs fried the air all around him and he managed to thumb off another shot. He was saved only because his horse spooked, rearing and taking the bit, and bolted back down slope. For a brief moment his own men put up a stiff fight, their pistols blending in a sustained roar. But then, as his maddened horse plowed through their ranks, they found themselves in the vanguard. A split second later, the opposing gunmen brought them under fire.

Their horses went berserk, wheeling and bucking, as the hillside erupted with rifle fire. Lead whistled past them like snarling hornets, and the first volley sent four men tumbling from their saddles. Others screamed and clutched at their wounds, and the fight abruptly turned into a rout. Three more men pitched to the ground as the survivors got themselves unscrambled and spurred their horses down the road. On the hillsides, a dense cloud of gunsmoke hung still for a moment, then scudded away on the breeze. A tomblike silence descended on the battleground.

Virgil sawed at the reins and finally brought his horse

under control. Before him, the roustabouts and teamsters turned en masse and fled for their lives. Some fifty yards downslope he hauled his horse around, prepared to rejoin the fight. The three gunmen who had escaped barreled past him, kicking their mounts into a headlong gallop. Uphill, he saw the Santa Fe grading crew slowly emerging from the rocky outcroppings, where they had taken cover. All around the roadbed, where Sontag and Roebuck had fallen, the ground was littered with bodies. None of the men moved, and wounded horses stood with their heads bowed low. The scene had the look, and the smell, of a slaughterhouse.

On the hillsides, four Santa Fe gunmen were down. Those who remained slowly stepped from behind boulders and moved into the clear. They stood staring down at the bodies, as though dazed by the carnage their carbines had wrought. A few of them looked toward Virgil, who sat his horse like a stone monolith. One of the men cupped a hand to his mouth.

"Go on," he shouted. "It's finished!"

There was no arguing the point. Within the span of a few heartbeats, thirteen men had fallen in death. A bloody price had been paid for the right-of-way, and ownership was no longer in dispute. The Denver & Rio Grande would never again return to Raton Pass.

Virgil rode toward end-of-track.

Nightfall settled over Colorado Springs like a funeral shroud. News of the battle, after being relayed by the telegrapher in Trinidad, had swept through town. There was no laughter in the saloons tonight, and men spoke in hushed voices. Their words were an obituary for the Denver & Rio Grande.

Virgil stepped off the evening northbound passenger train. His features were set in a somber frown as he crossed the depot platform. He blamed himself for the loss of Raton Pass and the needless deaths of so many men.

Had he reacted quicker, exerting greater control over Luther Roebuck, the bloodbath might never have occurred. Instead, as though struck mute, he had allowed Roebuck to force them into a gunfight. He took no consolation in the fact that he had killed Doc Sontag.

Beyond the depot, he saw lights burning in the Denver & Rio Grande offices. He hesitated, torn between hurrying home to Elizabeth and talking to Palmer. Guilt won out, and he walked toward the railroad headquarters. He saw no reason to put off the inevitable, even overnight. His report would be no less dismal tomorrow.

The outer office was empty. Virgil moved to the door of Palmer's office and entered without knocking. He found Palmer tilted back in his chair, a cigar wedged in the corner of his mouth. The railroader looked anything but distressed.

"Well, well," Palmer said, his voice icy with scorn. "Hail the conquering hero."

Virgil seated himself before the desk. "Keep your sarcasm to yourself," he said. "I've had all the trouble I want for one day."

"Trouble?" Palmer repeated loudly. "By tomorrow the story will hit the eastern newspapers. We'll be up to our eyeballs in trouble."

Virgil's jawline tightened. "Be sure to tell the reporters how you hightailed it out before the shooting started. That ought to boost your stock as a former general."

"We're not talking about my personal reputation. We're talking about the future of a railroad. Just imagine how Wall Street will react when the news gets out."

Virgil stared at him with a kind of contempt. "What the hell, we could always change our name to the Denver & Colorado Springs. It's a cinch we'll never make it to the Rio Grande."

Palmer flushed angrily. "If that was meant as a joke, it's in damned poor humor."

"I saw thirteen men killed today. As a matter of fact, I

almost got killed myself. So you'll just have to overlook my poor humor. I haven't spent a helluva lot of time worrying about the railroad."

There was a prolonged silence. Palmer puffed on his cigar, gazing across the desk without expression. Finally, he waved his hand in a conciliatory gesture. "Virgil, it occurs to me that you've lost your taste for railroading. Am I right or not?"

"Let's put it this way," Virgil said coolly. "I goddamned sure won't get any more men killed. You might as well forget about New Mexico."

"I already have," Palmer remarked. "When the news came through this morning, I immediately activated my contingency plan."

"What contingency plan?"

"In all truth," Palmer said matter-of-factly, "I had serious reservations about Raton Pass. However, there was always the chance you would pull a rabbit out of the hat."

The frown lines around Virgil's mouth deepened. "You really are a cold-blooded bastard, aren't you? You let me get those men get killed for nothing."

Palmer shrugged. "Command during wartime teaches harsh lessons. I learned that men are more expendable than cannon—or railroads."

"Maybe you were trying to get me killed, too. Was that part of your contingency plan?"

Palmer laughed too vigorously. A shadow darkened his eyes and Virgil suddenly realized that the accusation was true. A long moment elapsed as they stared at one another.

"What I plan," Palmer said at length, "is to build westward into Utah. I've already surveyed a route to Salt Lake City."

"You'll have to build it without me. As of now we're through."

"In that event, I suggest we sever our partnership. What would you consider a fair offer for your stock?"

Virgil looked at him quick, fully alert. "Where would you get the money to buy me out?"

Palmer's voice was guarded. "I have certain resources at my disposal. Of course, I couldn't pay anything near full value." He hesitated, tapped ash off his cigar. "What would you say to thirty cents on the dollar?"

Virgil laughed in his face. "I get the feeling you've found yourself a new investor. Which means you've got no choice but to buy me out." His smile broadened. "Or else you'd lose control of the railroad—right?"

"Not necessarily," Palmer said with wintry malice. "I simply prefer to have you out of my hair."

"Then it'll cost you," Virgil said evenly. "Four hundred thousand for my stock plus the half-million we borrowed from my father-in-law. Take it or leave it."

"You're mad!" Palmer flared. "That's highway robbery, outright extortion. I won't hold still for it."

"Yeah, you will," Virgil informed him. "Otherwise, I'll sit on my stock till hell freezes over. How does that jibe with your contingency plan?"

Palmer seemed caught up in a moment of indecision. His face congealed into a scowl and the cigar went cold in his hand. At last, he fixed Virgil with a haughty glare. "Very well," he said sharply. "I'll have the papers drawn up tomorrow. Anything else?"

"No, guess not. I'd say we're quits."

Virgil got to his feet and crossed the room. At the door, he paused and looked back. An ironic smile touched his mouth. "Give my regards to Brigham Young."

A merry blaze crackled in the fireplace. Virgil stood with his back to the mantel, silhouetted by the flames. His face was wreathed in a huge grin.

"So that's it," he said. "We're out of the railroad business—for good."

Elizabeth sat perched on the sofa. Her mouth was frozen

in a silent oval and she stared at him with shocked round
eyes. She shook her head in disbelief.

"Good Lord," she said softly. "You're like a phoenix,
Virgil. You always arise from the ashes."

"Not to brag," Virgil said expansively, "but I saved
your father's ashes too. Getting that half-million was a stroke
of inspiration."

"Wait till he hears about it! Honestly, he'll give you
anything you want."

Virgil looked at her questioningly. "What would I want
from your father?"

"Oh, I don't know," she replied airily. "Perhaps he'll
make you president of the bank, or president of the Denver
Pacific. Or maybe both!"

"No sale," Virgil said firmly. "I told you once before,
I wouldn't move back to Denver. That still holds."

A note of concern came into her voice. "What will you
do, then? We certainly can't stay here."

"How would you feel about New Mexico?"

"I . . ." she faltered, somewhat taken aback. "What's
in New Mexico?"

"The Santa Fe Railroad," Virgil said. "Or at least they
will be sometime next spring. When that happens, everything in New Mexico will skyrocket in value."

"You're not talking about the railroad business, are
you?"

"No," Virgil said, watching her face. "I'm talking
about ranching."

She appeared at a loss. "I don't know what to say."

Virgil moved from the fireplace to the sofa. He sat
down beside her and his voice mounted with enthusiasm.
He spoke of an expanding market for cattle once the
railroad entered New Mexico. By next year, he envisioned
boomtimes and a fortune to be made in ranching. There
were old Spanish land grants still available, hundreds of
thousands of acres to be had at reasonable prices. One day,
the land alone would make them wealthy.

"I'm through with railroading," he concluded. "It's a dirty, cutthroat business and I'm tired of feeling corrupt. I figure now's the time to make the break."

Elizabeth was silent a moment. "You've taken me by surprise," she said, "and it all sounds so risky. What do you know about ranching?"

"Not a thing," Virgil admitted. "But I'll learn, the same way I learned about railroads. And there's one other thing I haven't mentioned."

"Oh?"

Virgil's eyes took on a faraway look. "Beth, we've got a chance to build something of our own. Land and cattle—a ranching empire—something that will endure. A legacy for Jennifer and Morg."

His enthusiasm was contagious and her face quickly brightened with excitement. She nodded in approval. "I read somewhere that a man with a vision lives forever. I think that's why I married you."

Virgil took her hand. "Mark my word, we'll live to see it all come true. We're a team and we can't be beat."

Her eyes misted and she squeezed his hand. Then, suddenly, a thought flashed through her mind. She wondered whether or not the suffrage movement was active in New Mexico Territory. She made a mental note to write Susan B. Anthony and ask for the particulars. The challenge of organizing a distant land seemed to her somehow irresistible.

"Funny thing," Virgil said in a musing voice. "I've been thinking a lot about Earl and Clint. The kind of ranch I've got in mind, we'll need plenty of help."

A slow smile warmed her face. "Stop beating around the bush. What you're saying is that you'd like to have the family back together again. Isn't that it?"

"Yeah, I suppose so."

"Then ask them to come in with us on the ranching venture."

Matt Braun

"You're sure you wouldn't mind?"

Her laughter was a delicious sound. "As a matter of fact, I think it's a marvelous idea. Those two should have settled down long ago."

"Wouldn't that be something," Virgil said. "All of us together on our own land."

She scooted across the sofa. Virgil put his arm around her and she nestled against his shoulder. Her voice was oddly vibrant.

"I believe I'm going to like New Mexico."

29

SHORTLY BEFORE sundown, they came to the escarpment guarding *Llano Estacado*. Mackenzie halted the regiment and they sat for a time staring upward. The sight kindled a sense of awe and unimaginable wonder.

A wall of sheer cliffs rose straight up from the prairie. The plateau above was rimmed only by the sky and loomed like a vast citadel against the fading sunlight. Vertical outcroppings soared five hundred feet in the air, and the caprock, silhouetted by the fiery rays of sunset, gave the appearance of a weathered sentinel. The escarpment extended north and south beyond the vision of man, aged solid by countless millennia and seemingly invincible. It stood like God's fortress, barring the path of mortals.

At Mackenzie's order, Clint and his scouts took the point. The *Comanchero* prisoner, José Tafoya, led them into a maze of twisting ravines. The grade inclined steadily upward, and soon the regiment was strung out single-file through a tortuous labyrinth. Before dark, the moon rose behind them, round and full, floating free of the earth. The mellow glow cast a smoky haze across the landscape, lighting their path as they struggled ever higher. Toward the end, as the winding trail steepened, the troopers were forced to dismount and lead their horses. The moon stood at its zenith when at last they topped the caprock.

On the plateau above, Mackenzie again halted the regiment. He ordered a breather for the horses, and the men were given their first look at *Llano Estacado*. Throughout the day Clint had questioned José Tafoya as to what they might expect on the Staked Plains. Yet nothing the *Comanchero* told them had prepared either Mackenzie or Clint for the daunting sight before them. By comparison, the escarpment they had just climbed was a leisurely outing, hardly more than a stroll. Overhead, the stars glittered like ice shards in the moonlit sky, creating a spectral shimmer across the earth. What they saw left them chilled.

The plains swept onward to the distant horizon. The land was flat and featureless, absolutely empty, evoking a sense of something lost forever. There were no trees, no ridges or rolling swells, just endless space. It was as if nature had flung together earth and sky, mixed it with deafening silence, and then simply forgotten about it. Nothing moved as far as the eye could see, almost as though, in some ancient age, the land had been frozen motionless for all time. A gentle breeze, like the wispy breath of a ghost, rippled over the curly mesquite grass, disturbing nothing.

It was the unbroken emptiness, without movement or sound, that left a man feeling insignificant and somehow vulnerable. José Tafoya, speaking with a reverence normally reserved for the mystical, had told them that *Llano Estacado* did that to men. For in an eerie sense, the vast trackless barren was like the solitude of God. Distant, somehow unreal, yet strangely ominous.

Staring at the moonwashed landscape, Clint felt himself an intruder here. He had the spooky sensation that he was looking upon something no mortal was meant to see. About the still, windswept plains there was an awesome quality, almost as though some wild and brutally magnificent force had taken an expanse of emptiness and fashioned it into something visible, yet beyond the ken of man. A hostile land, waiting with eternal patience to claim the bones of those who violated its harsh serenity. A land where man must forever walk as an alien.

Mackenzie summoned Elijah Daniel. With the scout acting as interpreter, he questioned José Tafoya at length. The *Comanchero* submitted to interrogation like a condemned man mounting the gallows. His answers were quick and concise, and delivered without hesitation. He stated that Palo Duro Canyon lay some ten leagues north of their present position. Along the canyon rim, at a spot he had seen only once before, a steep trail led downward. He thought he could find it again.

"Tell him," Mackenzie said sternly, "that if he doesn't find it, I'll stretch his neck. And no reprieves this time."

When Daniel translated into Spanish, the *Comanchero* turned ashen. His lips peeled back in a weak smile and he rapidly bobbed his head. "*Sí, mi coronel.*"

Turning away, Mackenzie motioned to Clint. They walked off a short distance, halting out of earshot. In the moonlight, Mackenzie's features were worn and haggard. His limp was more pronounced; sixteen hours in the saddle had clearly taken its toll. He appeared to be in considerable pain.

"The men need a rest," he said. "I want them fresh when we strike the Quahadi camp. We'll hold here while you reconnoiter forward."

"Sounds reasonable," Clint said, nodding. "I'll take Elijah and the Mexican. No sense making a scout in force."

"One thing more, Mr. Brannock. In the event Tafoya does not find that trail, don't bring him back."

"Let's understand one another, Colonel. Are you ordering me to kill him?"

"I am," Mackenzie said shortly. "If he's led us on a wild-goose chase, then it's the least he deserves. Wouldn't you agree?"

"Yessir, I would."

"Then I suggest you move out, Mr. Brannock."

Some minutes later Clint rode off with Elijah Daniel and

the *Comanchero*. Before them lay the enormity of an
uncharted sea of grass, their one beacon the North Star.
They disappeared into a cold and silent emptiness.

The moon went behind a cloud. For a moment the earth
was cloaked in sudden darkness. Then the cloud scudded
past in a glare of moonlit brilliance.

"Jeezus Christ!"

Elijah Daniel hauled back on the reins. His horse snorted,
prancing sideways, and stopped dead. Beside him, Clint
and Tafoya jerked their own mounts to an abrupt halt. The
three of them sat staring into a black and seemingly bot-
tomless void. Their horses stood not ten feet from the rim
of Palo Duro Canyon.

From a short distance, even in bright moonlight, the
canyon was all but invisible. The earth simply dropped off
into a sheer precipice where only moments before the
plains appeared to stretch onward for miles. On a dark
night, as Clint suddenly realized, they would have ridden
over the canyon rim without a hint of warning. He understood now why the Comanche considered themselves in-
vulnerable on *Llano Estacado*. No white man would have
ever found Palo Duro.

Clint dismounted, leaving his horse ground-reined. Daniel pulled the *Comanchero* off his mount and the three of
them dropped to their hands and knees. On their bellies,
they wormed forward to the edge of the precipice. A
yawning crevasse opened before them, illuminated by the
shadowy light. The canyon appeared to be a mile or more
in width, and on either side the gorge walls rose in sheer
palisades of rock. From the top, the chasm gave the impression of an inky abyss, falling off into space.

Far below, Clint saw the telltale signs of an encampment. To the untrained eye, the canyon floor would have
appeared barren of life. But here and there he spotted the
flickering wink of dying campfires. A stream meandered

through the broad gorge, and along the banks, dimly visible in the pale light, he could make out the conical shapes of Indian lodges. Farther upstream the canyon widened in a vast fissure some three or four miles wide, with lodges scattered along the winding streambed. He estimated there were at least a thousand hostile warriors camped in Palo Duro.

Staring downward, he slowly inspected the canyon wall directly below. At first, the palisade appeared to be a series of craggy ledges and abrupt outcroppings. But then, José Tafoya nudged his arm and pointed with a thorny finger. Looking closer, Clint gradually discerned an irregular break that began some fifty yards from their position. The narrow trail dropped steeply off the rimrock and followed a perilous zigzag course down the face of the cliffs. Even in the moonlight, the precarious footing looked better suited to deer and mountain goats.

Elijah Daniel rose and ghosted off to examine the trail. While he was gone, Clint once more scrutinized the canyon floor. His estimation of the Quahadi took a sharp uptick and he felt a grudging sense of admiration for their tactical savvy. Palo Duro was a natural stronghold, and though hardly impregnable to attack, it would discourage all but the most determined force. Ten well-armed warriors at the bottom of the trail could hold off an army.

Upon returning, Daniel dropped to one knee beside Clint. His voice was troubled. "Ain't no way we'll make it down that trail on horseback. The troops are gonna have to dismount and do it single-file—on foot."

"Sounds dicey," Clint said. "Think we can do it in the dark?"

"Not without losin' half the regiment. One step the wrong way and you'd be walkin' on air."

"Looks to be a long drop, too."

Daniel snorted. "Squash a man flatter'n a bootheel."

Clint checked the angle of the moon. He judged the

hour at midnight, perhaps slightly later. A quick calculation of time and distance told him it would work. Give or take a few minutes, there were five hours until first light. He thought the regiment could be in position long before then.

On the ride back, Clint took the opportunity to question José Tafoya. Until now, the *Comanchero* had been interrogated only about military matters. At no time had Clint broached anything of a personal nature. But having seen Palo Duro Canyon and the Quahadi camp gave him an edgy feeling. Some sixth sense prompted him to ask the thing he'd avoided since Tafoya's capture.

Daniel translated for him. Whether or not the Seminole suspected the truth was impossible to guess. His features betrayed nothing throughout the entire conversation. He simply asked the questions and relayed the answers.

"How long have you been a *Comanchero*?"

"A long time, *señor*. Almost twenty years."

"And you operate out of Santa Fe?"

"*Sí, señor*. I have lived there all my life."

"Then you must know the one called Ramón Guerra?"

Tafoya suddenly looked uncomfortable. "We may have met sometime, *señor*. I do not recall."

"And the white *Comanchero*, the one who rides with Guerra? Have you met him as well?"

"*No, señor*." Tafoya seemed to squirm in his saddle. "I know nothing of such a *gringo*."

"You are a liar, but no matter. Tell me who Guerra trades with—which tribe?"

"The Comanche," Tafoya said in a shaky voice. "He alone trades with Quanah and the Quahadi band."

"Would he be there now—in Palo Duro?"

"*¿Quien sabe, señor?* All traders were late in coming to *Llano Estacado* this season. We waited for the *indios* to cease raiding."

"Which is why we caught you."

"Sí, señor."

"So Guerra could be there now. He and the white Comanchero as well. ¿Verdad?"

Tafoya shrugged. "Anything is possible, señor. Guerra travels with many carretas and therefore moves slower than traders such as myself. He may not yet have completed his business with the Quahadi."

Clint asked no more questions. He fell into a brooding silence that left both Elijah Daniel and the Mexican vaguely uneasy. Neither of them spoke their mind, but they both pondered the same thought. They wondered why he was so concerned about a white Comanchero.

The moon waned as they rode south. Thinking ahead, Clint decided that he would say nothing to Mackenzie. Instead, though he was not a religious man, his mind turned in another direction. There seemed nothing more, or less, to be done.

He prayed that Earl was not at Palo Duro.

Dawn was still a gray smudge on the horizon. The men of the 4th Cavalry quietly sat their horses in the sallow overcast. Nothing broke the stillness save the faint creak of saddle leather.

The regiment was arrayed in column of companies. Behind them stretched an umber plain shrouded in the dinge of false dawn. Before them opened the colossus of Palo Duro Canyon, with the northern plain dimly visible beyond the far wall. In the early-morning chill, their horses snorted frosty puffs of air.

Clint stood with Mackenzie at the edge of the canyon rim. Their gaze was directed downward, touching on the narrow, winding trail. Farther still, as though seen through a silty haze, was the Quahadi encampment. The lodges were spread along the stream, sheltered by stands of cedar and cottonwood. No smoke spiraled upward and there was no sign of movement. Even the village dogs still slept.

Westward, the canyon marched onward into infinity. A mile or so upstream was what appeared to be the outskirts of another encampment. Beyond that was yet another scattering of lodges, and faraway, still another. Across from the Quahadi camp, a herd of some fifteen hundred war ponies grazed on open grassland. Herds of a similar size were visible opposite the villages farther upstream.

Mackenzie's battle plan was dependent on surprise. The Seminole scouts would lead the attack, followed immediately by Captain Beaumont and A Troop. Then, with a foothold established at the bottom of the trail, Mackenzie would descend to the canyon floor with L Troop and H Troop. While Beaumont stampeded the horse herd, the other two troops would charge the Quahadi encampment. The balance of the regiment would file down the trail and join the fight as quickly as possible. Troop commanders were instructed to ride where the action was heaviest.

A faint blush of light tinged the sky. Mackenzie seemed to collect himself, nodding into the canyon. "I daresay we've found ourselves a wasps' nest, Mr. Brannock."

"Just offhand, Colonel"—Clint motioned toward the distant villages—"I'd say you're lookin' at Kiowa and Cheyenne, maybe some Arapaho. Probably a thousand braves."

"I'll settle for the Quahadi," Mackenzie noted wryly. "As for the others, I'd happily wish them Godspeed."

"Amen," Clint said quietly. "We'd be in a helluva fix if they decide to stick around and fight."

"Any cavalry commander survives on a mix of surprise and luck. I think today will test my luck to the limit."

"Yessir, I expect it will."

Mackenzie squared himself up. "Take your men down and open the fight, Mr. Brannock. Hold the hostiles until we can reinforce you—whatever the cost."

"We'll do our damnedest, Colonel."

*   *   *

Earl awoke to the sound of gunfire. Ordering Little
Raven and Lon to get dressed, he hurriedly pulled on his
pants and boots. He grabbed a Henry carbine as he went
through the door hole.

Outside, he found the village in a state of pandemonium. Quanah and the Quahadi warriors formed a ragged
line along the stream. They were exchanging fire with a
force of mounted soldiers to their direct front. Across the
way, another cavalry detail had stampeded the Quahadi
horse herd and driven it away from the encampment.
Dismounted troopers leading their horses surged down a
trail along the south canyon wall.

Women and children and old people were fleeing westward. But their retreat was blocked as another cavalry
troop formed and thundered across the canyon floor. Guerra
and his *Comancheros*, who were attempting to escape with
the women and children, found themselves cut off as well.
The Quahadi warriors gave ground slowly as the force to
their direct front pressed forward. Quanah was everywhere, shouting orders, retreating step by step in a stubborn delaying action. His intent was to buy time and cover
the withdrawal.

On horseback, the Comanche were invincible. Yet now,
forced to fight afoot, they were no match for the cavalry.
Looking westward, Earl strained for any sight of the Kiowa
and Cheyenne. He saw nothing and suspected that the
other tribes had fled at the first sound of gunfire. The
Quahadi's position was clearly hopeless; only a matter of
minutes remained before the village would be overrun. His
thoughts turned to Little Raven and the children.

The rattle of gunfire abruptly intensified. As the Quahadi
warriors were driven back from the stream, Earl hustled
his family to the western edge of the village. There they
joined the other women and children, who were scrambling up a trail on the north wall of the canyon. Earl pulled
Little Raven into a rough embrace, speaking rapidly, and her

eyes misted with tears. When he let her go, she obediently moved away, clutching the baby to her breast, and began climbing upward. He put his hand on Lon's shoulder.

"Listen to me," he said quickly. "I want you to go with Little Raven and the baby. They'll need help."

The boy shook his head. "I'm staying with you."

"C'mon, sport," Earl said, squeezing his shoulder. "We don't have time to argue about it. I'll catch up in a little while."

"You promise?" Lon demanded. "You're not just stringin' me along?"

"I give you my word. Go on now, get moving."

The youngster reluctantly obeyed. Earl hesitated, waiting to make sure he started up the cliffside. Lon looked back once and Earl motioned him onward. A moment later the boy caught up with Little Raven.

Earl turned back to the fight. He spotted Guerra and the *Comancheros*, who had taken cover behind an outcrop of rocks. They were exchanging fire with the cavalry troop that had flanked the village on the west. To the immediate front, Quanah and his warriors were in full retreat, scurrying toward the *Comancheros*' position. As they scrambled behind the rocks, their pursuers swept through the deserted encampment. The separate cavalry units, advancing from east and west, linked up before the canyon wall.

A furious volley forced the soldiers to halt their advance. At the forefront of the troops, Earl saw a band of dark-skinned Indians, led by a white man in civilian clothes. His breath stopped short and he stared hard at the man, gripped by sudden recognition. He watched as Clint rallied the scouts and motioned toward the rock-studded outcropping. Quanah and the Quahadi warriors held their fire, awaiting the charge, and a lull fell over the battleground. Then, splitting the silence, a single rifle shot cracked. Clint's horse went down beneath him.

Earl looked downslope. He saw smoke trickling from

the barrel of Guerra's repeater, and in the same instant he
caught sight of Clint struggling to free himself from the
dead horse. As Guerra took deliberate aim, waiting for a
clear shot, Earl shouldered his carbine and fired. The slug
whanged off the rock beside Guerra's head and he turned
in the direction of the report. For a split second, he and
Earl stared at one another across their sights. Abruptly,
almost as one, their carbines spat flame.

Guerra doubled over, his midsection spattered by a wid-
ening bloodburst. His mouth opened in a breathless whoofing
sound and he slumped forward on his face. One foot
drummed the earth in a death tattoo, then he lay still.
Upslope, Earl dropped his carbine and staggered sideways
in a nerveless dance. His hands splayed, clawing at empty
air, and he crumpled at the waist. He hit the ground hard
and rolled downhill, slamming into a boulder. His chest
was matted with blood.

Unnerved by Guerra's death, the *Comancheros* suddenly
quit the fight. They bolted from the rocks and clambered
up the steep cliffside. Quanah and the Quahadi withdrew
in a more orderly fashion. Firing from behind cover, they
moved swiftly, darting from rock to rock. The volume of
fire from their repeaters forced the cavalry to pull back
toward the stream. Some of the warriors died, brought
down by the longer range of the soldiers' Springfields. But
most made it up the north wall and disappeared over the
canyon rim. A final flurry of shots ended as sunrise crested
Llano Estacado.

Clint moved forward to the outcropping. He climbed to
where Earl lay wedged against the boulder. For a moment,
he thought Earl was dead and he sat down heavily. Then,
slowly, Earl's eyes rolled open. He forced a smile.

"Guess my luck ran out."

"Luck, hell," Clint said brokenly. "You could've got
away. Why'd you have to save my bacon?"

"You would've done the same for me."

Earl coughed and blood seeped out of his mouth. He gripped Clint's arm. "Little Raven . . ."

"Who?"

"My wife," Earl shuddered, drew a ragged breath. "Her and the baby . . . find them. The boy . . ."

A quicksilver splinter of time slipped past and Earl's eyes went blank. His mouth opened in a death rattle and his hand dropped to the ground. He stared upward at nothing.

Clint leaned forward and gently closed his eyes.

30

THERE WAS no pursuit. The men and horses of the 4th
Cavalry were spent, too exhausted to venture farther onto
the Staked Plains. Their fight with the Quahadi began and
ended at Palo Duro Canyon.

On the surface, the battle seemed an indecisive action.
Nearly fifty hostiles had been killed at a loss of only
seventeen troopers wounded. Yet the Comanche had escaped what might have been a slaughter, slipping away
over the canyon rim. Quanah and his people had once
again eluded the pony soldiers.

For all that, Mackenzie's victory was nonetheless real.
The Quahadi had been driven onto *Llano Estacado* with no
food, no shelter, and no ponies. A dehorsed Plains warrior
was unable to fight, unable to hunt, scarcely able to survive. Burdened by their women and children, the warriors
faced the threat of oncoming winter, and starvation. In
large measure, Quanah's brilliance at Palo Duro had merely
delayed the inevitable. His band had been reduced to a
collection of footsore wanderers.

Mackenzie ordered the village burned. In the abandoned
encampment, his men found several tons of winter provis-
ions. The lodges were torn down and used to kindle a
massive bonfire. To that the troopers added bags of pem-
mican and cured buffalo meat, and hundreds of tanned
buffalo robes. Flames leapt skyward and the conflagration

shortly resembled a second sunrise. A pall of smoke obscured the top of the canyon.

The pony herd was next. Mackenzie allowed the Seminole scouts to select twenty horses each as a prize for their services. The scouts quickly cut out four hundred of the best war ponies and hazed them down the canyon. The balance of the herd was driven to the south wall and held there by mounted troopers. On foot, troopers supplied with extra ammunition opened fire with their Springfields. The killing of a thousand horses was a slow, grisly business and consumed almost four hours. When the gunfire finally ceased, the floor of the canyon was slippery with blood and stank of death. High overhead, the buzzards began their circling wait.

Clint buried Earl underneath a tall cottonwood, not far from the stream. He fashioned a simple cross from poles and rawhide and burned Earl's name into it with a firebrand. Elijah Daniel helped him dig the grave, aware now why he'd been so concerned about a white *Comanchero*. None of the troop commanders questioned the fact that he had buried a renegade, even though the name on the cross sparked their curiosity. Nor did Clint volunteer any information about the man who had saved his life. He felt no need to explain himself.

The burial nonetheless drew stares. All the more so since the Quahadi warriors and the other *Comancheros* were left where they had fallen. Among cavalry units, it was common practice to leave enemy dead for wolves and scavengers. When Clint and Daniel lugged stones from the streambed to cover the grave, everyone within sight stopped to watch. A silence fell over the onlookers as Clint removed his hat and stood for a moment with his head bowed. Then he turned and walked away.

Farther downstream, Mackenzie was meanwhile overseeing the destruction. His game leg was bothering him and he was seated on a pile of buffalo robes. From there, he observed the burning of the village and, across the canyon, the slaughter of the pony herd. His mood was introspective, oddly saddened by what he'd done here today. Because of the slow passage down the canyon wall, he'd been unable to engage the Quahadi in force. The fight was over by the time the entire regiment had assembled on the canyon floor. Still, with only four troops in action, he had scattered the Quahadi and their allies.

The saddening part was that so few warriors had been killed. Mackenzie bore the hostiles no personal grudge, and by nature he was not a bloodthirsty man. Yet, unlike many military commanders, he realized that a Comanche would rather die in battle than be herded onto a reservation. By destroying the encampment and the horse herd, he had dealt the Quahadi the harshest of all blows. They would wander *Llano Estacado* without food or shelter, without protection from the winter storms. Finally, unable to watch the women and children starve, Quanah would lead his people into the Fort Sill agency. Mackenzie thought it an ignominious end for the last of the Comanche war chiefs, and he halfway regretted that Quanah had not fallen at Palo Duro. A man of such valor deserved a better fate.

The inequity of it triggered a darker thought. Mackenzie's gaze drifted to a copse of trees, where José Tafoya was being held under guard. His inclination was to hang the *Comanchero* and leave the body to rot. Still, whatever his personal preference, he'd given his word that Tafoya would be spared. But all that begged the question of what to do with the trader. A trial at Fort Sill would almost certainly result in a death sentence. On the other hand, the *Comanchero* simply couldn't be turned loose. Somehow, Mackenzie told himself, justice had to be served. Brooding on it now, he realized he was stumped for a solution.

Clint approached from upstream. Flames from the great bonfire cast an eerie glow over the campground. On the opposite side of the canyon, there were scattered gunshots as the last of the horses were dispatched. His features were drawn and somber as he halted before Mackenzie. He nodded without expression.

"Where to now, Colonel?"

"When we're through here," Mackenzie replied, "I plan to rejoin our supply train. The men need a few day's rest and some hot food. A good night's sleep wouldn't hurt either."

"After that," Clint asked, "what's next?"

"We resume the campaign, Mr. Brannock. Our mission doesn't end until *all* the hostiles are on the reservation."

"Way it looks to me, they're whipped now. I'd say it's just a matter of time till they come in on their own."

"Perhaps," Mackenzie conceded. "Nevertheless, we are under orders to pursue wherever the trail leads. I intend to speed their surrender along."

Clint frowned. "Without horses, the Quahadi won't last the winter. Why push 'em any harder?"

"That's a strange statement coming from you, Mr. Brannock. Have you lost your taste for fighting Indians?"

There was a moment of stiff silence. Clint finally shrugged, hands lifted. "An old scout once told me that there's nothin' like killing to tire a man out. I reckon I'm just worn down, Colonel."

Mackenzie studied him. "What is it you're trying to say?"

"Easiest way is just to tell you straight out. I'd like to resign."

"Here?" Mackenzie demanded. "Today?"

"Yessir, I reckon so."

"What would you suggest I do for a chief of scouts?"

"Give Elijah Daniel a crack at it. All you need are trackers, anyway. The Quahadi won't fight."

"Oh?" Mackenzie said. "What makes you so sure?"

"Quanah's no fool," Clint commented. "So long as he's on foot, he'll play hide-and-seek. He's got no chance against cavalry."

Mackenzie nodded agreement. "Have you considered the consequences, Mr. Brannock? Quitting in the middle of a campaign will tar you with the army. No commander would ever hire you again."

"I doubt that I'd try to sign on again. What you said a minute ago pretty much hit the nail on the head. I've lost my taste for it."

"I see," Mackenzie said, considering. "Tell me, does your decision have anything to do with your brother?"

"Maybe," Clint said evasively. "I haven't given it much thought."

Mackenzie's tone moderated. "I understand he saved your life."

Clint looked wooden. "The man he killed was Rámon Guerra. The he-wolf of all the *Comancheros*."

"Indeed?" Mackenzie said. "Well, in the end, perhaps he redeemed himself, Mr. Brannock. You might say he died a noble death."

"Nothin' noble about dying, Colonel. Anybody who's tried it would tell you that."

Mackenzie heard the hurt in his voice. A moment elapsed while they avoided each other's eyes. Then, with a crafty smile, Mackenzie looked at him.

"You've served me well, Mr. Brannock. Perhaps one good turn deserves another."

"I don't follow you, Colonel."

"Suppose there were a way around tarnishing your reputation?"

"How so?"

"I've been debating what to do with our friend Señor Tafoya. Would you be interested in escorting him to Santa Fe?"

"Santa Fe?" Clint said, astounded. "You aim to let him go?"

"Hardly," Mackenzie remarked. "I've decided to initiate a formal investigation into the *Comanchero* trade. Tafoya should prove to be a star witness."

"Maybe not," Clint said doubtfully. "From what my brother told me, the *Comancheros* have friends in high places. Who would you get to investigate them?"

Mackenzie chuckled. "I was hoping you might consider the job."

"Hell's bells, Colonel, I'm no detective."

"On the contrary," Mackenzie countered. "Your service record indicates you were once the special agent for a stagecoach line. And no white man living knows more about the *Comancheros*." He paused, smiling. "I'd say you're tailor-made for the job."

"I dunno," Clint said hesitantly. "It would have to be mighty damn official before it'd work. Half the politicians in Santa Fe are probably involved."

"Would a commission from General Sherman turn the trick?"

"You're serious, aren't you?"

"Never more serious in my life, Mr. Brannock."

Mackenzie went on to elaborate. His report on the *Comancheros* would hit Washington like a bombshell. Once the dust settled, he would arrange to have Clint appointed special investigator for the army high command. At Sherman's request, he felt confident that President Grant would order cooperation from the territorial governor. There was every reason to believe that Clint would have a free hand throughout all of New Mexico.

"One last thing," Mackenzie advised. "Until you've been commissioned, I suggest you stop by Fort Bascom and leave Tafoya in the guardhouse. We wouldn't want him assassinated before he had a chance to testify."

"Good idea," Clint agreed.

"Which brings us to the question of how you get from here to there. All we know now is that Fort Bascom lies somewhere west of the Staked Plains."

"Tafoya knows the way," Clint said with a hard grin. "I've got a hunch he'll be happy to show me. I'd even lay odds on it, Colonel."

"By God, Mr. Brannock, you're one of a kind. I hate to see you go."

Elijah Daniel and the Seminole scouts were equally reluctant to part company. As a gesture of their esteem, they asked Clint to pick himself a new horse from their herd of Quahádi war ponies. He selected a fiery-eyed *grullo* stallion, once the pride of some Mexican *hidalgo*. The horse was already broken to saddle and seemed content to once again have a steel bit in its mouth. The Seminole thought it a horse worthy of the man.

By early afternoon, the regiment was prepared to march. On the high plains above Palo Duro, Mackenzie and his troops rode south toward the Brazos. Clint and José Tafoya turned westward onto the ancient *Comanchero* trail through *Llano Estacado*. A short distance away he reined the stallion about for a last look.

Under a brilliant sunlit sky, the guidon of the 4th Cavalry fluttered proudly in the wind. He felt a part of himself riding with them, and then, curiously, he was reminded of a long forgotten adage. No man outdistances his past.

He thought it appropriate to the moment, somehow fitting. Just before he reined the *grullo* away, he marked the last sight of the regiment deep in his memory. He wouldn't forget his time on the plains.

A cold drizzling rain pounded the depot platform. As the train chuffed to a halt, the overcast lifted toward the mountains. For an instant, the westward skies were visible through the downpour. Then the clouds dropped lower, and gray twilight settled over Colorado Springs.

Clint stepped off the lead passenger coach. The date was October 11, almost two weeks since he'd ridden away from Palo Duro Canyon. After crossing *Llano Estacado*, he had deposited José Tafoya in the Fort Bascom guardhouse. Following a brief stopover in Santa Fe, he had then traveled north by stagecoach. Earlier in the day, he'd boarded the train at Trinidad.

Walking uptown, he was filled with a sense of dread. At first, he'd considered breaking the news of Earl's death in a letter. But then, upon reflection, he had decided it could only be done in person. Virgil was certain to take it hard, and he felt obliged to be there. Still, as he approached the house, he wished there were another way. He knew it wouldn't be easy.

Virgil answered his knock. The house was in disarray, with the walls bare and packing crates scattered about. Elizabeth hurried from the kitchen, greeting him with an affectionate hug. A moment later Morg bounded down the stairs, followed closely by Jennifer. Something in Clint's manner alerted Elizabeth and she intuitively sensed he'd brought bad news. She hastily shooed the children back upstairs.

In the parlor, the men took chairs and Elizabeth seated herself on the sofa. Clint began in a halting voice, first explaining Earl's involvement with the *Comancheros*. He went on to relate the events leading to the battle at Palo Duro Canyon. As he talked, Virgil merely listened, oddly silent, eyeing him with a mixture of dismay and growing apprehension. He concluded with an account of Earl's death.

For a long while no one spoke. Virgil stared straight ahead with a stricken expression, his features pale and drawn. His eyes glistened with emotion and there was a slight tremor at the corner of his mouth. Watching him, Elizabeth thought her heart would burst. In many ways, he'd been more of a father, rather than an older brother, to both Earl and Clint. She knew he was struggling to control his grief.

Virgil slowly pulled himself together. When at last he spoke, he'd regained some measure of composure. "Colonel Mackenzie was right," he said hollowly. "There at the end, Earl didn't show the white feather. He died an honorable man."

"No argument there," Clint said in a low voice. "Except for him, they would've buried me at Palo Duro. I've thought a lot about that."

Virgil's eyes were grim. "When all's said and done, he was your brother. He couldn't have done any less."

"All the same, I wish it'd worked out different."

There was a long beat of silence. When neither of them spoke, Elizabeth looked at Clint. Her voice was puzzled.

"What about Lon?" she asked. "Is he all right?"

Clint frowned uncertainly. "That's why I stopped off at Santa Fe. I figured I'd bring him here. Turns out he was with Earl the whole time."

"*No*—" she said on a sharp intake of breath.

"Just before he died, Earl said something that should've tipped me off. But it just never occurred to me that he'd take Lon into Indian country."

"Good God!" Virgil interrupted. "Are you saying Lon's with the Comanches?"

"I'm afraid so," Clint said gravely. "Near as I can piece it together, Earl's wife and baby took off with the rest of the women and children. Lon apparently went with them."

"That's monstrous," Elizabeth said, anguish in her eyes. "We have to get him back."

"I aim to," Clint told her. "Him and the wife and the baby, too. Way I see it, they're my responsibility now. That's the least I owe Earl."

Virgil appeared dubious. "How will you find them? And even if you do, how will you get them away from the Comanches?"

"Before snow flies," Clint said tightly, "the cavalry will drive Quanah and his bunch onto the reservation. I intend to be there when it happens."

"What if they decide to kill Lon in the meantime?"

"They won't," Clint assured him. "Once Earl married into the tribe, he was the same as a Comanche. They'll look after the boy."

Virgil paused, thoughtful a moment. "Maybe you could enlist the aid of these *Comancheros*. They might be helpful."

"Wouldn't work, Virge."

Clint briefly related his agreement with Mackenzie. His job now, he explained, would be to track down and destroy the *Comancheros*. Under the circumstances, he could hardly request their assistance.

"All the more so," he concluded, "since I plan to see every last one of them hung."

"Yes," Elizabeth said with sudden vehemence. "Destroy them the way they destroyed Earl. It's only fitting."

Not for the first time Clint marked that his sister-in-law was stronger than she appeared. Under her feminine softness, there was an iron will and a streak of tough pragmatism. She was much more the fighter than anyone suspected.

Virgil seemed somewhat taken aback by her fiery outburst. He stared at her for a time, clearly bemused. Then he looked across at Clint. "From the sound of it, you'll be headquartered in Santa Fe?"

"Yeah, I reckon so," Clint said. "Leastways that's where I'll hang my hat."

"Then you'll have to visit us on the Rio Hondo."

"What do you mean?"

"Those packing crates—" Virgil motioned around the room. "We're leaving tomorrow for New Mexico."

"You're joking!" Clint said, genuinely surprised. "What happened to your railroad business?"

Virgil quickly recounted his parting with the Denver & Rio Grande. He went on to explain that he had returned only yesterday from New Mexico. There, working through a land company, he'd purchased 100,000 acres of grazeland along the Hondo River. His plan was to establish the largest cattle ranch in the territory.

"I'll be damned," Clint said when he finished. "You aim high, don't you?"

"By next year," Virgil replied, "I'll be running ten thousand head of cows. I've already made an offer to lease another two hundred thousand acres."

Elizabeth cast a sly glance at Clint. "When you're through with the *Comancheros*—" She hesitated, her eyes merry with laughter—"perhaps you'll join us. We could make it a family venture."

"Not me," Clint said, grinning. "I'm a long ways from a rocking chair and a bunch of cows."

"Well, think about it," she said gaily. "We might even arrange a wife to go along with the rocker."

"That'll be the day!" Clint said, his grin broadening. "Besides, I've still got to find Lon and the baby. Let's take first things first."

"You'll find them," she said with conviction. "I just know you will."

"When you do," Virgil added, "bring them to live with us. So far as I'm concerned they're all Brannocks—the woman included."

Elizabeth nodded her head firmly. Nothing more needed to be said, for they understood that blood ties were the strongest of all bonds. They were, in the end, one family. The Brannocks.

The rain passed sometime during the night. At midday, with the sun at its zenith, the earth shimmered under glaring shafts of light. High overhead a ray of sunlight split apart and became a bronzed streak of feathers. Framed against the sky, it slowly took the form of a hawk.

On the depot platform, Clint watched as the hawk caught an updraft and drifted away. Beside him, Virgil was staring at the distant mountains, towering majestically against the muslin blue of an October sky. Their spell was broken as the locomotive chuffed steam and the engineer clanged his bell. The conductor's voice rang out over the depot.

"All aboard!"

Other passengers moved forward and began boarding. Elizabeth and the children walked to the last coach, which looked to be the least crowded. Their bags were checked through to Trinidad, where they would switch to the southbound stage. All the household goods and furnishings were to follow by freight wagon.

Virgil and Clint walked along the side of the coach. Through the windows, they saw Elizabeth and the children seating themselves. At the rear of the coach, they mounted the steps to an outside platform. Their eyes were drawn once again to the snowcapped mountains.

"Life's funny," Virgil said thoughtfully. "When we moved back here, I figured we'd never leave. Guess it wasn't in the cards for me to settle in Colorado."

Clint chuckled. "I don't put much faith in the cards, anyhow. I just go where the wind blows me."

"Well, for once, we're headed in the same direction. I'm damned glad it worked out that way."

"Hell, Virge, it couldn't have worked out any other way. Or haven't you figured it out yet?"

"Figured out what?"

"Except for Elizabeth, nobody else would have us. We're stuck with one another."

Their laughter was drowned out by the train whistle. The driving wheels on the locomotive spun and grabbed, and the cars lurched as the train got underway. For a moment, looking backward, the brothers watched the town fade into the distance. Then they turned, as though turning away from the past, and entered the passenger coach. Neither of them gave a thought to what was left behind.

Their destination now was New Mexico Territory.